MACKENZY FOX

BONES

BRACKEN RIDGE REBELS MC
BOOK 6

DEDICATION

While I never got to tell you that I'm a published author, knowing my books wouldn't be your cup of tea, I know that you'd be proud of me no matter what.

I miss you dad. Always and forever x

AUTHOR NOTE

CONTENT WARNING: Bones is a steamy romance for readers 18+ it contains mature themes that may make some readers uncomfortable. It includes violence, possible triggers such as cancer and spousal loss, guns, kidnapping and as always….LOTS of steamy love scenes!

BLURB

BONES

They say good things come to those who wait, and I can safely say I've waited a lifetime for her.

She's the new lawyer in town. She's feisty. She's got a temper. And I can't get enough of it.

The trouble is, she won't have anything to do with me, aside from getting me out of jail.

I know she feels something, I can tell by her body language and how she can't take her eyes off me when she thinks I'm not looking.

The question is, what is she running from?

If she thinks she can banish me and keep me away, then she can think again.

The chaos that surrounds me has got nothing on the hurdles I know we'll have to face.

But, I'm all in.

If it's a fight she's after, she may have just met her match… because I'm not going away.

KENNEDY

I came to Bracken Ridge to start a new life. To get away from the past and all I left behind.

But the more I try to forget, the worst it gets, like my ghosts are set to haunt me forever.

He's the bad boy biker who's got a lazy smile, eyes that sparkle and a dirty mouth that he can't keep shut. I shouldn't be attracted to him, he's exactly what I don't need.

But he calls to me on another level, one that I can't explain.

The trouble is, if I let myself fall again, I may not survive the fall out this time. And that's something I can't let happen, for both our sakes.

NOTE: This is book 6 in a series but is written as a stand-alone with no cliff hanger and a HEA. Recommended for mature readers only, it has adult content. Bracken Ridge Rebels rule...enter at own risk!

BRACKEN RIDGE
REBELS
ARIZONA
M · C

CHAPTER 1

BONES

I stare through the iron bars trying not to look at the clock ticking away on the wall.

When I do, it seems to go around extra slow because it knows I'm watching.

With every single second that passes, my fate lies in someone else's hands.

I called Rubble earlier to help me after being arrested and expected my club brothers to be down here, arguing and protesting for my freedom, banging down the doors until I'm released. While it's likely they'd end up being locked up in here with me, the thought is pleasing.

Instead, I'm throwing a ball against the wall just like in the movies, trading cigarettes with a dude called Albert, who smells like mothballs and piss, while avoiding eye contact with a guy called Bruiser. Things aren't looking good for me.

Hours have gone by, and there's still no sign of any of

my brothers.

I can't sleep. Either one of these dudes could slit my throat, or worse. Not that Albert looks like he'd be able to fight his way out of a paper bag, but desperate men can become unhinged and unpredictable. I've only been incarcerated for a few hours and I'm ready to crack.

Bruiser looks like he's all too familiar with how jail time works, and that isn't comforting, not in the slightest.

I hope I don't have to fight him.

Usually, I talk my way out of anything, and even though I'm wide-set and tall at six-four, he's still bigger. That, and I'd rather not have a murder charge added to my list of misdemeanors.

So far, I know all about Albert and what he's here for. Fuck if I care, but he seems like the lonely hearts type who hasn't had any human interaction in a while. He lost his job and has been drinking his way to oblivion, hence why he's here; he thought he'd be okay to drive and instead he hit a tree and almost killed himself. Talk about a wake-up call.

He seems harmless, even though I want to strangle him with my bandana because he's talked my ears off all fuckin' night.

I, on the other hand, am the proud owner of multiple outstanding warrants and unpaid fines. Oh, and a blunt charge from back in my younger days that I never showed up to court for. While it's not illegal anymore to possess cannabis in Arizona, it was several years ago.

I don't even know what the big deal is, but the cops don't seem to see it that way. So not only am I locked up in here with nobody coming to haul me out, but now it seems likely that I'm going to have drug possession added to my rap sheet. Just fuckin' great.

While my ultimate fantasy is to have that foxy lawyer, Kennedy Hart, come down here and bail me out, something tells me that Hell may freeze over first. For one, the woman has been ignoring my advances. She acts like there's a plague whenever I'm around and constantly gives me the stink eye when I try to be nice.

I'll have to rely on our usual lawyer, Stanley, a man who still wears a suit from the 1970s and thinks he's Colombo. I'm fucked in every which way.

The cops also took my phone away, hence why when they gave me one phone call, and the only number I could remember was Rubble's. My fellow club member and *supposed* brother in arms, though he's yet to show himself.

My job in the Rebels motorcycle club is the Road Captain, and that means I organize the club's weekly ride with all the patched members. I also take care of planning the route, setting the pace of the ride, and ensuring the safety of all the bikes. That's when the weather's good, since we don't ride a lot in the winter.

It's always a good time, when the colder months swing

around, to work on our bikes and get lone projects done. Lord knows there's always something to fix. The conditions in Arizona are harsh.

I live for the road. It's one of the few places I find peace in my life. I've had a love of motorcycles since I was old enough to ride one.

I sigh, not caring if my jail mates hear me. I'm done with this place; it smells funny and there's barely any airflow. I don't expect five-star treatment, but hell, I do need fresh oxygen.

Also, I need a shower to disinfect my body. I feel nasty.

They can't lock me up like this for half a blunt from a hundred years ago and some unpaid speeding tickets. I try to make peace with the fact that Stanley will get me out of this shit. He'll come through, then we can post bail and I can go on my merry way and life as I know it can continue.

And I admit, I live a good life.

I try to live every day like it's my last, always have, not that I plan on going anywhere, but who the hell knows what's around the corner. I don't plan anything, except the weekly rides. You could say I fly by the seat of my pants, but I like it that way. I like the unexpected.

I've got shit just how I want it. No ol' lady tying me down, unless it's to the bed – I'm up for that. No screaming kids, no huge mortgage payment that I can't afford.

Life's pretty sweet.

My business partner and the Vice President of the Rebels, Brock, owns the junk and scrapyard with me. It started off slow, but we've turned it into one of the biggest and most sought out yards outside of Phoenix. I'm fuckin' proud of it. It's been almost seven years of blood, sweat, and tears, and now we've got it running like a well-oiled machine.

Before this, I was hired by the military as a sniper. I was fresh out of college and was a master at my craft. After spending many years overseas in the line of duty, I got out of the game a while back due to injury. Even though I can't say I don't miss it; it also feels like a lifetime ago that I held a rifle in my hands.

People wonder why I'm the way I am. Most assume because I'm ex-military that I'm disciplined like Brock and Steel, the clubs enforcer, both are still set in their ways. But the truth is, when I left the military, I lost myself for quite a few years. I was too fuckin' serious. I vowed once I got through the downhill slope that happens when you're discharged, that I'd live each day to the full and try to connect to the person I used to be, back when I knew how to have fun. Life's fickle and way too short, that's what I know for sure.

I'm pretty sure a lot of people think I'm simple because on the outside I don't have a lot, and I'm a bit aloof. The truth is, that's how I've always lived; I don't have many material possessions. In fact, the only thing I really collect are tattoos and speeding tickets. Hence the reason I'm here.

Fuckin' Rubble. He was meant to be here hours ago and there're still crickets chirping.

I don't like being a caged animal. I guess nobody does, but this is different. Having my freedom taken away is proving to be a hard limit for me. I should've just paid the stupid tickets instead of being a lazy ass.

The echo of the door opening, followed by a gust of wind, alerts me that someone is here. Hopefully, my lawyer.

In my old occupation, I was designed for combat and excelled in enemy infiltration. That means I know how to stay camouflaged and observe what most people overlook, not that it's helped me right at this moment with my cellmates. I do not, however, predict the click-clack of heels that sounds on the concrete floor.

This is small-range combat on another level.

Kennedy Hart level.

Could I be so fucking lucky?

Surely not.

She might hate me, but I'll take her over Stanley any day of the week.

My heart races in my chest at the silhouette of a woman sashaying closer with every step of those clickety heels.

When she does come into view, I'm delighted to see Kennedy's beautiful face and flowing red hair. Fuck me if she's not a sight for sore eyes.

She's like a vision. One that makes my stomach clench and my heart beat faster.

Though I keep my poker face on, I'm ecstatic. There's no point in making it seem like I'm happy to see her. That technique hasn't worked for me yet, so I doubt being in the slammer is gonna change it.

Maybe I should try being an asshole – it's not like this predicament could get much worse.

Looking at her, she completely knocks me out of my reverie, and her fierce hazel-colored eyes drill into me. I can see that she's less than impressed.

Her red lipstick matches her hair, and I imagine her lips peppering kisses all over my body, wrapping around my cock as I take a fistful of that hair... *Wishful thinking?* Maybe?

But I deserve this indulgence after the night I've had, even if she isn't as pleased to see me as I am her. At least someone came to bail me out. No thanks to fuckin' Rubble.

I'll be having words with my club brothers when I'm outta this shithole.

Our gazes meet through the bars as I take in her stern expression.

"Mr. Romero, I'm sure we don't need any formal introductions, but for legal reasons, I'd like to state for the record that I'm Kennedy Hart and I'll be your attorney for your bail hearing."

I fuckin' love the way she says my name.

I can't help the smirk that appears on my face. *Is it just me, or does her gaze narrow even further?* She truly hates me.

From the minute I heard she was single, I tried my luck, hoping for a chance, but then so has every other red-blooded male in town and that just makes me more determined.

She might not be mine, and there's a high chance she may want my balls in a vice, but it doesn't mean any other fuckface can have her.

Over my dead body.

Instead, my eyes dip down her body to take in the feast before me, and I indulge.

She's all woman. Curvy, with an impressive rack that does things to my cock that no woman except her seems to manage lately.

All I seem to fuckin' do at the moment is fantasize about what it'd be like to have her in my bed. Or her bed. Or any surface that I can pound her on.

Oh, fuck yeah. That shit's hot and so is she.

She's wearing a floaty cream blouse tucked into a knee-length black skirt with a matching jacket, every piece of fabric molding to her perfectly. Miss Lawyer Lady has class and style, but then she'd look good wearing a paper bag.
I stand up from the hard bench I've been sitting on all night as I run a hand through my hair and try not to let my smirk widen any more. When my eyes meet hers again, she purses her lips.

"Well, well, sweet cheeks, it seems that Hell has actually frozen over if you're really standing here in front of me."

She smiles, but not in a friendly manner. More like she's shooting lasers out of her eyeballs and I'm the target. "Trust me when I say I'm being paid handsomely for it, and I'm only here because Stanley is on vacation."

"Still," I tsk. "You had a choice. You could've left me here to rot."

She leans toward the bars, and my eyes drop to her lips. "I would be smart and wait until you're a free man before you make *that* assumption, *sweet cheeks.*"

It doesn't put me off, oh *no*. Her backhanders only stoke the fire even more.

I fuckin' love the fact she's got a whiplash tongue; I can't get enough of it. Nobody else stands up to me like she does and I'm like a horndog just from the crumbs she throws me.

I may not act like a desperate man, but I certainly feel like one.

Bruiser snorts a laugh behind me as I shift my eyes sideways to frown at him.

When I look back at her, she has her own sassy smile going on that I'm not sure I like. It says she might actually follow through and leave me here… another night in this joint and I'll be climbing the walls.

I'm pretty sure that half a blunt charge isn't a felony

conviction, even though I can't be completely sure, but I'll still get a fine and possibly a conviction without serving. That's what I'm hoping anyway.

Surely she can get me out of the tickets I haven't paid, as those have definitely mounted up over time. The judge may cut me some slack since it's petty. The way I see it, there are worse criminals than me roaming the streets. Of course, they could make an example out of me, and then I'm truly fucked.

I'd love to see her in court, standing up for me, arguing to set me free. I know it's because she's being *paid handsomely*, as she so eloquently put it, but I don't care.

It'd be my fuckin' pleasure just to witness it, even if she didn't get me off.

That fuckin' skirt suit has me hard, and I definitely don't need any of that going on while I'm in here with these weirdos.

"Does that mean you're gonna use your powers of persuasion to get me out of this mess?" I grin, hoping for a fiery comeback.

She lets out a sharp exhale of breath, seizing the moment, before she says, "No, it means I'm going to use my *skills* that I learned in *law school* to have your charges lessened or even dismissed. While doing that, I'll make your sordid and somewhat questionable past disappear, along with the mile-long list of misdemeanor charges that I'll write off as you being young and stupid. Though the only thing that looks like it's changed over the years is the young part." She stares at me, unaffected, as I gape back at her.

"I'll overlook the fact you're in a motorcycle club where law enforcement and rules are considered non-existent. All while making you seem like Strawberry Shortcake, instead of a grown man who skipped out on a prior blunt charge, as well as a court date, *and* can't pay a simple thing like a speeding ticket because he has to prove something to the world. Now comes the part where I ask you if you have any questions, so I can go and prepare to defend your case."

I snort when I hear her say "blunt." It just sounds too comical coming from her prim and proper mouth.

I want to tell her that she's crazy if she thinks she'll ever get me to resemble anything close to Strawberry Shortcake. I want to tell her that she can't talk to me like that; I'm the client, after all. And what happened to Mr. Fuckin' Romero? But I do none of those things, and not just because Stanley – wherever the fuck he is– isn't here to rescue me.

The truth is, I can't wait to see her in action. This is almost worth being arrested for.

"I promise I'll be a good little boy, *Attorney Hart*," I mock while giving her a boy scout salute that has her rolling her eyes. "I'll even take you out for dinner if you can get my charges dropped. Any place you like, you name it. I'll even dress up for the occasion."

"That won't be necessary," she says drily, looking bored. "Your hearing's at three. I'll be back to collect you then. If you can, I'd suggest staying out of trouble and do as the guards say."

She may have heard about my mouthing off when I was arrested. Heck, the whole town would've heard.

My eyes go round as I glance at the clock and realize that's hours away. "It's only ten o'clock, though."

For the first time, I see her smile a genuine smile. So, she likes the fact that she's got one over on me, huh?

Well, I'll be happy when I've got one over on her, and that involves her lying over my lap so I can spank her ass for being a smartmouth.

It makes me wonder what she'd be like in the bedroom, and that just makes my cock strain painfully against my zipper.

"Well, I'm sure you can amuse yourself for a couple more hours," she replies, her eyes glancing at the nosy bastard to my right. She fixes him a look too.

"What if I'm being treated unfairly?" I whisper through the bars.

That only seems to amuse her more, when she asks, "Are you?"

"If I say yes, can we speed things up a bit?"

She shakes her head. "I'm not going to pervert the course of justice, Mr. Romero, just to suit your needs."

"Why not?"

"Because not only is that highly unethical as well as illegal, but it will also only land you in more trouble."

I rub my chin. Everything that comes out of her mouth sounds like it's sent to torture me.

"You're a lawyer, though. I'm sure you're used to shadier men than me?" I challenge.

I give her the one eyebrow lift that most women can't seem to resist. But with Kennedy Hart, it's like I'm her own personal brand of *not going there, ever.*

"You'd be surprised," she replies, holding her own. "Trust me, I've seen it all."

"Do you always talk in riddles?"

"I'm not going to discuss shadier characters I represent other than you, Mr. Romero. That isn't what you'd consider professional." She may actually be enjoying this. "Trust me, I'd find it a challenge to match the kind of juvenile record you have on your rap sheet."

I grin back at her. "I'm so looking forward to this."

She shakes her head, her curls bouncing as she does so. "I've got to go and prepare for your bail hearing, unlike *some* people I don't just fly by the seat of my pants, and judging by the charges against you, if you don't spend some time in jail, it will be an absolute fucking miracle."

I lean forward and whisper, "Are lawyers supposed to say *fucking?*"

She straightens her back as she takes a deep breath. I'm

a lot. I know that, but so is she. She's got a fire inside her that could see me burn in Hell.

"I'll be back at two-forty-five sharp. Try and stay out of trouble until then."

"It's not like I'm goin' anywhere!" I shoot back as she turns and stalks away.

I watch her fine, round, delectable ass swaying as she makes her way back up the corridor until she's out of sight. Her heels clickety-clack in her wake, echoing across the space between the bars and my freedom. It might be my most favorite sound I've ever heard.

That and her moaning while I fuck her into oblivion, which is inevitable, even if she hates me.

A good hate fuck is all somebody may need to brighten their day, and Kennedy looks like hers may need brightening just a little bit.

It's safe to say I have a crush on my lawyer. Big time.

Kennedy Hart is the epitome of sophistication and class. She may be able to fire lasers from her eyeballs, but she's also got the smarts to make most people cower. Not me, though.

Is she so far out of my league I'm in another state? Sure. But that's never stopped me before. And honestly, she can't hate me *that* badly if she's come all the way down here to haul my ass out of jail. She could've said no and left me here until Stanley returns from vacation.

I know Hutch, our club Prez, can be very persuasive, but

it doesn't seem to me that Kennedy is the type of woman that would let anyone, even him, boss her around. She's got nerves of steel. I kinda dig it.

"Who's your friend?" asks Albert from behind me. Not like anything is private in a shared prison cell.

"The devil in disguise," I reply.

"Do you think she does house calls?"

I turn to him and give him a pointed look. "Judging by the warm reception I got, I seriously doubt it."

He snickers. "She's a pistol, kid. I feel sorry for your ass if that's who's supposed to get you out of here."

I palm the back of my neck.

What would this old man know? Then again, he might be right.

"Don't I know it," I mutter, ignoring Bruiser who's just giving me the creeps.

"Best way to handle a woman like that is to make sure she knows who wears the pants," he continues.

"Is that right?"

"Swear it works like a charm."

I lean back against the bars. "You been married before?" I ask.

"Three times, none of 'em lasted."

I snort. "Figures, I'm not sure in the twenty-first century that women appreciate being shown who wears the pants, when, clearly, they're runnin' things just fine while we waste away here in jail."

He waggles a finger at me. "She's trouble. Don't say I didn't warn you."

I turn back to the bars and roll my eyes. *Stupid old man.*

I don't need him to tell me that she's trouble. I already know that.

And she's got the ability to bring me to my knees without even trying. That's the thing that lures me in because no woman has been able to do that before. Or maybe I'm just a schmuck after all.

There is no taming Kennedy Hart; that much is clear, and I'm not sure if I'd even want to.

I think I like her just like this, if only she'd agree to spend some time in my bed, instead of arguing with me about trivial shit like being arrested. We both know she'll get me off.

I want her.

And I plan on getting her.

That's what'll get me through until two-forty-five, when the woman who hates me decides my fate.

I can hardly fuckin' wait.

Bones

BRACKEN RIDGE
REBELS
ARIZONA
M · C

CHAPTER 2

KENNEDY

I sit at my desk and work out a strategy to try to get Ryan Romero, aka Bones, out of county and avoid time. I can't say it's going to be easy. It's not like he's citizen of the year.

The unpaid speeding and parking fines are one thing, but being caught with a blunt, albeit years ago, and never showing up to court, is just a headache I don't need. Since he had no known whereabouts at the time of the incident, the warrant for his arrest has been out for some time. It's comical that the cops in this town haven't tracked him down sooner, or maybe they already knew and didn't care. I don't know how much the club may be lining anyone's pockets, especially law enforcement's.

It all depends on the judge and how lenient they'll be with the fine and the excuse of not showing up for his hearing. I don't know if being young and stupid is going to cut it.

At the time, Arizona state law wasn't as lenient as

it is today. They've softened their stance on marijuana possession, and it looks like that may be my argument.

The thing I can't get over is his cockiness.

Granted, I thought he was a hot tamale when I first saw him that day six months back when I helped Angel out with her child custody case. Angel is Brock's partner; he's the V.P. and fellow club member.

Then he opened his mouth, and if the patches on his jacket and the fact he was sitting on a roaring Harley weren't enough to warn me off, his cocky attitude and the way he ogled my tits definitely were.

I don't dislike him *that* much. I don't know what it is if I'm being honest with myself.

Maybe it's the fact he's completely fearless that scares me because I've been there, done that, and I don't want a repeat of the resident bad boy. Of course, that was years ago, before my marriage…

I stare at the wall and shake the nostalgia off. There's no need bringing all of that up, especially at work, if I go down that train of thought, I'll never pull my way out of it and do what I need to do.

One foot in front of the other…

I also can't stop thinking about Bones behind bars.

The way he stood up straighter when he saw me, the smirk on his face, the way he filled out that Henley…

County looks a little different in most cities. Being that

Bracken Ridge is still a fairly small town with only one small police department, he's lucky he was just in a holding cell. The justice system for petty crime moves swiftly, so luckily for him he didn't get transported to Phoenix.

In reality, I've dealt with petty crimes like this for most of my career, oddly since I specialize in family law and custody cases. And divorces. Those are always fun.

I can't help the small smile on my face at the offer for dinner, or the code word meaning sex. The man just won't quit.

I know all about those boys over at the Rebels' clubhouse. Everyone in town does.

While they're not criminals per se, and all have legitimate businesses, there's always an air of distaste whenever they come up in conversation. I guess that's the reality of a small town; people talk, and word gets around, whether it's good or bad. And everyone has an opinion about it.

I think about Bones running his eyes all over my body as I approached his cell. The way he looks at me is different than how other men do. They just treat me like a piece of meat in a smart skirt suit. Generally, the men in my profession don't take me seriously. That tends to happen with male vs. female attorneys, which is utterly ridiculous but sadly true. You can't be sexy and successful at the same time; it's not considered professional. Lucky for me, I gave up caring what people thought of me a long time ago.

Sure, I know Bones wants to peel my clothes off, as he's made that part obvious. But there's something else in his eyes, something endearing and kind, and that's the thing I can't get away from. Stupidly, it's the thing that makes me want to high-tail it and run. I might be sassy and business-like in my profession, but the same can't exactly be said about my love life. Talk about a disaster area. And besides, I don't have time for a man. I'm far too busy.

Ever since I moved to Bracken Ridge to be closer to my sister, Stevie, I've not taken a break from setting up my own practice. It's been a life-long dream of mine to work for myself without an overbearing boss breathing down my neck, and it's been a labor of love. I love my office space and everything about it. I should, I've put my whole life savings into it.

It was a temptation taking this case on. For one, I don't exactly want to be around Bones as it only seems to encourage him.

I also can't explain why I'm being such a coward. We could have some no strings attached fun. Imagining him in the sack is too much, though. He's the type of guy where anything would go, I'm sure of it, and that makes my mind wander. Around him, it's like I have no filter in my brain.

I wonder if, like the rest of his body, how perfect he is under his clothes… is he well-hung or… *no!*

I do not need to be wondering about the size of my

client's dick. More to the point, I need to focus on what I'm doing for *Mr. Romero,* and stop distracting myself with this nonsense.

For someone that prides herself on a strong work ethic and taking charge, I'm certainly doing a lousy job of it.

Surely I've got the ability to resist a pretty face and dirty mouth? Then again, I am only human, and it's been way too long since I had sex…

Amelia, my new secretary and also Brock's sister, pokes her head around my door, interrupting my wayward thoughts.

"I've prepared the legal forms and contracts for the Smyths, and I've emailed you a copy. Their appointment is this afternoon, as soon as you're back from bailing out Bones." She does a bad job at hiding her amusement.

"That man will be the death of me," I reply, still half-reading an email. "If he was going to get off on cockiness alone, he wouldn't even need a lawyer."

"He's not that bad, once you get to know him, and look at what he did for Lucy when all that shit went down."

Yes, like I need a reminder of the Bracken Ridge Rebel Motorcycle club antics. They are well known around town. Lucy is Rubble's wife, another 'club brother' of the Rebels. She's a good woman. I've met her a couple of times in passing, and she always asks me to come out with her and the girls for drinks.

I heard through the grapevine that there had been an altercation with Rubble's former club and Lucy was threatened, resulting in Bones getting stabbed and winding up in the emergency room. Somewhere in all the craziness, Lucy's brother, Nitro, showed up out of the blue and they've since reunited. I've only seen him a couple of times around town on his very sexy motorcycle, and he's also very good looking in a rough and tumble kind of way. The Bracken Ridge Rebels prerequisite is obviously to be smoking hot before you're allowed to join. Even the club President, Hutch, isn't half bad, in a smolder, silver-fox kinda way.

Not that I'd tell Kirsty, his wife, that, especially since I'm on retainer with her business Bracken Ridge Real Estate. Kirsty has hired me to witness all the sales and contracts that go through on properties. The retainer is small change at the moment but it all adds up.

So yes, it was heroic, but the club still seems to be in a lot of hot water for a 'reputable' motorcycle club who apparently don't do any bad shit.

"I'm not sure I want to get to know him," I reply, *even if he is sexy as hell.* "But since he's now my client, I suppose I better put my game face on."

I obviously don't want to say too much to Amelia. Being part of the Bracken Ridge Rebels family, no doubt her loyalties lie with them.

"He's a dick for not paying his fines on time or at all.

You'll be able to get him off, won't you?"

"It's a hard one since he never showed up for his court date," I add. "It will depend on the judge, plain and simple. The judge won't take pity on him for not paying his dues, and his rap sheet leaves little to be desired."

"He's sweet on you, you know," she sing-songs as I try to ignore her.

"So? Most men are when you're new in town. I'm like the shiny new toy. It'll fade soon, and he can go back to banging those girls who hang around the club."

She gives me an eyeroll.

"What?" I argue. "Don't tell me girls don't hang there for sex and God knows what else."

"I won't refute that," she agrees. "But I've been there, and sure, they like to party, however, there's no hard drugs, and the girls are there because they want to be there. I don't see how it's any different than going to a bar and picking up someone random."

I realize she knows the life much more than what I do in terms of having a brother in the club. Whereas I don't know the first thing about it, only that they party hard and ride around on those noisy ass motorcycles, looking like they belong in jail.

Take Bones, for example. He looks like he needs a good, hearty bowl of soup and a hot bath. Not that I'd be the one to bathe him, but it's obvious he has nobody at home waiting for him… then again, maybe I'm wrong.

"That's a valid point, and I'm not judging. A client is a client, and he deserves a chance to explain himself." I say that with tongue in cheek because there really is no explanation why any judge will buy laziness and no respect for the law as excuses for his actions. And not showing up to court… that's not going to bode well, but I think he will escape jail time.

"Why does he get under your skin so much?" she probes.

Right here and now I realize that I'm obviously not as good as I thought at masking my feelings. Not that I have feelings toward a criminal and a smartass, no matter how sexy he is, but it does lead me to wonder exactly that; *why?*

Instead, I go with denial. "He's not under my skin. I just don't appreciate criminals clogging up the system. I know your family connection with the club, Amelia, I get it, but should I be worried if he does do time? Will I need to leave a forwarding address and update my will?"

Amelia snorts. "That's a little dramatic. You've been watching too much Sons of Anarchy."

"One can hardly blame me. I've never represented someone from a biker gang before." To say I have a little trepidation in this matter is an understatement.

She taps her chin as she crinkles her nose. "Just a tip. I'd probably not mention the words "biker gang" around any of them. They prefer *the club* or *M.C.* or anything that doesn't make them sound like outlaws, which they're not, aside from Bones's stupidity. Hutch won't be happy about any of it, especially with him being the Road Captain."

I've no idea what that even means.

I roll my eyes. "Well, I can't erase his criminal history, unfortunately. I can only hope we get a judge who will show him leniency. You never quite know how these things will go when so much time has passed, and he hasn't rectified his mistakes. Let's hope they don't choose to make an example out of him."

"He's a dick," she concedes. "But he's a good guy deep down, and he is pretty cute."

I know she'll say anything to stick up for her precious biker family, and I admire that kind of loyalty. My job, however, is to literally find a loophole and plead for leniency, rather than insult the judge's intelligence by making excuses they won't buy anyway.

"That remains to be seen in the courtroom. If he can keep his smartmouth in check for five minutes, then we'll all be better off," I say, ignoring the *cute* comment. I'm not even going to address that. Amelia just laughs as she wanders back to her desk.

If I don't care about anything other than trying to keep his ass out of prison, then why do my insides quake and my hands shake a little whenever I think about him in that

Henley, leaning against the metal bars, his deep hazel-colored eyes boring into mine like a wildfire.

That I don't care to understand.

"I'm not fuckin' wearing that shit," Bones says, nodding to the plain, white-collared shirt I brought with me. While I appreciate the Henley, I don't think a judge will, and his motorcycle jacket with the dirty, worn patches is definitely a no-no.

"It may be beneficial, Mr. Romero, to do just that. We are going for a plea, and in order to do that, we have to put our best foot forward," I reply, looking down at my papers. "So, if you'll kindly indulge me for a moment."

We sit down opposite each other in the room adjacent to the courthouse.

When he doesn't answer, I glance up at him.

"I wish you'd call me by my first name," he says.

I sigh. "Fine. *Ryan,* I think perhaps you need to listen to some sound advice for once. I can see where flying by the seat of your pants has gotten you and from where I'm standing, the judge will find any excuse to toss you back in there." I give him a pointed look. "That is, unless you don't mind visiting your friends again in the holding cell before they transport you to county for processing."

He palms the back of his neck, and my eyes wander to his large, flexed bicep. My throat thickens as I take in his hard, muscled body. It's like every muscle clings to that fucking Henley just to taunt me.

"First name's Bones, sweetheart, and that sounds more like a threat to me. And I thought you were on my side?"

I wonder how much time I'd get if I choked him to death, and if the judge would go lenient on me as I plead insanity. "It's Kennedy, or Ms. Hart when we're in public. And it's not a threat, it's a promise. I *am* on your side. After all, I showed up on short notice and bumped my other clients so I could fit this in given Stanley is on vacation. I've been preparing your case all morning." *Not that you seem very grateful.* I wave the file at him in my hand rather impatiently. He drives me fucking crazy. Maybe he likes getting me riled up.

His lips twitch. God, this must be so awful for him, having to not only sit here and listen to me give him orders about something trivial like what to wear, but he has no option other than to do exactly as I say. I can't deny that I like the role reversal just a little bit.

I'm sure that he and his biker brothers are used to calling the shots in their everyday life where women are often thought of as second class and definitely not in the same caliber just because they have a vagina. But he's in my playground now. My turf, my territory. And he will damn well listen, or he can plead his own case.

I try not to smile sweetly back at him, but it's kind of hard. He knows I've got him by the balls, he's not an idiot.

"I kinda like the idea of you working on me all morning."

I drop the manila folder on the desk with another sigh. "Trust you to turn everything I say into something sordid."

"Oh, I've got sordid down pat, baby doll. And you know what else?" He leans forward on the table between us and flashes me a shit-eating grin. "I kinda like you bossing me around."

I keep my cool. "I suppose a man like you doesn't get the opportunity very often, if ever, to have a woman do such a travesty like call the shots, right?"

"You got me there, babe. Most of the women I know don't talk like you. They don't act like you, and they sure as shit don't look like you."

"Can we get back to your case?"

"Do you have a boyfriend?"

"You already know the answer to that, not that it's any of your business."

"Married?"

"I'm about five seconds away from leaving your ass here," I say through gritted teeth.

"You gotta give me somethin'."

I open the file and pull out the plea deal and shove it

toward him. "Here's something, your signature stating that you've learned your lesson and as it's – by some miracle – the first time you were caught with an illegal substance, it was your first drug conviction. I'll add that you moved states without realizing your court date."

He stares blankly. "You been readin' up on me, bossy lady?"

"It's on public records," I shoot back. "We will hope and pray for a reduced class one misdemeanor, rather than a felony conviction. I don't have to explain to you how strict the state of Arizona laws used to be with marijuana possession charges, since that has now changed, but that doesn't excuse your negligence at settling this matter. The law at the time of the charges is all the judge will care about."

He stares back at me, and I know the word "felony" might have made him sit up in his seat a little higher.

"It wasn't even a whole blunt from what I remember," he clarifies. "It's not like I was dealin'. I used it to help me sleep. I had a lot of… stress when I was younger."

"Well, there is a clause in the paperwork that if you agree to participate, we can submit an ongoing drug test to –"

"Fuck that," he complains before I even finish, sitting back in the chair again, his hands splaying behind his head. "You gonna come over to my place and read me a bedtime story when I can't sleep, *Ms. Hart*. I'm not peeing in a cup every damn week or whatever. I'm clean. Haven't smoked the shit in years."

I stammer as he uses my name. If awards were going out for asshole of the year, he'd be getting the biggest prize. He doesn't know I've tried to pull a few strings with the local doctor who I've left a message with, not that I would expect his story of using for insomnia to be viable, but it may just keep him out of jail.

"Sure, I'll rush right over."

"Careful, I'll hold you to that." He smirks.

"You know, if you gave a little more concentration to your pending felony charges instead of trying to get me into your bed, then we'd get this over and done with a lot faster."

His eyes flick to my throat. "It's hard to concentrate with you around, and I don't mind if it's your bed or mine, or the floor, or the wall, or the kitchen bench. I'm adaptable."

My pussy clenches at his dirty talk, and I try to form words. When none come, I feign outrage.

"That's highly inappropriate, *Mr. Romero.* I could fire you as my client for harassment and sexual innuendo if I wanted to, then the least of your problems would be felony charges." I try not to let my cheeks redden at the thought of him doing just that in any or *all* of those places.

I don't get flustered. I don't get lost for words. I make coffee nervous, yet this thorn in my side is getting deeper under my skin by the minute, and I can't seem to shake him.

"But you won't." He smirks. "Tell me you haven't

thought about it.”

“I’m your lawyer!” I snap.

“So what? Lawyers can have sex, can’t they? Don’t tell me attorney-client privilege doesn’t roll over into the bedroom, *Ms. Hart,* because I don’t believe it.”

I glare at him. “Your comments are rude and, quite frankly, insulting.”

“Then why do your cheeks look flushed?” He fires back.

Damn my fucking pale as ass skin. I blame my mother. I have her coloring.

“They’re not, but I am surprised I don’t see any other sexual harassment charges in your long line of misdemeanors if this is how you woo women.”

He grunts. “Trust me, woman, I’ve never had to work this hard in my life to *woo* anyone.” He leans forward again, his eyes hungry. “Between us, since we’re besties now, I’ll let you in on a little secret; the only thing longer than my questionable line of misdemeanors is my cock.”

My eyes go wide, and I press my thighs together, subconsciously imagining such a sight. I don’t want to be thinking about his cock. I don’t want to be imagining what he’d do to me with it or me sucking him off under the table right before court, but my body has other ideas. My clit pulses with need as I do everything I can to *not* think about him without clothes on.

Your bed or mine, hell, even the floor, wall or the kitchen bench. I'm adaptable.

"Since warnings of unwanted lewd comments don't seem to be working, how about I leave you here to make your own plea bargain," I state more calmly than I feel. It could be me, but I'm sure his eyes dip down to my chest, where my nipples have pebbled just thinking about all of the things I shouldn't be.

"You wouldn't."

"Try me."

He runs a hand over his face and then smirks again. "Fine. I'll wear the shirt."

Finally, something that makes sense comes out of his mouth.

I'm about to hand him my pen to sign the contract we've agreed on when he shoves the chair back and stands. I'm momentarily confused, but then he makes his way to the door where I hung the shirt on the coat hook. Without any more words, he pulls the Henley up and over his body, revealing his back to me and a gasp holds in my throat as I check out his fine form.

He has tattoos over one arm and one half of his back, with the other side clean, and when he turns to reach for the shirt, tossing his Henley over his shoulder at the table, I get a glimpse of his toned abs and muscular, smooth chest.

Of course, he's an exhibitionist and turns all the way around to face me, shrugging the shirt on as his eyes meet mine and, without my consent, they dip down his chest, raking over that finely tuned torso. Greedily, I glance farther down to the boxer brief elastic showing over the top of his jeans. Finally, my eyes cast over the bulge at his zipper, and that's when I look away.

He grins as he begins buttoning up the shirt. "Like what you see, *Ms. Hart?*"

I swallow hard. He certainly keeps in shape… and that faint peek of hair leading from his navel into his jeans and toward his… *I've got to get a grip.*

"If you're quite finished undressing in a public arena, this document requires your signature. Unless you'd like to seek other counsel, and if so, that means we're done."

"Don't be a spoilsport." He gives me a wink. "It's all right to look. I don't work out at the gym for no reason, sweet cheeks."

My fingers itch to touch him, to run my hands over that crisp, white shirt and over his muscled body and rippled pecs, one hand wandering south to cup his dick. *I want him.* And I shouldn't want him. He's the epitome of what I really don't need in my life. Then again, carefree, no holds barred sex with a handsome stranger who spells a little danger and a whole lot of trouble could be just what the doctor ordered…once I get him out of this mess, of course…

I ignore his comment. "Are you going to sign this or not?"

He finishes doing up the top button and then gives me a

chin lift. "Got a tie?"

I blanch. "You want to wear a tie?"

"Didn't say that."

"Then what do you want a tie for?"

He gives me a waggle of his eyebrows.

Oh. *Duh.*

Now I'm picturing myself being trussed up by him and tied to his bed. This will not do.

He's about to say something else crude, when there's a knock at the door, followed by another officer, a female who gives me a curt nod. "They're ready for you, Attorney Hart."

I smile. "Thank you."

I flick my eyes to Bones. He's still standing, looming over me as I gather myself.

"Saved by the bell," he muses.

I collect the papers, noting he still hasn't signed them. "Please let me do the talking," I remind him for the fiftieth time. "Polite, honest answers are best, and do not, under any circumstances, seem like you're enjoying this whole thing."

"Why not? I kind of am."

"Please tell me your biker buddies won't be in court," I go on, ignoring his implication.

He gives me a shrug. "None of the fuckers bothered comin' to get me out, so who the fuck knows if they'll bother coming to my hearing."

"That reminds me, no cussing in court. We're going for

remorseful and contrite, so no eyeballing anyone either."

"You sure have a lot of rules, woman."

"And address me as your attorney when we're in court. It looks more professional."

He sweeps his arm toward the door. "Well, I'm ready when you are, *Attorney Hart.*"

I shake my head in exasperation as I point to the documents. "Sign."

He gives me a cheeky purse of his lips and bends down toward the table, scrawling his name on the bottom. His real one.

"Happy?"

"I'll be happier when I'm out of here," I mutter.

He pulls on the collar of his shirt. "Well, no time like the present. I might even let you buy me a coffee when we're done."

I place all the papers in my briefcase and snap it closed, ignoring his comment.

"Let's just get through the next half hour, and if I don't strangle you by then, it'll be a miracle." I smile sweetly as I button my suit jacket, his eyes watching my every move.

"That's not a no," he chimes as I stomp past him to the door.

The thing is, I'm not even kidding. I may go down for murder after all.

BRACKEN RIDGE
REBELS
ARIZONA
M · C

CHAPTER 3

BONES

I've never been so excited to be inside a courtroom in my life, even though I should be shittin' my pants they may cart me off to jail.

Obviously, I'm hoping for leniency, being I've somehow evaded the law up until this point.

It's probably best, as my hot lawyer advised me, that I keep my mouth shut for once.

I'm well aware that I tend to get myself in more trouble quicker than most people blink because I don't know when to quit, and it's not like Kennedy helps.

Especially when her cheeks flushed when I started with the dirty talk. That was pure delight.

I should stop trying. She's made it clear I don't have a chance in Hell, and while I can't argue with the fact she's got a stick up her ass, she hasn't exactly told me to fuck off.

She could. If she did, I'd back off, but it's like she keeps me hanging on the line, as if she likes the chase. That, or she really does hate me, and if that were the case, then why do I make her flush and stumble over her words? And when she pretends to ignore me, it makes me wanna take her long, red hair in one hand and kiss her plump lips until she begs me to stop.

I sneak a sideways glance and I'm rewarded with Miss Lawyer Lady in full professional mode. She's all business, her files neatly laid out on the table in front of her, along with a notepad and pen, like she's done this a million times.

"How long have you been a lawyer for?" I ask when we sit waiting for the judge to arrive.

She doesn't turn my way, but asks, "Are we making small talk now?"

I lounge back in the chair and cross my arms over my chest. "Why not? I don't bite."

She turns her head and our eyes lock. She's got a pretty hue to her hazel eyes today. They seem lighter than I remember.

"I don't usually engage in chit-chat with my clients." I like how she keeps calling me that. "I don't have to be your client when this is over."

"Mr. Rom –" I hold up my hand and she stops.

"Please, for fuck's sake, call me Bones."
She frowns. "How did you get that name anyway?"

I smirk. "I'll tell you when you answer my question."

Her chest heaves with what I think is a little exasperation, and I'm a sick son of a bitch for liking it.

"Eleven years."

I ponder that for a moment. "Got my name because I broke a lot of bones in high school, every bone in my body pretty much, and the nickname kinda stuck."

I see a small smile play on her lips as she looks away. "That's probably the most normal thing you've ever said," she muses.

"By normal, I'm assuming you think I'm abnormal the rest of the time?"

I don't see her roll her eyes, but I bet she just did. "Do you always have an answer for everything?"

"No, but I want to know something…"

"Is this where I pretend to be interested?"

"If you hate me so much, why did you agree to represent me?"

"I don't hate you," she whisper-shouts. "That's ridiculous."

"Is it?" I shrug. "Then answer me this, you're beautiful, smart – really *fuckin'* smart, you've got a whiplash tongue, drive a nice car and dress well, your body's hot as sin, you're single – and you don't have anybody in your life?"

Shit. Here I go again.

I see her shift in her chair as her eyes dart to me again, and there it is, deep beneath the fiery depths, I see something flash before me. If I'd blinked, I'd have missed it.

What am I not getting?

"You can't say things like that to me in court," she whispers, if not a little angrily.

"Nobody can hear us, just answer the question. It's not that hard. I get you don't like me, but I wanna know what kinda guys you're into – you do like dudes, right?" A thought crosses my mind, but I brush it off. Pretty sure her reaction to me changing my shirt cleared up any lesbian tendencies I've dreamed up.

"Of course I like dudes. I just… I just don't think that we should get involved or be talking about this, period. Not just in court."

"Why not?"

She sighs. "Aside from the fact I'm your attorney?"

"Only until you get me out of this mess."

She sighs again, a little heavier this time. "Not that it's any of your business, but I'm not ready to date."
I sit up in the chair and lean my elbows on the table. "Then tell me to fuck off."

Her brows furrow as her eyes dart to mine. "I'm not going to do that."

"I want you to, because if you don't want me to pursue you, Kennedy, you better tell me right now. I'd like nothing more than to take you back to my place and worship that hot, sexy body of yours wearin' those heels and make you forget about any other asshole that came along before me."

She blinks. "Who said he was an asshole?"

I frown. "Well, he put you off men, didn't he? You're not ready to date."

Her eyes glaze over, and I know straight away I've said the wrong thing. "It's really not like that."

"I'm tryin' to be a gentleman about it," I say. "But you're makin' it really fuckin' hard."

She's about to say something, but it's right at that moment that the judge decides to make an appearance. She's dressed in robes and looks about eighty years old. Hopefully, I look contrite enough to get a hall pass.

Everyone stands and Kennedy gives me a stern look, so I follow suit.

When the judge takes a seat, everyone sits down again.

My brothers showed up, and they refused to take their club colors off, so the bailiff kept them out in the waiting room. Not that I've got a nice word to say about any of them right now, since I've been here far too fuckin' long as it is.

"Ms. Hart," the judge begins. "Your client has been arrested for multiple charges and pleads guilty on all accounts?"

"No, your honor. On the first charge of drug possession and exceeding the allowable amount of cannabis in the state of Arizona for recreational use eight years ago, my client missed his court date as he was out of state. I do have a doctor's sworn statement the cannabis was in fact issued for medicinal purposes. My client suffers from insomnia brought on by his years of service in the military. As an upstanding citizen, you will duly note he's not had any other criminal charges in relation to drug possession prior to his arrest."

I turn to stare at her in shock. *What the fuck?* I'm beginning to love this fuckin' chick.

How the hell did she pull that off? I haven't been to the doc since I was a kid.

The judge looks far from impressed. "I'd like to see all of the paperwork and amount of cannabis found on the defendant at the time of his arrest along with the Doctor's sworn statement."

"Certainly, your honor." The deputy's assistant comes over to the table, and Kennedy hands him the paperwork while I continue to stare at her.

The judge takes her time scanning the documents over, like she isn't already aware of my case, which is pretty shitty judging if you ask me.

"Stop staring at me," Kennedy whispers out of the side of her mouth.

"I can't help it," I whisper back. "You just pulled a fuckin' rabbit out of your ass, and I'm supposed to just sit here and stare at the wall?"

"Don't swear in court, and the saying is; rabbit out of your hat. I told you before, Mr. Romero, you're not the only one who has friends in low places."

"Does this mean I owe you one?" I smirk.

She turns to look at me, her eyes ablaze with a look

on her face that kinda tells me she's in charge, and in this courtroom, she is. I respect that. It's a huge turn on when a woman can hold her own and is ten times smarter than you. I never knew I could be attracted to a woman's brain as much as her body.

"It means you owe me more than you can probably ever pay. Now shut up. We've still got to get through your *longer than my cock* list of unpaid fines, tickets, and warrants." My dick kicks in my jeans at her tone and her use of my words, thrown back at me, and I'm hoping the judge doesn't notice the boulder I've got goin' on front and center.

I'd love nothing more than to take Kennedy back to the nearest flat surface or, hell, her car even, and give her the best orgasm she's ever had in her life. She deserves it. I mean, she did say I owe her more than I'd ever be able to give, but clearly, she hasn't been in the sack with me before. I'm not a selfish fucker, which she'll understand if she ever lets me between her legs.

"Yes, ma'am." I resist the urge to salute and keep my chuckle to myself.

The judge finally looks up and over to me. "I will accept the documentation, but I have to address Mr. Romero's blatant attitude to not showing up to court and getting away with the charges by fleeing the state is a felony."

Kennedy doesn't falter. "While my client concedes it was not wise to move before receiving his summons and court date, he does accept that he made a mistake in not informing the Arizona DMV. Had he done so, he would have produced the court documents that would have cleared him from a felony charge, your honor."

The judge does not look happy. "With all due respect, your client has a blatant disregard for the law, Ms. Hart. I don't buy the excuse, which I'm sure is one of many."

"Your honor…"

The judge holds up a hand and Kennedy clamps her mouth shut.

"Since I've wasted enough time on this already, in relation to the medicinal cannabis charges, I will drop the felony charge. Thank goodness there is a doctor willing to vouch for Mr. Romero, otherwise this could have been a very different outcome since there was a warrant out for his arrest. However, since your client skipped out on his court hearing through his own negligence and less than par attitude, I will be insisting he perform community service at your supervision for a minimum of one hundred hours."

"Thank you, your honor."

What the fuck? Can she do that?

"I'd like to move on to the more serious charges of unpaid speeding tickets and the numerous parking fines."

"I apologize, your honor. My client was not being purposely obtuse. The fines were sent to another address through the DMV, and again, while that is no excuse, my client is more than willing to pay these fines and any penalties today. I have also put a proposal together for my client to commence voluntary community service in addition to the one hundred hours, which I will sign off on and make sure it is completed in a timely manner."

"This doesn't excuse your client's negligent behavior, Ms. Hart."

"You are right, your honor. My client was going through a hard time during his service in the Middle East while serving in the military, where he received a medical honorable discharge after suffering injuries while on duty. My client takes full responsibility for his prior actions, and I would like to note that he has not had any tickets in the last few…"

What the fuck? How does she know all that?

"Ms. Hart, while I appreciate the lengths you are going to in order to keep your client out of jail, I don't believe your client is taking the law seriously."

"I promise you, your honor, his past misdemeanors do not speak louder than the charitable work he has done including the Ride for Riches, the motorcycle riding challenge to help the needy and underprivileged, and more recently, he has partaken in donating materials to help rebuild the sawmill, which is being turned into a soup kitchen for the homeless."

The judge looks down at me skeptically. "The longer your attorney keeps talking, the more inclined I am to hear more about the ways you plan to redeem yourself in the eyes of the court," she says.

I'm about to open my trap when I feel Kennedy's hand on my forearm. She gives it a tight squeeze, and I shut my mouth.

"Your honor, I have also drafted a proposal including supervised community service with Faux Paws, the local dog shelter which is responsible for taking in stray and mistreated animals. They are more than happy for Mr. Romero to complete any remaining hours there, or at an institution as you see fit."

I keep my eyes down because I'm so fuckin' awe-inspired by what this woman is doing for me. As much as I don't like the idea of community service, I also don't want to go to jail either. It's a trade-off.

Faux Paws is the rehoming shelter that Steel, the Sergeant at Arms for the club, helped form with some other volunteers because he loves animals. In fact, I'd go so far as to say he loves his Pittie, Lola, and little scruffy terrier, Rocky, more than he does most people. This is going to be a piece of cake.

"While I appreciate your thorough readiness for this case, Ms. Hart, the bad attitude and blatant disregard for unpaid tickets are becoming an increasing problem, especially for vigilantes who think they're above the law."

"Your honor, I can assure you my client has learned the error of his ways."

She doesn't even spare me a glance this time. "I understand Mr. Romero likes to think of himself as an upstanding citizen, but the facts remain; he's had no fewer than twenty-three misdemeanors in the last three years alone and only one paid fine. Not a very encompassing track record. Disqualification of his license will be mandatory for a minimum of three months."

I stiffen next to Kennedy, my eyes rising toward the Judge. I'm the fuckin' Road Captain. I can't be without my goddamn license for any period of time, much less three months.

"Your honor, my client needs his license for his business at the junkyard. While he is on light duties due to an injury, he still attends the office daily and oversees deliveries and the collection of goods. He has to be able to drive to work."

She looks straight down at me through her glasses this time. She'd give Judge Judy a run for her money in terms of scariness.

"I will grant him an extraordinary license to and from work. That's it. If he's caught driving anywhere else in a car or a motorcycle, he will land right back in jail, permanently this time."

Shit.

I'm about to tell her she can't fuckin' do that or tell me what to do, and as if sensing my impending outburst, Kennedy tugs on the sleeve of my shirt.

"That won't be necessary, your honor, we are grateful for your leniency."

I use the closeness of her touch to slide my leg next to hers so we're touching, and fuck me if the heat from her body doesn't send an electric current through me. *She must be feeling this too?*

She flicks her eyes to Kennedy. "The fines will be paid today, as well as any interest accrued in overdue amounts and all the late payment fees. I am also issuing a fine for reckless endangerment for driving without a license, which would have been the case should you have turned up for your court hearing, that will also be paid today. You will be ordered to keep a clean record from now until a hearing date, which I will postpone for three months from now. Once all your community service is complete and there are no further infringements or arrests made in that time period, we can reconvene, and with any luck, Mr. Romero may finally learn his lesson."

"Thank you, your honor."

I don't know why she's thanking her. She may as well cut my nuts off if I can't ride my motorcycle.

"You can pay the fines before you leave and complete all the paperwork before collecting Mr. Romero from custody within the hour. Is there anything you'd like to add?"

"No, your honor, thank you."

The judge bangs the gavel down and the court is

dismissed. She doesn't spare us another glance before we all rise again, and she leaves the courtroom.

Kennedy sits back down and drops her hand.

"That was fuckin' amazing," I say, staring at her in awe. "Not about havin' to do community service or pay huge fines or not ride my motorcycle, but the part where you made a potential felony charge disappear, and that whole jail situation."

She pinches the bridge of her nose. "Well, hold on to your hat for a half an hour. The custodian will take you back to the holding cell in a moment. Once I've completed the paperwork, you can pay at the clerk's office downstairs, and we can all be on our merry way."

"You gonna drive me home?"

She spares me a look. "Not a chance."

"Aww, but we were having so much fun."

The officer comes back to take me away, and I stand and give her a wink. "Be seein' you later, sugar."

"Don't count on it," she replies without missing a beat.

"You're forgetting you volunteered to supervise my community service," I sing-song back as the deputy cuffs me again. "Which we can conduct in my bedroom, if you like?"

"That won't be necessary. Jayson Steelman has already signed off on your supervision for the cleaning and maintenance of the dog shelter, so I'd get used to poop scooping if I were you."

Shit. I forgot about that.

There's no way Steel is gonna let me get out of it, either. Still, I'd rather be there than be in fuckin' jail.

"I'll wear you down, you know," I call out as the officer leads me away.

She gives me a sarcastic wave of her fingers as I reluctantly follow the guard back to the courthouse holding cell. And it's the worst half hour of my life, not being back in the cell, though this one is deserted, but because I don't know if I'll get to see her again when I'm released. I never really said thank you.

Everything gets sorted out pretty swiftly. I pay my fines with the deputy's assistant supervising, and after that, they let me collect my belongings. The first thing I see are my club brothers, Rubble and Steel, waiting for me in the lobby.

We chest bump and Steel frowns when he sees the shirt I've got on. My Henley disappeared too. I left it on the table when I changed in the office adjacent to the courtroom.

Remembering Kennedy's eyes grazing down my body is enough to give me a hard on that won't quit.

"You know that material will make your skin itch," Steel says, giving me a chin lift and handing me my cut.

"Tell me about it. My sexy lawyer said it'd make me look better – guess she was right." I shrug. "Oh, and thanks for organizing the community service shit. Owe you one."

"You will owe me one when you're knee deep in it. I

needed all those cages cleaned out and we're gonna paint the outside next week. Guess it was good timin'."

I roll my eyes. "You're not actually gonna hold me to it, are you? I mean, my back and shit…"

"He's been using that excuse forever and a day," Rubble says, giving me a slap on my back, which makes me wince. "Time for a different excuse."

"Fine, I've gotta go find Kennedy. Shoulda seen her in there, fuckin' killed it."

"Don't look now." Rubble nods behind me. "She's at the clerk's desk."

I turn, and my eyes immediately drop to her ass. In that pencil skirt, she's all curves, and I want nothing more than to sink my teeth into her soft flesh.

"Bit of a looker," Steel grunts. "You gonna tap it finally?"

"She's playin' hard to get, nothin's changed on that front," I mumble.

"Maybe take some of Lucy's advice and be a little less Bones and a little more nice guy," Rubble puts in, like I need any advice.

"I am a nice guy," I snort. "I'm givin' her the option of which position she'd prefer. How much nicer can a man be?"

Steel shakes his head. "Not happenin', bro."

"I'd start with flattery before tryin' to get into her pants. Women wanna be wooed and all that shit," Rubble chimes, though I've heard enough about it from Lucy.

"Don't you fuckin' start." I *am* nice to women.

I don't treat them like shit or leave them hanging. They know what to expect when they get with me. I'm not opposed to a relationship; I've just never met a woman that would be a good match for me. Until now. There's something about Kennedy that pushes all of my buttons. Steel nods over my shoulder. "Better get a move on. She just spotted us, and ten bucks says she tries to hightail it outta here."

I spare another glance over to Kennedy, then turn back to them. "Meet you outside. Tell me you brought a cage."

"No can do. Might have to get a ride with the lawyer lady." Rubble looks a little too pleased with himself as I give him the middle finger. "Oh, and you owe me bail money!"

I ignore him as I make my way toward her, in case she does in fact decide to bolt for it.

"Long time no see," I say, sidling up next to her at the counter as she turns to look up at me.

"Feels like a lifetime," she replies, looking back at the clerk.

"See, didn't skip out on you, gotta start acting like a model citizen and pay my dues. Nice job, by the way." She snorts. "Is that your idea of thanking me?"

I lean closer, turning my head away from the clerk's window so I can whisper in her ear.

"No, my way of thanking you would be X-rated. I wasn't kidding about any of that."

Her breath catches in her chest ever so slightly and now that I'm towering over her, I'm rewarded with a nice view of her rack. I can just see the top of her breasts through the small V where her blouse sits. Fuck, I'd love her to choke on my cock.

"Mr. Romero, now that I'm done here, and it seems you're a free man, this is where we part ways." She thanks the clerk and pushes past me, her briefcase in hand as she swings those hips in her attempt to get away from me.

"The thing is," I say when I jog up alongside her, "I've no way of getting home. Boys only brought the sleds, and I'm not allowed to drive. Remember?"

She keeps her gaze ahead as she pulls out a pair of sunglasses and puts them on as the automatic doors open. "I don't see how that's my problem."

"Well, you have a car, don't you?"

"I'm not sleeping with you," she retorts.

Uh, okay, cut to the chase. "Why not?"

I like how fast she moves in those high heels. I'm literally power walking to keep up with her as she dismounts the steps toward the parking lot.

"There are a multitude of reasons, none which I care to disclose because I've already wasted enough of my time today."

"Wasted?" I snort. "Come on, you got paid and you got me off. We should be celebrating."

"Hallelujah. Does that feel better?"

I run a hand down my face. "Fine, have it your way. I'll walk, but it's kinda mean. I live the other side of town, and I've not slept all night. If I get hit by a car, you'll have it on your conscience."

I'm secretly kinda pissed. I thought we had a moment, but now I'm back to second guessing myself.

When we get to the bottom of the stairs, I go one way, and she goes another, but a few moments later, I hear her voice. "Fine," she calls out as I turn to look back at her. "But only because now you're probably going to purposely throw yourself in front of a bus so I'll feel bad."

I hide my grin, barely. "See, that wasn't so hard, was it?"

She turns again and her car beeps. Ah, I forgot she drove a Mercedes convertible. The top's up today. Pity. I'd love to see her hair blowing around in the breeze.

"Get in, before I change my mind."

Bones

BRACKEN RIDGE
REBELS
ARIZONA
M · C

CHAPTER 4

HENNEDY

I know I shouldn't, but a part of me does feel a bit sorry for him, especially paying all that cash out as well as the bail money, even though it is all his own doing.

Deep down, I'm not as harsh on the inside as I appear on the outside. In fact, I have a deep compassion for people, especially the under-privileged, which he isn't, or anyone down on their luck.

Ryan Romero, however, is a conundrum. On the one hand, he's paid some dues by the charity work I mentioned in court, and trust me, it was a surprise to me too. But on the other hand, he chooses to continually break the law and try to get away with it.

As he climbs into my convertible, I know this is a bad idea.

I know I'm attracted to him, and I think it was obvious when I stared at his naked chest, which is not something I tend to normally do. Then again. I've never had a man undress in front of me in a public place, much less a courthouse holding room. That's definitely a first.

His body is made for sin. He obviously works out and works out hard.

I can't deny that I appreciate the sight of a well-toned body, especially when it's accompanied by a nice face with pretty eyes. Let's face it, he's the whole package… until he opens his mouth.

"Sweet car," he says, glancing around my small interior.

I love my car; it's sleek, soundless, has all the modern touches and goes really, really fast. It was my one present to myself before I moved here… before things irrevocably changed for me.

"Thanks."

He turns and glances at the back. "No back seat," he notes.

"No shit."

"Makes fuckin' a bit hard, doesn't it?"

I sigh. "I don't fuck in my car."

"Huh."

"What does *huh* mean?"

He shrugs. "You're missin' out, babe. Fuckin' in the car can be really hot. The amount of room you don't have to work with for one, then there's the fact you may get caught, and you gotta be kinda quick, which I'm not." He gives me a wink as I glance sideways at him.

To say he doesn't wet my panties would be a lie. He does. And imagining us doing it in my car does turn me on, and now that I've had a visual, it becomes all the more apparent I may have a thing for my client… I just don't want him to know. I'm not ready to take that step… casual sex or not.

"Good to know."

"So, you do the casual thing?" he asks.

I want to beat my forehead on the steering wheel. *Is his mind always on the pepperoni?*

"Are we really going to discuss this like we're talking about the weather?"

I feel him looking at me. "We're grown adults. You can tell me to fuck off any time, or kick me out of your car, but since you've done neither, something inside me tells me that you secretly like it. You like the fantasy of me, don't you? *Ms. Hart.*"

"We're not in court now," I say. "It's Kennedy."

"Answer the question."

"I don't know what you mean, the fantasy of you?" I do know what he means, but I want to hear him say it. I also want the ground to swallow me whole.

"You don't want the real me, just the bad boy biker. The guy who can eat you out all night and fuck you just how you like it, raw, unbridled, and rough. I can be that fantasy for you, no strings attached. You should think about it. We'd be good together."

He's unbelievable. Cocky son-of-a-bitch.

I clutch the steering wheel, a retort in my throat, yet

it never leaves. "What, like our dirty little secret?" I find myself asking instead.

He grunts a laugh. "Now we're gettin' somewhere. Yeah, our dirty little secret. We both get what we want, and nobody has to know. You don't have to be embarrassed by me, or admit you slummed it for a while, and I can show you a good time, a really fuckin' good time."

My heart slams into my chest at his dirty words, but I frown at the "slumming it" comment.

Is this really what he thinks I think of him?
"Wait – that's not what I meant, I'd never… I'd never be embarrassed by you, Bones. I just…" *Shit*. Don't do it. My personal life is private… and he's a stranger. "I don't know how to do the casual thing…"

The comment really bothers me, not that it seems to bother him. I don't see myself as any better than him just because he's my client and he was in trouble. He doesn't seem fazed, like he's just stating a fact and he's accepted it.

"It's easy," he says. "Like ridin' a bike. Speakin' of which, how long has it been since you rode a bike?"

I swallow hard. *Two years*.

"Umm, I don't feel comfortable discussing that with you."

"A while, then? I don't see how, you're fuckin' gorgeous. Every man in the courtroom was picturing what's under that skirt suit and wishin' they had x-ray vision."

I tighten my hands on the steering wheel once more. My core is about to burst, and I might take him up on his offer to fuck in my car if he keeps it up. His downright dirty words both shock and thrill me at the same time. I've never had a man tell me exactly what he wanted to do to me, and I can't help but imagine him eating me out all night…

This wouldn't be a mercy fuck, though. Oh no, my body is begging me to take him home. Let him have his way with me. Fuck knows I haven't had sex for a very long time, not because I don't like sex… far from it, but because I'm broken, and a part of my soul may never heal from the past.

"Well, I guess I'm different than other people," I say finally, even though it sounds lame, and it makes me feel weak. I like sex. Hell, I loved sex. *Loved* being the operative word.

"You have a bad experience or somethin'?"

Jesus, he's so nosy.

"No."

"Then what?"

"Why do you have to be so goddamn annoying?"

He gives me a grin when our eyes meet. "If we're not fuckin' today, then can you drop me at work? Then I can get my sled."

"Sled?"

"Motorcycle."

"You're not supposed to ride that, remember," I tell him.

I don't know how I feel about being let off the hook.

I'm a goddamn roller coaster.

I don't want him. I do want him. I don't want him. I do want him.

I think about the implication of having random, casual sex with him, and it jolts me into a zone I haven't felt in a long time. Lust, I guess.

To say my body aches for a man's touch is putting it mildly, but Bones can't be what I need him to be. Not because he's a biker, or that I think I'm better than him, but because I have needs. I have singular, fucked up needs, and I can't ask that of a stranger. I just can't. So I stay single. Celibate, aside from my vibrator. Thank God for silicone.

"What's the address?"

He reels it off, and I make a right at the next street sign.

"You did good today," he says after a while. "I was impressed you got my doctor to sign off on shit that didn't even happen."

Yeah, well, I would suspect that had something to do with his 'biker' connections rather than me, but I won't question it.

"Well, it's clearly not what you know in a small town."

"Saved me potential jail time."

"Luckily I have friends in low places." I feel him watching me again as I turn into the high gates of the property labeled Bone Yard Junk on the sign. "Cute," I mutter.

"I might roll around in shit all day and get covered in stink," he goes on. "But I wash up good, babe. Just keep it in mind if you ever need a little relieving of your own, got me?"

I pull the car up alongside what looks like an old, rickety office.

"That won't be necessary."

He releases his seat belt and turns toward me, his face close to mine. "Every woman has needs, *Ms. Hart.* And I'm here to please you, so if you find yourself alone at night, wanting me to come over and eat your pussy and make you come with my tongue before I fuck you however you like it, then you've got my cell. Until then." He gives me a salute. "Thank you for haulin' me out of jail."

My eyes go wide as I swallow hard and continue to stare at him, watching as he lifts his large body out of my car, he slams the door, and saunters off to the office, tugging on the collar of his leather jacket.

I'm not often at a loss for words.

The white shirt I lent him makes him look like a walking contradiction. It's too crisp and clean to be worn with a leather jacket. I check out his ass. Small, tight, and goddamn perfect. I can imagine the sight of him, ramming his cock into me as I cry out his name, my hands restrained so I can't touch him as he draws out orgasm after orgasm, just like he said.

I groan out loud. *Shit, double fucking shit.*

He doesn't look back, and after he disappears inside, I snap myself out of my daze and put my car into reverse, ignoring the wetness I feel between my legs. Not only does he turn me on, but I'm actually considering using him for house calls in the very near future.

I forgot I had dinner plans with Stevie and Colt's girlfriend from the club, Cassidy. The two of them have become close friends since Cassidy moved to town. We spend most of the evening at Zander's, the upmarket tapas lounge in town that serves great cocktails.

Since I'm driving, I only have one and we eat tacos as Stevie tells us that Axton, Brock, and Amelia's jailbird brother will be joining her soon as the new bar supervisor when he gets out.

To be honest, I'm not entirely thrilled about the idea, but I can't voice it too much, and as he's also Amelia's brother, I've got to tread carefully around her because it's all she's been talking about.

"So, you've finally got the promotion in writing?" I ask, knowing that Richie Hutchinson, the Rebels President and the man about town, can be a little intimidating. I don't want Stevie getting ripped off. She's not as feisty as I am and has, in the past, had others take advantage of her.

"He's drawing up a contract, yes," she replies, giving Cassidy an eye roll. "And before you ask, I have accepted a pay raise, being that I'll be the new bar manager and also calling the shots."

I don't want to bitch about this in front of Cassidy, but she's the one who brought it up first.

"Are we sure we can trust this Axton guy? Between us girls, he was arrested for armed robbery. That's a little troubling, Stevie."
It makes my insides turn to mush. The thought of anyone hurting my little sister makes me want to commit murder. I'm very protective of her.

"Rumor has it the gun wasn't loaded, and he was high on ecstasy," Stevie says, twirling her strawberry blonde hair over one shoulder. "Young and stupid. He did almost ten years, and Brock's confident he's reformed."

"That's some scary shit," Cassidy agrees. "Even if he has reformed, have you voiced your concern to Hutch or to Brock?"

She frowns. Of course not. Maybe I should go and pay Mr. Hutchinson a visit and ask the questions for myself.

Axton will be on probation, obviously. Since I've never laid eyes on the dude, I don't have an opinion about whether he looks dodgy or not. I tend to get to know these things pretty swiftly… Like when I think about Bones, and I know that he isn't a bad guy. He's just done some stupid shit. I also can't stop thinking about what he said to me only hours ago. I'd be lying if I said I hadn't pictured him more than one time with his head between my legs.

"…I don't know how I would go about that," Stevie's saying. "I mean, they've given me a huge responsibility, and I know I can do it. I don't know that I can broach the subject without it seeming like I'm against the idea."

"Well, you should have been given a vote. You are the new bar manager," I reply, giving her a look. "Normally, it would be up to you to hire staff."

"I did agree to it when they asked me if I'd be comfortable working with him. Hutch was actually very forthcoming; he didn't want me to feel uncomfortable in any way…"

"But they were always going to hire him regardless?" I finish, because I know it's true.

"Everyone deserves a second chance, K, even crooks."

"Not all of them," I mutter.

"Amen to that," Cassidy says. "But on the bright side, I really don't think anyone at the club would put you at risk knowingly, or put you in harm's way. It won't work out well for Axton if he fucks it up."

I nod in agreement. "That's true, but it remains to be seen. It's a violent history – no matter how they sugar coat it. He was convicted for a violent crime, and I don't know how happy I am about you working with him and locking up at night with just the two of you…"

"K, you're being dramatic. I'm going to be fine," Stevie says. I know she's good at her job and she seems to have the bikers under control. They've never been rude or unkind to her, by some kind of miracle. She's a big girl now and has to make her own decisions, I know that, but that doesn't mean I have to be happy about it.

"I don't really care, as long as you're comfortable with it. It's all right to say that you're not, though. It's easy to be pressured into accepting something when you've been offered a promotion, especially when your employers are a biker gang."

"Club," Stevie corrects. "A gang implies they're outlaws. You know I wouldn't work for anyone who did anything illegal."

"I know you wouldn't."

"You worry too much. Hutch is the best employer I've ever had," she goes on, which does make me feel better. "And working with Ginger is a hoot. Summer's cool too, when she's there. She's started nursing school, so I don't see her as much anymore."

Summer is Gunner, the baby-faced charmer of the club's, little sister. She's striking just like him, but keeps to herself a lot. I haven't had much to do with her either, which just reminds me of how dull my social life actually is.

"Hey, you're going to the charity auction, right?" Cassidy pipes up out of nowhere.

"What?" I laugh.

She nods enthusiastically. "I've not been to one yet, but it's a lot of fun. The whole town gets involved. There're raffles, door prizes, and the highlight of the night is the bachelors of Bracken Ridge get to be auctioned off for a date."

Stevie and I both snort a laugh.

"Are you serious?" I splutter. "And here I was thinking Bracken Ridge was a hundred years behind the times."

"It can get a bit catty," Cassidy goes on as we continue to laugh. "Depending on who the bachelors are."

"God help us," Stevie says, then points at me. "You should totally come. Buy yourself a date, then you're obliged to actually follow through."

I wrinkle my nose. "I don't think that sounds like a terribly good idea. Have you seen some of the single men in this town? Mr. Carruthers from the convenience store, for one. Then Pete Williams that weird cat guy is another. Oh, and my personal favorite, Jack from the scrapyard. Apparently, his wife left him."

I know the Rebels had something to do with the fact that Jack had every single finger on his hands broken some months back. Now he's selling up, and rumor has it the Rebels are putting in a bid. The guys a crook from way back, but imagining him being up for auction makes me chuckle.

"Well, they've gotta get some decent guys," Cassidy goes on. "It's the big-ticket item of the night, and it makes them the most money, so the candidates can't be that bad."

"And this is why I moved to a small town," I muse as we continue to laugh.

I've had a good night, and I vow to do it again soon, once work slows down.

I'm known to be a workaholic. Starting from scratch in a small town has had its challenges, but I'm busier than ever now that the club has thrown work my way, and not just getting Bones out of jail. But also with Kirsty throwing her real estate contracts my way.

Going home to an empty house, I shower and fall asleep thinking about my ultimate fantasy, the one Bones put in my head. Not the part about me slumming it; that still churns my gut. I don't think of him like that. I was being honest when I said I don't know how to do the casual thing, and I definitely don't know how to do the *Bones* thing.

He's a lot.

A man who's as comfortable as he is with his sexual needs is a little unnerving.

He's confronting and deep down, I like it. I like a man who knows what he wants and better still; takes it. I don't know why I don't just sleep with him and get it over with, then I could actually stop lying to myself that he isn't under my skin, even though I know that's not a smart idea.

If I had half a brain in my head, I'd remember he's a criminal and a wiseass.

I just need to go to sleep and forget about him…

I know I'm dreaming, but I don't want to wake up. Not ever.

In my fantasy, he's in my room in the dead of night, uninvited, and he's peering down at me as I stare up at him in my dreamy, barely awake state. He's shirtless, his hair tousled, and he has that smirk on his lips that drives me insane. His eyes sparkle like diamonds in the night sky.

"I thought I told you to sleep naked," he drawls when my eyes finally focus.

"You never –"

He grins. "Peel back those covers, sugar. Let me see you." As I do, he drops his pants, boxers and all, and his huge cock springs free. It's fully erect, and he strokes it with his palm back and forth. I do as he says and throw the covers back, revealing myself to him.

His eyes graze over my body, and I gasp when he licks his lips. "Show me your pussy."

I let out a mewl at his dirty words and move my hand

down, spreading my legs and parting my pussy lips. His eyes drop down low as he keeps pulling on his dick. Seeing him sheath himself sends a spark of heat right through me, making me slick and ready for him.

"You been thinkin' about me? Pretty lawyer lady?"

"Yes," I whisper.

"You have, haven't you? Ever since I told you I'd eat you out and make you scream with my tongue."

Fuck.

I start to play with myself. I need to relieve the ache. I need *him* to relieve it, but I can't get the words past my lips.

He watches me as I watch him, both touching ourselves but neither of us touching each other.

His hand moves back and forth over his cock as he walks toward me, his pace quickening, his stomach muscles clenching with every pull.

"Such a pretty pussy," he murmurs, mounting the bed as he moves between my legs. "I need to taste you."

I swallow hard as he dips his head, licking through my folds as I buck off the bed. The bristles of his stubble scratching me, but instead of pain, all I feel is pleasure.

"Fuck," I mutter. "Jesus, fuck."

I feel him grin against my skin as he parts me with his fingers, licking my clit once, twice, then he sucks it into his mouth as I groan. I cup my breasts, needing to pinch my nipples, needing the pain as I soar higher and higher.

He keeps sucking as I reach my hands into his hair and groan. I come in seconds, squeezing my eyes shut and riding the waves of pleasure. But he's not done. Oh no, his annihilation of my body is just beginning. He inserts two fingers and blows on my sensitive skin. My eyes dart down as his meet mine. It's so sexy, naughty, forbidden, and I want all of him. I need him inside me.

"Fuck me, Bones. Fuck my pussy," I whisper.

He tuts. "Greedy little girl. Knew you'd be beggin' for my cock just like I told you." He licks my clit again, slowly, making me squirm as his fingers pump in and out as I try to hang onto my sanity.

"Please…"

He ignores me, running a thumb over my clit before he laps it with his tongue, unrelenting as he brings me to orgasm again with his fingers, spreading my juices, preparing me for his cock.

I want to suck his thick length so badly, but I can't tell him what I want. I can only be here, like this, his submissive.

I claw at his head as he brings his mouth up my body, kissing my skin at the navel and making his way north. He sucks on each of my nipples as his hips press into mine, and I feel his cock pressing into my stomach. Finally, his lips meet mine, and I taste my arousal as he plunges his tongue into my mouth. At the same time, he grabs my arms, pinning me at the wrists above my head, and I gasp, needing him to dominate me, needing him to take control so I can come again.

Without words, he reaches between us and grasps his cock, moving it to my entrance. He swirls the tip around my arousal, and then pushes into me full tilt.

His cock fills me up, just like I knew it would, so big that I cry out. Then he starts to move his hips, plunging in and out of me as I grasp his butt with both hands, gripping him tight, my nails clawing at him.

"You like my cock inside your tight pussy, baby?" he snarls, looking down at me as I gasp and groan at the intrusion. The pain sears through me, but it's a good pain, one I want, one I *need*.

"Fuck me harder, Bones, harder…" I cry out as he complies, the bed rocking violently as I wrap my legs around his waist, and he pumps me relentlessly. I come again as he grasps my hands to restrain me, licking his lips as he does so. His grip will leave a mark and that turns me on even more. I call his name over and over, and as he pumps me full of his cum, he shouts my name. Once he slows, we're both left panting like we've been deprived of oxygen…

And then I wake up.

My hand is swirling my clit, and I just came in my sleep.

Bones isn't on top of me, and I feel the need to have him inside me so much stronger than I ever thought possible.

Shit. Now I'm dreaming about him reaming me?

I shouldn't need his touch, but it's all I'm craving, even as I reach into the top drawer for my vibrator, knowing I need to get off properly, with it inside me while I picture his face.

And I do.

Plunging the vibrator into my soaking pussy, I hit the switch for the rabbit and it hums away at my clit. I groan as the full sensation makes me squirm around on the bed, wishing I had his ass to cling to as I come undone with him inside me, not a piece of machinery.

I imagine his cock filling me just like in the dream, pumping me, making me feel so dirty and so fucking good. I come hard, fast, my head spinning as I choke back tears at the strength of my orgasm. It takes a hold and won't let go of me.

And I send myself to Heaven, over and over again, calling his name each and every time.

BRACKEN RIDGE
REBELS
ARIZONA
M · C

CHAPTER 5

BONES

"Under five thousand?" Hutch raises a brow as he assesses the commercial kitchen Brock and I acquired for the Stone Crow, the local bar with a restaurant attached.

The club recently bought out Steph, the previous owner's share, and it's closed for major renovations. It was probably fashionable thirty years ago, and with new trendy bars and restaurants popping up all over the place in town, it's time to get with the times.

A lot of the other bars and eateries are upmarket, wine bar types. Hutch wants to bring this place back to the bare bones, turn it back into a family establishment with a buffet, home-cooked meals, and a bar that's for locals, homely and inviting. Being an original building, it's got character, but it's gonna take a lot of work.

When Axton gets out of jail, he'll be here to help get the place back on its feet, along with Stevie running the bar. Apparently, he got his electrician's certificate while he was in jail.

Stevie's pretty much the exact opposite of her sister. For one, she seems to like me. Not in *that* way, but she doesn't look at me with distaste or give me eyerolls like her sister does. She can also hold a conversation without insinuating I'm an idiot.

There's something going on with Kennedy that I can't put my finger on. I don't know what, obviously, but I'll be fucked if I don't make it my mission in life to find out.

"Would cost over twenty for stainless steel like this, and the appliances," Brock says, nodding to the large twelve burner stove with multiple ovens below.

A restaurant in Phoenix went into liquidation, so we picked it up for a steal. It's still in the back of the truck.

"That's a thing of beauty," Hutch remarks, looking pleased.

"Gas conveyor ovens have never been used, and the steel hotplate is still in the box," I say. "Cool room gets delivered Friday. It was too large to fit in the truck." "Fuckin' perfect. You boys did well." He slaps us on the back and actually smiles.

None of us like spending shit tons of money, especially when this whole place has to be rewired, walls have come down, the entire bar rebuilt from scratch. But it's gonna be worth it. When it's finished, it'll look a thousand percent better than it does now.

"Took us long enough to find it. Helped that we had

cash, and bein' in the right place at the right time," Brock says, giving me the nod. We knew this lot would go quick, but the bank had foreclosed on the restaurant and therefore they needed to get rid of it to pay back the loans. Their loss, our gain.

"We got the electrics gettin' done here Monday, then Axton can do the rest when he arrives," he goes on. "So if we can get all the shit in place and fitted out over the weekend, then the tiler could be here at the end of the week."

Brock gives us a chin lift. "Knuckles is gonna give the tiler a hand, bein' he used to do this shit for a livin'. Got Gears mixing concrete and bein' a general grease monkey. Kid needs to earn his stripes."

Knuckles is one of the old timers who helped form the club when Hutch took over. He's not around church as much as he used to be, only coming by when Ginger, his ol' lady, comes and helps out at the bar, which is most weekends. He's a crusty old thing but means no harm.

Gears is one of the newer prospects who came over from Jack's car and scrapyard. He was the one who let us know that Jack was ripping us off some time back with our deliveries.

"Colt's got Gash helpin' him with security. Business has gone nuts now he's got commercial properties on the books. They're gonna install cameras and a decent surveillance system, along with new locks, a safe for the back office, and electronic registers," Brock tells us. "Won't recognize the place when it's done."

Gash is the former prospect we called Lee, and he comes in very handy where odd jobs are concerned. He got stabbed in a brawl in Phoenix and the name kinda stuck.

"Can't fuckin' wait," Hutch grumbles. "Not makin' a dime with the doors closed."

He's not wrong there. "When do the new tables and booths get here?"

"Next week. Only thing worth salvaging were the floors. Under the fuckin' linoleum shit they put down is hardwood. Could never understand why people cover up shit like that. Just needs cleanin' and sandin' and a bit of polish. Prospects will be able to do it before the furniture arrives, all goin' to plan," Hutch explains.

No need to let Hutch know the schedules are tight, but we'll make it work. This is the biggest project we've taken on since Brock and I bought the junkyard together six years ago, and that paid off.

People scoff at other people's junk, but it's true what they say about one man's trash is another man's treasure, and we've made big bucks.

"Well, I'd love to stay here and chat, but I've got to go meet with Deanna to discuss paint colors," Hutch says as he rolls his eyes.

Deanna, his daughter and the interior decorator, has been sending us all texts of the paint and furniture colors as well as different material options for the countertops. Who knew there were so many decisions to be made about all these trivial little things you normally don't pay any attention to?

"Women are better at these things," I say. "They know how to put shit together, make it look pretty and tasteful and shit."

Hutch and Brock both look at me.

"What?"

"You growin' a pair of tits?" Brock grunts, a smirk on his lips.

"Don't fuckin' think so. Last time I checked, my nuts are still hangin' in place." I pat myself down, just to be sure.

He gives me a knowing look. "How'd it go with that lawyer chick?"

"How'd you think? She got me out of jail and nothin' else. She's got some weird hang-up about not mixin' business with pleasure."

I don't know why he's finding it all so amusing. It wasn't long ago that he was mooning over Angel and doing her on his desk at the office while I was out. So, I don't think he's got room to talk.

"Losin' your touch bro?" he scoffs.

"Nope. She just needs a little warmin' up."

"*Warmin'* as in she won't put out so you gotta use your hand?"

"Hey, I got sweet butts if I wanna get my dick wet."

"Yeah? Haven't seen you at church with any."

Why does he choose now to be so fuckin' observant? "Been busy. Got shit goin' on."

"Like gettin' outta jail?" Hutch puts in with a grunt.

"Had to pull some strings to get the doc to sign off on the cannabis shit."

"Well, the insomnia part wasn't a lie. I never slept back then."

"I know that, but it still doesn't account for all the other shit. Last thing I need is one of my boys in the big house. We might be a small club and stay out of one percent shit, but that doesn't mean we don't have enemies, especially with what went down with you and Lucy."

He doesn't need to remind me. I don't show it, but it has crossed my mind. If anyone retaliates, we've got the numbers with the Cali Chapter close by and the Sons of Phoenix Fury.

When I was a sniper, I never had a weak bone in my body, but you feel invincible in that environment. You're there to do a job and you're in the moment, every second, every day.

This is different.

If something had happened to Lucy and the baby, I don't know what I would've done. I could definitely never look Rubble in the eye again. I couldn't live with myself.

"I've wiped the slate clean," I tell him. "No more doin'

dumb shit."

Brock rolls his eyes. "How fuckin' hard is it to pay your fines?"

I flip him the bird.

"He's right. Club's no fuckin' good without a Road Captain," Hutch barks. "Doesn't look too good on a club who can't organize a simple run now, does it?"

Any one of my brothers could arrange a run in my place, but I hold my tongue. Hutch is like a father to most of us, and while I have loving parents who are still together and live in nearby Mesa, he's been a mentor to me since I prospected at the club.

If I ever let him down, for real, it would be the worst thing I could ever do.

"Well, lucky for all of us, Kennedy sorted it out."

"And still didn't fall into your bed," Brock mutters, just loud enough so I'll hear.

"Rome wasn't built in a day," I remind him. "She'll come around."

"When Hell freezes over." He gives me a grin he can't hold back. "Should ask her to come to the club. I'd love to see her kick your ass for real."

"That's where you're wrong. She's not the type to wear her heart on her sleeve, she might be a little feisty, but that can be worked out between the sheets, and I don't mind that kinky shit."

Hutch thumps me on the back. "If the woman isn't lookin' your way, son, it may be time to move on. Plenty more fish in the sea."

I don't want any other fish. *I want her.*

"The man's been in a committed relationship for over thirty years," Brock reminds me. "I'd listen to him; he may know what he's talkin' about."

"Never said I wanted commitment," I grumble. "Just a piece of the pie. Specifically, Kennedy's."

"Didn't you say she threatened to sue you for harassment?" Brock goes on, because he hasn't said enough.

Fucker can't keep shit to himself either.

Hutch gives me a side-eye.

"I was kidding." I shrug.

"Keep your nose clean," he warns. "Enough shit goin' on at the moment without your ass bein' in jail. Helped save your hide once, not gonna do it again. And next time, you'll have Stanley who, as we know, isn't exactly known for his ability to win cases."

"Maybe we should give Kennedy all our shit to deal with," Brock suggests. "Only a matter of time before Stanley retires anyway."

"She wasn't overly keen on representing me," I say. "Only did it because she didn't want to see me locked up until I could get another lawyer."

"Ah, the wonders of livin' in a small town." Hutch

grins. "The justice system works a little faster than in the city. But Brock's right, she did a good job negotiating. Could've been a lot worse. Woman knows her shit, so don't piss her off."

It makes me grow ten feet taller hearing him praise her, not that she's my girl, but if she were, I'd be pretty fuckin' proud. Not that I want a permanent woman in my life, but we'd have fun. I think about her curvy, sexy body and how confident she is in the courtroom, and I wanna do her so bad.

It's bad enough that now I've got my sights set on her, I don't wanna touch another woman. I'm resorting to pleasuring myself until I can score a date with her, and if that doesn't happen soon, I'll have to resort to drastic measures. And by a *date*, I mean full sex. It's not like I want to settle down with the woman, I just want her body. I want her mouth. I want every inch of her at my disposal.

I'm a glutton for punishment, even when I know it isn't just the thrill of the chase that has me begging for more, it's the fact that when I'm around her, even when she's in full-fledged lawyer mode, she lights something inside of me that I can't ignore. I want to explore it. I just wish she'd let me.

My phone rings, and when I see it's Steel, I groan out loud.

I've only been a free man for less than twenty-four hours and now he's gonna be on my case, for sure. I was thinking about paying one of the prospects to complete it for me; it's not like Kennedy's gonna know. What's she gonna do, come check up on me?

"Yup," I answer.

"It's almost ten o'clock," he says.

"Congratulations. Are we throwin' a party?"

"Very funny, smartass. I got a truck full of shit comin' in, and I need a hand haulin'."

"I regret to inform you that I have a full-time job," I tell him. "That requires almost all of my attention."

"He's slackin' again," Brock calls over my shoulder, down the phone. I punch him in the arm as he slaps me upside the head — his signature move, if he's fast enough.

I mouth *fuck off* to him as he laughs and Steel begins to ride my ass about responsibility and committing to something for once in my life. Honestly, I'm a little hurt. I can commit to lots of things, sleeping being one of the best hobbies a man can have. Drinking is another, along with pussy on the regular, not that I've been getting much action lately because I've been on pain killers for my back. It's not usually that bad, but when I lift heavy shit or move at the wrong angle, I'm in all sorts of trouble. It's an old injury that stopped me from continuing in the army. I still keep fit, but I've got to keep lifting to a minimum.

"I'll see you here in fifteen," Steel grunts.

"But –"

The line goes dead as I pull the phone from my ear, staring at it.

I know Steel's definitely not one for subtlety, but still, I am helpin' him for free, even if it is to keep my ass out of jail.

"Thanks, brother," I say to Brock. "Really fuckin' great."

"No problem." He tries to slap me around the head again, but I duck, and he misses.

"Gettin' slow, old man."

"How do you plan on gettin' over there when you can't drive?" Hutch gives me a chin lift.

I shrug.

He frowns. "You're only permitted to drive to and from work," he reminds me. "If you get caught, you'll be the new fish, and I'm not sure you're ready for that in state pen."

"Lucky for me, I've got a good lawyer. Anyway, can they really charge me for drivin' to my community service?"

"Don't look at me. I'm not givin' you a ride." Brock laughs. "Got shit to do here, and I need you back this afternoon so we can supervise the delivery at the Crow."

So much to do, so little time. It's aggravating.

"Who's gonna fuckin' drive me, then?"

"Call one of the prospects," Hutch suggests.

"Fine." I reluctantly go in search of Gears, he's around here somewhere. If I rope him in to help, Steel might sign off on extra time.

If it were anything else, except his precious dog rescue,

he wouldn't give a shit what I do. I suppose at least it is for a good cause, and it could be worse.

I wonder if I should text my lawyer now that I have her card, and ask if she needs to come and supervise. I can't help but grin when I think about my idea of supervision.

Wouldn't that be a hoot.

Two hours later, I'm hauling the last of the dog food boxes into the store cupboard and wiping my brow because I haven't worked this hard in a long while.

I've also managed to clean out five cages, helped Steel fix a loose rafter, and hauled rubbish to the dump.

"See, hard work doesn't kill you," Steel says when I drop the last box in the cupboard.

"It could, then you'd feel shitty about it," I grumble.

He's about to give me another task, no doubt, when Sienna waltzes through the door with an armful of flyers.

"Hi, babe," she says to Steel, then she smiles at me.

"Hey, Bones."

Steel bends down to give her a quick kiss, and I almost gag with how loved-up these two are. I remember when Steel wouldn't even let a chick stay over… Ah, how the mighty have fallen.

"What you got there?" I prod, nodding to the multicolored stack she's got under her arm.

"Ooh! I'm running errands and wanted to put these flyers up for the charity auction. We're still looking for donations," she says, looking excited.

I take one out of her hand.

"What's the occasion?"

"The Bracken Ridge annual fundraiser dinner party. Since joining the committee, it's my job this year to find a venue. I thought it would be a great idea to introduce the locals to the newly refurbished restaurant at the Stone Crow. It'll be big enough, and Hutch agreed to let us host it there." She beams. "There'll be all sorts of prizes, raffles and games, and a bachelor auction."

I frown looking down at the flier. "A what?"

She claps her hands together as Steel gives me an eye roll.

"Well, one of the ideas we came up with was a bachelor charity auction, where eligible men in town get auctioned off for a date. For the right price, of course."

"Is that even legal?" I scoff.

"Yes, of course it's legal. There's no... *funny business.*"

Steel grunts, which is his version of a laugh.

"You know, you'd get way more money if you included *funny business.*" I give her a wink.

She shakes her head. "It's all a bit of fun. Hey, why don't you put your hand up? You get a free meal, and the money goes to several good causes."

Steel laughs out loud this time as I give him a look.

"I don't date."

She puts her hands on her hips. "Right. And next your gonna say, *I only fuck*, right?"

"Sienna." Steel's shoulders shake.

"So glad I amuse you, bro," I say, wondering what the hell I'm doing here. First, I'm roped into community service, and now, Sienna wants to auction me off for money. They've got a whole lotta nerve these two.

"What?" she scoffs at Steel. "He's thinking it."

He gives me a onceover. "I thought bachelor auctions were for dudes that are good looking, rich, and can hold a conversation?"

"Very funny. Bit hard for a chick to hold a conversation when she's chokin' on my dick. Pardon my French, Sienna." She bug eyes me. "Ew."

"Anyway, which other shmucks do you have lined up?" I give her a chin lift.

"So far we've got four, whose identities will remain strictly confidential until the night." She taps her nose. "So, if you did sign up, your secret would be safe with me. Plus, you're a good-looking guy, Bones. You could fetch quite a bit of money."

"God, please don't encourage him," Steel butts in.

"That's all we need; another Gunner wannabe on our hands."

I chuckle at the thought. Nobody could've outdone that pretty boy in his heyday. Now that he's with Steel's sister, Lily, he's changed for the better, and though he still annoys the shit out of all of us, he's cashed his chips in and has settled down.

"All jokes aside, I'm not some fuckin' pretty boy. Those things are always so cheesy."

"Been to a few before, champ?"

I give Steel a look as he slings an arm over Sienna's shoulder. "It's an annual event, asswipe."

"Plus, there's one really big selling point," Sienna sing-songs.

I fold my arms over my chest. "What, puttin' out is optional?"

She waggles her eyebrows. "Kennedy will be there."

I act like I don't care; it's better that way. "What? Do you really think she's gonna bid on me?" I snort. "She'd pay you to get me out of her way. She hates me."

"I don't think so." Sienna smiles. "I mean, if she hated you, she wouldn't have bailed your ass out of jail, right?"

"She was bein' paid," Steel helpfully chimes in. "And anyway, Bones, you haven't thought this through. Aside from it being ridiculous. You might get an old woman, since there's plenty of lonely housewives out there too, lookin' for some action."

Sienna tuts. "Stop cheapening it," she scolds. "There is

no action to be had. It's a bit of fun, and it's tradition." She turns back to me. "Say you'll think about it? It would be really great to have a guy like you up for grabs."

The pleading in her voice tugs at my heartstrings, because I'm not a total asshole, and I do like the idea of Kennedy bidding on me. It's the ultimate fantasy when you think about it.

I can't imagine Little Miss Prim and Proper would put out on the first date, though, or the tenth, or pay one dime to even sip coffee with me, let alone dinner.

But… surely I can't be *that* bad.

I get a lot of chicks, never had any complaints, and Sienna seems to agree I'm good looking. I might not have movie star looks, but I do all right.

My lips twitch at the thought of what it'd really take to woo her.

"I'll think about it if Steel promises to never make me clean out a dog kennel again."

"Fuck off," he replies. "There's plenty more where that came from."

"Well, looks like I'm done here. Don't suppose you could drop me back off at the junkyard, and maybe grab some lunch on the way?" I ask Sienna, because there's no way Steel's gonna give me shit.

"She's not a fuckin' taxi service," Steel says, hands on his hips.

"It's fine." She waves him off. "But I've just got to pin these up to the notice board and put a few around town."

I give her a nod as she sidles off to post the flyers.

"You know, you probably should go in the auction," Steel says, turning back to the counter as I lean against it.

"Dating an old woman who clutches her pearls might be the change you need to get back on the horse."

I fake laugh at him because he thinks he's hilarious. "Don't knock older women; they know what they're doin', take charge, and don't lie there like a fish out of water."

"Thanks for that visual."

"Anytime."

"How's your shoulder healing?" Sienna asks, her back to us as she pins the notice on the bulletin board.

"Nice of you to ask," I say, givin' Steel the stink-eye.

"And it's healin' just fine. Doc says there's no permanent damage."

I got stabbed a while back, defending Lucy when we got jumped. I had to have stitches and had some nerve damage, but it's healin' all right. Of course, Lucy and Sienna are the only ones who take any notice of the finer details.

"That's good. You know, chicks love scars," she tells me, waggling her eyebrows.

I cross my arms over my chest. "What are you suggestin' exactly?"

"Just think about the auction. It'll look good for the judge."

I snort a laugh. "Not sure that's the kind of community service she had in mind."

Though, to get a glimpse at Kennedy Hart again in a more relaxed setting, other than my jail cell, would be nice. It'd be better than nice.

Maybe I'm just dumb enough to do it, given enough alcohol. I just hope Steel isn't right about old ladies and jumping my bones. This town does have a lot of retirees.

That's one problem I definitely don't need to have.

Bones

BRACKEN RIDGE
REBELS
ARIZONA
M · C

CHAPTER 6

KENNEDY

"She just won't see sense. I've tried everything. I'm not a bad father, I provide for my kid, always have, always will, but now she just wants to punish me because in her eyes I'm a fuck up." I stare at the poor bastard in front of me and nod as I listen to his tale. It's one I've heard many times before. The wife ended the marriage, they had no prenup, she cleaned out the bank account, now she wants the house, and to top it off, she also wants the kid full-time. Of course, I don't know the man in front of me from Adam, but he seems like an okay kinda guy.

Blue collar, steady income, lives in a decent part of town, and he's willing to pay his child support without any fuss. He's not super well-off but has provided for the family and is active in his child's life. There's just no need to punish the guy and use the kid to get to him. Sadly, I see this a lot, from both sides. It's all great until the going gets bad.

"I'm sorry to hear that. State law in Arizona states

that any property acquired by either party during marriage without a prenuptial agreement then becomes community property."

"In English?"

I smile. "Meaning, that both parties technically will own fifty percent of the asset after the debt has been paid out. It's important to let you know that your ex-wife is entitled to half the property, Mr. Gannon, and we would need to draw up a proposal for the divorce proceedings. I'm assuming that you're going to sign the papers?"

He runs a hand through his hair. "I never thought this could happen to me," he admits.

I nod sagely. *They never do.*

Forty to fifty percent of marriages in the U.S. end in divorce.

My eyes flick down to the white band around my ring finger where my wedding rings used to sit, and I push the pain away.

No, not all marriages end in divorce.
Now isn't the time or the place to go down memory lane.

"I know this is difficult for you, Mr. Gannon. Divorce is never easy; that's why I'm here to help you get through this transition and make it as smooth as possible."

He swallows hard. Poor schmuck. He's got no idea how bad this is going to get. Of course, I always hope for the best, but I'm a realist. And the fact that she's gone for the jugular with the kid only leaves me to believe that he's either a shitty father and husband and this is her payback, or she's a coldhearted bitch who wants to punish him.

It takes two to make a marriage work and two to make it come to an end.

"Can't make her come back to me, though, can you?"

It's worse when one person is still all in. Even after this, he still wants her back.

"Unfortunately not, Mr. Gannon."

He pinches the bridge of his nose, and I'm not certain for a second if he's going to lose it.

He really loved her.

"Are you all right?" I offer when he doesn't say anything more. "Can I get you a coffee?"

"How about a shot?"

I offer a small smile and let him take the time he needs to gather himself.

After a few moments, he nods, and his eyes flick back to mine. They're slightly glazed over.

"I guess I gotta be alright, for my kid's sake. She's only seven."

I nod. "It's always difficult when children are involved, but that's why I'm here; to help you understand the likely outcomes in terms of custody and the financial arrangements. While your wife has made it clear she intends to fight for full custody, it's important that we try and preserve the stability of your child. I'm sure all of this is difficult enough."

"You've no idea," he says, his voice low. "Trying to take Janie from me is the lowest blow she's thrown at me yet. I couldn't imagine Hell being much worse."

"I'm guessing that it isn't possible to remain in the same residence?" These questions have to be asked.

"You'd guess right. I'm living in the guest suite. She wanted me to leave, but I refused."

It's good that he has a brain in his head. It may be hard, but moving out is just one way for the spouse to commandeer the biggest asset. In this case being the family home.

"I won't beat around the bush, Mr. Gannon, but I will need to know if there is any reason that your wife is denying you access to your child in terms of concerns or safety?"

He looks at me sharply. "I'm a good father. I love my kid. If you're asking if I'm a deadbeat dad, I'm not, Ms. Hart. I made my marriage vows and I stuck to them. I took them seriously. And I've loved my kid since the day she was born and I held her in these hands." He holds both hands up to show me. "And I'll be damned if she's going to take the only thing in my life worth living for. I want to see my kid, it should be fifty-fifty, like we always agreed on. She can't do this to me!"

His passion says a lot.

"Glad to hear it. If your wife doesn't agree with the

provisional custody agreement I'll be putting into place, then it is likely we will go to court. In the meantime, I'll need you to provide me with any and all bank statements, including the mortgage payment activity, and any saving accounts, retirement accounts, and a copy of any other assets, like properties or vehicles. You should also get any valuables appraised, just to help protect your interests. Your spouse may attempt to prevent the fair division of the assets. I know it seems unlikely, but is there a chance that she will settle amicably?" I guess not, since he's here.

He shrugs. "I doubt it. She wants the lot. She's quite happy to clean me out, bleed me dry, and then toss me out on the street."

And I've got another humdinger for him. "This is a difficult question," I go on, "but for the purposes of building a case, I need to know if there is any infidelity on either party, or anything I may need to know that could reflect badly on you in particular?"

It's never a fun time asking *those* types of questions, but let's face it, I don't really know him. And if he's had an affair, then this will reflect badly should we proceed to court. It'll just make the spouse all the more determined to go after everything.

I don't judge people; I know how much effort it takes for a marriage to work.

"No, I never did. I was loyal to her throughout our

marriage, even when we were separated last year. I don't know about her, honestly, but I doubt it; she didn't even like sex."

I blink at him in rapid succession as I try not to visualize it and wonder why clients have to tell me absolutely everything.

I shuffle my papers and stack them into a neat pile. "Well, as soon as you can get that list of things to me, I can draft a document together, and we can go from there. Let's reconvene next Tuesday. How does four pm sound?"

"That sounds good." He nods as we stand. "Thank you, Ms. Hart. I'll see you next week. I appreciate it."

We shake hands, and I walk him to the door.

He leaves, and it's almost as if a trail of misery follows closely behind him. I have a bit of a sixth sense with people, call it a perk of the job, but he's telling the truth. He really is still in love with his wife, but at least he seems to have accepted that it's over.

As I turn to head back to my desk, Amelia calls out, "Your four-thirty's here!"

I frown. Mr. Gannon was my last appointment, and it's Friday. I'm ready for a glass of wine and to kick these heels off.

"I don't have a four-thirty…" I call back, and just as I swing my gaze that way, the tall, tanned cocky ass himself stands in the doorway, that annoying smirk on his face as our eyes lock.

"Sorry, *Ms. Hart,* thought it might be okay to pop in

since I was in the neighborhood and all, and you haven't been supervising me."

The way he says my name sends a shock through me, and I'm unsure if I want to jump him or give him a smack. He's wearing a tight, black, short sleeved Henley, his motorcycle jacket over the top, of course, and ripped jeans hugging him in all the right places.

My mind suddenly flashes back to the R-rated wet dream I had the other night where he had his head between my legs, then pumped me full with his cock, and I thank Christ he can't read minds right now. It also shocks me that I'm just realizing I full on orgasmed in my sleep while imagining him fucking me into oblivion.

Maybe I'm going through an early mid-life crisis. That must be it. I know I'm definitely older than him so it would explain why I'm having these unwanted and illicit thoughts that never seem to end.

He folds his arms across his broad chest as I clear my throat.

"I'm afraid that was my last appointment, Mr. Romero. Is it something urgent?"

"Very," he replies, walking in my office like he owns the place. I watch as he helps himself to one of the chairs in front my desk, and once seated, he leans back with his hands behind his head.

"Nice digs you got here."

I turn on my heel and round my desk but stay standing.

"Thank you for noticing. What is your emergency? You know you should call law enforcement if…"

"What if it violates my bail conditions?"

I regard him with sharp eyes as he watches me. If I didn't know any better, I'd swear this man enjoys getting a rise out of me.

"Does it?"

His eyes drop down my body as he rubs his chin like he's deliberating.

"Mr. Romero?" I prompt.

His eyes snap back to mine. "Sorry, I work with scumbags and deadbeats all day long. Admirin' a beautiful woman doesn't come around all that much during my day so I gotta take advantage while I can."

My lips twitch as I imagine how that scruff around his jaw would feel between my…

"What urgent matter do you have?" I repeat. *I need that fucking wine. Pronto.*

"I wanted to update you on my community service, since you are supposed to be checkin' in on me, makin' sure I'm all right and bein' treated fairly and sign this piece of paper." He grins, then wags a finger. "And I haven't had one phone call this week, askin' about my progress."

Treated fairly? He's helping his buddy out at the animal shelter. He probably didn't even show up.

"I don't need to check in with you every week," I remind him. "More like once a month to make sure you're attending and completing the tasks. The penalty for not completing it, as you know, is a one-way ticket back to the big house."

I can't help myself calling it that, as there's only one language this infuriating man understands.

It's an effort to keep my eyes from wandering down that fine body of his. I feel the telltale signs of my own body's reaction to him as I recall how hard he nailed me to my mattress in my dream, and I wonder if he'd be as rough in real life…

"Well, it's best to keep abreast of the situation, wouldn't you say?" He smirks as I place my hands on my hips.

"You're not going to leave any time soon, are you?"

He shakes his head. "Not unless you throw me out."

"Bones, I told you before…"

He holds up a hand. "I've tried to be a gentleman about this, *Ms. Hart*. I think if the judge saw how hard I tried to get a date with you, she'd give me a high-five and would've pardoned my sins rather than makin' me do menial shit that I don't get paid for."

"You're delusional as well as cocky."

I play with the ends of my hair and decide to sit down. Well aware that it'll just be an invitation for him to linger and backchat some more.

Doesn't he have a job to go to?

"I've come up with the perfect solution."

"God help me," I mutter.

"I can't deny this back-and-forth gets me goin' a little bit, and I'm up for the challenge, but I don't want you to fight me anymore."

"Mr. Romero…"

"Bones," he corrects. "You sound like you're addressing my father when you say it like that. Not a good look, babe."

I regard him levelly as I begin again. "Bones, I'm not fighting you. I'm your lawyer, and you're my client; it's pretty simple logic. It would be against all ethical reason to start something with a client."

"And if I weren't your client?"

I sigh. Not just because he's annoying me but because a deep, dark part of me wants to throw caution to the wind and let him have his way with me. Maybe then I'll get rid of him, and he can stop turning up unexpectedly.

The way he looks at me makes me want to die. It's full of lust, there's a fire behind his hazel eyes that I'd like to explore. Most guys dance around it, but not him. He goes straight for the jugular.

If he could really see to the heart of me, he wouldn't recognize what he'd find.

He'd see a woman who's hiding. She's a coward. She lives in the past and won't let herself enjoy anything for pleasure. She will continue to punish herself until her one-sided exile is over. When that will be, who can say. Even if I set the rules, I don't know how to break them.

I've never been able to break them.

"I don't get involved with criminals."

"Technically I'm out on bail, no record."

"I don't get involved with bikers."

He leans forward, his legs spread as he rests his elbows on his knees and gives me a chin lift. "Can't change that, babe, but I do want a date, and if you won't do it for the pleasure of my company, then do it for charity."

I frown. "What charity?"

"The Bracken Ridge Annual Fundraiser."

I bite my lip. So, he's going to be one of the bachelors? I can't help but snort a laugh.

His eyes drop to my lips and the fierce look in his eyes almost has me weeping. He looks like he's about one step away from ravishing me.

"Don't worry." He gives me a wink. "It won't be a full-service date. According to Sienna, sex is off the table. That is, unless you want it to be on the table."

"You'd like me to *pay* for a date with you?" I test the words out nice and slow, especially on the "pay" part.

"Yeah, I've been thinkin'. Everyone keeps tellin' me I'm never gonna score with you. I need to take you out somewhere fancy. Wine you. Dine you. Maybe on the third date, I'll get to second base, or maybe you'll make me wait. I have to warn you, though, I'm not a patient man."

"That's highly inappropriate…"

"That's just it," he murmurs, his sexy voice washing over me as I clench my pussy, suddenly feeling it throb between my legs. "I don't think that you do want those things. I think you want a man to give you the one thing that you can't ask for."

I indulge him with an obvious eye roll as he leans farther forward. "And what's that, exactly?"

He continues to come closer, lowering his voice. "A good, hard fuck with no strings attached."

I swallow hard. He doesn't take his eyes off me, his smirk long gone. He's absolutely serious.

"Look me in the eye and tell me you don't want my cock."

My eyes go wide at his vulgarity. "Mr…"

I hold up a hand. "It's Bones, babe, and I want to *show* you how I got that nickname. Trust me when I say you'll enjoy every minute of it. I'm done playin' fuckin' games. Come to the auction, bid on me, and I'll be yours for the night to do whatever you want with me. It can be our dirty little secret, remember."

I recover my jaw off the floor as I straighten my back, still grasping onto that slight glimmer of hope that the ground will swallow me whole any minute now. I feel my cheeks flush.

More to the point; why aren't I telling him to get the hell out of here?

"I – I'm not paying for sex!" I whisper-shout at him.

He shakes his head. "Technically, you're not. It's for charity, babe. I'm not actually gettin' the money. Just think of all the good your cash will do buyin' blankets and feedin' the needy. And it'll break the ice; a night of wild, all-night sex, doin' whatever you want me to do to that hot, smokin' body you've got under those fancy rags. You can pick where and when."

"You really are delusional." I can barely keep my expression neutral with my denial.

He goes to stand as I stay glued in my seat. "Just think about it. Nobody has to know. I want you, Kennedy Hart. You know I won't back down until you tell me to fuck off… let me hear the words spill from that pretty little mouth of yours, and I will."

The bastard cups his ear with one hand as I stare at him in disbelief. Confusion washes over me at his dirty words and how much I want him to nail me hard and fast, how much I do want every inch of that huge, hard body on top of me.

I open my mouth and close it again.

He smirks. "Thought so."

"Get out of my office," I say, my voice thick with temptation as I try and gather my thoughts.

I know I shouldn't let him affect me like this. It's all he wants, to get a rise out of me and to make me lose my cool. Maybe he enjoys being thrown out? Maybe I should threaten him with the police… not that that would do any good.

He points at me. "You better be there, because if not, I'm gonna punish that hot little ass for denying me all this time, *Ms. Hart.* And I won't be nice about it either. Somethin' tells me you like a man who likes to take charge, don't you?"

"You're disgusting," I manage, hoping it sounds believable.

He grins again, like nothing affects this asshole.

"You wish you found me disgusting," he chimes. "But you don't really, do you?"

I gape at him as he saunters off to the door, whistling as he does. I want to mutter a fiery comeback and tell him to never come back, that I won't be seeing him at the charity auction, and he can go fuck himself. But none of the words leave my mouth.

Arrogant asshole.

If he thinks he can come into my office and speak to me like I'm one of his stupid, cheap whores, then he can think again. Yet, I check his ass out as he leaves. I must have something wrong with me.

Maybe I'm a glutton for punishment after all, because all I can think about is taking him up on his offer… *nobody has to know.* No! That is wrong on so many levels.

Not that I'm against having casual sex. In fact, I think it may be healthy for me to play the field. But not with him.

My head tells me to run the other way, but my body tells me to let him have his way with me. Ravage me. Take me how he wants to; hard and fast.

And that'll be that.

The scary thing is, I'm actually considering it. So what does that make me?

BRACKEN RIDGE
REBELS
ARIZONA
M · C

CHAPTER 7

BONES

One of the things I like to do to stay fit is punching it out in the ring. Colt, the newest patched member to the club, and I usually have a sparring match at the gym. Though I don't always like sparring with him, since he used to be a professional boxer.

It is a good way, however, to get any anger and frustration out, and Colt knows how to rein it in and not beat my ass to a pulp unlike Steel and Brock. Those dudes don't know when to quit.

I've also just had some new ink done on the lower part of my torso, finishing off the tribal pattern I've been doing in stages, and it's been hurting a little. I love my ink, and I only have it down one side of my body, front and back, because I like the way it looks. Chicks love it too. One side half tatted and the other half bare.

"No punk ass moves," I warn Colt. "Angel just finished off my piece." I lift my shirt so he can see the covered patch low on my hips.

"Sting like a bitch?"

"Nothin' I can't handle. Though it was right on the bone, so it didn't exactly tickle."

Angel's Ink is one of the best tattoo parlors in Arizona, in my opinion. Clients come from all over the country to get tatts, and she's booked out months in advance, especially after being featured in Tattooed Ink magazine last summer.

Just because Angel's knocked up now, it hasn't seemed to slow her down; she's busier than ever.

There's really no-one else I would trust with my ink, not that she doesn't give me shit the whole time that I'm there about my personal life.

Added to that, my mom and dad are visiting next weekend, which means I have to have the house spick and span. No need to advertise. I'm known as a slob. I never used to be, bein' in the army for so long, but everything went out the window when I was injured. Even though I do still have a really messy office, my home isn't *that* bad. I just stopped bein' so meticulous because I didn't care anymore.

I'm lucky that I grew up in a loving household, my parents are still together and live in the next town about an hour away. They usually visit once a month.

You would think most parents, like Brock's, for example, would be horrified that their kid joined a motorcycle club after having a career in the military, but not my parents. They've always supported me no matter what

I've set my mind to, and they've always been proud of me no matter what I've done.

I have two other siblings. My adopted sister, Caitlyn, is a few years younger than me. She lives in Jersey now, and I don't get to see her much. We kinda fell out after high school. My other sister, Abbey, died when she was a child. She had a rare form of leukemia, and watching her go through that as a teenage boy kinda screwed with me a lot. She didn't deserve it. She was such a sweet, adorable kid, and she didn't make it past ten.

Caitlyn went off the rails a little after Abbey passed, as they were both incredibly close. I'd like to have a relationship with her again, but she only calls when she needs to borrow some money.

I also don't like that she put mom and dad through hell unnecessarily, especially after everything with Abbey. She didn't need to do that to them, but you can't say that to my parents. They don't see it that way and would do anything for either of us at the drop of a hat.

So, my teenage years aren't exactly a topic I like to bring up very often. I hide it deep down, the only reminder of my sister being her name tattooed across my heart.

"Thinkin' about gettin' myself some new ink, a back piece," Colt goes on. "Always wanted to get like a panther or a tiger or somethin' cool like that."

"'Long as your woman don't use her nails, you'll be

good." I chuckle. "Once had a chick do that to my shoulder and fucked my tatt."

"She goes more for the ass than my back," he muses.

The comment only reminds me of how much of a dry spell I've been having lately. Not from lack of chicks coming around to church; there's always pussy around left, right and center, but I'd be lying to myself if I said it's only because I've been busy with work and bein' outta town that's got my dick in the shade. That's just an excuse.

I know it's because I want the only chick in town I can't have.

I don't know what it is about me, but I'm an all or nothin' kinda guy. I've always been like that.

I can go a whole year of livin' like a bachelor and bangin' different chicks without a care in the world whenever the opportunity presents itself, but the minute I set my sights on a chick I really want – and subsequently – can't have, it becomes like a challenge.

I have to fuckin' have her. My dick is begging for her sweet pussy, which is why I'm staying away from church for a bit. I don't want the temptation, even though I know that I couldn't bring myself to bang another woman when I want someone else. Either way, I'm fucked.

Imagining Kennedy sleeping with anyone else is enough to cause an inferno of heat in my belly that could make me breathe fire. She doesn't seem the type to sleep around, not that I've been stalking her or anything, but she's the homebody type.

Better still, if she thinks she can flaunt another guy in front of me at any point in time, then she's got another thing comin'. And that's just the point. She makes me into a caveman.

I don't want to be this way, and I used to be completely fine with my everyday decision-making where chicks are concerned, but lately, things have changed.

It seems she's put a spell on me that I just can't seem to shake.

I don't usually give a fuck about who I do or who they do or any of that shit as long as we have a good time, but I can't even stomach taking another girl to bed even though I'm not technically with anyone else.

Does that make me a pussy? In the eyes of my brothers, that would be a yes.

I don't know why I feel this way, it's not like Kennedy Hart gives a fuck where I stick my dick, given I'm not stickin' it in her. But now that I've kind of implied I'll be at the bachelor auction, it feels kinda cheap to stick it somewhere else before I get to her.

I may have blue balls from lack of sex, but I know it's gonna be worth it.

And it makes me wonder if she'll chicken out. She may think she doesn't want my dick anywhere near her, but her body language says otherwise. I know that she's full of shit, and I intend to prove it.

Imagining her not showing up has me excited. I'd love to march into her office, locking the door behind me and bending her over the desk with force, givin' it to her hard and fast while she comes all over my dick. Just to prove a point.

The thought of her splayed out in front of me gets my dick twitching, her face squashed into her pile of paperwork while I hold her by the hair and fuck her. That'd give her something to dream about.

But it seems I might be the one dreaming. For one, she thinks I'm a dirty, low-down scumbag. Well, scumbags can still fuck, and I know I'm good. She just doesn't wanna let herself slum it.

I don't care what she thinks of me; it's just sex. I'm not looking for an ol' lady.

I'm not looking for a nag to tie me down and make babies with. I don't do that kinda shit, even if I have considered the option once or twice before in my life — Kennedy being one of those times. Like I say, she has me all mixed up.

Sometimes it'd be nice to have a hot woman on the back of my sled like some of the other brothers have.

Now I think about it, I've never had a woman on the back of my sled. I've never felt a woman's arms around me, hangin' on while I make her scream when I go too fast.

I chuckle at the thought of Kennedy on the back of my Harley. Oh, I'd make her scream all right.

Colt eyes me. "Your mind in the gutter, bro?"

"Always." I grin at him.

"Not seen you around church lately, you okay?"

I grab my gloves from the locker room. "Just busy. What with bein' arrested and shit, now I've gotta do community service, help out at the Stone Crow, and run the junkyard. I need a fuckin' assistant."

"Could get a prospect to help out, or is Gears using his injury as an excuse?"

Gears got clocked on the head with the butt of a gun when shit went down with me and Lucy, but at least he didn't get stabbed like I did. Couple of inches lower, and it'd have been closer to my heart.

"Fucker would use anythin' as an excuse if it meant he could sit on his ass and get pampered by sweet butts," I say, which he has no right to do bein' a prospect.

"Hutch had him and Jax dismantle all the old toilets at the Crow, and they had to cart them out, ready for the plumber. They complain' like bitches, the pair of them."

Jax, one of the new prospects, gets all the worst jobs, but that's just how it is.

"Not like it was when I prospected. Total fuckin' shit shoveler," I grumble, stepping in the ring. I pull my gloves on and start warming up. *Those were the days.*

"Worst job I ever had before I got patched in was watchin' Lily's salon," Colt goes on, facing me as he stretches.

"Doesn't sound so bad to me. Air-conditioned comfort." He grins. "Lotta nice chicks work in the beauty industry, and I couldn't touch one of them 'cause Steel was ridin' my ass. This was long before Cass came along."

"Fuck that. I can understand not touchin' Lily, but what about the other girls? They're not with the club."

He smirks. "I got told in no uncertain terms to keep my dick away from the staff. Last thing Steel wanted was a bunch of upset ladies in a beauty salon 'cause then he'd have Lily to deal with. It's not exactly good for business."

"Typical Steel, though I'm pretty sure he boned one of those hairdresser chicks, if not all of them, before Sienna came along."

Colt snickers because we all know the same rules don't apply to Steel that apply to the rest of us. He's also the largest, so it's not like anyone wants to get into a fight with him. Just ask Gunner; he lived to tell the tale but only because Steel didn't put all his weight behind the punches.

That's water under the bridge now because it was over Lily and Guns gettin' together, and I have to admit, I think Steel has mellowed somewhat since Sienna came into the picture.

She's good for him; he seems a lot calmer than he's been in years, not so high-strung. Though, gettin' it on the regular with a hot chick like Sienna, who also runs his office and takes care of all the paperwork, is every man's wet dream.

If I could find an office girl to do all my shit, it'd be in seventh heaven. Not to mention, she's also a good cook, lucky bastard. I keep myself alive, but I'm not always the greatest cook, even though my mom has Puerto Rican heritage, her mad cooking skills definitely didn't rub off on me.

We make it into the ring and Colt turns to face me. He's in good shape, shorter than me but wide set with large shoulders and has a killer right hook.

"Ready to rumble?"

"Never been more ready."

He grins in a way that makes me realize he's not playin' around.

Good. I need him to knock some sense into me and then maybe I'll stop fantasizing about a certain redhead who wants my balls in a vice.

I always get the shitty jobs.

Whenever there's a crummy job that nobody wants to do and the prospects are busy doin' other shit, they call me. And because it's Prez that's basically tellin' me and not askin' me, it's not like I can say no.

I think about the prospects haulin' the old toilets from

the restrooms and that makes me feel marginally better.

I'm hammering the bar shelves back on the walls since all the new glassware is being delivered and the handyman didn't show up.

At least this shitty job isn't hard, it's just time consuming and annoying.

"Hey, Bones," Kelsey says as I drill in a nail. It's not the world's most comfortable position, lying on my back on top of the bar, but shit happens.

I glance up and give her a nod. "Hi, Kels, what you doin' here?"

I know Kelsey was a bit sweet on me a while back when she was babysitting Angel's kid, but she was only sixteen at the time and she's only just turned seventeen. She's cute in a nerdy kinda way, but I don't – in any way shape or form – do underage girls, and I don't find them attractive in that way. So I've got to somehow try to not be a total asshole, but bein' nice only encourages her.

I'm almost twice her fuckin' age, and I watched her grow up. She's still a kid in my eyes, and in some way, she always will be.

"Kirsty wanted to come over and check the progress, and we need to check the supplies are all coming in as planned, so I tagged along."

I give her a nod and go back to the drill.

After I've stuck another nail in the wood, she's still

standing there.

"So, are you coming to the charity event?" Her eyes linger on my chest as I swallow hard.

I don't need her ogling me. Shit no.

"Uh, I'm not sure." I don't need her knowing I may have signed up to be auctioned off for money with the lure of a good time. "Not really my kinda thing."

She nods nervously.

Please just go away.

"Do you have to put all the shelves up?" She glances around the large bar area, now twice its size, and it spreads farther across the room since we opened the wall up that used to lead into the restaurant.

"Yup."

"That's a bitch. Maybe I can help?"

I take a long, patient intake of breath. *She's just a kid...*

"Nah, that's okay, I got it. If you wanna go find Stevie, she's around here someplace. I'm sure she'll have a job for you. This is kind of a one man show, darlin'."

Before she gets to answer, Jax sidles up to the bar, his eyes all over Kelsey's ass as he leans against it leisurely.

Is he lost?

I frown. Okay he's probably only twenty-one himself, but still. She's BRMC, and he shouldn't be looking at any chick from the club like that. Even if he will be patched in pretty soon, that's still no excuse. He's forgetting his place as a bottom dwelling prospect.

Kelsey turns to him. "Hi, Jax," she says sweetly. She's one of those innocent kids too, the needy type that are pretty but don't realize it, and that makes them very vulnerable. I bet she'd fall for any line in the book. Whether it was any good or not.

"Hi, sugar. What ya doin?"

I frown some more when his eyes dip to her chest. Looks like I might have to pound his face in if he keeps this shit up.

"Just asking Bones here if I can help some. I'm at a bit of a loose end."

Oh, I know exactly what he's thinking, but until she's of legal age and he's patched in, he can keep his dirty mitts off.

"Jax?" I say, linin' up the next nail.

His eyes dart to me.

"Yeah, Bones?"

"Fuck off." I drill the nail into place.

"Huh, uh… all right, I was just…" he starts.

"I know what you were just doin'. She's a kid and a part of BRMC, so don't even think about it."

Kelsey flushes bright red, but it has to be done. He has to learn to stay in his lane, and she's gotta learn to stop eyeballing. She might not hang around the club, but by association with Kirsty, she falls under the club's umbrella. And I wouldn't trust Jax or any prospect with her as far as I could throw them.

"I wasn't –"

"Bones!" she yelps, embarrassed.

I glare at her. "Trust me sweet cheeks, he's got one thing on his mind, and it ain't playin' patty cake."

Jax snickers until I turn my glare on him.

"You don't want me gettin' up to remind you where your place is, do you?" I turn the drill on, holding it up in the air.

He straightens and backs off. "Nah, man, just being friendly."

"Go be friendly somewhere else."

He grumbles as he stalks off in the other direction.

"Bones!" Kelsey whines, her skin still beet red. "That was rude."

"He's a prospect. Shouldn't be talkin' to you anyway."

"He was only being nice."

I sigh. "Trust me. Boys at that age have one thing on the brain and one thing only."

I use the word "boy" purposefully. He's still a little wet behind the ears.

She looks down at her feet awkwardly. Now may be the time to give her some unwanted but truthful advice.

"Stay away from bikers, darlin', at least till your eighteen. For one, Hutch would beat anyone's ass for so much as leering, let alone touchin'. You know what he's like with that kinda thing, and you wouldn't want that, would you?"

She shakes her head. "No, but I'm not a kid, Bones, and I don't appreciate you saying that and embarrassing me."

I roll my eyes and sit up on my elbows.

"If I were you, I wouldn't be in such a hurry to grow up. Be young for a while longer. You've got the rest of your life to be an adult and all the shit that comes with it, and…" May as well go in for the kill. "Don't be getting sucked in by the likes of douchebags like Jax who'll take your virginity and be onto the next chick by the mornin', not even rememberin' your name. You don't want that, now do ya?"

Her eyes go wide. "Who says I'm a virgin?" she splutters, her lip trembling slightly when she speaks.

Jeez. I don't want to think about it.

"Don't wanna know either way. Just sayin', boys take longer than girls to grow up. It's just a fact. You're a smart girl, gotta use that brain in your head. Don't be sellin' out. Save yourself for someone who's gonna appreciate it." That's not gonna be me. Then I add, just so we're clear, "Someone your own age, when the time comes."

"I… uh," she begins, but it seems I've embarrassed her enough. "Okay…"

"Kelsey?" Kirsty says, interrupting as she walks up next

to her. "Oh, hey, Bones."

"Hi, Mrs. H, you look ravishing today."

She gives me a little smile and turns to Kels.

"We can start marking the inventory off and sorting out the cutlery and plates and bowls for the kitchen."

"Sounds good," Kels says politely.

"Off you go, then."

Kels gives me a small wave as she takes off toward the kitchen.

Kirsty turns to look back at me. "Everything okay?"

I give her a chin lift. "Just givin' her a little pep talk about the birds and the bees, and to stay away from Jax." I grin.

Kirsty shakes her head. "Goddamn teenagers."

"We were all young once. No harm done. Jax got the message."

"Well, the last thing I need is a teenager knocked up by someone from the club. She's got too much potential to end up with a kid too soon."

"She's not stupid, though, just naïve."

"That's what worries me."

Hutch finally appears, heading toward us as he swings an arm around his ol' lady's shoulders, kissing her on the head, then giving her a peck on the lips.

These two are like a couple of teenagers; it can get a little sickening at times.

"Hey, babe."

"Hi, Sweetie. I brought Kelsey to help check off the inventory. Thought it would free up Stevie to do more important things," Kirsty says. "I know she's got a lot on her plate with things running a little behind schedule."

"Good thinkin', got more shit comin' in the next few days. Plasterer should be here tomorrow, and if we can get that done, then we may have a fighting chance at opening for the auction."

It'll be big pay dirt for the club and exposure for the new function room and restaurant, but even I have to admit, it's cutting it fine.

"When does the new chef arrive?" I ask.

"The weekend." Hutch turns to me. "All going to plan. She's got a great menu planned out and came with excellent references."

"She?" I quirk a brow. "Nice goin'. Love a woman who can cook."

"Let's hope she's a woman who can cook for many. Nothin' like bein' thrown in the deep end." Hutch is never a man to worry about things, but I can see the tension brewing over from getting shit ready for opening night.

It'll be great having a decent chef in the place. Means I'll get a good meal most nights, unless one of the club girls is offering or Colt whips something up since we live together. He's at Cassidy's a lot, so for half of the week I fend for myself.

Mom usually brings me frozen meals - she can't help herself - and I can make those last for a few weeks at least. Moms are the best.

"It'll be fine. We'll all pitch in," I say. "I'll have this done in a few, then I can move on to the kitchen. A few of the cabinet doors need fixin."

"Appreciate it," Hutch replies, his brow furrowing.

Just as I'm about to start putting more nails in the wall, I see a flash of red in my periphery that grabs my attention.

Sure enough, Kennedy appears right alongside Stevie as a slow smile spreads across my face.

This day maybe looking up after all.

BRACKEN RIDGE
REBELS
ARIZONA
M · C

CHAPTER 8

KENNEDY

I feel his stare from across the room before our eyes even meet.

Bones.

The man not only haunts my dreams but also my waking life.

And, though I'm not usually a fickle person, the attraction I feel toward him is more volatile each and every time we meet. It's not just how he looks, which I can admit, is pretty off the charts, it's his whole confident persona. The way he looks so sure of himself, even when I'm telling him how rude he is and to get out of my office. He's like forbidden fruit.

I barely know him, yet still my mind wanders to all the conversations we've had from when he was in jail to the last humiliating taunt in my office.

How I should have told him to take a running leap off a short pier. That I didn't, in fact, want him to *fuck me hard*, and I wouldn't be coming to the charity auction, but I know deep down, none of that is true.

Maybe I do want the bad boy biker, if only for a night. Maybe this back-and-forth banter between us has gotten me going. I can't lie that he's under my skin, like an itch that I just can't scratch.

"…so, that way people won't be lining up past the kitchen doors for the buffet on Sundays. What do you think?" Stevie asks, a frown on her face while she concentrates.

"I, uh…"

She turns her gaze to mine, and I feel guilty I zoned out thinking about the man that is still staring at me.

"I knew you weren't listening!"

"I *am* listening. I've just got a lot on my plate at the moment."

"Like a certain bossy biker we won't mention?" She taps her nose a couple of times, and I swat her hand away.

"Definitely not."

"He's staring at you," she whispers. "I think he's got a bit of a crush. That's so sweet."

I shake my head. "There is nothing sweet about it. The man's a walking one-night stand, ready to put another notch on his belt with the new girl in town. It's nothing to be flattered or smug about."

She shrugs. "So what? How long's it been now, K?"

I take a long deep breath before saying, "Let's not go

there."

She walks around the other side of the bar to fish around for something. "I'm not going to; I was merely pointing out a very obvious fact."

"Which is?"

She stops hunting for whatever she's looking for and gives me a grin. "He'd be good to have some fun with. He's got a hot body, isn't a total ass, and won't remember to call you the next morning. It's a perfect situation."

I put my hands on my hips. "Thanks for the vote of confidence, sis, but I'm not in the market for a one-night stand or anything close to it."

Her face softens, and it makes me feel all the more pitiful. "Hey, it's just a joke. I just want you to not take life so seriously, K. Things have been stressful for you for so long."

"Who says I'm taking life so seriously?"

She gives me a pointed look, leaning on the bar across from me. "It's been two years, sis. It's time."

I swallow hard, then look around quickly. "I don't think here is the time nor the place."

She squeezes my hand as I tuck a lock of hair behind my ear. This is a sore subject for me, and Stevie is the only one, aside from a few close friends at home in Cali, that really know about my past.

"I'm sorry. I'm just trying to make light of the situation, and it's just like you to overthink it. He's a good-looking guy, and he clearly likes you, that's all I'm saying."

I look sideways and he's gone back to drilling, his body splayed out on the other end of the bar as he holds up a plank of wood, affixing it to the wall.

"Well, keep those thoughts to yourself. The last thing I need is him distracting me," I whisper-shout.

"Aha! So, he does distract you?"

"I've got eyes," I huff. "I'm not totally immune, but you know I don't do the one-night stand thing."

"That's because you've always been in relationships. Sometimes it's nice to just let loose, you know?"

A slow smile spreads on my face. "Are you trying to tell me something?"

She frowns. "What?"

"You're still in a relationship, apparently, so what would you know about letting loose?"

I know she misses her boyfriend, Trent, that it's hard with him being away. I take my hat off to anyone in a long-distance relationship, especially when the other person is deployed. It can't be easy, and I know she's loyal, despite how tempting it may be at times when you're lonely.

"What do you mean *apparently?*" She tries to whip me with a dish rag, but I dodge it.

"Who's getting her panties in a twist now?"

She rolls her eyes at me. "I wouldn't know about letting loose *lately.* All I'm saying is, you're way too serious, K.

We never have any fun anymore."

"Hey, we had fun the other night at Zee bar, didn't we?"

"I worry about you," she whispers.

Ever since we've been back together, Stevie has taken on the role of protector, which is funny because that's always been my role. She's certainly spread her wings since starting this job; it's done wonders for her confidence, and I can't deny that. I never thought my little sister pulling drinks at a biker club would be the thing to bring her out of her shell, but she seems a lot happier than she has been in a while. Despite the fact she basically pines for this man she's been with since college.

I don't dislike Trent, but I also don't think that he's made any real commitment to my sister. They're not engaged, there's no talk of marriage, and they've barely lived together. I don't know how she's going to fare up being by herself for years at a time.

"You don't have to worry about me," I tell her. "Honestly, I'm fine. I'm loving this fresh start, Stevie. I'm getting new clients every day, I like where I live, and my apartment is really nice. Life's good right now. I feel like things are on the up and up."

I purposely don't mention my love life because, frankly, it's not up for discussion, and she knows it. And now definitely isn't the time with interested eyes and ears all around us.

Her voice still holds concern as she says, "Well, that's good, and I'm glad you're finding your feet. I told you it wasn't so bad here."

I smile, trying to seem reassuring. "I like small towns. You get to know everyone, and it's more personal. If you've been in one city, you've seen them all."

"Hey, do you want to grab some lunch? I'm starving."

"That's what I came to ask you," I muse.

"Great minds think alike." She goes off to get her purse, and I glance back over to the bar where Bones was lying. Only his drill and some loose nails lay there now. It looks like he's putting together a long shelving unit that goes right across the wall, likely for the bottles of alcohol that will take up the entire space. So he's very handy with tools, and his hands…

"Hey, Kennedy."

I turn as I see a very pregnant Angel come up alongside me, perching on one of the high stools.

"Hi, Angel, how are you?"

She smiles as she pats her swollen belly, and my eyes dart down. "I'm well, thanks Kennedy. How are you doing?"

"I'm fine, busy. Hey, I'm just taking Stevie to lunch if you'd like to join us?"

She groans. "I wish I could, but I've got to get Rawlings in less than an hour, and then she's got an after-school recital that we need to get to. Brock doesn't want to miss it.

He'll be the big ass biker blocking everyone's view because he wants to video her singing."

I smile to myself. The men of this club are certainly very involved with their family lives, which is nice to see and not often all that common. From what I've seen and heard from Stevie, they do seem like a brotherhood who sticks together and looks out for one another.

That is one aspect I do respect.

"That's so sweet of him. How's the pregnancy and the baby?"

She winces slightly as the other hand rests on the bar. "This pregnancy's been giving me hell," she says. "I think the baking time is almost up, I feel like a Walrus."

I laugh, she certainly doesn't look like one. "I'm sorry to hear that, but you definitely don't resemble any kind of Walrus I've ever seen. You look great."

"Look at the size of my ankles!" she exclaims waggling one foot at me. "My feet protest every day, I think this baby is going to resemble it's daddy more than it is me."

I gasp, her ankles are pretty bloated. "Shit, woman, you should probably elevate your feet and put them in some ice."

"I know. I'm meant to be at home taking a load off, but I had a client this morning that I couldn't put off."

"Angel, you work way too hard," I tell her.

"If Brock catches me here…"

"Woman!"

We both turn our heads simultaneously.

The massive figure of the man in question stands in the doorway to the bar with his hands on his hips. Brock is a very large man, and scary if you don't know him.

"Uh oh," she says, though she gives him a big cheesy ass grin as he stalks toward us.

I try to diffuse the situation. "Hello, Brock, I was just taking Angel to lunch, thought she might like to put her feet up for a little bit."

He glances at me and gives me a chin lift, but his eyes dart back to her.

"Was over at the salon. They said you just left," he says.

"I'm here now, aren't I?"

These two have fire. You kind of get that first impression from the get-go.

"So, you were at work again?"

"Brock," she says, rubbing her stomach. "I'm not an invalid. I'm going to work right up until I have the baby. I'm fine. We discussed this. It's good for me to do a couple of hours a day to get the circulation going."

"I've got better ways to get the circulation goin', just gotta call me."

She glances at me with a smirk. "Sorry, Kennedy. Can't take the man anywhere."

Oh, but he's not done yet. "You look exhausted, and I don't need my heavily pregnant wife passin' out because she's been told to stay home and rest." He glances at me. "Doctor's orders before you go gettin' any ideas. Tryin' to tame this one has been a work in progress for the last twenty years and then some."

I smile despite myself. "How's that working out for you?"

He grunts. "Not so great, obviously."

"I'm going to have lunch with the girls. I don't see how that's overdoing it," she argues.

He cups her face with his hands and goes in for a kiss as I look away. "Fuckin' drive me bananas," he mutters. "Lucky you're carryin' my kid 'cause I'd put you over my knee for smartin' me."

"Promises, promises."

Stevie finally comes back from out the back with her purse. "Oh, hey, Brock."

He gives her a chin lift too. "Make sure she eats," he replies. "If this kid is anything like me, then he's gonna need all the nutrients he can get."

"What if it's a *she*?" I quip.

Brock frowns. "If it's a girl, then I'm gonna be outsmarted and outnumbered. Fuck knows I'll have my ass handed to me for the rest of my life."

"You love being surrounded by women," Angel says. "Now you've got your wish."

He shakes his head. "If she's anything like you, then I'm well and truly fucked."

Angel leans toward him as she mutters, "Such a sweet talker." They kiss again and Brock moves one hand to her stomach, holding it there.

These two are well and truly in love, it's plain to see.

"Pass me a bucket," Stevie sing-songs. "If you wanna break it up, lover birds, I've only got a small window of time to snarf some food down before I've got to get back." I glance around again and don't see Bones anywhere. I wonder if he left, and I feel a little bit miffed he didn't come over and say anything. No wave. No chin lift. Nothing.

Not that I care.

The more I stay away from him, the better it'll be, and hopefully he won't star in any more of my illicit dreams where he's the main attraction, using my body like it's an amusement park.

Brock helps Angel off the stool and gives her a squeeze on the ass as she waddles past and we head out.

The more I hang around the girls, the more I see that these men I thought were mindless barbarians aren't all just brutes who pound their chests. Brock had very good reason to tell Angel to get off her feet; her ankles look terrible.

All the while, I can't help but wonder where Bones took off to and why he's now ghosting me. Maybe he's finally gotten the hint and he'll leave me alone, and I can get on with my life as I know it.

If that were the case, then why do I feel bitter

disappointment running through me that I didn't get to talk to him? Not that we talk – I'd call it more like annoying banter with a hint of dirty flirting and a lot of sarcasm, mainly from my side because he seems to bring out the snark in my personality.

Even from across the room, it's like he's undressing me with his eyes, and he doesn't give a shit who sees. Those butterflies go off again in my stomach, and I can't deny the tempting idea of his offer.

I mean, even when he's disappeared, he's under my skin.

Maybe now he's choosing to play hard to get.

I have wondered if it's because I do like the attention, but only from him. I don't usually want or like guys ogling me at the best of times, but he doesn't do that. He looks at me with something else that I can't put my finger on, which is stupid. He's made it clear what his intensions are, and all they include is fucking me, as he so eloquently put it.

Still, I think about the day I went to see him behind bars, and I know that I shouldn't be feeling the things I'm feeling after seeing him locked up with that smirk on his face. A beautiful disaster.

He has a body made for sin. I got the memo on that, well and truly.

You better be there, because if you're not, I'm gonna punish that hot little ass for denying me all this time, Ms. Hart. And I won't be nice about it either. Somethin' tells me you like a man who likes to take charge, don't you?

Maybe I do. Maybe I do want him to secretly sneak into my bedroom in my fantasies and ravage me like he hasn't a care in the world. Maybe I do want him to spank my ass and tell me I'm a bad girl. The thought has my pussy clenching as I try not to let the arousal flood through me.

Again – he's nowhere in sight and he's under my skin.

I've got to break this cycle.

Maybe Stevie is right. Maybe I just let loose and see what happens. Forget the fact he's my client on probation who I am meant to be monitoring…. I can safely say I've never been attracted to a client before, much less slept with one.

Look me in the eye and tell me you don't want my cock.

His dirty words have me wanting to show him just exactly how much of a bad girl I can be.

Bones

BRACKEN RIDGE
REBELS
ARIZONA
M · C
BRACKEN RIDGE
REBELS

CHAPTER 9

BONES

My place isn't exactly the type of house you want to bring your parents back to without prior knowledge of their visit. You never know what may crawl out of there at any given moment. I try not to let mom in without prior warning, unless she's bringing food, but she's a bossy little woman who won't take no for an answer.

Even though, contrary to popular opinion, some say I'm a slob, I do know how to work a washing machine. And I pay one of the club girls or sweet butts to come clean my place once a week to keep the place tidy, though Colt isn't a bad roommate and does his fair share to keep it livable.

Not that any woman has shared my bed here for a while. I tend to keep all of that at church. Yet, I can't even imagine taking Kennedy Hart up to my rickety single bed upstairs at the clubhouse and bangin' her. For some reason, it feels wrong. Dirty. She should be in clean sheets, in a bed that won't sound like I'm tryin' to murder it, and more to the point; I wouldn't be able to do all I needed to do on a single bed. Hell no. The thought stirs that fire inside me, the same inferno I've been feeling for months now.

When I take Kennedy Hart for the first time, it's going to be in a bed big enough for me to maneuver around. I want every damn inch of her beautiful body.

I saw her today, and I stayed away, but fuck knows how. I know she kept looking over at me, though. If she hates me as much as she claims she does, then why did she keep checking up on what I was doing? A slow smile creeps on my face that I left her hanging. She can deny it all she likes, but she's into it just as much as I am.

Maybe if I leave her hanging a little bit more, she might come running into my arms. Here's hoping. I'm gonna have blue balls for an eternity if this keeps up.

Just the thought of sinking into her sweet pussy is enough to make me wanna hold out for the rest of time because there ain't no cure for what I got. Only her. And the thought of her finally giving in to me sends my pulse racing so bad that I'm not sure I can't hold out much longer.

It's that very notion that has me creaming into my hand all week, like a fuckin' pussy boy, and then havin' Sienna call me to make sure I wasn't chickening out of the bachelor auction which I didn't even officially agree to.

To be honest, I've thought about it. I mean, it is a bit embarrassing, not that I'm unsure if anyone will bid on me, because I'm sure someone will. But if Kennedy doesn't, then it'll be a shot to my ego that I really don't need. As well as the ribbing I'll get from the boys. That, I'll never live down.

Of course, Steel has taken it upon himself to tell everyone at church that I'm volunteering to be auctioned off, so now I'm a laughingstock. They're just jealous because they didn't get asked to be raffled off. At least that's what I tell myself.

I don't give a shit what they think; it'll be me in Kennedy's bed by the night's end. I'm counting on it. There's no way she can avoid me forever. I told her what'd happen, and while she likes to think I'm disgusting and have a dirty mouth, I did see her skin flush when I spoke dirty to her. I also noticed her chest rise rapidly and her eyes drop to my mouth more than once.

She can act like a prim and proper little lawyer lady all she wants, but I know women like her, they're wound so fuckin' tight that they wouldn't know a good time if it bit them on the armpit.

I don't give two shits about what anyone will think when I show up in my club colors. Everyone knows that the Rebels now own the Stone Crow. We're not promoting it as a biker bar, but a family friendly pub and bistro with home-cooked meals. We want to bring the locals back in when they've had enough tapas and overpriced finger food.

The whole renovation has been tedious, but finally it's

finished. And what a transformation. It went from dull and dingy and smelling like stale beer to being bright and airy. The restaurant now boasts new flooring, countertops, and restrooms as well as a state-of-the-art kitchen.

I can see that we're gonna be hangin' out a lot more down at the Crow, especially if the new fancy chef Hutch hired is as good as he says she is.

Things could be lookin' up on the takeout menu.

I spray some cologne as I slick my hair back, letting my mohawk grow out some. I still have it longer on top, but I wanna look good tonight so I go all out. All my jeans are ripped, so I pick my most comfy pair with less holes and then shrug on my cut and lock up.

Mounting my vintage Harley, I fire up the engine. I love the sound of my bike when I first start her up. It's like music to my ears. There is no greater feeling in the world than a Harley takin' full flight, gliding effortlessly along the asphalt. Destination anywhere.

That's what I live for. Even though I'm technically suspended from driving and shouldn't be going anywhere, I don't give a shit.

When we don't get to ride as much in the wintertime, I get withdrawal symptoms. I'm not really a car guy like Steel and some of the other brothers are. I love my bikes, period.

When I have to ride in a cage, it's only for short distances or if it's too cold out to take the Harley.

I hope tonight isn't a drag, and I also hope I don't look like a damn fool. The only reason I even contemplated this is because I wanna break the ice with Kennedy.

I pull up and the first thing I see is a row of Harleys lined up in the lot. Fuckin' great.

So all my brothers have come to watch the spectacle, just what I need.

That's the trouble in small towns; you can't get away with shit.

The kitchen had a trial run last night with a few of the club members. The new chef Roxy seems enthusiastic and capable, from what I've heard. I didn't get to meet her, nor did I get to eat.

The place looks incredible, shiny and new, the old floorboards under the shitty old carpet came out great, looking brand new with the dark stain.

I spent most of the night helping Colt rig up the security cameras again now that everything is back in order. He also changed all the locks, added a new alarm system, and installed motion sensors for the cellar where all the booze is kept. It's like Fort Knox.

Stevie will move into the apartment upstairs, and Axton will occupy Sienna's old place when he gets out in a few short weeks.

It's sure to be strange having Axton around, not that I really know the guy, but the pressure's on if he's ever gonna live up to Brock and Hutch's expectations.

He'll help Stevie run the bar, though she'll be the one charge, so it'll be interesting how he takes direction from a chick after getting out of prison. I'm all for it. Stevie's capable and dependable, and she's got the chops to see it through, but she's gonna have to have her wits about her with an ex-con. We all are. But there's also a certain amount of trust from Brock and Hutch. They wouldn't purposely put anyone, much less a woman, in a situation that would be harmful to them.

Axton will also be prospecting for the club, earning his dues and proving his worth. All of it falls on Brock if this doesn't work out, and I know for a fact my fellow business partner and friend will not put up with any shit should this go south, even if Axton is his brother and has been inside for the better part of ten years.

I'm all for givin' second chances, but I'm cautious. Ex-cons aren't always reformed.

We all trust Brock and his decision-making, but the truth is, he hasn't been around Axton for ten years. He's only seen him on the visits to prison he makes up in Stradbroke. He doesn't really know anything about him or what kind of person he is now. I've only been in jail for twelve hours and it changed me, so I can't imagine what doing hard time in the state pen would do to you. Ten years has gotta do something to the psyche. I dread to think of the horrors that could've occurred. Being locked in a concrete cell is the reason I've always toed the line, aside from the tickets and the blunt incident.

I never did get into heavy drugs as a kid or now as an adult, it just never interested me. Though you'd be surprised how many people judge you because of the fact you have tattoos and a mohawk, even before they see the patches on my jacket.

I've never been ashamed to be who I am. I've never been anything other than this. And while I'm nowhere near perfect, I'm not full of horseshit either.

My parents taught me to be honest and see the good in people, and I guess that's one of my downfalls. I've let people take too much of me in the past and not give back; it's probably the reason I haven't had a girlfriend in years, not anyone permanent anyway. I wouldn't say I'm the biggest manwhore around, since I do actually have to like the chick before I bone her. That's gotta count for something, even though there's been a definite slight dry spell lately.

I park and head into the back, not wanting to announce my presence by going through the front doors.

When I head inside, Colt is in the back room, still pouring over the elaborate computer system he's set up.

"Hey, dude," I say, leaning against the door jamb.

He looks up from the screen. "Sup?"

"Gettin' organized." I nod behind me, like that says everything.

He smirks. "So, the rumors are true? Thought they were just shittin' me."

"It's for charity." I shrug, like that's the only reason.

"Right."

The realization I'm an idiot suddenly strikes me.

Before I can back up and get out of there before anyone sees me, I feel a hard slap on my back.

"Finally, Sienna's gonna hand you your ass if you don't get in there. The dinner is about to start," Steel says, his hand gripping my shoulder with force, just in case I had any plans to make a swift exit.

"I thought I had time for a beer for fuck's sake." I shake my head.

"No time for that. Tryin' to get some funds for a new van for Faux Paws," he tells us. "So, if you're our only hope, you'd better get out there. Work your magic."

Colt's shoulders shake as I give him a look.

"Not fuckin' workin' shit. Said I'd show up, and I have, like this isn't humiliating enough," I complain.

"There's nothin' humiliating about being ogled and auctioned off when it's for the needy," Colt says, once he's recovered from laughing at me. "Think of it like a service to the community."

"I'm not sure how needy the over fifties women's shake

n' bake club is, but you'll see for yourself soon," Steel goes on, really rubbing it in now. "Most of them are out there with their paddles, ready to snap up a bargain. I'd be careful, though, some of them don't get out much. Hope your health insurance is up to date; they may bite."

Colt snickers into this bourbon as I shove Steel's arm off my shoulders.

"Very funny. There's a very high possibility some hot chick out there will snag me and make me her slave for the night."

Steel shakes his head. "If you're talkin' about a smokin' hot red-headed lawyer, then I'm afraid you're shit outta luck, bud."

I frown.

This isn't good. Wasn't my warning enough? This doesn't deter me; it only makes me all the more curious to find her and ask what the hell she's playing at.

"She'll be here," I maintain. "Practically unzipped me in her office the other day. If it weren't for another client comin' in, she'd have sucked me off there and then."
Steel grunts. "This is the same woman who threatened a restrainin' order against you?"

"That was hearsay," I remind him. "And I doubt she came all the way down to county to bail my ass out if she really had an issue with me."

"Who could resist you, right?" Colt says, trying not to choke on his drink.

"More like she saw pay dirt and took it," Steel adds, like I asked for the commentary.

"You'll both be laughin' on the other side of your faces when I nail her. The only restrainin' goin' on will be her hands bound to my bed."

"Does she know that?" Steel cocks a brow.

"You'd think she'd know a good thing when she sees it. After all, you do throw yourself in the way of crazed gunmen as well as put up a good fight occasionally," Colt puts in.

I pull on the lapels of my cut. "Thanks, Colt, at least there's one person around here in my corner."

"Hey, I'm all for you taking a knife on behalf of Lucy," Steel replies. "But you can't milk the heroics for the rest of time."

"I'll remember that when you ever need my assistance or need a knife pulled out of your shoulder," I add, giving him a look.

We all stop our banter when Sienna comes storming through. She frowns when she sees me, then frowns even more when she sees Steel.

"Bones!" she cries. "You were meant to be here fifteen minutes ago."

I give her a lazy smile. "I'm late to everythin', sweet cheeks. It's gonna be all right."

She gives Colt a wave, but narrows her eyes on Steel.

"What did I do?" he grumbles.

"Don't be putting him off. We need all the available bachelors we can get," she goes on. "Two haven't shown up, and I'm in half a mind to get you to go round them up."

I cup my good ear. "Say that a little louder, and I might even start to think you haven't got me here to fill in a few gaps."

She turns her gaze on mine. "You don't want all those little kittens and puppies over at the shelter to be homeless out onto the streets now, do you, Bones?"

"That's great. Bribe me with cute fluffy animals I can't say no to."

She beams. "Stop being a baby. It'll be fun, I promise. But you need to get your ass moving."

Famous last words.

Despite her storming around and her whiplash tongue, Steel is one lucky man. She's not only beautiful but smart too. I don't know where she finds the time to set all of this up with running Steel's office and keeping everything in line there. She's really landed on her feet here in Bracken Ridge, and though Steel is still a grouchy asshole and always will be, she's been good for him.

Steel had PTSD for quite some time after he came back from duty in Afghanistan, but he manages it well. I think settling down has really grounded him, and while it hasn't improved his overall temperament, it has at least softened the blows somewhat.

"Fun like a hole in the head," I grumble, running a hand through my hair.

"Get on over here and give your man some lovin'," Steel says, eye-fucking her in the short dress she has on.

She waggles a finger at him. "No time for that, babe. I'm running seriously late."

I've never heard him let anyone get away with any kind of rebuttal, but he just shakes his head in an exasperated way as one corner of his mouth curls up.

"What?" he says when I can't help a snicker.

"Oh, nothin'."

Sienna links her arm through mine and steers me out of the room, giving Steel a finger wave as his annoyed gaze follows us until he's out of sight.

"You know you've just earned me a punch in the face," I tell her as we walk down the corridor to the front of the bar.

"He's a big pussy cat, really," she whispers with a laugh.

I look down at her. "Maybe to you, but not to the rest of us who get manhandled by their women."

"Well, he should know by now that I only have eyes for him."

I smirk. "You two are pretty loved up. It's kinda sickening."

She rolls her eyes. "You won't be saying that when you find the right woman."

"Hey, I find the right women all the time."

"Woman wasn't plural."

"Oh." I smile. "This is why I'm here, isn't it?"

"No, you're here for charity."

"Oh right, sorry. I thought the whole reason I gave up my Saturday night was to come and sweep my lawyer off her feet and land her in my bed. For a price, that is. My bad."

"Is that all you guys think about?" She sighs. "And I don't think that is quite the idea of the auction."

"It's fine. I don't mind bein' a manwhore if it's for her. I'm open at that particular junction."

She face-palms herself. "I'm far too sober for this conversation."

Kennedy better be here. If she's not, I might just go pay her a little visit tonight. Finding her place shouldn't be too hard, though I've no idea where she lives because I'm not quite at the stalker stage yet. The possibility that she really isn't comin' is makin' me a little crazy. The notion that I may get stood up rattles my brain as I wonder why the fuck I'm even here.

I don't bother to glance around the bar as Sienna drags me along.

I've got a part to play and tonight it's the bachelor with a penchant for redheads.

If I get bought by an old woman with a glint in her eye,

I will be even more of a laughingstock with the brothers. They're all lurking around here somewhere because they've nothing better to do, but that's the least of my problems.

Gettin' Kennedy into my bed is gonna be a challenge, but no one said life was meant to be easy, especially where women are concerned.

BRACKEN RIDGE
REBELS
ARIZONA
M · C

CHAPTER 10

KENNEDY

I don't know why I put my favorite dress on tonight, or let my hair go wild and applied far too much makeup than should be humanly possible. Then again, I do know why.

Not that I have any intention of placing a bid on Bones at the fundraiser. He can politely threaten me all he likes; I'm not going to give into his whims. Not just because he's my client who's still under my jurisdiction until his probation expires, and that in itself is unethical, but mainly because I don't know if I can handle being alone with him, as weak and pathetic as that sounds.

A man like Bones wants a strong, confident woman in the bedroom, and while I might be many things at work and in the courtroom, hell, in everyday life, I don't exactly carry the same confidence into the bedroom. I haven't for a long time.

I could always threaten him with getting arrested again, not that I really want to do that, but he's persistent. It kind of comes with the territory and the whole alpha male biker vibe he sports so well.

It doesn't matter that the air hissed out of my lungs when he cornered me in my office or the fact my heart beat so fast I was sure he could hear it. None of it matters, because he's not good for me. I can't get involved with a man like him. A man who can't take no for an answer, for one. The nerve!

That doesn't explain the exotic dreams I've been having, but I know it's just my mind playing tricks on me because he's forbidden and wild and all the things I *shouldn't* be attracted to.

Bones would probably brag about the whole encounter with all his buddies after the deed, and then where would I be? Having to put up with their snickers and taunts every time I run into any one of them. Men love to brag, that's all I can say. Why would he be any different?

When I finally arrive, I find Stevie behind the bar and she shows me to the reserved table where the wild child of the club, Deanna, the club Prez's daughter, Lily, and Summer are sitting, already getting sucked into what looks like a round of martinis.

"Can I get you one?" Stevie asks as I nod gratefully.

Before I even take a seat, Kirsty spots us and makes her way over. She's wearing a leather, tight-fitting dress with red shoes that match her lipstick. She's a very elegant woman and is still very attractive at her age. You'd never think she was married to a biker.

"Keep them coming!" Deanna calls out to Stevie as she retreats to make me a cocktail. I need it after the week I've had. It's been all doom and gloom with child custody cases and divorces.

At least the girls of the club are nice and easy to get along with. That's a bonus I never expected. They're not your typical *biker babes* or like the women I would have imagined that hang around a motorcycle club.

They keep telling me they're not an outlaw club, and aside from Bones's petty misdemeanors, they seem pretty low-key. Tonight, for example, sure, it's a good way to reopen the Stone Crow with its new look and family friendly appeal, but it's also even better to give back to the community.

One reason I moved from the city was to be in a smaller, more close-knit town that didn't have the hustle and bustle of city life. I've done all of that, and I certainly don't miss the commute for an hour each way just to get to my office.

Kirsty gives me a warm smile. Now that I'm on the club's payroll, as well as receiving a generous retainer for Kirsty's real estate business, I technically work for her now.

She's never done me wrong and has been kind to me. I feel like she's a genuinely warm person. She also has that air about her that spells trouble if you ever crossed her. I respect that. There is nothing wrong with speaking your mind and sticking up for yourself. Sometimes people see kindness as weakness and that really bugs me.

In my line of work, I have to keep an open mind, and I also have to use my gut instinct.

I'm pretty good these days at making fair calls on most people. It's like you develop this sixth sense and can read people really well.

"I'm so glad you could make it!" Kirsty says to me, slinging her arm around her daughter, Deanna.

"Wouldn't miss it for the world. I like supporting a good cause," I say.

"And we get to check out the available horndogs," Deanna sings with glee. "Not that there's anyone in this town I'd want to put my hands on."

"That's just being negative," Summer says. "I'm sure that there will be other desperate men up there other than Bones."

They all laugh.

"It was super nice of him to donate his time, though," Sienna says, sidling up next to Kirsty. "I hope you're not all going to give him a hard time for being generous and putting himself out there on stage." Her eyes fall on me for just a fraction of a second.

"Generous?" says Lily, spluttering her drink. "We all know he wants to get bid on so he can –"

Sienna tuts and cuts her off, clearly trying to save Bones's bacon, like I don't already know he's probably got chicks ready to crawl all over him. I wasn't born yesterday.

"Well, you could do the honorable thing and place a bid to get the donations up a bit," she says sweetly. "Nothing like a bit of competition to get the high rollers interested. Remember, it's all for a good cause!"

"Yeah, I'm sure there'll be some *stiff* competition up there tonight," Deanna chortles just as the chair next to me moves.

Angel slowly plonks herself next to me, holding her belly as she lowers herself.

The girls all turn to her.

"Hey, stranger!" Deanna says with a grin. "The old ball and chain let you out?"

She rolls her eyes. "That ball and chain put this huge baby in my stomach and I've got ankles the size of an elephant's balls if that answers your question."

More laughter ensues.

"Well, you choose to do the wild tango with a giant, what do you expect?" Lily pipes up, pointing the finger.

"You've still gotta squeeze that kid out yet."

Angel winces. "Don't remind me. I'm not one of those people who have an easy time being pregnant. I've had morning sickness every day for nine months, and most days I just feel like the side of a barge."

I give her a sympathetic smile. "So, you're due any day?"

"I'm overdue, which is why Brock didn't want me to come," she says. "But my mom and dad have Rawlings for the weekend to give us some alone time, and he's been here all week long, getting stuff organized for the Crow's reopening. I don't want to sit at home all night with my knitting needles, waiting for my water to break."

I nod. "Fair enough, it's probably good to get out. Are you feeling any pain now or just soreness?"

"Every freaking minute it hurts." She smiles. "But it's more uncomfortable than anything, like you can't get comfy any which way. It's all worth it, though. To hold your baby for the first time, you forget everything else. Time stops."

I've never really been a person that wanted kids, but I can certainly appreciate that it would be pretty extraordinary. Time's ticking for me, I'm thirty-eight but then again, so is Angel. "I can imagine."

"Brock's always wanted a big family, but I think I draw the line at two."

"Well, two's a good number. Do you know the sex of the baby?"

She shakes her head. "We wanted it to be a surprise. Brock doesn't care either way. He adores Rawlings. She's turning into a bit of a tomboy. Then again, she's always been a free spirit, ever since she could talk and tell me to mind my business."

I laugh at the thought, though I've met little Rawlings and she definitely has a big personality.

Before I can say any more, the emcee for the night

appears on the makeshift stage and gets our attention.

"Good evening everyone! I'd like to welcome you all to our annual charity fundraiser! We will start off tonight's event with spin the wheel and door prizes, followed by the entrée, then a pop quiz for each table followed by the main course, and for dessert we get the big headliner; the bachelor auction."

Everyone claps and wolf whistles when the auction gets mentioned, like the men are pieces of meat. If it were women up there on stage in bikinis or otherwise, being auctioned off for a date, there would be a holy uproar. The joys of living in a small town where nobody cares.

The buzz around the room at the tables is surprisingly upbeat. I guess this is an annual event for the good people of Bracken Ridge, and I don't get out much myself. I'm sad to say that since starting up my practice, my social life has taken a backseat. Not that there is a boatload to do around here, but there are still some nice restaurants and the Zee if you want a quiet drink with a sophisticated edge.

All in all, I really like Bracken Ridge. It has no memories of… my husband or my past life.

I swallow hard; knowing this was inevitable. It's like I punish myself every time I feel one iota of happiness or enjoyment. Bam! It hits me full force. I don't know who I'm trying to kid. Grief lurks where you least expect it.

My husband died two years ago, and I nursed him while

he slowly slipped away from cancer.

He was so young.

I look up from the table and everyone is clapping, so I do the same, mechanically, because I've no idea what just happened, but someone is going up to the stage to collect a duo of wines in a box.

Kirsty catches my eye and I smile at her, giving her a chin lift. *Shit.* She's observant.

She smiles back, but it doesn't reach her eyes. Concern flashes across her features.

Thankfully, the first course arrives, and everyone tucks into what I have to say is the best prawn salad I've ever had. There's some kind of citrus dressing that gives the whole dish a zing.

The new chef in town, Roxy, has only been here a week, and I should take it upon myself to be neighborly and introduce myself sometime. I know what it's like moving to a new place where you know nobody, though I'm lucky that I have Stevie and that we get along so well. I'm not sure where I would be without her sometimes, even when I know I rely on her too much emotionally. You would think being as hard hitting as I am in my day job that I'm tough as nails in all aspects of my life, but the truth is, I'm not. When it comes to relationships, for example, that's where I fall short. I don't let other people see that inside, I am an emotional person. I do let things get to me when I shouldn't, and when it comes to men, I am a complete failure.

I keep myself guarded because of the fear of being hurt again. My husband died; he didn't leave because he wanted to, and the guilt and shame rises within me like it always does because I know what comes next. He wasn't a bad man, not one bit, but the cracks were starting to show in our relationship before he got sick. We were more like roommates, buddies, than a married couple.

Do not go there tonight.

No. I can save it for later, when I'm safely tucked away in my own room, where I can reflect and punish myself some more. The good people of Bracken Ridge, especially my new big client, Kirsty Hutchinson, don't need to see me break down.

I'm tough, I'm ballsy, and that's what I have to keep showing people.

If they knew the real me, they'd think I was a fraud too. I can't let that happen.

The salad plates are cleared, and then Sienna and another couple of volunteers begin passing around a large piece of paper with a thick marker for each table. It looks like it's time for the pop quiz. These are usually fun. I can't say I've had one of these since my college days and that feels like an enormously long time ago.

The subject is eighties music. My favorite. And I do have a bit of a competitive edge ever since I was on the debate team in high school.

The questions are actually quite hard and since it seems the rest of the table also has a competitive streak, we keep our answers fairly guarded.

"Which album topped the charts in nineteen eighty-six, dubbing the artist as the most successful singer of that year? Double points for the name of the album and artist."

God! I was born for this quiz.

I ding the bell.

"Table six?" the emcee says, looking over at me.

"*True Blue,* the artist is Madonna," I say with confidence.

She looks down at the card. "That answer is correct. Five points for the correct album and a bonus five for the artist."

My table erupts in cheers and claps as I take a fake bow, knowing that this is my third cocktail and I need to slow down, though I'm having too much fun to care.

The next few questions we get two out of three because our rival table seems to have a bunch of people from around that era as well.

"It's a tie between table six and table twelve; the final question will determine the winners." More hoots and cheers go around the room. This is quite a serious business.

"The final question is multiple choice, so hands on the bell. For the table to win an all-expenses paid day out at the spa, courtesy of the Lodge… which song went to number one in nineteen eighty-two and stayed in the charts for several weeks, is it A. Eye of the Tiger, by Survivor, B. Let's Get Physical by Olivia Newton-John, or C. Ebony and Ivory by Paul McCartney and Stevie Wonder."

Table twelve are quick on the bell, beating Deanna by only a half a second.

"What's the answer?" she whispers.

"It could be any one of them!" Lily cries, clearly on the edge of her seat.

"I don't fucking know, but I need that foot spa, so somebody better start racking their brains."
Summer glances over to the other table a few up from us.

"I don't think they know. They're conferring for a little too long."

"I think it's Olivia Newton-John," I whisper. "In fact, I'm sure of it. How could any of us forget those leotards and leg warmers?"

"I think she's right," Deanna agrees, "not that I remember much about the eighties…"

"Eye of the Tiger, by Survivor," calls one of the guys from table twelve.

We hold our breath as the emcee looks down at the card, then back up to them. "That answer is incorrect." She glances at our table. "Table six, do you have the correct answer?"

"I love a smart lawyer who knows her music," Deanna chimes, looking very sure of herself. I'm only hoping that I haven't ballsed this up completely. She turns over her shoulder and calls out, "Let's Get Physical by Olivia Newton-John."

The emcee nods and throws the card behind her in dramatic flair. "That answer is correct! Table six, you win the magnificent day out at the Lodge spa, which includes a full body massage, facial, and a manicure and pedicure, courtesy of the Lodge owner, Vanessa, who generously donated this prize."

Our table erupts into fits of cheers and hugs, and I feel quite proud of myself. Plus, I really do want that massage. I freaking need it.

"Well done, girls!" Kirsty says, coming over to us from her post by the door. She's been keeping an eye on how things are running with the wait staff and the drinks being served. From what I can see, it's a well-oiled machine. I'm so proud of Stevie for organizing her staff on such short notice.

"I'm so in need of that day spa, like pronto!" Lily chimes, jumping up and down with glee in her chair.

"I've never won anything before." I laugh. "Though it is kinda hard to forget that video clip. It kinda sticks in your brain."

Claps and applause ring out as Deanna gets up to accept the voucher from the spa.

I can't say I've been up in the mountains to the retreat that I've heard so much about, but something tells me we ought to make a girls' weekend out of it.

Deanna does a happy dance on her way back. "I'm so excited about this!"

"Me too. I've never been up to the Lodge, so maybe we should all take off for a weekend? Just us girls?" I suggest.

"Fantastic idea," Summer agrees. "I need a break from study and classes. This is the perfect excuse."

"Let's throw some dates together. Get me your schedules, and we can work something out," Deanna says happily.

"All I have to do is get Saturday covered at the salon, and I'm good to go," Lily replies.

"And I just need this baby out of me, then I'm good too," Angel quips, taking a sip of her lemonade.

The main courses are delivered. I'm having crumbed chicken on a bed of mashed potatoes with steamed vegetables. It smells absolutely delicious and being I haven't had anything since lunchtime, food is a welcome sight. Everyone eats away happily; except Angel, as she's having a hard time getting comfortable.

By the time dinner is over, the main event is humming to a new tune as the table chats excitedly about the mystery men. Little did I know, the men coming out to be bid on are supposed to be a secret. Though it's a small town, and I'm betting most people know who they are anyway.

When the lights dim, the emcee announces the lineup of six eligible bachelors who will win a lunch or dinner date with the winning bidder, courtesy of the Coffee Bean.

I see his silhouette straight away, even though his body and his stature are not things I should be so familiar with. In fact, they should be foreign to me.

The fact that they aren't, as I press my thighs together, tells me everything about how my body reacts to him, even if my mind has a little catching up to do.

And, of course, he's wearing his worn leather jacket with the filthy patches. I can just imagine him grinning like the Cheshire Cat in the dark, knowing he's all that and loving every second of it.

I wonder if I've actually had enough alcohol to even think about bidding for him. Just as I'm contemplating that, a round of shots appears from the waitress. I glance over at the bar and Stevie gives me a wave.

It's like she read my mind.

BRACKEN RIDGE
REBELS
ARIZONA
M · C

CHAPTER 11

BONES

You know when something seems like a good idea at the time?

And then you get stuck on stage, waiting for a room full of strangers – who're eyeing you up like a slab of meat – to bid on you for a "date," which now that I'm thinking about it, could be code for something else. Some of the chicks in this place seem a little eager.

Here I was thinking Sienna was all Miss Goody-Two-Shoes, and behind our backs, she's secretly pimping us out on the side.

The other chumps stand beside me, and one guy, who I don't know, is literally sweating like a pig.

I feel like giving him a slap on the back and tellin' him it's gonna be okay. This is for charity, right? No need to go gettin' all panicky over it. Though I can't talk, I'd let Kennedy do whatever the hell she wanted if I got to be in her bed for a night.

I don't wanna think about that while I'm standing

here in line, I don't exactly want to showcase a boner in my jeans, it's not a good look where these women are concerned. Some of them look like they don't get out much.

As if the humiliation isn't enough, my club brothers all sit lined-up at the bar, laughing and cajoling at my expense when we're led out onto the stage. We do get applause and someone wolf whistles, though I've got a good mind to think that was probably Gunner. He seems to be finding this a hoot. I have no doubt that if he were single, he'd be the one up here with his ass hangin' out. Trouble is, the fucker would enjoy it too much.

The emcee introduces us all by first name. I give them all a salute when my name is called – thank God Sienna told them my club name – I don't need everyone knowing I'm Ryan Romero for Heaven's sake. Like this isn't embarrassing enough.

Of course, my club colors raise a few eyebrows, but that is the point. I like to shock.

I grin at the crowd, scanning for the only woman in this joint that can hold my attention, and I don't see her anywhere. *She better be here.* I don't wanna get snapped up by Betty Crocker.

Once the formalities are over, the first contestant gets a nice shiny spotlight on him while the rest of us fade into the background.

I look out amongst the eager faces as the room dulls. I

still don't fuckin' see her.

I'm aware Kennedy Hart isn't one to take orders, especially from me, but I was there when her skin flushed as I told her what I wanted to do to her, and she didn't kick me out on my ass.

I know one thing; she better not leave me here hung out to dry because I will pay her a visit later tonight if that's the case, and if that means banging down her door and waking her neighborhood, so be it. One thing about me that's 100% consistent all the time – I keep my word. Sometimes that's not always a good thing because I tend to overpromise, and then I really get myself in the shit. But I have to finish things. I might be known around here as the guy who's late for everything, or I tend to find better ways to spend my time other than workin', but at least I'm consistent.

The first guy up for dibs is called Pete. He collects stray cats and is pretty weird. He has a rocky start to begin with. Poor sucker was the one sweating just earlier, and it seems bein' under the spotlight is doing him no favors.

The emcee tells the room he enjoys: Gaming, ten-pin bowling, and collecting cat figurines.

Go figure. He probably still lives with his mom; he looks like the needy type.

He ends up selling for $150.00

If that happens to me, I don't think that's even going

to buy Faux Paw a jumbo bag of biscuits, much less a new van.

I contemplate giving them a flash of my abs. I mean, what's the point of working out if no one gets to see what's under the leather. I'm only thinking of charity, after all. And Kennedy's eyes did wander when I stripped for her in the courthouse holding room.

The guy next up, Mr. Carruthers from the convenience store, is a seasoned pro. Now that he's recently divorced, he's got the whole world at his feet. Or at least the good women of Bracken Ridge.

"When he's not supplying the locals with groceries and fresh donuts," the emcee croons, "he enjoys watching cowboy movies, collecting vintage coins, and candlelit dinners."

The crowd claps, and bids immediately go a little nuts for a minute or so. Honestly, these chicks are hardcore. I mean, Mr. Carruthers is about sixty years old.

I still can't see Kennedy, not that you can see anything once the lights dim and the spotlight blinds you.

"Sold for three hundred dollars!"

The crowd claps and cheers, and the bar coos and whistles as Mr. C takes a bow.

I feel like slapping my forehead.

Dan from the laundromat is next; he's tall and lanky like his father, and I think he's about a year out of high school. It's obvious by the socks and shoes he's wearing that he still lives at home and his mom does his laundry, though he's gone wild with a Darth Vader t-shirt.

"You nervous?" I ask, because he looks like he's about to shit himself.

"A little," he replies as I nod and give him a squeeze on the shoulder.

I should tell him that this is just dinner, it's not *actually* a date, but it looks like he might need a little advice on the female front.

"Women are a little hard to figure out," I say as he looks at me weird. "But they're really not so bad, as long as you take the lead and shit. Chicks love that. Open doors, give them a compliment, and definitely don't go in for a kiss unless they're giving you the right signals."

His eyes go wide as he looks at me like I'm the I-Ching.

"What signals?"

"She'll play with her hair, look down, then back up at you under her lashes, and she might touch you."

"Touch me?"

"Yeah, like some chicks make it obvious they're into you." I think about Kennedy and smirk. "And some chicks really don't. So don't get the two confused. Some chicks really won't be into you, point blank. Accept it and move on. There're plenty more fish in the sea."

"Wow," he says. "That's the best adv–"

"Dan, are you with us?" the emcee calls as we both glance her way.

I pat him hard on the back. "Go get 'em, tiger." Poor Dan, he looks like a deer caught in headlights. He swipes his mop of dark hair back and it flops straight back down again. The bidding starts a little slow, but he does have a kind of endearing quality that might make someone feel sorry for him.

"…going once, twice, sold! For three hundred and fifty dollars!"

He turns to me with wider eyes than before, and I give him the thumbs up. Poor kid looks like he might puke.

I pull on the collar of my cut as the emcee introduces me. "Contestant number four is Bones. He enjoys tinkering with his engine parts, sucking on… juicy… peaches… and… bare horseback riding." Yes, my introduction questions are all laced with innuendo, and I'm pretty sure the woman with the mic is now blushing.

I fist pump in the air, waving to the crowd, ignoring my brothers at the bar who are all falling over laughing like the dumb fucks they are. The more engagement I get with the crowd, hopefully the more money I'll raise. Now that I've spent some time at the shelter, I actually do want to see those upgrades happen. And it'll do my ego some good if I can make some good coin, maybe even shut the idiots up at the bar who shouldn't be here.

I do a full circle so they can see the goods. The spotlight is bright, it blasts my eyes as the lights dim once more.

"Can I see a hundred…"

"One fifty!" yells a bidder.

Phew. The first bid is a welcome relief. I wouldn't want to do the walk of shame with my tail tucked between my legs.

"One seventy-five," calls out another.

"Two hundred!" is yelled from somewhere down the back.

I put my hands on my hips and scan the crowd, giving them a show as I give a cute Grandma at the table in front a wink.

"Two-fifty," the first bidder yells.

"Three hundred!"

"Three hundred is the current bid," the emcee says into the mic. "Do I have any higher bids –"

"Three-twenty-five."

"Three-fifty!"

"Four hundred!"

Jeepers. I don't know what these ladies have planned for me, but I'm starting to think I should quit the theatrics. I step toward the emcee, startling her for a second, and give her a chin lift.

She hesitates, then I summon the mic with my two fingers. She holds it out for me.

"Calm down, ladies," I say out to the room. "There's enough of me to go round… for the right price, that is."

Emcee lady takes the mic back as she sizes me up, but the bidding has begun again.

"Four-fifty!"

"Five hundred!" yells a loud male, booming voice. Everyone looks toward the bar and there is Brock, holding up a beer toward me.

I grab the mic this time without warning. "If you want a date with me, lover boy, all you gotta do is ask!" I say, giving him a thrusting gyrating motion with my hips. Shocks and gasps ring through the crowded tables.

Brock shakes his head as Colt slaps him on the back, chuckling, as I hand back the mic.

Two can play at that game, funny fucker.

I think the emcee lady wants to remind me this is a family friendly venue, but instead she stares at me with her mouth open.

"You gonna outbid him, sweetheart?" I whisper-shout. "Or do I have to do something drastic, like drop my pants?"

She blinks rapidly a few times and then recovers herself.

For fuck's sake, someone outbid fuckin' Brock! Although, it would be funny to see him five greens out of pocket, I would laugh my ass off at that.

"Do I see any raise on five hundred from the… uh… large man at the bar…"

"Five twenty-five," calls the bidder at the front again. It could be the old lady I winked at; I'm not sure, they're all blurring into one. I am glad that she outbid Brock, though.

"Five-fifty!" the same chick in the back yells out.

It's a kind of nice feeling, two women battling it out over you, even if neither of them are the woman that you really want raisin' their paddle.

"Five hundred and fifty dollars, everyone! Going once, twice… are we all done at five –"

"One thousand dollars!"

Everyone gasps at the same time.

I glance over to where I think the voice came from and try to see who the heck the crazy person is.

"A thousand dollars?" the emcee lady repeats like she can't believe it, and honestly, neither can I. Now I'm really starting to consider what the hell I'm doing here, meanwhile Steel is laughing all the way to the bank with that new van.

"You heard the lady!" I holler.

"A thousand dollars! Sold to the lady from table six…" The lights come back on, and I see a flash of red hair as the girls from the M.C. all give Kennedy Hart high-fives.

That sly little fox.

A slow grin spreads across my face as our eyes finally meet. So she was here all along.

Good girl, I muse to myself. *Good girl.*

I can hardly fuckin' wait to get off this stage.

I have to wait another half an hour before going to congratulate the big bidder of the night. Everyone is going on about it. Way to make an entrance, *Miss Lawyer Lady.*

I didn't even have to flash many of my body parts in order to do it. That's a first.

After the auction finishes, we're free to leave and meet up with our bidders, who will get the Coffee Bean voucher. I wouldn't be caught dead in that place. It's where preppy kids hang out during the day and schoolteachers eat at night.

The only thing I want to be eating is Kennedy's…

"Hey, fuckface," Gunner calls as I get to the bar and, if I'm not mistaken, some of the boys have the smiles wiped off their faces. "Did your lawyer lady really just pay a thousand bucks for you?"

I spread my arms wide. "It seems she knows quality when she sees it."

This makes him, Brock, and Colt snort with laughter.

Steel tips his beer to me. "Did good, brother."

Hutch appears behind the bar and tips his bourbon to me, too. "Looks like the night went off without a hitch. Grub was good, drinks are flowin', good to see this place full, with people spendin' money."

"Can't argue with that," I say. "Though I haven't had any grub yet, been too busy makin' money off my ass to think about silly things like eatin'."

"Help yourself, Roxy's got plenty left over." Hutch nods

toward the kitchen. Unbeknownst to him, I've got more important things on my mind than sampling the menu, not when I could be sampling Kennedy.

Stevie hands me a beer, which I think I've more than earned tonight. I turn and rest my back against the bar and seek Kennedy out. She's sitting with Deanna, Summer, Angel, and Lily. They're all deep in conversation. Deanna is animated with her hands, and the girls are all laughing.

Kennedy is a vision when she's relaxed. You don't see it very often because she's so guarded, but when she lets her hair down and really smiles, the whole world lights up. I should tell her to smile more.

"You gonna go claim your prize?" Brock gives me a shove with his shoulder.

I give him a sly smirk. "I don't think this is gonna be too much of a hardship, fellas. After all, she is smokin' hot and bailed me out of jail, so at least we have somethin' to talk about. Not that there'll be much talkin' goin' on." Gunner all but chokes on his beer.

"Don't go gettin' all frisky on me," Hutch warns. "We're not licensed for anythin' except food and drink."

I smirk. "Well, if she paid a thousand dollars to go on a date with me, I'm pretty sure she wants to get her money's worth."

Brock rolls his eyes. "In your dreams. She hates you."

"Hate is a strong emotion," I remind him. "She thinks

she hates me because she likes control in her world, and I'm not some little puppet dancin' on a string that she can pull this way and that. I know her type."

"Is that right?" He takes a chug of his beer. "You sure you're not just goin' soft, brother?"

"You almost found out with that half-assed bid you made." I cup my dick. "And I prefer redheads."

Brock shakes his head. "There's no hope for you."

I grin as I push off the bar and saunter over to table six, flipping them the bird in my wake.

When I get there, Angel is doin' some weird breathing shit and Kennedy is looking around, a little frantic. The other girls at the table have disappeared on a bathroom break.

"Hey, Ange. *Ms. Hart*," I say, my eyes on Kennedy, then they dart to Angel. "You all right?"

She's rubbing her stomach while breathing two in and two out. I frown as I watch her.

"No, I'm… I'm having contractions, big ones." My eyes go wide.

"We need to find Brock and get her to the hospital," Kennedy says, and I realize she isn't kidding around.

I turn and signal to Brock to come over, his eyes darting to Angel as he stands and makes his way over.

"Should I call an ambulance?" I ask, totally out of my depth here.

"Quicker to drive. They're coming faster… oh, shit…"

Angel winces as she clutches Kennedy's hand.

Kennedy and I look at one another as Angel makes another face I never want to see again.

"Oh, crap. My water just broke."

"Babe?" Brock kneels down next to her as she turns to him.

"The baby's coming," she breathes hard and fast. "The baby's coming now."

His eyes go wide too as he takes in the situation. "Holy shit."

The girls return from their bathroom break.

"What the hell?" Deanna exclaims, seeing Angel breathing hard and fast and Brock holding one hand on her stomach and the other on her back.

"The baby's on its way," I tell her. "We gotta get her to the hospital."

"I can drive her," Summer says.

"You've been drinkin'," Brock replies. "We all have. *Fuck!*"

"I only had two," Deanna pipes up. "I should be okay."

"You had a shot as well," Lily reminds her. "I lost count of what I had. Shit, sorry, guys."

I wave my still full bottle of beer in the air. "I didn't even get to have a sip."

Brock throws the car keys at me, and I catch them in one hand.

Angel starts making noises that don't sound human as Brock lifts her into his arms.

Hutch and Kirsty come racing over too.

"I knew you should've stayed home," Brock curses as he carries her across the room. I clear the path for them to get through the crowded space.

"Where's your truck?" I ask Brock.

"Out back," he grunts. He looks a shade whiter than pale.

I feel sorry for Angel, she's the one who's about to squeeze a mini-me of Brock out of her. I'd be frantic too.

We cut through the side entry that leads to the back door and make a swift exit.

I get the door to the back seat, and he places Angel inside as she keeps doing rapid, shallow breathing.

"You sure she's not gonna have that kid on the back seat?" I say.

"Fuckin' hope not, just had the seats recovered," Brock replies.

"Stop being asswipes and move it!" Angel snarks at us.

I turn and Kennedy is by my side. "Get in," I tell her with a firm chin lift.

To my delight, she follows suit, going around to the passenger side and climbing in next to me.

I fuckin' like it when she listens to me, which isn't very often.

But I can't bask in that revelation, as Angel sounds like

a heavy steam train about to go off the rails.

I turn as Kirsty, Hutch, and Deanna climb into the truck next to us. "I'll call your mom and dad," Kirsty says through the window.

"Appreciate it," Brock replies as Angel rests against him.

I start the car and put it into reverse.

"Buckle up, sweetheart," I say to Kennedy as I swing an arm over the seat to back up. "It's gonna be a bumpy ride."

BRACKEN RIDGE
REBELS
ARIZONA
M · C

CHAPTER 12

KENNEDY

Bones drives with precision and doesn't even exceed the speed limit, even when Brock yells at him to step on it.

I refrain from reminding him that he shouldn't be driving and telling him another speeding ticket will land his ass in jail for good this time. I keep my mouth shut because there's enough going on in the back seat without my five cents.

"Bet you're glad you went to pre-natal classes now, aren't ya, buddy?" Bones quips, looking in the rear-view mirror.

"Shut the fuck up," is Brock's reply.

I stunt a chuckle. I cannot imagine a man like Brock at a class like that, but it is kind of sweet all the same that he would. There is no shame whatsoever in supporting your wife, no matter how big and burly you are.

I wish there was something I could do for poor Angel. I know this isn't her first rodeo, but still. The woman is a machine. She's holding it together better than I ever could, until…

"Motherfucker!" she yells out as Bones and I side-eye each other, followed by, "Sorry guys. Contraction, a bigger one than the last."

"You yell and scream all you like," Bones says. "No judgment here, babe. If I had that man's baby fightin' to get out, I'd be screaming too."

I roll my lips to refrain from laughing, and I hear Brock tell Bones to get fucked while he soothes Angel at the same time.

I don't know why, but there's something very attractive about Bones in this moment. Like he's gone all alpha, but he's also sweet and quite endearing. I don't know where to look.

Without a doubt, this whole club screams alpha, let's face it, the way they all take charge. The way Bones just does what he wants without question.

If only I didn't question myself so much. I wish I could throw caution to the wind like that and not give a damn. I guess I do take the job home with me; it's an occupational habit. I don't know when I became a soccer-mom without any kids.

Meanwhile, in the back, Brock is freaking the fuck out.

I glance sideways at Bones and he turns and gives me a wink. I swallow hard and look away, trying to concentrate on the road instead of him.

While Bones takes the streets swiftly but carefully, Angel breathes in and out loudly, panting and cursing.

Brock tells her over and over that it's going to be okay, that he's here and he's not going anywhere. It makes me wonder if she had a hard time with her first pregnancy.

I know Rawlings isn't Brock's biological child because I helped out Angel with her custody case. But I do know that he loves that kid like she is his own. He dotes on her, and it's not hard to see why; she's adorable.

To my surprise, Bones doesn't run any red lights. I'm not saying he's driving like a saint, but he's certainly keeping to the speed limit. I guess a night in jail did something to his psyche after all.

The fact that I just bought Bones tonight hasn't even come up yet. I can't wait to have *that* conversation. I don't know if it's because we have company, or if he's concentrating really hard on getting us to the hospital, but he doesn't say anything at all about the subject.

In less than ten minutes, we're pulling up at the hospital. Gotta love small towns.

Bones drives into the lot and immediately jumps out, opening the passenger door. I follow suit behind him as Brock slips Angel into his arms and he carries her across the lot, rushing toward emergency.

"My wife's in labor!" he yells out to a couple of nurses hanging out front. They take one look at Angel and rush toward her, and another calls to the orderly inside for a wheelchair.

"How far apart are your contractions?" one of the

nurses, a young, blonde woman asks Angel.

"I had two big ones, and they were about five or six minutes apart," she says as Brock holds her hand, brushing her hair back off her face. "I had one earlier at dinner, but it was mild and went away quickly."
Brock frowns but doesn't say anything.

They admit Angel right away and page Dr. Stevens, her obstetrician.

Everything happens so fast, the wheelchair arrives and Brock places Angel in it, refusing anyone's help to do it for him, and then he follows the nurses as he wheels her off to a private room.

We sit in the waiting room, the others arriving a few minutes later.

"How is she?" Kirsty asks, looking worried as she rushes in.

"She's doing good," I tell her. "A real trooper."

"How far apart are the contractions?"

"She said five or six minutes, the baby's close. She went from zero to a hundred, literally."

"Looks like the kid takes after its father," Bones muses. "Not gonna wait around for anyone to get comfortable and is about as subtle as a sledgehammer."

More people gather in the waiting room. And now it's a waiting game. Deanna, Sienna, Kelsey, and Lily all lounge in the uncomfortable chairs as I watch the clock.

"How long do babies take to come out?" Bones calls out.

"That's a loaded question right there," Kirsty muses. "If the contractions were that close together though, I doubt it will be long."

I glance over to Bones leaning against the wall, one ankle crossed over the other. When our eyes meet, he gives me a chin lift, beckoning me to him.

Swallowing hard, I'm unable to bring myself to jump to his command. A few moments later, he kicks off the wall and struts off outside, giving me a head nod in that direction.

A few minutes later, I excuse myself to get some air.

When I step outside, Bones immediately grabs me by the wrist and pulls me around the side of the building, away from the entrance. I don't have the will nor the want to stop him.

When we get out of sight, he pushes me up against the bricks.

"You know what you've done to me, placin' that bid?" he growls as I stare up at him. I'm fairly tall, but he still towers over me, his face no longer teasing.

My heart races in my chest as I take in his scent, his body, and his proximity.

"I thought you'd forgotten all about that?" I quip, trying to hold my own.

His lips twitch. "Hard to forget when I've had a wood all night just thinkin' about what I'm gonna do to that pussy."

My eyes go wide. "I did not buy you for sex!" I

whisper-shout. "Now that I'm thinking about it, I clearly realize I had too much alcohol and it affected my judgment. Maybe I'm regretting it…"

He presses me farther into the wall, completely ignoring me. "You smell so fuckin' good." He runs his nose up my neck, a shiver flowing through me at the sensation, as I press my hands flat against the wall behind me.

"You know I don't like this cat-and-mouse game, babe. I told you before that if you bid on me at the auction, I'm yours for the night to do whatever you want with me."

My heart races when I imagine such a beautiful idea. *No!* This devious man haunts my freaking dreams, and here he is, telling me he'll do whatever the hell I want.

"Or give me a good, hard fuck with no strings attached?" I throw his words back at him from the other day. Who could forget that encounter?

"That too."

"Well, if you think that, then you're sadly mistaken."

He smirks. "I don't think so. The only thing that'll look better than your mouth around my dick is me drivin' it home into that sweet, sweet pussy." He pushes his hard dick into my stomach as I groan. "You know you want me to do it. You want to take a walk on the wild side, don't you, *Ms. Hart?* See if this bad boy biker can really fuck?"

His dirty words make my throat dry, and I know what I want, but I can't just go out and ask him about starring in my fantasy. That would be downright weird, and he'd think I was a freak.

Yet, it *is* what I want.

As if reading my mind about the short, sexy dress I have on he says, "And don't think I don't know that you wore this sexy thing for me, because I know you did and it's turnin' me on so fuckin' bad." He reaches one hand to cup my breast and it's like my blood turns to molten lava as he squeezes.

I roll my lips because I can't speak.

"I wish I could stop," he mutters in my ear, rubbing his dick against me as I squirm. Every nerve ending in my body is literally on fire. "Do you want me to stop?"

"Not here!" I breathe. "We can't do it here."

He nips my neck with his teeth, and I wish he'd kiss me. I wish he'd take control and own my mouth like he owns everything else.

"Where, then?"

"I –I don't know…"

"Don't play coy with me now, sugar. We both need this. You make me fuckin' insane, woman."

What I need is air, and a lot of it, but he takes up all the space in my immediate proximity, making that little luxury impossible.

"Bones…"

"Tell me what you want." He pushes back to look at me again. His eyes serious. His jaw ticking. "Tell me!"

"I want you to break into my house and crawl into my bed and take my body however you want," I stammer.

He cocks a brow, his chest rising rapidly, like he's out of breath. "What else?"

I swallow hard. "Come into my bedroom without saying a word, take my body, restrain me, show me no mercy, …" I feel heat rising in my cheeks at my admission.

His lips quirk. "Fuck yeah."

I can't meet his eyes. I feel the throb of my pussy from the heat of his gaze and the sheer size of him.

He leans closer to my ear. "Where do you want my mouth, Kennedy?"

"On me."

"Whereabouts?"

He reaches down and cups my sex over my dress, his fingers grazing my lace-covered pussy. I'm so wet, and there's no doubt in my mind he can feel it.

"Oh God…"

"Say it."

I roll my lips. "My pussy," I whisper.

He groans, nuzzling into my neck as I move my hands into his hair, inviting his touch, my core slick and wet with arousal. He could nail me against the wall if he wanted to, and I'd let him.

What the hell has gotten into me?

I'm a respectful member of the community, and he's

turning me into a dirty whore. But I want to be his dirty whore, at least, right in this moment, I do.

"I need you so bad," he mutters, nipping my neck, still refusing to kiss me. I don't know why, but I'm dying to feel his lips on mine for the first time. Literally dying.

"Then come to me," I whisper. "But don't tell me when. Just come."

I bite my lip as he raises his eyes to mine, gripping my chin. "I knew you were a dirty girl underneath all this pretty shit."

"If you knew, then it shouldn't be too hard to please me, then, should it?" I throw back, fighting for some self-control.

He grabs one of my hands and places it between us and straight onto his dick. I gasp as he holds his hand there. "That feel hard enough for you?"

I bite my lip. "Kiss me, Bones."

He shakes his head. "If I kiss you now, babe, I'm not gonna be able to stop. And though I want to, we both know how this will end if I do."

I need friction so damn bad.

His length is rock hard and thick. To say I knew he'd be big is an understatement. Everything I thought I knew turns upside down. I squeeze my hand around his bulge, and he curses growly and low.

"You're only gettin' away with this because Brock and Angel are about to be parents," he goes on. "Otherwise, I'd drag you home right now and make you empty my balls with that pretty little mouth of yours."

I bite my lip as I look up to the sky and wish we weren't backed up against a brick wall outside a hospital.

"Do you always talk so dirty?" I wonder out loud.

He pulls back. "What's up? Don't like it, babe?"

"It's not that, it's just… I'm not used to it…"

"You'll get used to it."

"That's not what I meant."

"Are we gonna argue over mixed metaphors?"

I shake my head in exasperation. "Did anyone ever tell you you're extremely annoying?"

He pretends to think about it. "Lucy used to. But then I saved her from being shot and stabbed all in one night, so she's a little more appreciative of my *annoying* habits. I'm not a man without skills."

"Skills?" I laugh.

He grins. "Good with my hands, babe." He waggles them at me.

"Have you been keeping out of trouble?" I try to change the subject.

"Why, you gonna spank me if I've been a bad boy?"

"You know what I mean."

"Maybe you need to spell it out to me."

I continue to fondle him until I hear someone clear their throat.

We both look sideways at the same time. Steel stands in the alleyway, his eyes flicking down to my hand between Bones's legs, and I quickly snap it away.

"Thought you two lovebirds might like to know, the baby's here," he says.

"Fuck, that was fast," Bones replies, not even attempting to move off me. "Kid must've been dyin' to get outta there."

"What did they have?" I ask, trying to shove Bones off me.

"Brock's about to come out and tell us." His lips twitch as he turns, then adds over his shoulder, "Might wanna do somethin' about that boner, brother, before you scare everyone in the waitin' room."

I feel my cheeks flush red as he disappears and Bones finally moves off me, reaching down to adjust his dick through his jeans.

"Jesus, got a fuckin' missile in my pants," he mutters.

"Great, now Steel's going to think we're… you know…"

He looks back at me. "Who gives a shit. Trust me, he's seen a lot worse."

"Your lawyer giving you *benefits*. Ugh! I don't think so."

"Hey, you haven't given me any benefits yet, to be fair." He leans in and kisses me on the forehead, further fueling my lustful thoughts because he STILL WON'T KISS ME!

"But I plan on changin' all of that real soon."

He holds out his hand to, I assume, help peel me from the bricks I'm plastered against.

It flashes through my brain if I should have said anything about my fantasy, but it's out in the open now, and I have to admit, it is kind of exhilarating imagining it.

"You're optimistic."

"Nah, babe, I'm a realist. You just gotta give me a spare key. Don't wanna have to break in through a window to get to you. You know I'll do it if I have to, though."

I can't even believe I'm contemplating this. This is exactly what happens when you have too much liquor and get together with girls who encourage it. Not that I can blame them; this is my own doing and my own mess, and the hole I continue to dig is just that.

I can do this, I tell myself. *I can have one night of passion with him and that'll be that.*

We can go our separate ways and pretend like it never happened. Sex is a natural part of life, something that I haven't had in a while. Okay, a long while.

I just hope I don't wake up tomorrow and wonder what the hell I've gotten myself into, but heck, it wouldn't be the first time. My life is one long rollercoaster ride, one where you're never really sure where the ride ends and real life begins.

*

BRACKEN RIDGE
REBELS
ARIZONA
M · C

CHAPTER 13

BONES

"It's a boy!" Brock announces the minute we step back inside the waiting room.

Cheers, applause, and hollering rings loudly around the room as we all congratulate Brock. He's wanted this for a long time; a baby with Angel and to give Rawlings a brother or sister. The look on his face is priceless; I've never seen him so happy with a grin so wide.

Aside from running the business together, we've been good buddies. As much as we take the piss out of one another on a daily basis, he is like a brother to me and the closest thing I've ever had to one.

Angel's mom and dad are in the waiting room with us, and they leap up, tears leaking from their eyes. Rawlings runs to Brock the second he appears and he picks her up, twirling her around in the air as she squeals.

"A baby brother?" she calls as he stops and rests her at his hip.

"Yep, didn't mommy do a great job?"

"Can we call him Rupert?"

Brock kisses her on the forehead. "Definitely not."

Brock's idea of cool baby names include: Hawk, Wolf, and my personal favorite, Maverick.

"How's Angel doing?" Sienna asks, clearly chomping to see mom and baby.

"She's doin' fine," Brock says. "They're just nursing at the moment and gettin' the baby checked out before they can have any visitors."

"Can I see him now?" Rawlings asks, swinging her arms around Brock's meaty neck. "Please, Dad?"

"In a few minutes, sweetheart," he replies, kissing her on the forehead. "Gotta make sure Mom's okay first. Frankie and the nurses are takin' care of her."

She nods. "Five minutes."

I guess the apple doesn't fall far from the tree.

Deanna, Kelsey, Lily, Sienna, and Kirsty all squeal and clap their hands excitedly at the news. In fact, most of the waiting room is BRMC by now. Good news sure does travel fast.

The vicinity is abuzz with noise and chatter. Brock gets backslaps from all the brothers and then Hutch produces a box of cigars which he hands around to all the guys.

A nurse quickly runs over and tells them they better not even think about lighting those up inside, which was exactly what was about to happen.

I don't think I've ever seen Brock so chatty in his life. He and Angel were high school sweethearts and best friends for a long time. They split up, then got back together, but it was on-again-off-again for quite some time. With Rawlings in his arms, it sure is pretty cute.

I never thought I'd ever see him settled down, but if it were to be with anyone, it was always gonna be Angel. Even at their worst, they were devoted to each other and now they're in a good place and have a family of their own.

I turn and see Kennedy chatting with Summer, Cassidy, and Lily as Rubble and Lucy come through the door. Lucy's holding little Avery in her arms as she comes over to where we're congregated.

"Oh my God, did we miss it?" she asks, tears rolling down her face.

"You tell Lucy who you're about to go meet," Brock says to Rawlings.

"My baby brother!" she calls out loudly for the entire waiting room to hear.

Rubble slaps Brock on the back and Lucy turns to me. "Hold her for a sec, hon."

She places little Avery in my arms and goes in for a hug with Brock and, of course, she wants all the details.

After the whole incident with Tex, Rubble's old club Prez, tryin' to kill us, Lucy and Rubble asked me if I'd be Avery's godparent. Heaven knows why they'd want someone like me; I don't know the first thing about babies, but I couldn't really turn them down. And she's a pretty good baby. She doesn't cry a lot, which is a bonus.

I frown as I look down at the kid wrapped in a swaddle. She's only three months old, and though I'm not a kid person, she really is as cute as a button.

"Don't go gettin' all clucky on us," Gunner says, nudging me in the ribs as he passes. "Babies will do that to you."

"Yeah, don't look now, bro, but that hot lawyer chick's givin' you serious eyes holdin' the kid. Babies are fuckin' chick magnets," Colt adds as I look up and see all four of the girls staring at me.

I give them an eye roll. Can't a man hold a fuckin' baby without things gettin' weird?

I think about Kennedy's belly swollen with my kid and my pulse quickens, a sharp pain lodging in my chest.

Where did that come from?

I've never wanted kids. I mean, I don't hate kids or anything, but I've never been into having my own or even thought about settling down. Maybe one day, but it's not on my radar right now.

"Don't drop her," Deanna says, peering into my arms, trying to sneak in a coochie-coo.

"I'm not goin' to fuckin' drop her!" I retort, indignantly. "She's safer in my arms than in yours."

"That's probably true," she muses. "It does kinda suit

you, though."

"Don't you start."

"What? I'm saying it's cute."

I shake my head. "Wake her up and you can have her all to yourself."

I can feel Kennedy still watching me as I cradle the baby.

It's nice to see that she fits in with most of the girls from the club. Not that it's mandatory. Girls don't always get along, but it certainly helps where small clubs are concerned. Not that she comes to church, like ever.

It remains to be seen if she'll step foot in the joint. Now that Stevie has left the bar and gone over to work at the Stone Crow, she's got even less of a reason to be there.

We've got to wait for a little bit until we're allowed to go through and see Angel, though Brock takes Rawlings and her parents through first.

I feel sorry for her, the last thing she probably wants is a bunch of us barging our way into her room while she recovers from childbirth.

Seeing the look on Brock's face, though, that's priceless. He's one proud papa.

When I finally get to hand Avery back, Lucy gives me a peck on the cheek. She's like a sister to me, and that is a bittersweet feeling. Bitter because it makes me think of Abbey and makes me wonder what kind of young woman she would have grown into and how unfair it is. It also makes me think of my other sister, Caitlyn, and how we don't have a relationship and how much I'd like to. The sweet part is looking around this very room, knowing I've got the best friends I could ever wish for and an amazing family right here, and parents who love me. I can't say the same for most people. That makes me feel like the luckiest bastard on the planet.

I glance back at Kennedy, and she turns her head away just as I do.

Was she still looking at me? I notice that the corner of her lips turning up as she tries not to smile.

I can hardly believe my luck that she's up for a roll in the hay, and she's got kinks. She's so fuckin' beautiful. Every damn inch of her hot, curvy body. I need to be in her bed as soon as possible. I might even make a whole day out of it.

Thinking about her ultimate fantasy has me wild inside, even if I really want to take her home tonight and bang her stupid. Maybe if I can get her alone again...

A few hours later, after we've seen Angel and the new baby, it's time to head out. I've got to drive some of the girls home, since they all had a decent amount of alcohol tonight at the event.

Annoyingly, Kennedy's apartment is the closest from the hospital, so it means that I'll be stuck in the car with Summer and Deanna for the duration.

They gush about the baby and make plans to go back tomorrow with presents, now that they know it's a boy, and flowers for Angel.

I want to reach over and squeeze Kennedy on the knee, slide my hand up her thigh, and take that mouth of hers when she least expects it. I'm twitchy as hell that I can't do those things.

I want her to fish around in her purse and dig out that spare key to her apartment and give it to me, but she doesn't do that either.

"You all right?" I give her a chin lift while the girls are preoccupied cooing over the photos they managed to snap.

"Fine," she replies.

"You don't seem it."

"I'm just tired," she says.

"I need that key," I mutter. My balls are gonna be fuckin' blue by the time I get around to doin' what I really want with her. Clearly, it ain't gonna be tonight. Just as I contemplate dropping the girls off and going back to Kennedy's, my phone rings.

I put Gears on Bluetooth. "Sup?"

There's only one reason why a prospect is ringing me so late and none of those reasons are good.

"The alarms are goin' off at the junkyard," Gears says through the speakers. *Shit.*

"Are you there now?"

"Few minutes away. Took Jax with me, just in case."

"I'm droppin' the girls home. I'll be there in ten." There go my big plans to go back on over to Kennedy's after. I hang up and run a hand through my hair.

"A biker's work is never done?" Kennedy says quietly.

I shift in my seat, annoyed that I'm now making another diversion, but being it's the junkyard, I've gotta go check it out. "Somethin' like that. Probably just kids, nothin' to worry about."

I turn onto her street. It's a new neighborhood, and I'm glad she lives in the nicer part of town. It's a small apartment complex that was built late last year, and looks like it has good security, not that it's usually an issue around here. Hearing that the alarms are going off at work from Gears, however, has me re-thinking that.

Kennedy turns to the back. "See ya later, girls. Thanks for a great evening."

"You're welcome," Deanna replies. "I'm stoked we won the pop quiz. Can't wait to get pampered!"

"Yeah, I'll send a group text around so we can get some dates planned," Summer pipes up. "Before they start to get busy again when the tourists come rolling in."

"Sounds like a plan." Kennedy smiles and turns back to me and says, "Thanks for the ride, Bones."

I unbuckle my seatbelt as she does the same. "I'll walk you to your door."

"That really isn't…"

I look up at her, and she shuts her mouth. "Which apartment is yours?"

"It's on the top floor."

It's only three stories high. I exit the car, keeping it running and walking her to the elevator.

"I usually take the stairs," she says.

I frown. "It's not safe for a woman to be takin' stairs at this time of night."

She folds her arms over her chest. "I'm sure I'll be fine. I've got pepper spray."

I shake my head. "You can never be too careful, even in a small town."

We climb into the elevator and take the short ride to her floor.

"Are you always like this?"

I glance at her. "Like what?"

"Looking around for potential threats?"

I shove my hands in my pockets. "I didn't realize I was. Occupational habit, you can't take some traits out of a soldier."

She presses her lips together. "I can't imagine you as a soldier."

"I bet you couldn't imagine me between your legs a week ago either. Life works in mysterious ways, sweet cheeks."

"Are you always this romantic?" she splutters, shaking her head.

I turn and grin at her. "Never promised to be anythin' except myself, and I'm crass. I should probably warn you that I'm not like a fine wine, I definitely don't get better with age."

She stares straight ahead. "That doesn't sound good."

The door pings and we step out. I follow her up a short corridor, and she rummages around in her purse.

"Speakin' of which, you didn't elaborate on that key situation," I remind her again.

She shakes her head. "Is that the reason you walked me up here, to make sure you get it?"

I lean against the wall. "Why do you always think the worst of me?"

"I don't."

"Yes, you do. Admit it."

"I have to get one cut for you," she says.

Great, so she does still really wanna do this.

"Better get on that first thing tomorrow, babe."

"It's *Ms. Hart* in public." She bites her lip, and I know she's kidding, but I strangely like hearing her sass me.

"Oh, right," I say mockingly. "Wouldn't want to give anyone the wrong impression now, would we?"

I don't know what I see in her eyes, but something flashes there quickly. If I'd blinked, I would have missed it.

"You know I didn't mean it like that."

I run a hand through my hair as her eyes flick to my bicep. "You always seem to be backtracking whenever we get into a disagreement. I don't mind a woman speakin' her mind. Long as I get to have the last word."

A smile forms on her lips. "I'm a lawyer, Bones, so it's a given that *I'm* the one that is going to have the last word." I push off from the wall as she steps back, startled. "Jittery, babe?"

"No," she lies.

I grin and walk her back into the door. "Maybe I should give you a little partin' gift."

"I already had my hand on your cock today…" Fuck. I love the way she says that. "I think we're good."

"That wasn't a parting gift, *Ms. Hart,* that was absolute torture." I press my forehead against hers. "Wanna kiss you."

"But you said –"

"Don't listen too much to what I say," I whisper. "I'm pretty much full of shit most of the time."

I reach up to cup her face and she instantly settles into my touch, then I finally press my lips to hers. Her lips are soft, plump, and beautiful. I fuckin' love the feel of every inch of her.

A soft mewl leaves her mouth as my tongue seeks entry. Slowly, the kiss deepens, turning more urgent and needy. Her hands reach for me and run up my biceps, feeling my muscles as my dick hardens at her touch. It makes me want more, but I know I've got the girls waiting downstairs and a potential threat waiting for me at the junkyard.

When I pull back, she's just as breathless as I am. I adjust my dick, and her eyes flick south.

"Look what you did, again."

"Well, I'll need to do something about that, won't I?"

"Fuck yeah." I lean in and kiss her again quickly, once, twice. "I gotta go."

She swallows hard as I back off. Her lips look bruised and swollen from my brutality. Good. I can't wait to see what they look like with my cum all over them.

"I'll be seeing you," she says, as I walk backwards.

I point to her as I step into the elevator when it pings open. "Get me that key."

She nods as the doors close, and she's gone from sight.

I've never been so wound up over a chick before… that fuckin' kiss. I touch my lips, and I can't help the smirk that forms as I adjust my dick once more. She's absolute perfection.

She'd better get me that key pronto or, fuck it, I'll just knock the door down and buy her a new one.

I get back to the car and climb into the driver's seat.

Deanna, still in the back, leans on the back of my chair. "You're gettin' quicker. That was less than five minutes."

She and Summer laugh like little school kids.

"Very funny. I like to make sure women get home safe,

like I'm doin' for you two," I say, putting the car into reverse.

"Do we get a goodnight kiss too?" she coos.

"Uh huh, is that why you two also snuck outside at the hospital for a bit of hanky-panky?" Summer joins in, leaning on the back of the other seat.

"Will you two seriously shut the fuck up?" I growl.

"Ooh… getting touchy," Deanna sing-songs. "You must really like her."

"That's no secret," I mutter, knowing I shouldn't engage with either of them. "Trust me when I say, when I do nail her, it's gonna take longer than five minutes."

They both guffaw, and I'm tempted to make them get out and walk if they keep it up.

Deanna ruffles my hair as I slap her hand away. She's like an annoying little sister that enjoys tormenting me.

When I do eventually kick them out at Summer's place and make my way across town to the junkyard, I find Jax and Gears at the front of the property, the large flood lights that light the front are completely blown. Clearly, they've been smashed, as I see glass all over the pavement.

"What the fuck?"

Jax gives me a nod. "There's a smashed window too, but the alarm must've scared them off. There's no evidence of a break-in."

Bracken Ridge isn't the type of town that has a high crime rate, so this is unusual. We don't keep cash in the office, though. In fact, besides our two computers, there's nothing of value in there.

The junkyard itself is all completely sealed off at nighttime, with high fences and wiring, and the best security system you can get, so they didn't get that far. Colt installed everything, and we'll have CCTV footage.

"Clean this shit up," I say, pointing to the window. "Board up the window for now. I'll get it repaired in the mornin'."

"On it," Gears says and heads off toward the junkyard to get some materials.

"Probably just kids," Jax adds, as I study everything silently. Something about this just feels off. I don't know why.

"Probably."

"Anything else you need me to take care of?"
I flick my eyes to him. "Don't say anythin' to Brock. Fucker just had a kid, so this can wait till the mornin'."

"Got it."

"I'll go check inside, make sure everything's in order. I'll reset the alarm in case they're stupid enough to come back."

He nods.

I spend the next hour securing the property, though I can't do anything about the lights until tomorrow. We'll need the cherry picker to be able to replace them. Whoever did this, they definitely weren't kids. You'd need one hell of an aim to knock them out. It seems a little more professional.

I'm beat by the time we finish and it's almost two in the morning.

I'm ready for sleep.

I'm ready to go dream about my girl and what I'm gonna do to her.

For what I have in mind, I'm gonna need a shit ton of beauty sleep.

BRACKEN RIDGE
REBELS
ARIZONA
M · C

CHAPTER 14

KENNEDY

THREE YEARS AGO

I stare at Dean as the doctor delivers the prognosis.

"It's terminal?" I whisper, like I've misheard.

He grips my hand and I glance down and stare at it like I'm having an out-of-body experience.

"I'm afraid the chemotherapy and radiation haven't shrunk the cells," Doctor Allen explains, looking grave. "In fact, this type of carcinoma is rare, and it's aggressive, it's also usually quick to grow."

Dean was diagnosed less than six months ago. Six months of hell, going to the hospital every single week. He doesn't even look sick.

I've read up on every single piece of information I can get on merkel cell carcinoma, and I know all of that. I know that it's painless, almost undetectable, and is developed from excessive skin exposure. With Dean being in construction, he's outdoors a lot.

I'm in shock. I mean, I always thought we had a fighting

chance at beating this thing.

"It's going to be all right," Dean whispers, like I'm the one who needs the pep talk.

"No, it's not!" I all but yell at him. "It's not going to be all right, Dean. That's what the doctor just said! You're going to… you're going to…"

"Die?" he finishes. Another trait about him that drives me nuts is his ability to be real.

I shake my head. "Don't say that."

"We have to face reality."

"How can you be so calm about this?" I cry. "The doc just said you're going to die, and you're just sitting there like you've given up the fight."

His face falls, and I feel terrible. I know how hard he has fought; I've been there right alongside with him.

"I haven't given up the fight," he says. "But we always knew the chemo was a longshot."

I don't want to hear it. I don't want to hear anything like this. I just want it to all go away.

My husband is going to die.

I turn to the doctor. "How long?"

He looks to Dean and steels himself. "I would say between six and twelve months."

I grip the side of the chair and a strangled noise comes from the back of my throat.

"You can't be serious?" I whisper, though I don't even

know if any sound came out.

"I know this is a shock for you both, and we can discuss the options going forward…"

"Options?" I splutter. "What options do we have now?"

In truth, Dean has been a lot slower lately and out of breath. He's also lost weight. A lot of weight. But he doesn't seem like he's at the end of the road. He's still walking around, talking, eating…

I'm angry. Shocked. Emotional. And I can't even imagine what's going through Dean's mind.

"We knew it was a longshot," he says again, ever the truth teller between the two of us. "It didn't work."

We may have been hoping for a miracle, but they can happen, just not to us.

"We should get a second opinion," I say quietly, even though Doctor Allen can hear me.

"I'm sorry that this isn't the news you were expecting," he goes on, "but the cancer has spread to Dean's lungs and lymph nodes. I wish I could be sitting here giving you better news, but I'm afraid I also have to be real with you both."

I feel my axis spinning. My world falling apart.

Dean and I met in college and fell in love. We married young and thought we knew what we wanted early on. I'd not had very many relationships before him, and when we started dating, everything fell into place, at least for a while.

Dean's face is grave. I cannot even imagine what he is

thinking right now, faced with his own mortality. "We knew we were at stage four, sweetheart. We were hoping for a miracle."

"But people can beat it," I fire back, fear and trepidation running through every molecule in my body. "We just need to keep fighting…"

Dean glances at me. "Honey, I'm done with chemo. I don't want to go to into hospital three times a week, it's no way to live. I want to experience life with what little time I have left. I want to do those things that we've always wanted to do."

I stare at him but I'm not really seeing anything. I feel my head spinning.

My husband is going to die, and now he wants to go on a road trip? That's the thing he's always wanted to do; drive along Route 66.

Emotions run through me, and the guilt swallows me whole.

I was supposed to leave him. Almost eight months ago to the day, I'd even planned it out. That was before we got the diagnosis.

Dean and I grew apart a long time ago, but neither of us wanted to admit it. There wasn't anybody else, but we'd become more like roommates than a married couple, and I, for one, was deeply unhappy.

I wanted to make a clean break, slip away quietly as to not hurt his feelings. Even though I know we still love each other, we're not *in love*.

I love and care for him deeply, and I always will, but the magic died long ago.

A few weeks before I planned to sit down and talk it through with him, because I'd never just leave, he went to the doctor to get a lump looked at on the back of his neck and got the diagnosis of skin cancer.

I was in shock, and so was he. Being out in the sun all day for years obviously didn't help, but having his own construction business and building it from the ground up meant long, hot days in the sun.

After that, we found out the diagnosis was already past stage three, almost at stage four, already having spread to other parts of his body, but we were hopeful. I stuck by him, for better or worse, never telling him my original plans. That would seem callous and uncalled for.

Now I sit here in this doctor's office after the last eight months of watching him undergo treatment with agonizing guilt at what I could've done to him. And he still has no idea. None.

I feel like the most selfish person in the world.

I don't get how he can sit there so calmly while he's been given this information, discussing his demise with rational. I get he's in shock too, but I feel like I'm a complete basket case.

It's a helpless feeling, because really, all you can do is

be there for support, but that's it. There is no miracle cure. There is nothing that's going to change the outcome. This is it.

I pat my chest and go to stand. I feel a panic attack coming on.

"I need some air," I say, motioning to the door. "I'm sorry…"

Rushing out of the room and through the surgery doors, I double over as I gasp for air. I try to slow my breathing down, but the attack comes out of left field. I've been having a lot of these lately. I start to shake and walk over to the wall, leaning against it. The loss of control is too much for me. I wouldn't say I'm a complete control freak, I just like things how I like them, everyone does, but this is something else. This is just plain evil and cruel.

He's only thirty-five years old; he's a good person, he doesn't deserve this.

Pull yourself together!

I try again to slow my breathing, and I steady my thoughts which are spiraling out of control.

We will get through this.

I don't know how, but we will.

I just need to breathe…

PRESENT DAY

There's a knock at the door as I'm working on my deposition.

Kelsey sticks her head in and gives me a wave. "Hey, Kennedy."

"Oh, hi, Kelsey, thanks for popping by."

"No problem at all. Kirsty said you might have a few hours for me in between the real estate."

"That would be great if you want some extra cash," I say. "I've got a ton of filing and copying to do, and you can fit it in with your other job if you'd like. Poor Amelia is swamped, and I'm looking at hiring an assistant."

I have been thinking about this for a few months and have been hoping that another lawyer may join the practice being I am constantly busy and business is picking up. Now that I also have legal contracts with Kirsty, word is getting around.

"Sounds good to me. I can start now if you like. I've got this afternoon free, and I can work a couple of mornings a week if that helps?" She smiles.

I like Kelsey. She's got a good head on her shoulders, and she's going to go places if she keeps up with her studies and work experience. I like how independent she is already at a young age.

"That would be great if you can fit it in." I glance at the envelope on my desk, then clear my throat. "I have a couple of things to take to the post office and an envelope for Bones, if you wanted to take those as well?"

"Sure thing," she says happily.

"Perfect, just go and find Amelia. She's out back and will give you a rundown."

"Thanks, Kennedy, I really appreciate it. I'm saving up for my first car." She beams.

I smile back. "It's great to have a goal like that. The money will add up in no time."

"I'm hoping so!" She takes off to find Amelia, and I can't help my smile. She's such a nice kid.

My heart hammers in my chest because I got the key cut first thing this morning, and I'd rather not leave it under my doormat for anyone to just find and help themselves to my apartment.

This is really freaking happening.

I try not to let those thoughts distract me, because if I think about it too much, I know I'll chicken out.

Ever since I lost Dean, my priorities changed, and I lost a piece of myself. I threw myself into work like a woman possessed, and really, it was all to avoid dealing with the trauma. I thought I could outrun having to face it, but it all catches up with you in the end.

I may not have been the love of his life, but I stuck with him and made sure he had every single thing he needed. He passed away knowing I truly did love him.

And I feel like a fraud.

The last few months were the worst…

"Would you like a coffee?" Kelsey interrupts as she passes by a few moments later.

I give her a cocky grin. "You know, I may never want you to leave."

She comes over to retrieve my mug. Half my coffee went cold, as usual, and I didn't get to drink it. It's the story of my life.

"Fine by me. How do you like it?"

"White with half a sugar."

"Strong or weak?"

"Strong please. We also have a coffee card at the Coffee Bean, so feel free to use it if you fancy a bit of fresh air every once in a while."

"Cool, thanks!" She skips away, and I sit back in my chair and smile to myself.

To be sixteen again. The whole world at your feet, no problems on the horizon, and nowhere to be.

Nobody tells you that adulthood is going to be so hard. Nobody tells you the perils that you will face will not just test you, they'll cripple you. And time doesn't stop just because you want it to, not even for a second.

The thing is, if I could turn back time, I question if I'd have done anything differently. Nothing is in your control, that's one thing I've learned. It's taken me years of therapy to come to that understanding, and even now I struggle with a loss of control. Which is why I strongly need Bones to take charge in the bedroom. I have a hard time climaxing unless it's a little… rough.

I contemplate running back out to Kelsey and taking the envelope back, but I know deep down I want this. I deserve it, even if he will just see it as a one-night stand, another notch on his belt. He banged the new lawyer in town, bravo.

I try not to think if he's been with another woman since we made our little deal, not that I expect him to be exclusive, but it kinda does turn my stomach a bit. Maybe I should have specified.

It's been so long since I dated that I'm not even sure how any of this works anymore. I'm pretty sure that agreeing to one night of passion with a man who is my client, and is currently on probation, doesn't allow me to tell him he can't sleep with anyone else.

The next day, I have a couple of meetings and all I can think about is the fact that Bones did not come over. I thought he'd be there the first chance he got. I wore my good silk pajamas and everything.

I know he got the envelope because Kelsey said she left it for him on his desk when she went out to the junkyard, and he was sitting at it.

Anxiety sweeps through me as I second guess my decisions. *Maybe I got it wrong?*

Then I think about that kiss, the way he backed me up against my door. In the alleyway at the hospital, where he put my hand on his dick. I don't think I got it wrong, no, in fact, I'm certain.

Maybe he really is waiting it out, and I have to admit, the anticipation is kinda killing me. It makes it all the more exciting; the not knowing when he's going to sneak into my apartment. Because I know, or *hope,* he's coming over at some point, and I'm not just left out here high and dry.

The evening rolls into the next day and he still didn't come.

I'm starting to really wonder now. I don't like that he's got me on edge, like a volcano about to erupt but not quite ever getting there. I don't like how this is affecting my psyche.

I've got clients and contracts and judges to deal with, and here I am pining and daydreaming about this man, I don't even know, coming over and nailing me without any warning.

I need to get a grip.

Maybe I've finally cracked? Maybe I'm suffering from some sort of brain meltdown from not having sex in so long. Is that a thing?

I drink way too much coffee, but I need it to get through my afternoon in court. I've got a divorce lawsuit and a bail hearing. I seem to be doing a lot of those lately, not that there's an abundance of crime in Bracken Ridge, but the town is getting busier with the new land development and business opportunities. With growth comes the good and the bad.

The youth don't seem to be too much of a problem here. I did text Bones to make sure that everything was okay at the junkyard the next day after he dropped me home, and he said it was nothing to worry about. And that was it. For three whole days.

After court, I decide to go home early and make something nice for dinner. I invite Stevie over, but she's got too much to do with decorating her apartment. Not to mention, Axton gets out from prison next week, and I've got a shit ton of paperwork for him as well. I wasn't involved with his initial court hearing for parole, but I will be taking over once he's released. And yes, I still have my reservations because I've been around enough ex-cons to know that leopards very rarely change their spots.

My feet are tired and aching, but I still go to the gym after work and do a spin class, then I stop off at Quickie Mart to grab a couple of things for dinner.

I watch Grey's Anatomy and almost fall asleep on the couch. I have a quick shower and, once again, pull my nice silk pajamas on… just in case, though it seems perhaps someone else has caught Bones's attention. That wouldn't surprise me with some of the scantily clad women that hang around that club.

I don't get to bed till after midnight, and as I slink down into the soft, comfy mattress, I'm glad I got through another day; it helps doing what I love. I'm lucky I found my calling early on, and I couldn't imagine doing anything else.

After Dean passed, I decided then and there that I would only do things that make me happy. All the self-doubt and guilt and worry I feel when it hits me, is all my own doing. It has nothing to do with my career, my friends, or the town I live in. It's all me. And working on bettering myself is a work in progress. I like to feel I'm getting better at it.

I do know that I'm happy I moved to Bracken Ridge. It's just the kind of place that is bustling enough to keep my active mind occupied, yet still has that country town feel.

I fall asleep exhausted, dreaming of my mystery man who may not even show up.

2 HOURS LATER

I roll over in my sleep. I've been restless a little tonight, and I know it's because I've been thinking about Dean a lot this week, more than ever, in fact.

I yawn loudly, then something out of my periphery catches the corner of my eye. My heart races, but I stay completely still.

I don't dare to turn my head, even though I know it's him.

Shame on me for knowing *exactly* how he smells. It's a heady mix of spice, smoke, and gasoline. And I can't get enough of it.

The mattress dips as he kneels at the foot of the bed, and my heart beats so fast and so loud that it may explode out of my chest at any minute. I feel my pussy clench with forbidden arousal at giving him access to my apartment whenever he wanted, and access to my body at his leisure. But I fucking need it.

I want to pull him down to me, kiss him roughly, grind my sex into his hard, fat cock, but I don't do any of those things. This is his show, and he's got center stage.

I feel him shift again, crawling up the bed until he's straddled over me.

My eyes pop open.

"I thought I specified that you're to sleep naked," he growls, looking down at me fiercely.

I swallow hard at his words and the fact he's shirtless. He's got this five-day beard thing happening that makes him look oh-so-sexy and very rugged.

"You never specified that," I whisper.

A slow smile creeps across his face as his eyes sparkle with delight. "Well, I'm specifying it now. Naked from now on, got me?"

I bite my tongue from telling him to get fucked, and instead, I nod.

"Yes, what?"

I roll my lips. "You're not expecting me to call you Sir, are you?"

His eyes dip to my lips as he hovers over me. "No, but I guarantee you'll be saying the lords name in vain when I'm done with you, baby doll."

He crashes his mouth down onto mine before I can reply, and I whimper as I grasp the bedsheet under me and kiss him back, our tongues colliding.

"You look so fuckin' beautiful," he tells me in between kisses. "Like a fuckin' angel."

I pull him back down to me as he chuckles, and we kiss for a long, long time. I run my hands along his bulging biceps, and down his chest. The man is all muscle, with a small smattering of hair on his chest. He lifts off me enough to pull the covers back and tosses them behind him, then he straddles back over me. In the dim light, I see he's wearing jeans, unbuttoned, and oh how I long to feel that cock inside me.

"You kept me waiting," I murmur when he presses his body against mine, nipping my neck with his teeth while he skims down my body.

He reaches my breasts and I almost buck off the bed when he sucks a nipple through the material of my loose silk camisole.

"Like you in fuckin' silk," I hear him mutter. He pushes my top up with urgency as it bunches at the top of my breasts, and he groans in appreciation when my tits are on display for him. "Fuck."

He licks one nipple with his tongue, his fingers

tweaking and plucking the other as I gasp. He's so strong, hard, and fucking beautiful, and he's got me trapped underneath him. I know in this moment I don't want to be anywhere else.

His dick pushes into my thigh as he sucks on one nipple, all the while I squirm beneath him, making sounds that I've never heard myself make before. I try to rub against him, needing friction between my legs, but it seems he's just warming up.

A few moments later, he grabs my wrists and pins them above me, securing them to my bed post with what may be his bandana. He ties the knot tight as he looks down at me.

When our eyes meet, he says, "Feisty little thing, aren't you? Least this'll keep you contained for a while."

"I need to come," I tell him, pulling on my restraints.

His grin widens. "Words I never thought I'd hear come out of your mouth, babe."

I want to push his head down farther. I need his mouth on my pussy. I need to scream his name while he makes me come undone. I'm so flushed and hot and horny for him, I almost can't bear it.

"Fuck me, Bones… *please*."
He chuckles but ignores me, snaking one hand down into my shorts and between my legs. He hisses when he feels how wet I am.

"Jesus, you're soakin' for me. Bet you've been thinkin'

all week about what I'd come here and do to you, haven't you?"

I don't get time to answer, as he grabs the elastic at my hips and yanks my shorts off, dragging them down my legs. Then, I'm bare for him. He tosses my shorts across the room and then nuzzles his nose into my pussy.

He's teasing me, seeing how far he can push me before I beg him, and I have to admit, I'm pretty close.

His prickly beard tickles my sensitive inner thighs as he runs his tongue through my folds, then he spreads my legs wide.

I gasp as he begins to eat me like I'm his last meal, and I mean *his last meal.*

With my hands restrained, I can't touch him as he licks me, nice and slowly, up toward my clit and back down again, his tongue circling the spot that has me ready to burst. He spreads me apart with one hand and latches onto my clit, and I'm done. I begin to come, and he not only sucks but he rubs his tongue gently as I gasp and flap around, swearing and calling his name until the crescendo. And I fall mercilessly. The orgasm hits me so hard it feels like a freight train.

"Eyes on me," he growls as my eyes pop open, and I look down at him.

He licks his bottom lip as I watch him insert a finger inside me, then another, his motions smooth but firm and excruciatingly slow.

"Yes, Bones…" I cry when he licks my clit and keeps fingering me. "Right there, oh God… oh God…" I explode again as he keeps watching me, one of his hands moving up to cup my tits and rub my nipples as I go off like a firecracker.

I flop back down onto the pillows, panting and breathing hard.

"Don't get too comfy, babe," he tells me with humor in his tone. "Your night of pleasure is just beginning."
I'll never ever second guess myself again.

BRACKEN RIDGE
REBELS
ARIZONA
M · C

CHAPTER 15

BONES

Seeing Kennedy Hart beneath me while I finger fuck her into her third orgasm in minutes is enough to drive a sane man mad.

She's so beyond beautiful, I can hardly contain myself. I want to push inside her bareback and fuck her raw. But I know I'll come too quickly, and I want to make this last. My dick, however, has other ideas. I need to get these jeans off because there is no more room left in there for what I have going on. And I need relief, soon.

I push off the bed to stand and shove my jeans down. "You got a rubber?"

"No, I mean, yes. I bought some the other day," she says, her eyes dropping to my cock as they go slightly wide. Yeah, I'm big.

I give her a chin lift. "You have any before that?"

Her eyes are still on my cock. "Uh, no."

"Good."

She flicks those pretty eyes up to my face, looking

slightly miffed. "What do you mean, good?"

I fist my cock as she watches me. She licks her lips, and I know I need those lips around me, strangling my cock.

"While we're fuckin', it's just me, yeah?"
She frowns. "I'm not fucking anyone else, asshole. I don't just give out my door key to any old body."

I lean over and undo her restraints, letting her arms free. She rubs her wrists for a moment, and I can see they're slightly red.

I've fuckin' marked her. The thrill that runs through me makes me feel like a schoolboy again who's up to no good. I smile at her temper. *There's my girl.* "No need to get those non-existent panties in a twist, sugar. Now sit up and get on your knees."

She hesitates for a second as I give her a chin lift, but it doesn't last long before she complies, and I almost come all over her pretty sheets at her obedience. Crawling to the end of the bed toward me, I jerk off in front of her. She watches me as her perfect ass sits up in the air. I'm dying to take that ass, too.

"Like this, *Mr. Romero?*"

"Careful, *Ms. Hart,*" I drawl. "Say that again, and I might come all over that pretty mouth."
Her breath hitches as I summon her with two fingers to come closer.

I lean down and push her hair back out of her eyes, then

reach farther behind and grab a handful of her ass, giving it a squeeze. I slap it once, twice, as she cries out, and then I feel her tongue on the tip of my dick. I lean back and the greedy little thing sucks the end as I stop fisting myself. The sight of her mouth anywhere near my dick has me more than ready to blow my load.

"Your cock's so big, *Mr. Romero*," she whispers as I stare down at her swirling her tongue again, lapping up my pre-cum. *Fuck yeah.*

I groan, still holding it as she pulls on my wrist to stop me. "Allow me," she says.

I watch as she grips me at the base and takes me deeper into her mouth. I have to close my eyes for a second or else I'm not going to make any of this last, and I don't want to blow in the first minute of her sucking me off. This is a night I want to remember vividly in my mind.

"Fuck," I mutter as with each suck, my cock gets swallowed even farther into her mouth.

I open my eyes again and grasp her hair, pulling her down so she almost gags, then I pull out and thrust in again.

"Kennedy…" I call out, gripping her with both hands. I know I'm being rough, but how can one blame me. She's utter perfection.

She mewls and groans as I fuck her mouth, slowly, in and out as she jerks me off at the same time. I know I'm not gonna last, especially when I look down and see her huge tits out on display, bouncing around and out of control, and that ass in the air. Fuck, that's ripe for the picking.

"I'm gonna fuck you so hard," I mutter. "You got that, *Ms. Hart*? You're not gonna be able to sit down for a week." She garbles a groan as I reach the back of her throat, and I'm so tempted to blow my load right down it, but I pull out as she looks up at me in surprise.

We stare at one another as I catch my breath. I turn and grab my jeans and pull a rubber out of my wallet, then roll it on as she watches and I tell her to turn around.

Before she turns, she says, "So you have condoms?"

"Of course, I was just checkin' to see if you really were prepared." I spank her ass again as she yelps.

She shakes her head as I chuckle and my reward is the full view of her perfect round ass and her pussy.

I stand flush up against the bed and grasp her hair as I lean down. She turns, and my mouth crashes against hers, our tongues colliding as I rub her ass with one hand and pinch her nipple with the other.

"I can't wait for that tight little pussy to swallow me," I whisper as she pushes back against my thighs. "You want it too, don't you, my dirty little lawyer?"

"Bones…" she cries. "Hurry, I need you inside me…"

I'll never get sick of her beggin' me like this. I pull back from her mouth and dip my head between her legs and lick from her ass to her clit, spreading her folds with my fingers, she's sopping wet, literally dripping. I insert a finger and spread her slickness around everywhere, even her ass as she whimpers.

"Anyone ever been in here?" I grunt. Hoping no is the answer.

She shakes her head.

"Good. Not tonight, babe, we'll work up to that, but I want every inch of you, includin' your ass." I hold my cock as I slide it between her folds and down to her clit, back and forth. I love teasing her; I think it might be my new favorite pastime.

"Bones…" she groans.

"Yeah, babe?"

"Oh God…"

I line my dick up with her entrance and push inside. She gasps as I slide out and push in again, harder. I grip her ass, slap it, and push in again.

Jesus Christ, I'm gonna die happy.

Then I hold her hips at a slight angle and amp up the tempo, taking her harder, faster, pistoning into her tight little hole as I feel her clench around me.

I knew we'd be good together, but that's an understatement. She's fucking delicious. That tight little pussy taking all of me, squeezing the life out of my cock.

I reach one hand into her hair and pull her head back.

"Next time you come, call me Ryan," I tell her.

She swallows hard, and I move in and out faster, harder,

I climb on the bed, straddling over her as I quicken until I feel her pulsing, our skin slapping together as she cries out in pleasure.

"Oh God…" *Say it. Fucking say it.* "Oh God, Ryan… Ryan… Oh yes, yes, yes!"

I ride her through it, and as soon as she's done, I pull out and flop down on the bed, my head on her pillows.

"Sit on my dick," I tell her. "Ride me, Kennedy."

She crawls over me, and I sit up for a second to suck on her tits, goin' back and forth between the two, kneading and squeezing as she holds my cock with one hand and then sits down. I hiss as I glance down at her pussy swallowing me. *Fuck, this is so good.*

Our eyes meet once more, and I kiss her hard as she holds onto my shoulders and bounces up and down on me. My hands grip her hips, controlling her movements as I enjoy the look of pleasure on her face. Every inch of her body is on fire, and so is mine. I move a hand to grip her throat, remembering how she asked me for it rough.

"Never gonna have a man fuck you like I do," I growl.

Oh yeah, I forgot to tell her I'm a possessive son of a bitch when I'm fucking. Especially when it's a girl I'm crazy about.

I fight the urge to push up into her, meeting her thrusts, but I want this to go on for as long as I can.

"You can hold it for a while," she gasps, her head lolling

back as her tits bounce in my face.

"Oh, sweet cheeks, you have no idea. I can go all night."
I kiss her again and then lie back onto the pillows as she
continues to ride me. My hand slides from her throat as
our fingers interlace as she begins to move back and forth
instead of up and down. I know she's hitting her clit on my
pubic bone, and I tilt my hips so it'll graze her even more.

"Yeah, you like that, babe?"

She cries out as I hit the spot roughly, sending her
over the edge, and when she leans down and bites on my
shoulder, I lose all sense of control. I flip her over, and she
yelps as I pull her down the bed.

I push back in, fucking her hard. I can't take anymore
teasing as I ride out the orgasm she was just coming down
from. I bury my head in her neck as I groan.

"Fuck, gonna come, babe, gonna come…" I explode,
and it feels like my soul leaves my body as my cum shoots
out. I wish I didn't have a fuckin' rubber on.

I still and empty myself, groaning like a man possessed,
and then collapse on her, completely spent.

"That was so hot," she whispers.

I roll sideways and crash on the other side of the
mattress. Her pillows are like a cloud, not like my lumpy
pillow at home.

"Yeah," I agree, trying to catch my breath. It's been a
long time since I've felt like I've run a marathon after sex.

We both lie there, staring at the ceiling. I raise both my arms and rest them behind my head.

"All we need now is a cigarette," I muse, flicking my eyes to her.

"Definitely not in my freshly painted house," she says, her chest moving rapidly. It makes me happy that I've still got it and she seems to be out of breath too.

Her long red hair splays out on the crisp white of the pillows, and she looks like some kind of goddess. I'm not an idiot. I know she's upper class and too good for me. I'm sure she thinks she's slumming it, but at least I seem to have sated her for the time being.

I roll on my side to face her. "You're a very beautiful woman, Kennedy," I say, running a hand across her belly. I love her curves. I love how she's got meat on her bones, and she's confident in her body. She doesn't try and cover herself up like some girls do. I love nothing more than a woman who's confident in herself. There's nothing sexier.

"You're not so bad yourself."

I grin as she turns to face me. "You ready to go again?" Her eyes go wide. "Again?"

I brush her cheek with my knuckle. "I'm kiddin', better give that pretty pussy a break before I pound it again."

She bites her lip. "You're right. I'm probably not going to sit down for a week. Thank you for that."

"Anytime." I watch as a sadness crosses her eyes, and it

prompts me to ask, "How long's it been?"

Her eyes flick to mine. "Since I had sex?"

I nod.

She winces. "Uh, a while."

"How long's a while?"

"Um. About two."

"Months?"

She bites her lip. I've never seen her like this, kinda vulnerable. "No, Bones. Two years."

My eyes go wide. "Two years?" I splutter. "What the fuck?"

She shrugs. "I don't really want to go into it right now."

I guess now isn't the time, post coital, to get into it.

I make a cross-eyed face, and she laughs softly. "My dick would fall off if I had to wait two years," I say, trying to imagine it. "That would feel like a lifetime."

"It wouldn't, you know. That's all in your mind."

I give her a chin lift. "But, why so long? You're stunning. Any man would be happy to take you to bed."

"I already told you, I don't want to get into it. I guess I just haven't found anyone I was really compatible with in *that* way."

Even though I know she's hiding something, I let it drop. For now. "Except me?"

She shakes her head, but she can't hide her smile. "Don't go getting a big head."

"How can I not? You've not had a man in your bed for two years, and here I am with the keys to the kingdom."

She tsks. "I'd hardly say you have the keys… oh wait, you *do* have the keys." She laughs and her whole face lights up. It's the sweetest sound I've ever heard. "God, I'm losing my mind."

There goes that pain in my chest like before. It thrums, and my mouth goes dry as I look at her. *Why does it keep doing that?*

"Yep, does that mean I get to sneak in here and do that to you again tomorrow night?"

"I love your optimism."

"No, you love my dick."

"That too, it is very nice."

"*Nice?*" I splutter.

"Okay, sorry, you're very well-endowed."

I chuckle. "I'll take that as a compliment."

"You can certainly last a while too, they're not bad attributes to have."

"Oh, that's nothin', babe," I say, cupping her cheek. "That was just a warmup."

Her eyes go slightly round. "A warmup?"

"You didn't think you were gettin' away that easy, did you?"

"You just pulverized my vagina."

I burst out laughing as she slaps my hand away.

"Stop laughing at me!"

I lean over and brush her lips lightly. "Why? You're funny. I don't think I've ever been accused of pulverizin' someone's vagina before."

"Do you not do that to all the other women at the club?"

I rub my chin, thinking this is a trick question for her to see how many women I've slept with. She's a lot smarter than me, and I know how her brain works.

"I can't say I have."

"Are you lying right now?"

"Why would I need to?"

She bites her lip, and I pull it out from her teeth and kiss her again. "You wouldn't."

I grin. "You want me to do that again?"

"I think I need a little nap first," she replies, and I can't help but think how adorable that is.

I am a little beat myself, but I know I've got plenty more in me.

I kiss her again before getting out of bed. "Don't worry. I've got plenty more in the tank for later."

I pad over to the ensuite bathroom and pull the rubber off, discarding it into the trash. Then I take a leak and marvel at how neat her place is. Expensive creams and lotions line the little shelf to one side of the mirror, but nothing is out of place. I bet if I looked close enough, she'd have her initials imprinted on her towels.

"You've got a real nice place," I say, making my way back to bed as she watches me. My dick's still at half-mast, and I know we're not gonna be gettin' a whole lotta sleep tonight, whether she needs a nap or not.

"Thanks. Are you staying over?"

I glance at her. She's rolled onto her back but still watches me carefully.

"Yep."

"Do you snore?"

I laugh. "Not that I'm aware of." I turn and pull her to me as I nuzzle into her neck. "And if you're a good girl, *Ms. Hart,* I might wake you up later with dessert."

"You brought dessert?" she asks, confused.

I laugh as I brush her lips with mine. "Nah, babe, you're the dessert."

"Oh."

"Yeah, oh."

Pulling her closer, she turns around and we spoon, *fucking spoon,* and it feels like the most natural thing in the world.

I fall asleep within minutes, wondering how I've managed to not fall into bed with her this whole damn time since I first laid eyes on her, but I plan on making up for lost time. Oh yeah, that's a given.

Whether she knows it or not, she's fuckin' special, and I'm gonna hang on to this slice of paradise for as long as I can.

BRACKEN RIDGE
REBELS
ARIZONA
M · C

CHAPTER 16

KENNEDY

I don't know what I dream of, but I know it's delicious. I feel happy, sated, and my skin tingles all over. My body aches with a need that I've never known before, and I feel… *oh God, what's that?*

I wake with a start, and it takes me a few moments to realize what's happening. I look down and see Bones between my legs, and he's eating my pussy like there's no tomorrow.

I'm spread eagled on my back as he eats me out, probing my entrance with his tongue. I sigh and spread my legs wider. His tongue is so fucking good. He swirls it up and down and all around, his hands reaching underneath my body, gripping my ass. It's like he can't get enough of my body, and who am I to stop him?

He latches onto my clit and tugs gently as I buck off the bed, his tongue not letting up, and I start to feel myself lose control. My orgasm comes on fast and furious as I groan and reach down to clutch onto his hair, not that he has much hair to grip. His tongue does such amazing things that I'm just about seeing stars when I come down from Heaven.

"Oh God…"

"You like that, babe?"

"Oh, yes," I hiss.

"Like my dick?"

"Fuck yes."

I hear him chuckle, then he reaches to the side table where I see a bunch of foil packets strewn across it from last night. He rips the foil with his teeth and rolls it on his fat cock. And my, my, I wasn't kidding when I said he was well-endowed. I am a little sore, but not so sore that I don't want him inside me again.

He grabs my thighs and pushes my legs back so they're bent, then he tilts my hips slightly. He enters me slowly at an angle, and I groan out loud at how tight I feel with his cock sliding inside me full tilt. It feels like I've gone to Heaven all over again.

"Fuck, I love this pussy," he groans as he slides in and then out again, pressing his body down onto the top of my legs so they're pushed up against my chest. He goes deep. So fucking deep.

"You make it hard for a man to last," he grunts, his eyes sparkling as his lips twitch. Well, good morning to me. I could wake up like this more often.

"I wish I could say the same," I whisper as he watches me, and I close my eyes from the sensation as my mouth forms an 'O' every time he enters me.

"Open your eyes, *Ms. Hart*," he tells me as I my eyes snap open. "Eyes on me. I want to watch you when you come all over my dick."

I bite my lip as he picks up the pace, hitting my G-spot at just the right angle. My eyes flutter at the sensation, and I feel the heat in my skin as he fucks me.

"So good," I murmur.

"You like wakin' up like this?"

"Mmhmm."

He slows the pace, but thrusts hard at the end, changing the speed. My body aches with a need that I didn't know was possible. He's so fucking good. Now I've had Bones heroin, and there's no going back.

"Gonna kick me out of your bed?" he asks out of nowhere.

"If I was going to, I would've by now."

"Good answer." He thrusts even harder, his biceps and chest muscles flexing as my eyes devour his body. He's in damn good shape. Every line of his body ripples. And in the morning light, I see he's got tattoos over one side of his body only and not the other. It's so damn sexy.

"Call me Ryan again when you come."

"You're hittin' the spot."

"Yeah?"

"Oh God, yeah," I moan.

"Tell me…"

"Oh God… Oh, babe… Oh, Ryan... Ryan… fuck, *fuck*... "

"That's it, baby." He rocks his hips as my clit throbs against his pubic bone. "Come for me…"

I cry out as he rides me through it, slow but hard, and I clench my pussy around his thick cock.

I grip his ass hard as he reaches down and kisses me.

"You're really good at this," I murmur as his bristly beard, which I'm really digging now that he's had his head between my legs, *twice*, tickles my skin.

"Need to give you a parting gift."

Holy fuck. Work! "What time is it?" I gasp.

"Who the fuck cares?" He grinds into me as he reaches up and grips the headboard, then he spreads his legs wider and moves up to his knees. *Oh, holy hotness.* I wrap my legs around his waist. He's so fucking deep now.

"Don't stop," I moan, not even recognizing my own voice.

He chuckles and picks up the pace, and I'm really glad my bed doesn't make a noise. I grip his ass again and dig my nails in.

"Fuck yeah," he growls. "Don't ever wanna stop drivin' into you, so fuckin' tight. Your pussy chokes my cock so damn good, babe."

I hope I'm making it hard for him to hang on because when he loses it, I want to lose my mind just watching him.

"Gonna come, babe," he says, as if reading my mind.

He pistons his hips at an angle and fucks me harder, then reaches between us and pinches my clit. It sends me over the edge.

I cry out and come all over his dick, again, not even caring I'm so slick and wet I'm going to have to change the sheets after our night of debauchery. I feel him tense, then still as he shoots his load, his face fucking picture-perfect as he calls my name. It's so fucking hot.

He pulls out and rolls off me a few moments later, collapsing onto my pillows. We're both panting and sweaty.

I lie there, feeling like the sensations in my body may never end as I catch my breath. He's so good in bed.

"I fucking love your dick," I can't help but whisper as I fight for air.

"You sound like you do. I fuckin' love that tight little pussy. Wanna do that again."

"Right now?" I gasp, alarmed. He's just annihilated me again, and I'm barely recovered from last night.

He grunts a laugh. "Not right this minute, but later tonight. You want that?"

As if I have to think about it. "Definitely."

"Want me to sneak in again? Take you by force?"

"Hell yes."

He chuckles again, then reaches over and cups my sex. "This is mine."

"You going to go all alpha on me now?"

"Like you don't want it."

I can't deny it. I do want it.

He plays with my pussy gently, stroking without penetrating, and it hits me how affectionate he is. How playful and sweet. I thought he'd be all caveman and out of here the minute he got off. I didn't think he'd stay and that I'd wake up to him eating me out under the covers.

That was so hot.

"You're insatiable," I say. "I've never really had a sex marathon before."

He turns his head to look at me. "Like I said, that was just a warmup, baby doll. When we've had a marathon, I won't actually let you get any sleep."

"It'll be our little secret," I muse, happy and sated while we lie there in companionable silence as he rests his hand on my pussy. I'm sure he just fell back asleep.

I didn't even correct him about saying my body is his. He doesn't get to dictate anything like that, yet, but I know that he's absolutely right. There is definitely no other man that I want in my bed. And that thought should disturb me more now that I know we've crossed the line.

But it doesn't.

With him, nothing seems to be off limits.

An hour later, Bones is gone, and I'm in the shower, washing the smell of sex off my body with my creamy body wash.

I touch between my legs and I'm sore, but I don't care. It was worth it.

Ryan Romero owns my body, there's absolutely no doubt about it.

The things he did… the way he woke me up… Goddamn.

I wanted to so badly reciprocate and suck him off. In fact, I can't wait to wrap my mouth around him again tonight. He deserves it after the five hundred orgasms he gave me in the last eight hours, and now I've basically given him the keys to my place to come and go as he pleases. I shouldn't be so cavalier, but what the heck. The man's a goddamn sex machine. To think I've been holding him at arm's length for months and I could have been doing, well, *that* this whole damn time.

The phrase *ruining you for any other man* rings true, and I don't want to be a foregone conclusion, but how he plays my body like it was made for him, it stirs me to new heights even now when I think about it.

And I can't stand here in the shower touching myself; I need to get to fricking work. I've got a day ahead of me.

For some reason, I have a spring in my step once I'm ready and off to work.

Half-way through my morning, I get a knock at my

door, and when I glance up from the mountain of paperwork I'm sifting through, Brock is standing in my doorway.

"Hey, Brock," I say as he doesn't wait to be asked in. "Congratulations again on the baby. How are you settling in with him?"

"Great, thanks. He's a real little charmer, just like his papa. Thank God he looks like his mama, though."

"How's Angel doing?"

"She's good, exhausted, but good. I'm headin' over there now to pick her up."

"That's great." I pause and smile. "I'm taking it that this isn't just a social visit?"

He sits in the chair opposite me, but it hardly holds his frame. "You know Axton's gettin' out this week."

"Yes," I say. "I received the documents from his parole lawyer, and I can liaise with them on his parole conditions on a weekly basis. Of course, he'll still check in with his parole officer, it just means he won't have to travel to Phoenix every week to do so. I've arranged a local officer since he won't have a current driver's license. As long as he doesn't breach his bail conditions, we're set." Which is the million-dollar question. Yet Brock seems a little… worried. He gives me a nod. "Appreciated."

"Is everything all right?"

He rubs his chin. "Can I be frank?"

"Of course." I stand and go to close the door. Amelia

is just outside in the reception, and I don't need her overhearing our conversation. She's so excited about seeing Axton again. It's been ten years, and her perception of him is clearly very different from Brock's. Amelia was only thirteen when Axton got sentenced.

He palms the back of his neck. "Now that it's really happenin', I'm havin' some… strong…"

"Feelings?" I finish when he pauses like he can't spit the words out.

"Yeah."

"What about?"

He looks down at his boots for a moment like he's uncomfortable. "Of him failin'."

I walk back around to my desk and take a seat. This is heavy. I know Brock is a proud man, like most of the men in the motorcycle club. I respect it would have taken a lot to come on over here and tell me this. Not that I'm a therapist or can even help him, but he's looking at me like I have all the answers.

"We'll create a support system for him," I say, racking my brain to think of something encouraging. I mean, in the end, it is up to Axton to stay on the straight and narrow. He's got to want it enough, but I can't really come out and say all that without it sounding condescending. "He has a family who loves him and friends that will motivate and uplift him, and that's a pretty good place to land. He's got job security, a place to stay. He's going to have to put immense effort into staying out of trouble, but let's face it, I think he'll have enough to deal with at the Stone Crow to keep him busy."

Brock's lip twitch. "He needs to keep busy, never could sit still as a kid."

"The big part is, he's going to need you now more than ever. I don't need to tell you that prison changes people. He won't be the same person you remember when he went inside, you'll probably want to brace yourself for that."

"That's the problem. If he fucks up and lands back in jail, it'll kill our mother."

"Are you close with your parents?"

Stevie and I don't see our mom as much as we would like as she lives in California, but we talk once a week. I don't remember much about my dad. He left when I was small.

"Mom and I always have been, but Dad and I have just repaired things recently. It's taken a lotta fuckin' years to put past shit behind us, pardon my French. My parents have never visited Axton in jail, and he feels a little bitter about that. Not that he'd want mom to see him in there; it'd break her heart, but dad could've made the effort."

"Maybe he will now, once Axton is out in society and sees he's making amends to prove he's a decent member of the public. It takes time to heal old wounds."

He nods. "You're right. I just know it'll break mom in two if he gets sent back again. She wouldn't survive it."

I nod. He's a man who obviously cares a lot about his family.

"Well, they did do something right; you and Amelia turned out okay, and from what I've read on Axton, he got caught up with the wrong crowd. He was very young, and I'm sure that had a lot to do with his mistakes."

"If you think I'm okay, you're more screwed up than I thought," he muses. "As for Amelia, she can get into trouble faster than you can blink, but she's a good kid, always has been."

"She's an excellent secretary. I'd be lost without her."

"Appreciate you givin' her a chance."

"It's a small town, so we've got to stick together. That's my motto anyway. I've got Kelsey helping out too around the office. May as well keep it in the Bracken Ridge Rebels family."

His lips twitch again. "What about you, you fuckin' Bones?"

My eyes go wide, and I tuck a strand of hair behind my ear. That went south fast.

I'm actually a little lost for words that he just came right out with it.

"Uh, I don't usually discuss my sex life with… people." Or members of the Rebels Motorcycle Club.

"Despite the fact he drives me completely fuckin' crazy,

he's a good guy. Loyal, dependable, knows what he wants, and he doesn't treat women like shit. In case you're in the market, that is."

"That's… very good to know, even if you do make it sound like I'm shopping for a car," I say, shuffling the papers on my desk. I need to keep my hands busy. "But it's strictly professional. I can't get involved with a client…"

Am I going to get white spots on my tongue for lying? Probably.

"Right, uh huh." He doesn't seem convinced.

"But I'm sure what you're saying is true," I go on. "He does seem like a stand-up guy, when he's not getting himself into petty misdemeanors and stupid shit."

He levels me with a look he probably reserves for those he's trying to interrogate. Lucky for me, I've got a similar look down from my years of being an attorney, though I doubt I'm half as frightening as he is.

"Should come to the club more, hang out there a little bit, get to know everyone. We're not so bad."

Why does that sound like more of a summons than an invite?

"Is that an open invitation?" I ask, trying to make it sound light.

"Obviously. Stevie's a good sort, got a good head on her shoulders. Everyone likes her."

"We're very close, we always have been since we

were little."

"How'd you feel about her workin' with Axton?"

I swallow hard, but I can't lie to the man. Something tells me that he'd see right through the bullshit radar anyway.

"To be perfectly honest, I have my reservations," I tell him, looking him in the eye. "It's nothing personal. I'm sure he's learned from his mistakes and he's wanting to start afresh, but he's an ex-con. And excuse my being blunt, but I've seen a lot of them. Not all parolee's get on the straight and narrow and stay there; half of them end up back inside." He nods. "I understand your concerns. Trust me, I've had them myself. It's my neck on the line if he fucks up. My reputation and the thought of him goin' back inside is concernin'."

It's also a probability. For Axton's sake, I hope he's got his shit together.

"There's a lot riding on it, but I'm sure after ten years, he wants to be out and never go back in there again. As we've established, he has an amazing support system. It's the best thing that could happen to him. He's one of the lucky ones to land on his feet like this."

"You can say that again," Brock says, rubbing his chin, then he stands abruptly. "I gotta go. Thanks for everythin'. Text me when you have the paperwork we need, and I'll make sure he fills it all in."

"Okay." I stand too, then add, "Thanks for dropping by. Everything's going to be okay, Brock. I really believe that."

He points at me when he gets to the door. "Don't forget the club. Havin' a shindig on Saturday night to celebrate the baby, be nice for the girls to see you there."

"I'll give it some thought, thank you."

He nods and opens the door, striding out as he stops to talk to Amelia on the way.

I sink back into my chair and face-palm myself.

You fuckin' Bones?

At least it was a question and not like he actually knew anything. It makes me wonder if Bones will tell the guys. I mean, I only left him a few hours ago, so he may not have had a chance yet.

Bones wasn't kidding about not being able to sit down for a week. I can certainly still feel where he's been. He's such a dirty man, and I can't help the smile that creeps on my face, wondering if I'm going to see him tonight and have a repeat.

Here's to wishful thinking.

Bones

BRACKEN RIDGE
REBELS
ARIZONA
M·C

CHAPTER 17
BONES

I hold my hands in Kennedy's flaming red hair as she sucks the tip of my dick into her mouth. *This mouth…I could watch her do this forever.*

I didn't waste any time letting myself in tonight after dark to find her reading in bed, with fuckin' glasses on. I'm making her wear them now while she sucks me off without any clothes covering her up.

Her tongue swirls around my tip as she hovers over me, fondling my balls and making groaning sounds as she grinds down over my knee cap. She's a fuckin' vision sitting over me like this, her tits out on display as I pinch her nipples and cup the weight of them.

It makes me wonder if she actually knows how beautiful and sexy she really is. She's confident in the courtroom but seems to lack the same kind of knowing attitude when we're alone together. I can tell she enjoys submitting to me and likes me takin' charge, and I don't mind it one little bit.

"Think I could get used to this," I mutter, looking down

at her as she looks up at me with heated eyes. "Especially with those fuck-me glasses on."

She licks my dick like a lollipop, and I groan, hardly daring to believe that she's up for it again tonight. I half wondered if she'd change her mind after last night's romp; not because it wasn't good and she didn't enjoy herself, but because of her lawyer principals.

She questions everything, like she's cross-examining me instead of shutting that pretty mouth and enjoyin' the show. I seem to have shut her up for the moment, though.

I don't dislike her principals. I dig it that she's got morals and standards; it's another thing about her I admire. I don't really know many people like that these days.

This thing may only be temporary, but I can pretend that she's mine for now. That she'd be happy to be seen with me and not embarrassed by being with a biker with a mohawk and a criminal record. I know she can do better. I know she probably wants better, and it leads me to thinking about what kind of guys she's usually into. *Other lawyer types?*

Does she like a man in a suit and not a guy who wears overalls and operates machinery in a junkyard. I make good money. I make more than some lawyers. It's all about semantics.

We'll have even more club coffers come in after we purchase Jack's used car and parts lot. He's selling up due to falling on hard times. He's a piece of shit for beating on his wife, but at least this time she had the good sense to leave him. One thing the club never tolerates is violence against women.

My hips rise off the bed as Kennedy changes pace, sucking me harder, faster, licking my tip as she gently nibbles with her teeth. *Fuck.* It feels so fuckin' good.

"Your tits look so good bouncin' like that," I tell her in a husky voice. "Want you to sit on my face after this."

At least she listened tonight and was naked under the silk robe she had on. I peeled that off of her real quick.

She makes a garbled sound in the back of her throat as her hand strangles my cock.

If I look away, it might be able to make it last, but then again, if I come now, I'll get her pussy on me faster. I begin to move my hips, hitting the back of her throat, and keep pushing my way in until she gags.

"Gonna come. You gonna take it?" I choke out, spreading my legs even wider.

"Uh huh," she garbles as she jerks me harder, squeezing my balls as her mouth sucks me so fuckin' good. I'm there in seconds. I come hard, spurting down her throat as she laps me up, and I grip her hair, making sure she takes every last drop of me.

I don't have words for how she looks with her lips wrapped around me, on her knees, takin' every inch that I've got to give her.

"Fuck, that was good," I pant as she releases me and

continues to lick the end of my tip, cleaning me up. "Think I like you with my cum all over your face."

She wipes her mouth with the back of her hand, and if I hadn't blown my load then, I would by now.

"You taste so good. I couldn't waste a drop." She cups her tits and straddles across me as I stare at her.

"You're the fuckin' woman of my dreams," I tell her before I can stop myself. "Need to taste you."

"Bones, I can't sit on your face."

"Like fuck you can't. Hurry up, I need to be inside you." I'm greedy for her tonight.

She climbs farther up my body, resting her arms on the headboard as her knees come to either side of my head. I spread her folds and lick through her wet center. I can taste her arousal, and she groans when I do it again.

"Such a pretty pussy," I mutter, holding her by the back of her thighs as I lick her, then suck on her clit as she cries out. It's swollen and probably throbbing from need, and I'm gonna give her the release I know she so desperately craves.

I insert a finger as I suck her hard, then another, working my tongue across her sensitive nub as she cries out my name, *my real one*.

"That's it, fuck yeah," I mutter in between licks and sucks.

She starts rubbing her pussy on my face as she rides back and forth, and in no time at all, she cries out as she comes gloriously hard on my tongue. The sounds she makes are like nothing I've heard before and it makes my cock swell.

I pull her down roughly, so she's straddled over me again, sitting up, so we're face to face. Her legs are spread wide, her thighs clenching around my waist. We're so fuckin' close. I kiss her hard, her arousal still on my tongue as she groans and wraps her hands around my neck.

"Sit on it," I tell her, in between kisses. "Sit on my cock and ride me."

"We need a rubber."

"Don't like em'. You on birth control?"

"Yes, but you need one."

"I'm clean, babe. Always use a rubber."

"Bones…"

"Lean over and grab me one, put it on me, but fuckin' hurry."

She does just that and pulls the tab off the foil packet, rolling a condom down on my cock with ease. I'm so aroused I'm ready to fuckin' blow again.

"Not gonna be wearin' one of these forever," I tell her. "I fuckin' mean it."

"Play your cards right, and next time, maybe you won't have to."

I feel like pulling the thing off and shoving my cock into her, burying myself deep inside and filling her with my cum, but I hold off. That's her choice to make, and I know it'll feel all that much better for the both of us.

She sits up slightly, holding me at the base as she slides down onto my cock and we both moan. I hold her hips and begin to slide her up and down, biting down on her neck as she rides me.

"God, Bones, that feels so good."

"Bet you've been thinkin' about this all day, haven't you?"

"Yes," she admits. "All fucking day."
I grin into her shoulder as we move up and down in unison.

"I'm gonna come to your office, lock the door, and take you over your desk, and there ain't a darned thing you can do about it," I growl. "I wanna fuck that ass while your clients sit outside waitin' for you."

"Yes!" she cries out at my dirty words.

"But you're gonna have to be quiet. Don't want those nosy bastards in the waiting room hearin' you come now, babe. Those sweet curse words are only for my ears."

"Oh God…"

"This is my pussy," I reiterate. "It's fuckin' mine…"

"Yes, it's yours."

I thrust up to meet her, and we fuck fast, hard, as I bounce her like she's made of plasticine. I grip her throat and she cries out, coming hard as I ram into her sweet, tight hole over and over until I'm seeing stars.

"Comin', babe. Oh fuck… oh fuck yeah…"
I still and spurt my load, for the second time, moaning

as I hold her hips tight, then I flop back onto the pillows, bringing her with me.

"That was so good," she pants.

I hold her to me, running a hand down her back as I cup her ass. "Love havin' your mouth on my cock. You look so fuckin' good chokin' on me."

She murmurs into my shoulder as we lie still, and a wash of peace, or some shit, washes over me.

I'm really comfortable with her, I realize. It's not like with other girls when I fuck and run. I'm there to get off, and so are they; it's not like this. There's no small talk, I barely know anything about them, and I don't care to. But with her, everything's different.

We shouldn't work, we're so obscure together, but we fit so fuckin' well.

She should be with some business type, one who can give her the highfalutin' life that she deserves and all the pretty things in the world money can buy.

I might be earning good money, but I'm never gonna be driving a fancy BMW or taking her out to flashy restaurants while she shows me off to her friends.

I don't know what the fuck we are, and I don't dare ask, but I don't want this to end. I know that much. It isn't just the sex for me, though my dick right now is still at half-mast even after I've blown my load twice in one night. It's what she does to me.

It's what she did to me the first time I met her and what she's been doing ever since.

It's that feeling in my chest every time she looks at me with those sparkling eyes full of promise.

"Brock came by today," she says, after a while.

That is *not* what I was expecting to come out of her mouth as we cuddle. "What did he want?"

"To talk about Axton, since I'll be liaising with his parole lawyer when he gets out."

"That it?"

"He was giving you a plug."

I grunt a laugh. "He was? He never has anything nice to say about me to my face."

"Maybe he's gone a bit softer now he's got a baby in tow."

I nuzzle her shoulder, kissing her pretty skin. "I doubt it."

She lifts up, resting one elbow on my chest as she gazes down at me. "He more or less told me to be at the club on Saturday night. Surprise, surprise, there's a party."

I smirk. "And are you gonna come?"

She shrugs. "Why would I do that?"

I reach up and kiss her gently. "Because… I can show you around."

"Like your bed?"

"Fuck no." I laugh. "I wouldn't take you upstairs to that dump. I meant my place, the house I share with Colt. Though I'll have to tidy up a bit if I know you're comin' over."

"Not very domesticated?"

"I was in the army, old habits die hard and some I let go completely. But my mom spoilt me rotten, so I blame her."

She smiles. "Do you get along with your parents?"

"Yeah. They're the best. They're comin' up next weekend to visit. What about yours?"

She flicks her eyes away momentarily. "I don't know my dad. He left when I was young. Mom and I talk every other day, though. She lives in Cali with her new boyfriend."

"Does she ever come out?"

"She wants to, now that Stevie and I are both settled."

He frowns. "What about Stevie and this guy she's been datin' that we've never seen. Does he actually exist?"

"He exists."

"And?"

"And what?"

I run my fingers down her clavicle bone, admiring every inch of her body. "And do they really make the long-distance thing work?"

"I guess." She shrugs. "She's sensitive about it. Personally, I don't think she should have tied herself down so young. I know from experience."

My eyes go wide. "You do?"

She pales ever so slightly. "I mean, I dated young too and had relationships and stuff."

I narrow my eyes. Why does she feel like she can't be honest with me? I know when someone's lying.

"Right."

"Do you want to take a shower?" She tries to divert the conversation, but I already got the memo. I don't get to learn anything about her that's too deep or personal. I get it.

I'm still inside her, and I don't actually wanna move from this spot, but she once again dismisses me, and I can't help but wonder why.

"If it means I can bend you over and take you from behind."

She chuckles, kissing my chest as she looks up at me while she does it. "You have a very high sex drive."
I watch her, brushing her hair back off her face. "I do when you're around. I can't get enough of you, especially in those tight, pencil skirts and those glasses. I meant what I said about comin' to your office and doin' you from behind. That's a promise and a little fantasy of mine that I'll be happy to fulfill."

"You can't do that at my workplace. Amelia is there, and Kelsey…"

"Watch me, or better still, feel me. I'll be the one fuckin' you into submission just how you like it."

"Bones…"

"Don't Bones me. You want it. Admit it, me fuckin' you at work turns you on."

She licks her lips, and I smile triumphant.

"Asshole," she whispers.

She slides off me, and I pull the rubber off and knot it. I meant what I said about those too. If we're gonna continue seeing one another, I'm not gonna keep wearing one. Ain't no other guy having a slice of what's mine.

Soaping her up in the shower ultimately leads us to makin' out again. Around her, my cock's always ready for action every second of the day. I've never gone three times in one night since I was in high school.

I lather up her tits with suds and pull her nipples while our tongues go at it, exploring each other as my hands move up into her wet hair. She groans as I press my cock into her stomach, pushing her against the tiles.

Reaching between her legs, I rub her clit gently, knowing I've been a little brutal with her tonight so I've gotta be a little more tender.

"You like my face between your legs, don't you, babe?" I whisper, rubbing my nose against hers.

"I like the beard," she admits, tugging slightly on my tuft. My dick swells at her touch.

"Yeah? Well, this thing hanging between my legs likes you a whole lot."

She reaches down and grabs my cock in her hand. "You're so fucking big."

"That's it, babe, talk my dick up."

"I don't have to. I think it speaks for itself."
She fists my cock harder, and I groan.

"Fuck, babe." I love the feel of her wet body beneath me as we make out under the spray of the water.

She reaches up and kisses me, and I lose all train of thought. She's so goddamn beautiful. And I know she's got a bag full of secrets, just like her sister Stevie. Maybe the two of them are unlucky in love. Then it hits me… *am I falling for this chick?*

Those heart palpitations and the happy feeling I've had all day every time I think about seeing her and climbing into her bed... I may have it a bit bad for my lawyer lady, but how can one blame me?

She's smart, she's funny, she's sexy as hell – but I know she thinks this is just fuckin' and that's all it was meant to be. Just a little bit of harmless fun with no strings attached.

If that's the case, then why does imagining another dude in her bed make me want to shove a gun down his throat for even thinkin' about my girl, much less bedding her. *My girl?*

And it shocks the hell out of me. I've never really wanted a steady girlfriend. I've never really found anyone that I clicked with so much that I'd want to get to know better. And women make men messy. It ain't all roses.

I know things have worked out for some of my other brothers, but what happens when it doesn't work out? Steel got divorced before he met Sienna and it was a disaster.

The bitch took him for everything and even lied about bein'
pregnant to get him to marry her in the first place.

Nobody talks about what happens if shit goes bad.

Yet would it all be worth it? To love a woman like
Kennedy even for a little while and then lose her. I don't
know. I've never been in love, so I can't really say, and I
don't know if that's what this is– but I do know I want to
see her again. I do know that I've imagined takin' her to
church with my arm slung around her shoulders while I tell
everyone she's mine.

I've even thought about her wearing my cut and riding
on the back of my sled.

I don't know if there's something in the water, but
this feeling isn't something I'm familiar with, and it's
downright terrifying.

As I deepen the kiss, our tongues collide… I could
never fuckin' get enough of her sweet lips, her soft touch,
the way her eyes look at me intensely when she comes.
That's the shit that gets me off; seeing her pleasure, making
her feel good, knowing that she's enjoying it.

I slide into her from behind without a rubber and she lets
me, pressing her body into the glass and slapping her ass.

It feels so fuckin' good as the water cascades around
us, and I fuck her slowly, peeling her back slightly so I can
reach around to cup her tits and pinch her nipples. I know
playin' with them gets her off and makes her orgasms more

intense, and I'm all for women's liberation. In fact, I'm front and center.

She cries out as I thrust a little harder as I hit the end of her, and she plants her hands on either side of the glass.

"Want your ass," I whisper in her ear. I want it so bad. I run my thumb and fingers along her crease, and she bucks back against me. I rub some of her arousal on the tip of my finger and rub it over her ass back and forward. "It'll feel good, till we work up to my cock."

She groans as I slowly insert and feel her clench down.

"Bones…"

"Relax," I tell her, biting down on her shoulder. "It'll feel good if you let go. I'm not gonna hurt you. I'm never gonna hurt you…"

To my delight, she does as I say, and I slowly move my finger in and out of her as I resume my thrusting. To my surprise, she bares down on my finger, wanting more.

"That's it, baby. Does it feel good?"

"Y–yes..."

"Imagine it's my cock," I whisper. "Soon, you're gonna take all of me, and I'm gonna come in your ass. Then you're gonna beg me to do it again."

She mumbles something incoherent as I move one hand to grasp the back of her neck, then I move it around to her throat. I know she likes it when I hold her throat or her wrists and subdue her, and she likes it even better when

I'm rough. I wonder if she'd let me tie her to the bed by her arms and legs.

I move to smack her on the ass, then I do it again as she cries out.

"You like your ass being spanked while I fuck both holes?" I grunt.

"God, yes, *Ryan…*"

I chuckle into her skin and bite down on her shoulder as I move back to squeeze her throat, thrusting my dick deep, as I fuck her ass with my finger. She's takin' it so well. I watch as she moves a hand between her legs to rub her clit. Every fuckin' sensation. Oh, yeah.

"I don't ever wanna stop," I mutter, loving every single moan that escapes her lips. "I fuckin' love doin' you, babe."

"Gonna come, Bones…"

I revel in the feel of her clenching down on me as I squeeze her throat tighter as she comes hard, and I speed up, needing my own release as I shove my finger deeper, wishing I could put another in there, but I don't wanna scare her. Seeing her ass and her pussy take me is too much, and I spurt hard, coming deep inside her as I call out her name, stilling when I'm spent and she's gasping as I release her neck.

"This whole fuckin' body is mine," I growl in her ear. "You hear me, *Ms. Hart?*"

I smack her ass when she doesn't answer.

"Yes," she whispers, pressing her ass back against me as I slowly remove my finger. The greedy girl wants so much more. I can't wait to explore every inch of her body and do all the erotic things she wants me to. I'm gonna do it all.

"Anyone even looks at you twice, I'm gonna hurt them."

"Then I'll have to bail you out again," she says, panting.

"I can pay you back like this."

"You're gonna be doing a lot of screwing, then."

"Touché." I laugh. "Spoken like a true queen."

BRACKEN RIDGE
REBELS
ARIZONA
M · C

CHAPTER 10

KENNEDY

I can't even believe the week I've had. I never knew seven days ago I'd be not only sexually satisfied by a man who is totally wrong for me, but I'd be drinking and mingling at the biker clubhouse on a Saturday night. Yet here I am.

And Bones can't take his eyes off me.

I told him I was coming via text message, and aside from one night midweek when he was working late, we've spent every night burning the midnight oil.

And he keeps me awake all night long with that big, fat cock of his. Or his mouth. To say he enjoys going down on me is an understatement.

Tonight, I purposely wore something casual to not draw too much attention to myself, but his eyes are all over my tits and my ass. I guess the low-cut tank top and ripped jeans I thought were low-key are just the thing to get the man's head turned in my direction.

He went to the bar to get us some drinks and left

me with Amelia and Lucy. Then he told me if anyone approaches me, as in a member of the opposite sex, I'm to tell them that I'm with him and to fuck off.

Like I don't know how to ward off unwanted attention. Honestly, some of these men are so archaic in their ideologies, and it amuses me more than it annoys me. I'm a big girl. I can stick up for myself. And they don't seem like the kind of biker club that are going to be brawling and fighting over women.

"…and then they tried to break into the workshop," Lucy's saying as I turn my attention back to her. We take a seat on one of the leather couches near of one of the pool tables.

The girls have been telling me about the spate of break-ins that have been going on this last week, and after Colt's viewed the security footage, it seems they knew where the cameras were and never showed their faces. And worse, they don't seem like kids as everyone first thought.

"Did they get away with anything?" I ask.

"It seems like they're more or less hell bent on causing destruction, rather than actually breaking into the premises and stealing anything," Lucy goes on. "Rubble is starting to think it's someone with a vendetta."

"Bones's place got broken into too," I say, remembering the night that he dropped me home. "They didn't get anything either but smashed the flood lights and caused quite a bit of damage."

"That's so annoying," Amelia groans. "Last thing this town needs is a crime spree. What are the cops actually doing in this town?"

Lucy shrugs. "It happens a few times a year, blow-ins come around town and wreak havoc and then take off. They target smaller places with fewer police presence and raid small businesses, trying to get easy cash. Most of the time, they're teenagers on drugs, looking for a quick fix."

"That's awful," I agree, "but it doesn't look like they got away with much by the sounds of it. Most of the businesses around here seem to be fairly secure."

"Colt's wired everything up through cameras for all of our businesses," Lucy tells me. "But other shops don't have that kind of technology. It'll probably create some new business for Colt. He's already got Jax and Gears pretty much helping him full-time."

"Not a bad business to be in when shit like this happens," I agree.

"It sucks, though," says Lucy. "Our town is pretty much crime-free. Not saying the cops don't do anything, but the threat of BRMC usually sways most people into not doing any shady shit. Just ask Jack."

I shake my head. If I never hear that story again, it'll be too soon. "Yeah, I heard about him. I guess that's what you get when you cross a club full of angry bikers. I don't suppose the club has any other enemies. Maybe one of Jack's employees, for example. Now he's selling up, they could be a little disgruntled."

Lucy taps her chin thoughtfully. "Hey, that's not a bad idea. He does have a couple of goons and a son who's a bad apple, though what can you expect from a role model like Jack."

I shrug. "Just saying. It makes sense if there's a vendetta and obvious bad blood."

"I'll mention it to Rubble."

"So," Amelia says, her eyes going round. "Did you come here with Bones?"

I have to think fast. While I don't want to outright lie, I knew this was a bad idea from the start.

"No, I got invited by Brock," I reply, which isn't a lie, and I technically did drive here in my own car. So that isn't coming with anyone. "To celebrate the baby and meet everyone, since I'm going to be doing a bit of work for the club, mainly with Kirsty. I thought it was a good idea." Amelia doesn't look convinced, and to be honest, neither does Lucy.

"How long?" Lucy gives me a chin lift.

My eyebrows rise in surprise. "How long what?" She spares Bones a glance at the bar, then her eyes flick back to mine. "How long have you guys been going at it?" Amelia snorts her drink and then begins to choke. I give her a hard pat on the back.

"We're not going at anything. He's a client and –"

She holds her hand up. "There's no fooling me, honey, and nobody really cares about the attorney-client privilege crap except you. There's only one reason why Bones has had a shit-eating grin spread across his face all week, and now I know why."

My heart hammers in my chest. This isn't what I needed, and had I known Lucy was a detective and able to sniff out bullshit faster than a sniffer dog, I wouldn't have even come here. Amelia also works for me, so I don't need her thinking I'm unethical. Or anyone else.

I don't even know what *us* even means.

We're fucking, that's it.

"Well, I'm afraid I can't kiss and tell," I reply, hoping to hold on to my dignity for a fraction longer.

"He is pretty cute," Amelia goes on, looking over at him as I give her daggers. "And I've heard he's good in the sack. Not that I would know."

I'd honestly rather not think about it.

Lucy chuckles. "He hasn't been seen around the sweet butts or the cute single hang-arounds at all this last little while." Her eyes dart to mine mischievously. "Looks to me like he is pretty smitten."

I like hearing that, as much as I know we're not betrothed or anything, but I feel a little bit of fire when I think about him with another woman. Yeah, that's not happening as long as I'm around. Exclusivity works both ways.

"You two are as bad as each other," I sigh, trying to play it off, hoping they'll drop it. It's bad enough I'm getting a few looks my way of people wondering who I am and what the hell I'm doing here.

I guess I do stick out like a sore thumb, even though I tried to dress a little less conservative.

"Hey, Luce," a deep voice says, and I turn to look straight at a beautiful pair of green eyes and dark brows. The dude talks to Lucy but is looking right at me.

"Hey, Nitro!" Lucy leans up and gives him a hug. "Have you met Amelia?" He nods. "And this is Kennedy, the club's new attorney. Kennedy, this is my little brother."

Brother? Ah, this is the guy who helped Bones and Lucy when all that shit went down. I still have no idea what actually happened aside from Nitro stepped in and Bones getting stabbed.

The club's new attorney? I want to face-palm myself.

"Pleased to meet you." I stick my hand out to shake his as he looks down at it and a smirk forms on his lips. He takes my hand in his, clad in a million silver rings along with silver, leather and cloth bracelets all the way up to his wrists. He has this whole long-haired, bohemian rockstar vibe going on, and those eyes…

"You new around here?" he asks.

"I've been here a little over six months. What about you?"

"Just got to town." He gives me a chin lift. He's intense and doesn't smile.

A few moments later, I feel two hands snake around my waist and a muscular chest press into my back.

"Nitro," Bones says as I swallow hard.

"Bones," Nitro replies.

I don't need to face Bones to realize that there may be a pissing competition going down, and as I glance at Nitro, I see that I'm not mistaken.

"You all right, brother? Need a drink?" Bones offers, though his tone is clipped.

"I was just headin' that way," Nitro replies.

"Ask Ging for the top shelf shit, otherwise you'll be drinkin' that shitty moonshine Rubble likes."

Lucy play punches Bones on the arm.

Nitro saunters off without another word as I try and unravel Bones's arms from around me.

Amelia's lips roll inwards as she watches the spectacle and Lucy turns to Bones and points at him.

"That was kinda rude."

"Why? Got rid of him, didn't it? Had his hands on my woman."

Oh, here we go.

I spin and turn to face him. "I'm not your woman!" I whisper-shout. "And I don't need you defending my honor when it's not wanted, nor is it asked for."

He releases his hold slightly, but I still feel his hands hovering around my hips.

"Doesn't matter if it's asked for. You're in *my* club now, sugar. Man's gotta let another man know where it's at. Dressed like that, you'll be gettin' plenty of unwanted attention. Best he knows now you're off limits."

Off limits? Holy heck.

Lucy bites on her lip to save from laughing.

I shake my head. "Dressed like what, exactly?"

He nods down to my tank. "That's at least a size too small."

My mouth opens, and I close it again, my eyes narrowing. "It actually *isn't* a size too small; it fits me just fine, and more to the point, I like it."

"Didn't say I didn't like it either. I said it looks a size too small. Makes your tits look bigger."

"And that's a bad thing?"

"When other men notice, yep." He smiles without humor.

"Are you going to tell me what to wear now?" I demand.

He chuckles. "Nah, babe, but if you don't want every available dude in this place hittin' on you and starin' at your tits, then it might be best next time to wear somethin' a little more… covered."

I lose it. "You don't get to tell me what to wear, or what to do!" I poke him in the chest as I hear one of the girls laugh out loud. "I didn't ask for it, and I definitely don't need your approval."

He holds his hands in the air in surrender, then leans to my ear and whispers, "Save that fury for the bedroom tonight. You've just earned yourself punishment."

Even though his words hit a spot deep down inside me, I still think he's out of line with my attire comments. "You've got nerve."

"Don't get mad, I'm just sayin'. I've got a hard on just lookin' at you in those tight jeans, and I can see down your top when I'm hoverin' over the top of you."

"Well, stop hovering!"

He brushes the hair back off my shoulder. "You don't really mean that."

"Why don't we go get a refill?" Lucy says, clearing her throat as she drags Amelia away from the spectacle.

I try to keep my temper in check and my voice as low as possible. "If a man wants to talk to me, he can. I don't need you beating your chest like an ape, telling me that I shouldn't wear a goddamn tank top."

He leans down and bites my pulse point. Clearly not fazed at me basically yelling at him for being an ass. "You're so fuckin' feisty when you're mad. I'm gonna tie you to my bed tonight and spank that little ass red until you realize the error of your ways."

I swallow hard again, trying desperately to think of a comeback to hurl at him when there's a loud *ding, ding, ding*.

My eyes snap to the large make-shift stage that has an open outdoor area in the summer, where people can sit at little tables and enjoy the music. Tonight, though, there's a jukebox, and Angel and Brock appear with the baby. It's so sweet seeing Brock holding the baby in his arms, with Rawlings's hand in his as well.

While the party technically isn't until tonight when the kids have gone home, the barbecue is a little more child friendly. There're a few other older kids running around, playing chase while they dodge around the tables.

"Oh fu… uh, I mean… Dudes! Listen up!" Gears calls out.

Bones's hand slide down my ass, and he gives it a squeeze, then feel his erection digging into my back. I think our little fight got him going, and while I'm mildly turned on myself, he's still not going to tell me what to wear or what to do. I can talk to whoever I like. Even if Nitro was making the moves, then what was Bones going to do about it, fight him? I mean, it's not like Bones and I are dating, we're messing around. That's it.

Then why does my heart thump in my chest when I imagine him wrapped around another woman.

I am a jealous woman, not going to deny it, but he isn't mine to get jealous over. He hasn't even taken me out on the date I paid for at the charity auction!

"We'd like to thank everyone for comin' here today to celebrate our happy news."

Angel beams at Brock as they look at one another. "Those of you that know us realize how long we've wanted this, and to give Rawlings a sibling. In my opinion, it's long overdue."

Rawlings fist pumps in the air and everyone laughs.

"And we just wanted to thank everyone for your love and support," Angel goes on as Brock ruffles Rawlings's hair. "And for being there for us when times got really rough. It has been a hard road, but we've always had the love and support of the club behind us."

"That's what families are for!" Hutch yells out from the bar. Kirsty sits between his legs on a stool, her head resting back on the crook of his shoulder. They still look so in love.

Brock nods in his direction. "Those of you that know me know that I'm a man of few words, but I do appreciate everything the club and its members have done for me since I left the military. I've been able to accomplish everything I ever wanted, and now we have a complete family of our own, and hopefully… more babies to come!"

Angel shakes her head while Rawlings gives Brock a high-five. I can't help but chuckle.

I feel Bones rumble behind me and his hand at my hip touches my bare skin where my tank has risen up. His touch still sets me on fire. I can't stay mad at him for long, and I don't want to ruin the weekend by losing my temper. I know what I can be like sometimes, but he also has to learn that

I'm not property.

"I think one ten-pound baby delivered naturally without time for an epidural is enough for a little while," Angel muses, giving him the side-eye. "That being said, Rawlings would like to tell everyone the baby's name that we've all chosen. Don't you, sweetheart?"

They look down at the little blonde-haired replica of Angel who's dressed in the same outfit as her mom, little denim overalls and a black t-shirt, with a long swinging ponytail.

Brock places a protective hand on her shoulder.

"We'd like to present…" She does a fake drum roll that's so darned cute. "Baby Ethan Wolf Altman," she calls out in a big voice, then Brocks whispers down to her ear, and she adds.... "Oh, and we are accepting gift cards for mom, or dad's favorite bourbon as baby-warming house presents."

Angel slaps Brock on the ass as he booms with laughter. Laughs and hoots ping around the room, followed by applause and loud-pitched whistles.

"She's adorable," I say, clapping my hands.

I feel Bones at my ear. "I don't envy Brock. She's worse than her mama and more like Brock every day."

If I didn't know she wasn't Brock's biological child, I wouldn't know any better. And it's clear he dotes on her, on all of them. It's really heartwarming to see.

I think about the day he came into my office, and I know he's a good man. Deep down, he's a family man and just wants what's best for the people in his life.

"And here's to Rawlings, big sister to Ethan Wolf!" Kirsty calls out between cupped hands.

I notice Angel's parents sitting next to Hutch and Kirsty. It's really cool how they're part of the M.C. as well. They beam with pride, and I see Angel's dad wipe his eyes.

As if reading my mind, Bones says, "See, we're not so bad, really. Are we, babe?"

"That's debatable," I reply. "And will you stop feeling my ass? People are watching."

"Do you think I give a shit?" he growls in my ear. "You won't be saying that when I'm makin' you scream the house down."

I can't deny that Bones is the best lover I've ever had, not that I've had that many. There were only a couple of men before I married Dean. I've avoided the whole 'men' situation after him. I didn't think I deserved to be happy and still feel that gaping hole of guilt inside of me.

Guilt because while I was there for him for better or worse, I was going to leave. I didn't want to be married anymore.

The thought makes me go rigid in Bones' arms.

"What you thinkin'?" Bones asks quietly.

"How sweet they are," I reply honestly as I watch Brock, albeit reluctantly, hands little Ethan over to Lucy who cradles him in her arms.

"I can't help thinkin' how sweet your pussy is," he says

in my ear as I close my eyes. "Let's sneak away."

"I thought you said you wouldn't take me upstairs to that shithole?"

"I wouldn't, but my place is closer than yours."

I can't deny that a thrill goes through me at the thought of rolling around with him tonight, and I definitely don't resist when he drags me out of the club and over to his monster bike.

He should not be riding this, but I can't help but notice the beautiful Harley with a gleaming paint job and flaming orange down one side.

He pulls me to him, and his tongue is in my mouth before I can blink. Cupping my face, our tongues clash, and he kisses me with passion.

When he pulls back, he says, "When you're in my club, I'll put my fuckin' hands wherever I want, and I'll do whatever I need to in order to show everyone that you're with me."

I stare at him with wide eyes.

"What are we, Bones?" I reply, feeling the conflict rise once again in my chest. "It isn't like we're dating, and now you're warding off other men for just saying hello."

"So what? You're with me and no fucker is gonna come up to you and try and take what's mine." His eyes are fierce as he pierces me with his gaze. "And trust me, he wasn't just sayin' hello."

"What's *yours* exactly?"

"You know what I mean."

"Uh, I don't think I do."

"We're fuckin' exclusively," he grunts.

"We are?"

"Well, you're not takin' any other man while I've got a say in it, and I definitely only want your pussy…"

"Last of the romantics," I mutter.

He presses against me again, and I feel his hard cock against my stomach. "Get on the back of my bike. I need to fuck, and if we don't go now, I'll mount you on the back of my bike."

I roll my lips as I can't help but shake my head and smile at his ridiculousness. There is never a dull moment with Bones around.

"Where the hell did I find you again?" I muse.

"Jail," he reminds me.

Oh yeah, that's right.

BRACKEN RIDGE
REBELS
ARIZONA
M · C

CHAPTER 19

KENNEDY

ones runs his tongue through my folds, and I buck off the bed.

"Oh God," I groan.

He lived up to his promise and tied me to his bed, using a belt to secure my hands while my legs are bent and spread wide for him. He's been at it like this for ages, soft, slow, sensual licks, and he won't let me come.

"Tell me you're a bad girl," he whispers.

"What for?" I sigh.

He pinches my clit as I cry out. "For bein' a snotty little bitch to me at church and tellin' me off."

"I wasn't –"

"Have it your way, then…"

He continues to lick and suck me, then two fingers slowly curve inside me as he strokes my G-spot. I think I'm going to have a heart attack.

"*Please…*" I beg him.

"Say the words." He doesn't let up, and I'd probably

agree to anything right now just to be able to come.

I try to grind up into his face, but he pins me down harder.

"You can't use my own orgasm against me!" I cry.

He chuckles. "Try me."

He keeps me on the brink, and I cry out in frustration. Just as I'm about to climax, he stops, then he starts the whole process again.

"Fine. I'm sorry, now do it…"

I feel him smile against my core, his bristly beard – which he has not shaved since I told him I liked it – brushes against my clit just how I like it. God, I'm so fucking sensitive to his touch…

"What are you sorry for?"

"You son-of-a-bitch!"

"Now, now, there's no need for name callin'."

He continues his slower than slow ministrations as I flop my head back onto his pillows with an exaggerated sigh, pulling on my restraints.

"I'm sorry that you're being a dick about other men talking to me."

"That doesn't sound like an apology to me. It sounds more like I'm bein' smarted, babe, and I can drive you wild like this all night. I love eatin' your pussy…"

I groan as he rubs his chin over my clit, his beard scratching me in all the right places. I buck off the bed and cry out.

"*Jesus!* Fine! I'm sorry I was a bitch to you about the other guy and being weird about you touching me in front of the others."

"Because why?"

Oh, I am so going to repay the favor. He just doesn't know it yet.

"Because I'm –"

He stops, looking up at me, my slickness all over his mouth, and I almost convulse looking at him. His eyes are predatory, and I know he's going to fuck me hard in a matter of moments.

I pull against the restraints… this is so fucking hot!

"Because you're?" he prompts, like I need reminding. I close my eyes and puff air out of my cheeks. "Because when I'm at the club, I'm yours, Bones."

He grins, then blows on my sensitive flesh. The fucker still has his jeans on, but half his ass is hanging out, and I see the tuft of hair at his naval as he moves up to his elbows, slinging my legs over his shoulders… oh so help me God. "That wasn't so hard, was it?"

He doesn't wait for an answer, just thrusts his tongue inside me where his fingers just were and then swirls my arousal over my clit with his thumb as he drives me into the mattress. Watching him eat me like this sends a huge, pulsating orgasm right through me as I come, pushing more of myself into his face, and he rides me through the most earth-shattering experience I've ever had. Just as I'm shuddering from the aftershocks, he blows on my pussy again, his fingers replacing his tongue.

"Your clit's so swollen it's fuckin' pulsin," he says, licking it gently with his tongue as I thrash around. I need to touch him. Not being able to just makes it all the more frustrating, which is what he wants.

"I need you inside me," I cry out. "Bones, I need you now!"

"Patience, baby. You'll learn it one way or the other." He drives his fingers into me faster as his other hand parts my folds and he sucks my clit hard while I whimper over and over.

"Oh God, oh my God…" I come again as he drives his fingers deeper and faster, drawing out my climax as he sucks on me like a sweet peach.

"Fuck, I love the taste of you when you come," he drawls, then he pushes my legs off his shoulders, and before I even have time to react, he pulls his jeans off and kicks them away, then dives his cock into me and begins fucking me hard, rocking his hips back and forth while I cry out and shudder against his solid body.

"You're so fucking good," I cry out. "So good. Don't stop, Bones…"

"What do you call me when I'm fuckin' you hard?" he mutters, his hands moving up my arms to my bound wrists, and they stay there.

"Ryan!" I call out. "Oh God, please, Ryan, like that, just like that…"

This man can move his hips like nobody's business. I've never had a man who paid my body this much attention and got me this worked up. Even if the bastard did have me apologize before he let me come. I'll get my own back. The lawyer in me is always scheming.

"Yeah, baby?"

"Oh God, yeah."

He starts to move faster. "Gonna come too. This tight little cunt's got me hard as fuck."

I mewl and yelp as his bed hits the wall. Unlike mine, it protests loudly and squeaks like it's in pain. The sound goes straight to my core. I may never, ever get enough of Ryan Romero.

I can't form words, my body's primed for another build up…

"You like me fuckin' you hard, tied up, baby, don't you?"

"Yes, that's it, right there… don't stop…"

I lose it again, seeing stars as my climax feels like thunder rumbling through my entire core. He stills and then shoots his load inside me, cursing and calling as he drains his balls and then collapses on top of me while we both fight for breath.

"See what happens when you defy me in front of my

brothers?" he pants, kissing the top of my head.

"Remind me to defy you more often. That was so hot."

"You're fuckin' hot," he growls. "And you're not gonna be gettin' any sleep tonight because I need your hot little sassy mouth suckin' on my cock."

"Are you sure there's anything left in there?"

"Five minutes," he breathes, rolling off me. "I just need five minutes."

He rolls off the bed and returns with a washcloth, wiping his dick as he saunters back to me.

"Are you going to untie me?" I ask, as he seems in no hurry to do any such thing.

"I'll think about it."

"Bones!" I shout.

He chuckles and reaches over and unties my hands from the bed, then quite unbelievably, begins to clean me up too. I've never had a man do that before. It's always a mad dash to the bathroom if you don't have tissues by the bedside table.

"Lost my mind doin' that," he says as I pull him down for a kiss. He deserves it after the ripples that just shook through me. When he pulls back, he's grinning from ear to ear.

"What?"

"Nothin', just admirin' the view."

I close my legs and he pushes them back open by my knees. "Don't spoil a pretty view."

My cheeks heat as I take him in. I know that I'm feeling

things that are much deeper than just screwing. I take a moment to get my shit and my thoughts together.

"I'm sorry," I say quietly. Before he can ask what for, I add, "for acting like that when you were going all alpha on me. I'm not used to a man taking charge. I've always kind of been the one who had to take the reins in my past relationship."

He studies me quietly without a word.

"I still don't think it's a good idea to grope me in full view of the club members, but I wouldn't really like another woman coming up to you while I was gone for five minutes."

"You wouldn't, huh?"

"If I'm being completely honest, no, it'd be a little shitty."

A slow grin spreads across his face. "Yeah, would you fight for me?"

I shake my head. "The only fighting I do is in the courtroom."

"I don't know, you do a pretty good job of it in the bedroom, too, my little spitfire."

He kisses me lightly, then goes to dump the washcloth in the hamper.

"Where are you going?" I ask as he pads to the door, butt naked.

"Fancy a snack?"

I laugh. "You're going to go make a snack dressed like

that? Don't you have roommates?"

He shrugs. "Colt's at Cassidy's tonight, and I'm way more comfortable without clothes on."

"Wait, I thought you didn't cook?"

I lean down and pull his ripped, black Harley Davidson eagle t-shirt over my head. It sits just below my thighs and smells exactly like him. I refrain from taking a deep inhale at his intoxicating scent.

"I don't, but I do make a mean grilled cheese."

My stomach practically rumbles with hunger. "Oooh. Yes, please."

I quickly go pee as he waltzes down the hallway toward the kitchen. His ass could be a wonder of the world. When I finish up in the bathroom, I laugh out loud when I see he's put an apron on while he fixes our sandwiches.

His lips twitch as I snake behind him and slap his ass with one hand. God, his butt's so damn cute.

Everything about his body is off the charts hot. The muscles and ripples run all down his back and his butt and legs. I admire the view of half his body tatted up at the back, while the other half is bare. One butt cheek blank, the other covered with swirly tattooed patterns.

He's the epitome of sex.

Staring at him like this does things to me. I don't know what I'm thinking right now because I can't explain it, but I do know that I freaking love everything he does to me and how sweet and caring he is with me. I wonder what the catch is. Like, he must have something wrong with him. Nobody is *this* perfect.

I stand behind him and feel his ass, then run my hands under his apron and feel up his front too, loving how his muscles feel smooth under my hands. His rippling six pack is like God's gift to women. I run my fingers through the tuft of hair at his navel, and he groans.

"Touch my dick," he gruffs.

"Now, now, you're making grilled cheese," I sing-song. "A girl needs to eat."

He turns as I step back. "Yeah, she does. You can eat my dick."

I squeal when he lunges for me, and I'm not quick enough. His mouth is on me before I can run off, and I know for a fact he'd chase me.

"Feed me first," I groan when he finishes assaulting my senses. "Then I'll give you dessert."

He picks me up and places my butt on the counter, right next to the bread and the bag of grated cheese.

"I'll feed you, all right." He runs a hand through my hair as we stare at each other.

What the hell is happening?

If he feels it too, he doesn't say anything, but I'm pretty sure he knows we just shared a moment.

I cling to his shoulders as he rips the t-shirt from my

body and then pulls his apron off.

I can't freaking fall for him… The trouble is, he's making it so damn hard not to.

I wake wrapped around Bones. Who'd have known from looking at him that he's a snuggler.

He's hot too, as in, like a thermostat.

Lifting his arm off me, I slide out of bed and pull his t-shirt on. After he ravaged me on the kitchen counter, he made grilled cheese and brought it back to bed to eat as we watched TV.

I didn't expect any of this. I just wanted a good time, a roll in the hay with the resident bad boy with no strings attached. I didn't expect to be in his bed every single night.

After I use the bathroom, I go in search of coffee. Thank goodness he has a Keurig coffee machine. I almost die when I open the drawer closest and see the Original Donut Shop pods.

I set about making us two cups as I clean up last night's mess. It seems Bones doesn't like to bother too much about tidying up after himself, though the house isn't as untidy as I first thought it would be. At least there are no dirty dishes, aside from the couple of plates we used.

After a quick sneak in the pantry for sugar, I can see that he lines up all his canned goods which makes me chuckle. I guess you can't take everything out of the army guy after all.

I'm quite pleased with my efforts as I add half a teaspoon of sugar to mine, and not knowing if Bones takes sugar or not, I dump half of one in his too. Just as I pick up the mugs to take back upstairs, the back door swings open, and a small, petite woman chatters away to a middle-aged man in another language a million miles an hour. I halt in my tracks as they both stop talking, and we stare at one another.

It feels like eons pass before my words can form.

"Um, hello?" I say. "Can I help you?"

I mean, they don't seem like they're breaking in to rob the place or anything.

The woman takes in my attire. I don't know if she notices that I have Bones's shirt on, but I get the suspicious feeling they may be his...

"We're Ryan's parents," the man says, offering me a kind smile, then his hand. I'm holding both mugs, and I'm aware that I'm wearing a shirt that barely covers my ass... with no panties on.

I could offer him my elbow...

"Uh... hi," I reply, unsure if I should turn and place the mugs down on the counter and reciprocate the shake, but he waves his hand away, seeing I'm a little stuck. "Sorry, I wasn't expecting to run into anyone..."

When his mom recovers from her shock, she claps her hands together. "We never thought it would happen!" she cries, her smile exactly like her son's.

"Uh, never thought what would happen?" Jeez this is awkward…

"That he'd finally have a girlfriend!" she exclaims like I'm stupid.

I laugh. "Oh no, no, sorry, there's been a misunderstanding. I'm not his girlfriend." Great. So, awesome way to go and announce you're his fuck buddy... "I'm his lawyer."

I could slap myself. Seriously. *I'm his lawyer?*

His father's eyes go wide, and his mom claps her hands again like this is good news. Oh God. *Kill me now.*

"Well, I'm Henry, and this is my wife, Isobel," his dad says, thankfully keeping his eyes at head height. "I'm surprised Ryan didn't mention we'd be coming over. He must have forgotten, since he's always got a lot going on." I don't know what I would ever have expected from Bones's parents, but it isn't this. They seem so… *normal.*

"I'm Kennedy," I reply because I should really tell them my name.

His mom says something to his father in what I think is Portuguese, and I smile kindly, having no idea what she just said. Probably that I'm a tramp who's wearing her son's clothes.

"We know, we've heard all about you," Henry goes on, ushering past me toward the Keurig. "Since Ryan was in jail and all."

"Oh." I realize. *His parents know about that?* I don't know where to look. If the ground could open up and swallow me whole right about now, that would be completely awesome.

"Well, I'll just go and… and umm… find him for you."

His mom, who I realize is holding an armful of what looks suspiciously like frozen meals in containers, gives me a warm smile. "Lovely to meet you, Kennedy. I'll make us some waffles."

My eyes go wide as I smile and do what any woman would do under these circumstances, I agree. "That would be lovely. Uh, thank you."

I take off, hoping neither of them watch me leave because my ass is more than likely hanging out.

I race as fast as I can back down to the master suite without spilling the coffee everywhere. When I get back in there safely, I shut the door firmly, leaning back against it.

This could only happen to me. I swear to God.

"Bones!" I whisper as I set the cups down on the dresser to one side. "Bones!"

He doesn't move. He's rolled up in the sheets, on his front, half his ass peeking out and, my, my, is it a glorious sight. I stare at it for a second in admiration before I internally slap myself. I crawl onto the bed and shake him. He barely moves.

"Wake up!" I whisper-shout a little more firmly.

He begins to stir, then when he looks at me with one eye open, a slow smile spreads across his face.

Before I can stop him, he reaches out and pulls me to him, rolling me with his body until I'm straddled over him as he tugs my t-shirt up.

"You wearin' my shirt's got my dick hard," he tells me, yawning. "Look what you did." He nods down to his very hard, very fat, beautiful cock that springs to life between us. I stare at it like it's the eighth wonder of the world until I shake myself out of my daze.

Before I can blurt out his parents are out in the kitchen and I just ran into them *looking like this,* and now his mom's making us waffles, he tries to jack up my shirt higher as his other hand grips my ass and squeezes. "Fuck, I love morning sex. You gonna ride me, babe?"
My eyes go wide as he leans up and takes my nipple in his mouth and starts to suck it.

Oh, my fucking God, this man is insatiable.

"Bones... I... Oh..."

"You diggin' the beard, aren't you?" He gives me a wink as he moves his mouth to my other nipple.

And then we both hear it. "Ryan!"

He freezes, his eyes darting to the door. "Who the fuck is that?"

I shake off the lusty sensations of impaling him while

his parents are down the hall making us breakfast and finally find my voice.

"That's what I'm trying to tell you! I just ran into your parents in the kitchen."

His eyes go wide. "Dressed like that?"

I nod. "Afraid so."

"Oh, boy." He wipes his face, then he calls out, "Comin', Mom. I'll be there in a second!"

Thank God she doesn't barge in here. I think one scantily clad meeting half naked is enough for the rest of my lifetime.

"Do they usually just barge in your house unannounced?" I whisper.

Unbelievably, he moves his mouth back to my nipple and begins sucking again.

"Nope. I forgot they were comin' over." That's it. That's what he says, as though we're discussing the weather and not my bare ass hanging out for all to see.

"Bones!" I admonish. "Quit it! I've got to get up."

"I've got to get down," he complains. "You've got me rock hard. Can't go see my parents with this between my legs."

"Suck it up, buttercup. I'm not having sex with you while your parents are out there making us waffles!"

His eyebrows shoot up. "Mom's makin' waffles?"

I slap my forehead.

"Well, why didn't you just say that?" he says,

continuing to play with my breasts as my shirt bunches up under my arms. "Mom makes the best waffles ever."

"Stop it!" I try to climb off him, but he holds me down with both hands at my hips.

"It is kinda naughty, fuckin' quietly so my parents don't hear my squeaky bed."

"It isn't *kinda naughty*!" I fire back. "It's not happening, not now, not ever."

"You know, I'm only going to tie you up again for denying me."

My pussy clenches at the thought and how hot that was last night.

"Next time, it'll be your ankles tied too," he says, caressing my face as he plants kisses up my neck, and I almost lose myself, until I hear…

"*Ryan!* Hurry up whatever you're doing in there. The food's almost ready!"

"Oh. My. God." I close my eyes and die a little inside. "Your mother thinks we're having sex in here."

"Well, we could be if you weren't wastin' time talkin' and tryin' to stop me pleasin' you."

I shove him back and manage to escape. "Seriously, not funny."

"Do I smell coffee?" He yawns, stretching his fine body upward as he, albeit reluctantly, climbs out of bed. I can't help but stare at his dick and wonder if I shouldn't just lock the door and ride him quickly. *No!* "My eyes are up here, beautiful!" He laughs, sheathing his cock as he heads to the bathroom.

I roll my eyes as he passes, taking a long sip of the coffee I just made.

"Oh, and I'd put some pants on, baby girl," he adds through the open door. "I think Mom and Dad may have seen enough of your ass for one morning."

I curse the ground Ryan Romero walks on as I flip him the bird and hunt around for something to cover up with.

This is just my luck and Bones isn't one bit put-out, like it's all a big joke.

As soon as I gobble down those waffles, I'm out of here.

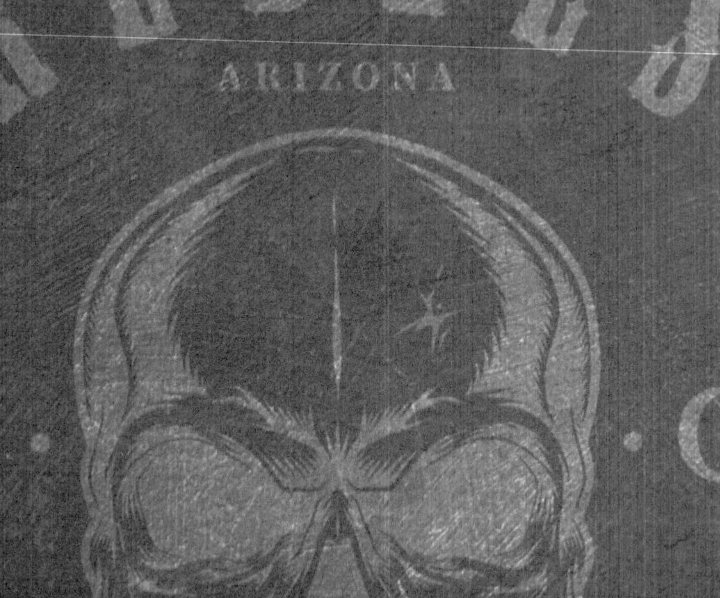

BRACKEN RIDGE
REBELS
ARIZONA
M · C

CHAPTER 20

BONES

I wander down the hall, dragging Kennedy by the elbow as she tries to wriggle free.

I can't help the huge grin on my face at my parents seeing her dressed like that, or the fact she thinks they'd care. They don't question what I do or who I do it with.

Dad gives me an equally bright smile as we clasp hands and hug. "Nice goin', son," he whispers proudly as I turn and kiss my mother on the cheek.

She ruffles my hair and stands back to look at me. "You look thin," she says, assessing me.

I roll my eyes. "Mom."

She turns her gaze on Kennedy. "So do you. Sit down and eat. I've made plenty and whipped up some bacon and brought some homemade maple syrup. Lucky I did, you only had that store bought trash that's full of refined sugar and loaded with calories."

Kennedy stands there and looks like a deer caught in headlights. I'm not sure where my strong, sassy, lawyer lady has gone, but at least she's got shorts on this time.

"You could actually knock next time," I say to mom, giving her wide eyes.

She waves a hand at me. "You knew we were coming. Anyway, your papa and I aren't old prudes; we know you like to have your fun. We're all adults here."

"Mom!" *Fantastic.* Humiliated by my own mother in front of the woman I'm trying to impress.

Kennedy rolls her lips inwards and tries to fight a smile. At least she's not running out the door.

"Isobel, leave the boy alone. You're embarrassing him," says my dad.

"He's had enough years to know by now that I won't sugarcoat things," she retorts, one hand on her hip. "And he's thirty-two years old. I still don't have any grand babies."

I face-palm myself as Kennedy looks at me, alarmed. She's definitely gonna head for the hills now. Way to go, Mom.

"Mom, why don't you take a beat and enjoy the waffles and not scare my girl away."

Kennedy goes to open her mouth, to no doubt protest, but then closes it again.

"Since when has your mom ever taken a beat?" Dad muses, giving Kennedy a wink.

"Maybe she could start," I reply more firmly.

Mom is one of those little, scary women that most people are deadly afraid of. She cuts to the chase and reads people like a book. And she never stops feeding everyone.

She waves me off. "So, Kennedy, how is Ryan's probation coming along?"

I shake my head as Kennedy spurts her coffee out all over the table. I pat her back as I give mom daggers.

"Sorry," she says as I grab her a handful of napkins from the middle of the table. "The question caught me off guard."

"It's fine," dad says, trying to smooth things over as mom looks between the two of us like she's done nothing wrong.

"He's doing just fine," Kennedy goes on, color rising in her cheeks. "And I just want you to know, since we're on the subject and this is quite unorthodox… I don't usually umm… sleep with my… umm… clients." Wow, Kennedy Hart tongue-tied. I never thought I'd see the day.

Mom tilts her head and nods like she understands. I am, in her eyes, after all, the catch of the county. Why wouldn't someone like Kennedy want to bag me?

I try hard not to chuckle.

She pats Kennedy on the hand good-naturedly. "He's a wonderful boy," she says with a firm nod. "Top of his class, and we were so proud of him when he went into the military. Though, like any mother, I didn't want him to go to war and be put in danger. He's a very loyal person, despite the fact he continues to deny me grandbabies and instead collects God awful tattoos and motorcycles," she admonishes as I run a hand over my face. Dad chuckles, looking between us like he's watching a tennis match.

"I think it's probably time that I drove Kennedy home," I say between clenched teeth. The last thing I want Kennedy knowing is any of these things. "Seems as I'm the hot subject of the day."

"Well, it isn't very often I get to see you, and I've never seen you with a woman I'd be happy to call my daughter-in-law."

"Mom!"

"It's fine," Kennedy says, biting her lip as she sips her coffee politely. "My mom is always trying to marry me off to the nearest available bachelor with a good job too. It's like a rite of passage."

Mom claps her hands together. "See."

"Can we please talk about something else?" I huff.

Mom turns to Kennedy, like they're besties now. "Have you ever been married Kennedy?"

She eyes her hands, looking for any signs of a wedding ring.

I glance at Dad as he eats his waffles, chuckling to himself as I shoot him daggers. I'm sure to never see Kennedy Hart ever again after this.

She looks momentarily stunned by the question, and I'm about to tell mom to back off and drag Kennedy out of there, when she surprises me by saying, "Yes, I have, actually."

I stare at her.

"Oh, dear." Mom shakes her head. "It's all right, these things happen. Did you remain on good terms?"

Kennedy swallows her next mouthful with vigor, and then says, "We did, and then he died."

My heart races in my chest at her admission. Shock and disbelief run through me.

I didn't even know this vital piece of information and she just confessed it to my mom. A woman she's known for all of five minutes.

Mom pats her hand. "I'm sorry to hear that."

Kennedy smiles gratefully. "It was hard," she says, and it seems she can't meet my gaze. "But let's not get caught up in all of that. How long are you in town for?"

Mom glances at me quickly but doesn't say anything, instead she tells Kennedy that they're here for today and will drive back this afternoon. Not before adding she'll clean my house, stock up my freezer, and make sure I have clean clothes to wear. It isn't helpful.

Now Kennedy's going to think I'm a thirty-two-year-old serial bachelor who has his mom come cook and clean for him. The reality is, I can't stop her.

I have been known to house dishes in my bedroom for weeks at a time, but I'm getting better at it. And I do know how to work the washing machine, despite popular opinion that I don't.

If Kennedy was considering anything other than a roll

in the hay, she's sure to run a mile as soon as she can escape the Spanish Inquisition.

She doesn't leave the table, however, instead she sits through mom's barrage of questions, and they even have a second cup of coffee.

When it's time to drive her home, dad shakes her hand and mom gives her a big hug and tells her not to be a stranger.

As I walk out to my sled, I turn to her as I hand her the brain bucket. "I'm so sorry about that."

She nods. "It's all right. I know how to handle moms."

I look down at my boots. "I didn't know… you were married. Why didn't you tell me?"

"You didn't ask," she replies. "Anyway, it's in the past."

I palm the back of my head. "But, he died?"

"Yep."

"Do you wanna talk about it?"

"Nope."

"So that's it, then?"

"What do you mean?"

I shake my head. "You can't just say you were married and he died, and that's it."

"Why not?"

"You told my mom, and you don't even know her."

"She asked me a question, and I didn't want to lie."
I stare at her, the feeling of regret swirling through me that I've been a dick. I haven't even gotten to know her one tiny

bit. We've been at it like rabbits, exploring each other like teenagers, and I know nothing about her. Nothing at all.

"When did he…"

"About two years ago."

"Can I ask what…"

"Cancer," she says abruptly. "He had cancer, and it was a slow and painful thing to watch and go through. That's it. Can we go now? I really need to get home and get things organized for work tomorrow."

She's shut down again, like she does so well, and it bothers me.

"I want you to open up to me." Thoughts of my sister hit me with full force, and it's like I've swallowed a mouthful of cement. One thing is for sure, you never get over the loss of someone you loved deeply.

She puts her hands on her hips. "Why? We're not dating."

"But we're exclusive."

She takes a long, impatient breath. "I don't want to talk about it."

"You don't, huh?"

"No, I don't. You can't possibly understand what it's like, all right? So, let's just let the matter drop."

Anger surges through me.

"I couldn't possibly understand," I mutter, as I climb on my ride and turn the key to roar my beast to life. "'Cause

I'm not capable of having any human emotions, right?"

"That's not –"

"Get on," I growl.

It takes a lot to piss me off, but that comment has just taken the prize.

It's not like she's gotten to know me either, so she can't act all pissed off because I didn't think to ask her if she'd been married before. It works both ways. The nerve of this woman.

She wraps her arms around me as she climbs on, and normally, I feel warmth and a surge of pride when she's on the back of my sled. Now I just feel cold, like the warmth we had has just dissipated.

I drive fast to get her home. I don't want to linger; I just want to go.

When I get to her apartment block, I park in the lot but don't turn the engine off. She climbs off just as my phone rings in my back pocket. I fish around and see it's Colt.

"Hey, brother," he says when I answer. "Emergency meeting at church. Three more businesses were hit last night, including the shop."

"Shit, was anything stolen?"

"Alarm scared them off, but they smashed all the windows at Steel's auto, then mine and Rubble's before leavin'."

"Holy fuck."

"Gotta be someone with a vendetta."

"Be there in five."

"Gotcha."

We hang up.

Kennedy holds the helmet out to me as she shakes her lovely, red locks out, and I try not to notice. She's never looked more beautiful than when she's natural like this. With no makeup on, her pretty skin flushed, her eyes bright and sparkling.

But I'm pissed with her. She doesn't just get to dismiss me when it suits her.

I hang it on the handlebars. "See you around." I give her a chin lift.

She narrows her eyes, clutching onto her purse. "Is that it?"

"What else do you want me to say?"

"Are you mad with me right now?"

I roll my eyes. "If you can't figure that out, then maybe you're not as good of a lawyer as you might think you are."

Her lips part as I give her a salute and rev the bike, taking off with a squeal down the street as I leave her standing there.

I tell myself it's for the best. She'll only hurt me in the end, and I'm already starting to fall for her and feeling things I shouldn't be.

She thinks so little of me that I wouldn't understand or comprehend what simple heartbreak feels like. It's a fuckin' joke.

My sister had leukemia. She was fuckin' ten years old.

I feel like smashing something.

Maybe this is how it should end. I should never have pursued her, knowing that she had some power over me with her tough talking and her undeniable beauty.

My mom always told me to stay away from all the pretty girls who had a brain; they were trouble. I guess she was right.

I know I'm not good enough for her, I get it. She's a lawyer, and I'm a guy who can't even clean his own house and runs a junkyard for a living. I've nothing to offer her. I don't even have feelings, according to her.

Women make men weak, and this is exactly why I've never had a real relationship and why I'm stupid to believe it was possible in the first place.

I get to church, and my mood has not improved.

Ginger is making coffee behind the bar and Gash is helping her do a stock take.

I give Ginger a nod. "Hey, beautiful."

"Hi, Bones. Ugh, you look like shit."

I raise my eyebrows. "Thanks a lot, nice to see you too." I give Gash a chin lift.

"Hey," he says when he sees me. "Meeting's about to start. Want a coffee?"

Gash, formally known as Lee, just got sworn in not long ago, but he still likes to do menial jobs that the prospects normally do. We can't kick the habit out of him. He's a good guy, and I have a lot of time for him, but I need something stronger than caffeine.

I shake my head. "I'm good."

"Who died?"

I shoot him a look.

He raises his hands in surrender. "Chill, man, I was just kiddin'."

Wrong choice of words. I run a hand through my hair. "Grab me a shot."

He grunts a laugh as Ginger shakes her head. "It's ten am," Gash tells me.

"Yeah, you grown a pussy since I saw you last?"

He cups his dick and shakes his head. "Nah, anaconda's still hangin'."

"Please, God no," Ginger says, slapping her forehead. She's probably old enough to be my grandma, but she's seen and heard it all. Her ol' man, Knuckles, has been hangin' around the club more and more lately, not that he's all that heavily involved anymore unless we're having a shindig or something big.

I roll my eyes as he snickers and reaches for the Jack, pouring me half a glass. I down it, wincing at the burn and hit him up for another.

"It's gotta be a woman," Ginger says, leaning on the bar. "It's always a woman that leads you to the bottle."

"When is it anything else?"

Gash points at me. "Said a mouthful there."

"Not that redhead, Stevie's sister?" Ginger continues, always alert and aware of anything going on with the boys.

"The very one."

She shakes her head again. "That's what happens when you jump right in the sack and don't get to know the woman. Let's hope she's not carrying silver bullets."

"When did you get so wise?"

"Always been wise, sugar," she tells me with a wink. "Nothin' can't be fixed with a little persuasion."

"It's persuasion that got me into this mess."

She shakes her head, turning to finish the coffees. "There's always sorry, honey."

"Maybe I'm not the one who has anything to be sorry about."

Gash snickers as I give him a look.

I push off the bar and walk toward the doors to the meeting room, which are wide open.

Colt is the new addition to the weekly meetings. Normally, it's longstanding and original members of the Executive Committee only. But Hutch has made a new position of Regional Officer, or RO for short. Being Steel has two roles in the club, Enforcer and Sergeant at Arms, his duties are more than most of us have. With things being so much busier lately at the club, Hutch wants more structure and to relieve Steel as much as possible.

As Road Captain, I handle all the club outings and trips. Gunner is the club Treasurer, who looks after the books and finances. While he might seem aloof and all over the place, he's great at making money and keeping track of it. Rubble is the Secretary and keeps track of all the members and dues owed to the club. And Brock being the Vice Prez can step in if Hutch is away or ever incapacitated.

Colt's new role will be reporting back to Prez about any new movements in town, carrying out duties that comply with our club's laws, and fulfilling any requests from Prez or any of us around the table. The middleman, so to speak.

While Steel manages the prospects entirely, Colt will now have a hand in taking some of the workload when there's a confrontation or problem with members that can be resolved without taking it higher. The next port of call would be Steel, then Brock and lastly Hutch if there is no resolution.

Being a small club, the chain of command is a little loose and not as strict as it is with bigger clubs. Steel and Hutch both like to know everything that is going on within the club at all times, but I suspect as Hutch is getting older, taking some of the petty problems away will help free him and Steel up a little.

Most of the prospects are pretty good but sometimes

they need to be slapped around like a little bitch to knock some sense into them.

Ginger enters with the coffees and takes them around the table. She stops beside me and places another bourbon down on the coaster in front of me.

I give her a wink.

"Thanks, darlin'," Hutch says as she leaves. "So we know we've got a problem. The question is, who the fuck is targeting us?"

"Better not be anythin' to do with the shit with Rubble," Steel grunts, looking down the table. "I didn't exactly enjoy the idea of bein' around the Vipers and the Sons shit the first time round."

The Vipers and the Sons of Phoenix Fury had unfinished business, all around the time when I got stabbed by the Fury's old Prez.

"If it were retaliation," Brock points out, "they wouldn't bother with petty shit like breakin' windows to prove a point. They'd tear gas the clubhouse."

Steel doesn't look convinced, but he's suspicious of everyone.

"Got footage of the premises. Trouble is, they know where the cameras are and they've got face masks on," Colt says, taking up residence opposite me, next to Gunner. "But I have an idea that might work."

"Shoot," Hutch says with a chin lift.

"We set up a sting, lure them in, and then wait to nail their asses. Then we'll know exactly who it is, and we can deal with it without involving the cops."

"That's not a bad idea," Rubble agrees. "The pigs aren't doin' shit to find out who it is. They took some fingerprints and that's it, not like the culprits are gonna leave any evidence layin' around, and they seem hellbent on makin' a mess, rather than actually stealin' shit."

"If they touch the Crow, they're dead," Hutch affirms. "I'm gonna get the prospects on it, night and day. Be good when Axton's here, as we need some solid muscle on-site for any shit goin' down. I know Stevie can hold her own, but a little brawn won't hurt as a deterrent."

Brock nods. "Steel and Colt can arrange the prospects. I'll debrief Axton. He's well and truly gunnin' for release day."

"You headin' up to Stradbroke?" Hutch asks.

"Yep. Bring him back same day."

"Think we should have a welcome party," Gunner puts in. "Gotta be rough spending that long in a concrete cell, watchin' your ass twenty-four-seven. Man's gonna need some pussy, too."

"Shit, yeah," I add, wincing at the idea of not having sex in ten years. "Ax could probably do with a beer or two and meet everyone at the same time."

Axton will be technically prospecting, but he won't be wearing the cut while he's at work. And I don't know how that's gonna fly because he's almost thirty. I doubt he's gonna like being told what to do. And, Stevie is his new boss.

I hope he likes takin' orders from a chick because Hutch has her up on a pedestal.

"I'll get Ginger and Summer to organize a get-together," Brock says. "The girls can organize a spit roast. Nothin' too fancy."

"He got a sled yet?" Steel gives Brock a chin lift.

"Yeah, I can lend him my old bike until he's back on his feet with his own wheels."
Not like you can join an M.C. without a set of wheels, temporary or not.

"Speakin' of which, need to discuss Nitro. Give him an ultimatum about joinin' us if he's gonna be hangin' around the club," Hutch says around the table. "Know he's been helpin' you out Rubble. We're all short-staffed, and I can use him at the Crow as security. But I've been thinkin' about puttin' him to work in the car and scrapyard, once the sale goes through."

Brock nods. "Could be good. He's good at fixin' shit. Not sure he's very customer focused, though."

A few chuckles go around the room. "Gears knows that place like the back of his hand. While he's still prospecting, I don't wanna give him too much responsibility to take control, but what does everyone think about Gash? He's just doin' odd jobs and shit right now. Seems like a waste,"

Hutch goes on.

"Probably not a bad idea. Nitro is strong; he could keep the yard clutter-free and tidy shit up. Gears could oversee sections, and they can both do the haulin' for deliveries back and forth from Mesa and Phoenix," Rubble puts in. "He's a good worker."

"Question is, does Nitro want in?" Steel asks, looking down the table. "Fucker's had long enough now to decide if he's a Rebel or if he's joinin' Smokey and the Sons of Fury."

"I'll talk to him," Rubble says.

"Send him in to see me," Hutch adds. "Brock and Bones can run it by Gears. Can be a trial run to see what he does with the responsibility, see how serious he is."

"Good plan," Gunner continues. "Especially if Nitro also wants to prove himself to the club. It's not a free ride, just because he's Lucy's brother and all."

Nods go round the table in agreement.

Hutch points at Colt. "You and Steel work out a game plan for the sting. Let me know what you come up with by this afternoon. I wanna set something up tonight."

Colt nods. "We'll hash some ideas out."

"Use Gash if you need to. He's stock takin' and doin' shit for Ginger. Since the prospects are out fixin' windows and shit, an extra pair of hands won't hurt. Bones and Gunner can join you later."

"What about us?" Brock thumbs to himself and Rubble.

"We're chopped liver now that we've got babies?"

Hutch sits back in his chair. "All I ever hear is Angel naggin' that you work too much and since your baby is less than a week old, it might be considered gentlemanly of me to let you off the hook." He turns to look at Rubble. "Then I got Lucy bustin' my balls because he's always out late, and she doesn't get enough time with him. Since you're both new fathers, I thought it might be nice to spend some quality time with your women," he grumbles.

"That's what got them into that mess in the first place," Gunner snickers. "Too much fuckin' quality time."

Hutch's gaze flicks to Guns. "When are you and Lily gonna get a bun in the oven? I'm not gonna be young forever."

"Let's not get crazy," Gunner says. "Got a little bit of freedom ahead of me before we start thinkin' 'bout that shit."

"Please God, do not let them reproduce," Steel mutters, looking up to the ceiling.

Hutch looks at me.

"Hey, don't look at me. I got nothin'," I say, holding my hands up.

Hutch bangs the gavel down. "I need somethin' stronger than coffee to get through any more of this shit."

Bones

BRACKEN RIDGE
REBELS
ARIZONA
M · C

CHAPTER 27

BONES

"Whoever it is has been watchin' and waitin'," Steel says, unimpressed. In fact, he looks ready to throttle someone. "Love to get my hands on the fuckers. It'll make what I did to Jack seem like a walk in the park." Nobody wants to relive that day, least of all Jack, but Steel is the hardest out of all of us.

"Seems like the timing couldn't be any more suspicious," Colt agrees as we watch the security footage. We've got a partial number plate, but I don't want to go to the cops just yet."

I scratch a hand through my beard. "So, the club's buying Jack out in the next couple of weeks, and there's bad blood there. I think it's a no brainer. They want to cause as much damage as possible in as little time."

"Seems about right. Just got word from Lily that the front of her salon got spray painted over last night." Steel grunts. "They didn't break any windows, but that's probably because the salon is in the main street and they only had limited time. Hers was the only place hit in the street, so they're definitely sending a message to BRMC."

"Jesus. Not good," I agree, liking the sound of Colt's sting plan more and more. "Sounds like we need to give them a taste of their own medicine. Don't like it they're now movin' on to the women. After the shit that went down with Lily last year at the salon, she doesn't need to be too scared to go to work again."

About a year back, Lily was attacked by a deranged woman in the salon who was out for revenge when the dude who drugged Lily didn't succeed in abducting her, thanks to Sienna's intervention. The woman was his sister, as far as I can remember. The guy was caught up in people smuggling and sex trafficking. When he got caught, he hung himself in jail before he could be prosecuted. Steel's – normally placid, wouldn't hurt a fly Pittie Lola – attacked the woman and kept her subdued until backup arrived.

Lily's the total opposite of Steel, but the one thing they have in common is they're both as tough as boots.

"She's gonna be fine. Gunner's piercing three days a week now, so he'll be there to keep watch. Need some more prospects. Jax is almost ready to be patched in, so only got Gears and Axton, when he arrives." Steel nods to Colt. "We can start recruitin', see who's new around town, who might be interested."

"Sounds like a plan," Colt agrees, and we continue to sit

in Steel's office, bouncing ideas around.

"I think Colt's idea about settin' a trap at the Stone Crow could be our most obvious next choice. I know Hutch doesn't want to lure them there, but let's face it, they've hit every one of our businesses except the clubhouse. It's only a matter of time." I suck in a breath, hoping that they don't hit anywhere else, but it seems inevitable.

Colt nods. "They seem to favor weekends, Friday or Saturday nights. Let's stick to that. I'll set up extra cameras and check all the alarms. We can camp out here and post Gash and a couple of the prospects at church; that way, it's halfway between the two. They can stay here tonight and keep watch until we set things up."

Steel flexes his hands like he's ready for a fight. "I'm so looking forward to this."

I give him a chin lift. "Me too. Been a while since we hauled some ass and smashed some skulls."

"In the meantime," Steel goes on, "I'll get Linc to see if he can tap into the main street cameras for town, where the street parking is. If they were dumb enough to pull up, then we may get lucky with a full plate number."

Linc is Steel's Go To guy when it comes to information he needs that fly's under the radar.

"I tend to think things like this only escalate," Colt says gravely. "They've gotten worse each time they've broken in somewhere across town, like they're gettin' desperate."

"Might be an idea to get Jax and Gears to watch the two goons we've put out of a job. It would make sense that they'd be slightly pissed that Jack's sellin' up, and they've now got no job at the yard," I add. "It can make a man do some crazy shit."

"Good idea," Steel agrees. "Hutch is meeting with Jack's realtor about the settlement. Seems like retirement can't come soon enough for the old bastard. That family ain't right in the head."

"Probably best off layin' a low profile," Colt says to me. "If shit goes south, it won't take much to see you back in prison."

"I'll be fine." I nod. "And thinkin' about it now, doesn't Jack have a son? Could be doin' his dad's dirty work for him. Just a thought."

Steel looks lost in thought. "Could very well have a point. Means we better watch him and hopefully catch whoever this is soon. Jenkins saw the damage done to Lily's, so she's had to report it. No way around it." He pulls out his phone. "I'll text Linc now. Soon as I have the footage from the main street cameras, I'll let you know."

Colt nods. "Sounds good."

I go to stand. I've got to get back to my parents, since it's been a few hours since I left. "If I can do anything before then, just gotta say."

"Appreciate it, brother," Steel says as Colt gives me a chin lift.

I jump on my sled and head home.

All the way there, I can't stop thinking about Kennedy. About how closed off she was earlier. It sounds like she's obviously had a traumatic experience, but how can she assume that she's the only one that's had a bad run in life.

I speed home, realizing I am reckless because if I get caught, I'll end up back in jail again. Maybe that wouldn't be a bad thing because it means Kennedy could come bail me out.

But would she? Or would she just let me rot in my cell this time around.

I don't get to find out because I don't hear from her for a whole week. No text message. No visits to check my community service. Nada.

I don't know if I'm to be pissed or worried, yet I also don't want to be the sap and cave first. In reality, I want to barge my way into her office and demand what's up her ass.

In her eyes, I don't have a right to feel anything because I'm a biker. I get the stigma, trust me, I wrote the damn book. What she doesn't know about me is that I do have all those emotions, even if I keep them closely guarded.

Being part of an M.C. comes with a lot of judgment, I get that. I get that she hasn't been around the club for any length of time. But I've never treated her like shit. I've never cussed at her unless it's when I'm fuckin' her and she's digging her nails into my back. I'd never even dream of laying a hand on her in vain. Yet, she has the right to treat me like I'm a neanderthal who shouldn't feel bad when she closes off and insults me. Well. I've got news for her, and it doesn't just involve me spankin' her ass for talking to me like that. It involves me potentially never seeing her again.

I drop by the Stone Crow to check on Stevie, at Hutch's request, on Friday while we wait for the cartons of alcohol to be delivered. Colt and Steel figure if these hooligans are watching, then this would be an easy haul for them to fuck shit up.

I personally cannot wait to see if they show up, so I get to go postal on their asses.

Stevie's polishing glasses at the bar, getting ready for the lunchtime rush.

"You all right, darlin'?" I give her chin lift as she greets me when I come through the back.

"Hi, Bones. I'm fine. You good?" She gives me a bright smile. Everyone loves Stevie because she looks like homemade sunshine, but she's got a mouth on her that nobody expects, if and when the time calls for it. I chuckle to myself when I think about where she gets that from.

If I'm tellin' the truth, I didn't mind dropping in because, hopefully, she'll inadvertently tell me what's goin' on with her sister.

"I'm all right. Waitin' for the alcohol delivery. Jax will be here soon to help offload, and Brock's collectin' Axton in the mornin'."

"It'll be good having him here," she agrees. "We're short-staffed as it is. Hopefully, he's a fast learner." She's the opposite of Kennedy too. Blonde. Bubbly. Lanky. And she doesn't have that air of sophistication about her that her sister does.

"You feelin' okay with Ax bein' here?"

She shrugs. "I had my reservations, but in the end, it isn't up to me. I trust Hutch and the club; he wouldn't put me in danger, and he's been good to me. Pays me well. I live rent-free. I haven't got much to complain about."

I nod. "Glad to hear it."

She reaches to put the clean glass back on the shelf. "So, did you stab my sister in the eye with a pencil or something?"

My eyebrows shoot up in surprise. "Why, did she say somethin'?"

Stevie shakes her head. "Not exactly, but she's been quiet this past week. It's not like her."

I rub my chin. "We had a fight."

She raises her eyebrows, but keeps polishing glasses. "So, you two are a thing?"

I lean on the side of the bar and run a hand through my hair. "I don't fuckin' know what we are. It was just a fling at first, just havin' a bit of fun, or that's what I thought. Then she told my mom she was married and that her husband died. When I questioned her about it, she got all cold and hostile."

Stevie glances up at me, and I know I've struck a chord. "Yeah, she's very sensitive about that. It's still pretty raw, even though it's been over two years."

"I get that, but the thing is, she brought it up. When I tried to talk to her, she told me I couldn't possibly understand what it's like and shut me down. Kinda got the feelin' that she thinks I'm incapable of having any emotions."

Stevie winces. "It's a hard limit for her. She honestly has a hard time dealing with it."

So do I. Not that she'd know that. "Yeah, I get it. I don't expect her to tell me shit just because I asked, but it's like she's completely shut me out. If you haven't noticed already, I'm really diggin' your sister, and I don't know what to do about it."

Stevie stares at me for a few moments before realizing I'm serious. And I sound like an absolute pussy.

"Hey, don't feel bad about it. This is what K does. She tends to shut down and go into self-preservation mode when she's tested or is uncomfortable. She's good at it."

"I've noticed," I mutter.

"In the courtroom or in a legal battle, she can hold her own, skin you alive with words, but when it comes to *him,* she punishes herself."

"Why, it isn't like it was her fault. She stuck by him;

she's got nothin' to feel bad about."

Stevie shakes her head. "It's not my story to tell, Bones. I'm sorry. But talk to her. I know she likes you a lot. As much as she keeps shit to herself, she's been the happiest I've seen her in years. Whatever it is you two have been up to"—she gives me a pointed look—"I'd say, keep doing more of that. She's miserable this week, so that's got to mean something."

I give her a half smile. I know she's trying to cheer me up, but I'm still mad. Though, hearing she's miserable doesn't sit well with me. And I want more.

I want more than just a quick fuck on a Friday night, sneaking around, not being able to throw my arm around her when I want, not being able to go meet her for lunch in case any of her colleagues or clients see us together because I wear leather patches. Fuck that shit.

She's either with me or she's not. Maybe I'm tired of bein' a dirty little secret.

"I don't know about that. I haven't heard from her all week. I don't think she appreciated me droppin' by her home after takin' off the way I did."

She smiles kindly. "My sister is a lot, Bones. I'm gonna be straight with you. I love her a lot, she's my best friend, and we're protective of each other. But you're a good man. I've seen you around the club and how you treat the women, and I think you're good for each other. My take on it is this, *show* her, rather than *tell* her. And stand up to her; it's what she needs."

I frown at her words as Nitro comes through the front doors, and I give him a chin lift as I shift off the bar.

"You open yet?" he asks Stevie.

"Just about to," Stevie says. "What can I get ya?"

"Cold beer would be great."

I glance at him. "What's got you all flustered? You meet a chick in the back alley?"

He gives me a smile. "Nothin' that exciting. Just doin' a job for Rubble, then I gotta meet with Hutch."

I give him a chin lift. This could be his lucky day, after all.

"Heads up, you might wanna be thinkin' clearly between now and church about what your intending plans are with the Rebels."

"Been thinking about it a lot. I need to plant some roots, can't keep flyin' by the seat of my pants forever. Shit gets old."

Stevie returns with his beer, and he hands her a bill, telling her to keep the change.

She smiles and takes off to open the front doors.

"You're tellin' me. Lucy's been enjoyin' havin' you around. Nice for her to have that after all the shit that went down and the years you both missed out on."

He's a mysterious dude, a bit of a dark horse, but I don't dislike him. He keeps to himself a lot, not that there's anything wrong with that. All of us here at the club, besides maybe Gears, being the newest member, have known each other a long time. There is something about him, though. He has this kind of quirky vibe about him that's a cross between bohemian and cowboy.

"She deserves to be happy; she's always been a good sister. Lotta regrets, bro, but I'm here to rectify them. Find myself a good woman and hopefully settle down," he says. I raise my eyebrows in surprise. It's not like I've really taken a lot of notice of his comings and goings – aside from the time he made a pass at Kennedy, then I noticed.

"Can't turn tricks forever," I say, as it seems like he might need the moral support. "We're all more like family than a club; we've got each other's backs. I know some shit went down in the past with the Fury, but we run a tight ship here. No illegal shit, obviously, but we help each other out. In fact, we're gonna do a stakeout tonight to try to catch who's been sendin' a message to the club. Can come along, if you want."

He nods. "Sounds like an idea. Does it mean I get to break somethin' if we catch them?"

"Freakin' A." I laugh. "You'll have to get past Steel first. He gets first call on who gets pulverized and how."

He grunts. "Don't wanna mess with the big guy."

"Definitely not."

Both our heads turn as a group of girls from the hospital roll through the door, and Stevie stops to talk to them.

One has scrubs on while the others have white nurse's uniforms on.

"Fuck, those uniforms are hot," Nitro mutters.

"Can say that again."

The one in scrubs, I realize, is the new doctor, Frankie. She delivered Lucy and Angel's babies. She laughs at something Stevie says and then she turns her head our way.

She's got a flowing, auburn-colored ponytail and long legs that seem to go for miles.

She does a double take when she sees Nitro staring at her. I chuckle into my fist.

"See you haven't met Frankie yet," I mutter as she gives us a small wave.

I give her one back as Nitro just nods his head.

"Frankie?"

"Yeah, she's Lucy's baby doctor."

"Guess that's where I know the name from then. She seems a little familiar."

We watch as she follows the other girls over into the dining area, and one of the waitresses shows them to a table.

Stevie comes back, swinging a rag over her shoulder as she shakes her head at us.

"Good to see the local community coming together over lunch," I muse, looking back at her.

"Right, well, now the Crow isn't a cesspit, we tend to attract better clientele. The Friday lunch special is the hottest ticket in town since we reopened." She looks down at her watch. "And my part-timer's late. Another great start to the day."

Poor Stevie. Everyone is feeling the pinch at the moment with a shortage of good, reliable staff. Maybe Gears or Nitro may be better suited over here. Then again, they'd never get any work done if that's the caliber of clientele the Stone Crow's now sporting.

Nitro is still looking over there.

"You wanna go join 'em?" I laugh.

He turns back to me. "Could swear I've met her before," he says, then shakes it off. "Must've been in my dreams, sure I'd remember a pair of legs like that."

"Not like you'd forget."

"Definitely not."

I check the time on my phone. "I gotta go. If you wanna come back tonight, shoot me a text later."

"Gotcha."

We fist pump, and I holler out to Stevie as I head out back.

I can't say I got any closer to knowing what the fuck's up with Kennedy. It's not like I don't wanna see her again, but this is all new territory for me.

I've never thought twice about an ol' lady, for fuck's sake, but now she's got me questioning everything I know and what I thought I wanted.

I can't work out whether I'm a stupid motherfucker

who's a glutton for punishment, or if should I just go out and get what I want.

She made it pretty clear this was just casual, and so did I.

But things have changed now.

I don't need to rationalize anything to anyone, much less to myself, but I know I don't want her to be with anyone else. I know I would rip some fucker's throat out if they even so much as looked at her. That's gotta mean something.

Each time I try and convince myself to forget her, I know I can't. I want to wrap her in my arms and kiss those pretty, soft lips. Get under her skin, but for the right reasons, not like what I've been doing.

Then I remember that in her eyes, I'm just a dirty biker. Someone she can dispose of when she's done. Someone who isn't capable of having feelings or emotions, because I'm in an M.C. I've never been an emotional kinda guy, but this woman has had me in a spin for the better part of six months. And it's been a long week since I was in her bed, holding her close, listening to her laugh.

She's cast a spell on me that can't be ignored.

I'm fucked if I walk away, and I'm fucked if I don't.

If this isn't real and what I'm feelin' is all just bullshit, then why do I yet again ache that pain in my chest? The one that makes it hard to breathe when I think about her takin' up with some other guy. When I think about what we could be together if we were to seriously give this a shot.

Trouble is, I've no idea what she's thinkin', or if her headspace is anywhere close to what mine is.

From the deafening silence, I'd say that I've got my answer.

BRACKEN RIDGE
REBELS
ARIZONA
M · C

CHAPTER 22

KENNEDY

It's been five long, horrible days without hearing from Bones. Each time I try to pick up the phone, everything just sounds so wrong. I never meant to insult him or make him feel bad, but inadvertently, I did.

I went back to being my usual self and shut him out. I've been going over and over things in my mind, and I don't know how to fix this.

Last night, I heard the rumble of a loud Harley Davidson driving down my street. I didn't need to look out of the window to know it was him. Driving past my place, idling at the sidewalk, but he never came up.

I wanted him to. I would have gladly taken him back in my arms, and my bed.

I would have loved nothing more than for him to park his motorcycle, sneak into my room, and take me like he did the first time. It was so raw, so intense, like there was an inferno between us that couldn't be doused.

I've never had that before, and I loved every fucking

minute of it.

When I arrive at work Friday, ready to start my day, I do not expect to find the office completely vandalized with the door kicked-in and the windows smashed.

Amelia stands next to me when she arrives and gasps in shock.

"Oh my God," I whisper-shout. Glass is smashed all over the front walkway, and it looks like the inside of the reception area has been ransacked.

"We need to call Brock," Amelia says.

"No, I need to call the police," I reply, ignoring her, pulling out my phone as I dial 911 and give the operator the rundown and the street address.

When I hang up, Amelia still has her hand over her mouth. "Who would do this?" she whispers.

"Assholes," I mutter. "This is un-fucking-believable."

It's devastating. My beautiful office front is completely destroyed. The person who took the call told me not to go inside or touch anything so they can fingerprint and look around.

We stand out the front and in less than fifteen minutes, a police car pulls up alongside my car.

"I'm Officer Jenkins, and this is Officer Peters," the larger of the two cops says as I give them a nod. "We'll need to fingerprint and take a look inside before you can enter the premises, ma'am."

"Sure." I nod.

"There has been a spate of break-ins over this past week," he goes on. "So it could very well be related."

When I glance over to the door, I see the reception desk ransacked and Amelia's desk turned over, files strewn and scattered everywhere.

What a fucking mess. I shake my head just looking at it because I have no words.

"What the fuck happened?" asks a voice from behind us. Amelia and I both turn and see Nitro standing behind us, assessing the damage.

"Looks like someone decided to ransack my office," I sigh, my anger about at its boiling point. I don't know the extent of it yet. We haven't been allowed back in.

"Better stay put, let them do their job."

"We'll have to reschedule all the appointments," I mutter to Amelia, pressing my hand against my forehead at the amount of work we now have to do.

"It's fine. I'll deal with it," Amelia reassures me.

"I'd be canceling the rest of your day," Nitro puts in helpfully. "Looks like it's gonna take awhile to clean this shit up." He turns and walks away, holding the phone to his ear.

I try not to feel defeated, but this is exactly what I don't need.

Not even three minutes later, I hear the very distinct sound of bikes rumbling in the distance. Not just one, but by the sounds of it, more like an entire tribe.

I groan as I turn to look at Amelia, and she just shrugs. It looks like the cavalry is on their way.

What amazes me most about Amelia is how innocent she is. Her eldest brother is the Vice President of the Rebels and a tough as nails dude who you wouldn't mess with in a dark alley, and her other brother has just done a ten-year stint in Stradbroke.

You'd think she'd be hardened and tough, like they are, but to be honest, it couldn't be further from the truth. I mean, she tells it like it is and she can be a little wild, but there's not a mean bone in her body.

"Nitro called them, right?" I groan.

"I sent Brock a text." Amelia shrugs.

I turn and give her a look. "Well, it's a police matter now."

"I know that, but they'd want to know what's going on. Anyway, I'm Brock's sister and you're with Bones."

"I'm not *with* Bones," I whisper-shout.

She frowns. "Okaaay."

"You don't have to say it like that."

"Like what?" she defends.

"Like you don't believe me."

"I didn't mean you're *with* him. I meant, you're involved by association."

I frown a whole lot more. "What the hell is that supposed to mean?"

Involved by association?

This is *my* office. I know Amelia is Brock's sister, but it has nothing to do with the club.

Jenkins and the other officer look up the street upon hearing the sound of the bikes getting closer, then Jenkins says something to Peters, and he nods.

"It means what you think it means. There's no escaping it. You chose to be the representing attorney for Kirsty Hutchinson, and therefore, you're now on retainer. You bailed Bones out, and you're the club's attorney, one way or the other. They protect what's theirs."

I stare at her with a newfound realization. *Holy crap balls.*

It was decent of Nitro to stop; he lounges against his motorcycle as he looks over at us.

"I don't even know where to begin answering any of that," I say, rubbing my temples.

"That Nitro guy is kinda cute," Amelia whispers, ignoring me.

I have to agree, he is pretty hot. His shoulder length dark hair hangs around his face as he tucks it behind his ears. He's broody and has an air of mystery about him.

"Is he staying in town or going back to Phoenix?"

"I don't know," Amelia says. "I heard from Deanna that Hutch called him to the clubhouse to discuss some business, and Hutch doesn't just call you out to church for no good reason. Could be he's going to be patched in."

"Like an initiation?" I snort.

She smiles and turns her gaze back to mine. "Snicker all you want, but they fix what's wrong in this town quicker than the cops can."

"I don't want to hear any of this," I reply. "So you're either going to stop talking, or I'm going to jam my fingers in my ears and say *la la la.*"

I don't want to face Bones, not like this.

I'm not sure when this turned from fun into a disaster, or why talking about anything to do with Dean and that whole situation is a hard limit.

Somewhere in the mix, my feelings have gotten in the way. It's like I have no control over my emotions. I've only been sleeping with him for a few weeks.

I barely know the guy.

Yet, I felt fine enough to tell his mother, who I'd only just met, all about my past. I felt fine to fall into his bed without thinking about the consequences, and I sure as hell felt fine about continuing this thing that we have between us, which feels like the most natural thing in the world.

All of a sudden, four loud, obnoxious motorcycles roll into the lot.

Bones is clad in his usual sleeveless motorcycle jacket with a plaid long sleeved button-up shirt underneath, except it's not done all the way. My eyes wander down his body to his torso, his tattoos peeking out as he parks and pulls his helmet off. He's got a bandana on, tied around his head like a total badass. I swallow hard. My attraction for him hasn't wavered, it seems.

Next to him are Steel, Brock, Gash, and Gears.

But Bones is a sight for sore eyes. My stomach flutters with nervous little butterflies as he looks across the throng of people now gathered, and we make eye contact.

I wish I could tell him that I didn't mean what I said, that I'm sorry. I tend to push people away if they get too close. They never get to see the heart of me because sometimes I'm not even aware of it myself.

I fucked up. I know I did. I just hope he doesn't hate me for it.

"Kennedy!" Bones calls, as he rushes toward me, concern in his eyes as he approaches. His hands cup my face as he looks me over, and I feel myself relaxing into his touch. "Are you all right?"

"Yes," I whisper, sounding more vulnerable than I ever have before. "I'm fine. My office got totaled. I wasn't here when it happened."

He looks toward the office doors and frowns.

"Who called them?" Brock nods toward the cops as he slings a meaty arm around Amelia.

Amelia flicks her head toward me as Brock frowns. "I don't know why I'm getting all the pouty faces and furrowed brows," I snap. "That's what normal law-abiding citizens do when they get broken into."

I don't add that I'm not going to run to Bones or the club every time I have problems, even if I am *involved by association*. It *is* what normal people do in these types of situations, isn't it?

Bones kisses the top of my head, and it douses the fire in a matter of seconds. I look up at him, astonished. He pulls me away from the others so we can talk in private.

"Shoulda called me first," he says in a low voice.

"I didn't think we were speaking," I fire back.

"Trust you to have a smart answer," he mutters. "Can't just put it aside when you're in trouble, can you?"

"Does this have something to do with the break-in at the junkyard, and at Rubble and Steel's?"

"We assume so, but don't know for sure yet. Workin' on it. You got an alarm or a camera?"

I shake my head. "I moved to a small, quiet town because I thought it was safe."

"It is safe, but there are opportunists in any town, anywhere, and you should have better security. I'll see to it."

I put my hands on my hips. "I don't need you to see to it, Bones."

He frowns. "Why not?"

"I don't really have anything of value here, except the computers and my client files."

"You could've been in there when these

motherfuckers struck."

That's not the point, but his concern is kinda unnerving. "But we weren't."

He leans toward my ear, his beard tickling the side of my face as I take in his masculine scent and his growly voice. "You still fightin' with me, *Ms. Hart?*"

I look down at the ground. "Bones," I whisper back. "I haven't heard from you all week. You completely ghosted me. What am I supposed to think? I'm sorry I shut down, okay? I really feel bad about it, but that's no excuse to dump me off, and then charge away like a bat out of hell and that's it."

He pulls back and stares at me, his lips twitching tightly. "I didn't dump you anywhere. Last time I checked, you had a cell phone too. You could've called me if you were feeling so bad about it." He gets right in my face as he says the next part. "It's not over, Kennedy. None of this is over until I say it's over. You hear me?"

My stupid heart flutters, even though it's a traitor.

I poke him in the chest but lower my voice. "You can't just come here and make it all okay by looking at me like that, making your demands and going all alpha on me."

He looks down at the offending finger and then smirks. "Least you're touchin' me, babe. That's better than the alternative. And I don't seem to remember you caring about my demands when you rode my face."

My eyes go wide. "Jesus, Bones."

"You know it's true."

I look down at my feet. It bothers me that he thinks I don't care about him, or that he isn't enough for me.

"Listen, I've not been sleeping really well," I say, desperate to get it off my chest. "But I'm sorry I snapped at you about not being able to understand. That was awfully presumptuous of me and so very wrong."

He stares at me, his features rigid. Something crosses his eyes. "I just wish you'd open up to me. I, of all people, can understand more than you know, Kennedy. You're not the only one who's lost someone close to you." He's using my first name, meaning he's deadly serious.

I feel a tight knot it my chest. "You?"

He pushes my hair back off my face. "I don't wanna get into it here," he says. "Later. But know this, I'm frustrated because you told my mom things that I don't even know, and that's on me. I should have asked. I should have gotten to know you better. I should be the one askin' those things instead of pretending we're just fuckin' and nothin' else. And I need you to stop fightin' with me, unless it's in the bedroom, but you'll be tied up so it won't matter, I guess."

He cradles one side of my face. He looks so… *vulnerable.* Then a smirk appears as I realize what he just said.

"I just expected a one-night thing. A good time. Great sex. Maybe a few laughs. But not to feel like my world has crashed down around me because we fit together so well."

"So, what's the problem?"

"I don't actually know. I guess I need to figure some shit out, and that starts by taking things slow and not fucking it up."

It's not like he thinks it is. I'm not ashamed to be with him, even if at first him being in the Rebels M.C. was a cause for concern. He's told me before I'm out of his league, but that isn't true.

Whatever bad things he's thinking, he's wrong. I'm the one with issues. I'm the one who carries the past around deep inside me, unable to let go. The minute I feel happy about anything, I push it away, like I don't deserve it.

I have no right to be mad with him when I made no effort to ask him one thing about himself or his family either. It's hard for me to admit, but it's true. I haven't really taken any of it seriously.

"I guess you do."

I could get lost in the way he looks at me. His face is utter perfection and so very easy to love. *Love?*

"I never wanted to fall again, Bones. I wanted to concentrate on my career and make a name for myself. Set up my own business, have a career, and make a life I can be proud of.

I never once thought about having a man in that equation. A deep part of me doesn't ever want to go there again because I failed in my last marriage."

"It's not a failure, babe," he says, tenderly. "All of it is just life. Nothin' is perfect, nothin'. You can only take each day as it comes. I'm no fuckin' expert on any of this shit, but I don't let it worry me. Day by day, that's all you gotta do."

I'd never want to fail Bones. That scares me because I don't even know him, yet it feels so very real.

His deep honey colored eyes on me make me want to die. Sometimes it feels like he looks right into my soul.

"I guess I've got some thinking to do then, don't I?"

He gives me a chin lift. "I guess you do."

I swallow hard as I assess his face. He's so endearing to me that I feel like a first-class bitch forever doubting him.

"Amelia said that you got called because I'm involved by association," I say out of nowhere, staring at him. "What does that mean exactly?"

"You know what it means."

"That I'm on retainer for the club as well?"

"With Kirsty you are, but it's not *just* that."

I smile. "Did anyone ever tell you that you talk in riddles?"

He smirks back. "Says the lawyer with the smart mouth."

"You're not going to pound your chest now, are you?"

He shakes his head. "I don't think it would do me much good."

Jenkins comes over and interrupts us. He nods at Bones and gets a chin lift in return.

"We've done all we can do here. We took some prints from the door, but it will be hard to determine." He looks over at Bones. "Lily's salon also got defaced last night. Got anything going on that I should know about?"

"Trust me, I wish I knew," Bones says. "Whoever they are, though, it was a pretty cowardly dumb fuck move to begin with. They obviously don't wanna fight fair."

Jenkins looks like he disapproves. "Ring your insurance, then get this cleaned up. I'll send you a copy of the police report," he says to me.

"Thanks," I mutter, dreading having to come to fix all of this.

When he walks away, Bones turns back to me. "Wish you hadn't involved him," he mutters.

I raise a brow. "I'm an attorney. I abide by the law. Like I said before, if I get broken into, I call the cops, so get used to it."

His lips twitch. "You're goin' the right way about gettin' a spankin'."

"This isn't funny."

"Does it look like I'm laughin'?"

"What isn't normal is calling on the local motorcycle club to come and sort out my problems."

He shakes his head, adding an eye roll in for good measure. "One thing you'll learn if you stick around here long enough is, in Bracken Ridge, we're a family. We help each other out. It's not about me or anyone tryin' to take over," he says. "But you can't clean all this shit up yourself.

I'll send the prospects over and get the glazier organized to come by and fit new glass."

"That's kind of you," I reply. It's not like I'm going to refuse help when it's offered. "I literally have a whole entire building to put back together."

He holds my chin, staking his claim. "I'll find them, and when I do, they'll wish they were never born."

"I don't like this," I whisper. "It makes me uneasy."

"It's gonna be okay. I promise. You don't have to worry about anything, and…" he goes on, intercepting my objection. "You need to learn to let others help you once in a while."

I know he's right, but relying on other people isn't what I'm used to, and I know that I have to get better at it. My head's all over the place right now. I can't think straight.

I glance over his shoulder, and Steel is looking over at us, concern on his face.

"Steel is looking at us," I mutter.

Bones's lips twitch again. "Who cares?"

"I think he thinks we're fighting."

"He's makin' sure you're okay. Like I said, it's what we do."

Steel, by far, towers over all of them, with Brock coming in as a close second. And being the enforcer of the club, I've heard it means he keeps everything in line with safety and security. I mean, I certainly wouldn't mess with him.

"You're a good club," I say quietly. "I can see that, and I can feel it. It's like a family, one who sticks by one another. I do appreciate you coming, even though the cops…"

He places a finger over my lips to quieten me. "How about you give me some sugar and shut that pretty little mouth of yours up?"

I shake my head, though his dirty talk goes straight to my pussy because I remember how I had him in that pretty little mouth of mine and how good it felt.

"Not in front of everyone." I don't even get the words out as his lips crash onto mine.

It's harsh, brutal, and sensual all rolled into one. Every bone in my body lights on fire at his slightest touch. His lips alone send me to oblivion.

When he pulls back, we're panting.

"Wanna see you tonight," he mumbles against my lips.

"I want that," I agree.

"Gonna give it to you so fuckin' hard."

"I want that too."

"Your ass is mine."

I swallow hard. "Bones…"

"And if you're not naked with those hot lawyer fuck-me-glasses on, I'll put you across my knee first."

"Don't be late, then," I whisper back. Forgetting about all this shit might just be the medicine I need. "I'll be waiting." He gives me a knowing smile, and I want to just jump on the back of his motorcycle and disappear from all the chaos.

Patience. I tell myself. *It's all going to be okay.*

I only hope it's true.

Bones

BRACKEN RIDGE
REBELS
ARIZONA
M · C

CHAPTER 23

BONES

I don't get to go to my girl's bed and wrap myself around her and bury my aching dick into her sweetness. Instead, I'm fuckin' staking out the Stone Crow, waiting for an attack that may never come.

Nitro sits opposite me, and as we're outside, I'm freezing my balls off.

Steel and Colt wait inside, and Gash keeps watch by the back wall, just in case they decide to jump the fence. And that's a big *if*. Nobody knows if they're comin', but we can't take the risk of havin' the place unmanned. They slit their own throats when they decided to fuck with Lily and Kennedy.

Tomorrow is the welcome home party for Axton, so it's gonna be a fuckin' shitshow if we don't get these bastards tonight. The fact they're now goin' after club girls means this is personal. And Hutch isn't gonna let anyone get away with that shit, not on his watch.

"How'd it go today?" I give Nitro a chin lift, referring to his earlier conversation with Hutch.

We're all on board with him coming to the club. The question is, does he want to?

"Good, actually. I guess there was already a majority vote at the table about my joinin' the club without prospecting as long as I can prove my worth, and for that, I feel grateful."

Kinda nice and unexpected. "Appreciate that."

"Hutch also mentioned that he'd offer me employment, once the car and scrapyard goes through. I guess you could say I owe this club a lot. Seems like I landed on my feet, so it's a no-brainer, one I can't pass up."

I slap him on the back. "Nice goin', brother, glad to have you in the club. Will get Colt to sort your patches and cut."

He gives me a chin lift. The fucker doesn't smile a lot, but his eyes crinkle ever so slightly.

Ever since he shot Tex in front of me and Lucy, I guess you could say we've kinda shared a bit of a bond. Long as he keeps his eyes off Kennedy when she's around the club, we shouldn't have any beef. That's my only requirement.

Despite the fact I don't know what Kennedy and I are, that doesn't mean anyone else gets to have a poke. Over my dead body.

"Lookin' forward to it. Gotta find me a place to crash, can't stay at church forever."

"Well, you're lucky right now there's only two prospects up there, and Gash, but he's lookin' to move out.

Maybe you could share a rental?"

"Could be worth askin'."

Property is pretty scarce these days with the new subdivision being highly sought after. The town is still fairly small but has still grown some over the years. I hope it never gets so busy that you gotta look over your shoulder. I moved to a small town for a reason, and I like it here.

I like it even better knowing that Kennedy has bought her apartment and opened her own business. It means she's planting some roots. I never thought I wanted any of that shit until she showed up and turned my world upside down.

Now I feel like a fuckin' schmuck for ribbing Steel, Brock, Gunner, and Colt. Here I was thinking they were just pussy-whipped – now I know what I was missing out on.

And that's exactly how it happens. They sneak up on you, into your life, get under your skin. *Women.*

They make you fuckin' crazy, but I can't deny the thump in my chest whenever she enters a room or whenever I hear her name. She's like a siren, calling to me, and I'm a sucker because when it comes to her, I have literally zero control.

And I also need to tell her about my past, about Abbey. *I have to...*

"He'd be your best bet. He's not a troublemaker, and he's got a good head on his shoulders, unless you're lookin' for a party house, then I'd suggest stayin' at church."

He shakes his head. "Kinda think my partyin' days are

over. I started pretty young, and I've done it all. Could've written the whole damn book."

I grin. "Gets like that. We still have some kickass parties, plenty of chicks, plenty of grub and live music. Don't mean you gotta get shitfaced."

"I've probably been in the life too long, feel like an old fuckin' man sometimes," he goes on. "Seen too much shit. Sad as it sounds, I need some fuckin' peace and quiet to gather my thoughts, get life back on track instead of bein' stuck in a rut. Seems like a nice place to do it. I've got Lucy now too, as well as the club."

"Glad you two found one another again," I say, knowing how much Lucy feels about him and what they've been through together. "I know only too well that shit gets even more tiresome when you get older. See these gray hairs?" I point to my head, and he chuckles. "All women-related." He turns to look at me. "Ain't got no gray hairs, thank fuck."

"They'll come. Don't worry about that. Hang around the women of this club a little longer, especially that sister of yours, and you'll know what I mean."

"Chicks are the same everywhere," he muses, with that twinkle in his eye that makes me wonder if he ever had a girl and lost her. He seems like the broody type. But it's not like we're gonna chat about it.

"You said a mouthful there, brother."

"We got a lot to catch up on, me and Luce, but we'll get

there."

"I know she never stopped yappin' on about you over the years, *Adam* this and *Adam* that. Wish my sister cared as much."

"You two don't talk?"

"Nah, man. My other sister, Abbey, she died when I was young. We were close, but Caitlyn and I don't exactly see eye-to-eye."

"I'm sorry, dude, about Abbey. Shit's gotta be rough."

"Damn straight. Fucked if I know how this life shit works."

"All I know is it's fuckin' hard, bro," he goes on. "Just gotta live each day how you wanna live it. Tired of doin' what others want me to do. It's why I'm here, to start fresh."

"Good enough reason," I say, feeling his sincerity, and frankly, it shocks me a bit. He's always so closed and guarded, doesn't let anyone in. I'm glad he feels comfortable around me enough to share it. "And livin' here is the best. You'll get to go on club runs too, not that I'm meant to be drivin' anywhere at the moment."

He gives me a chin lift. "So, are you and that lawyer chick gettin' it on?"

"Got that right and then some. Never expected it to be more, but it happened."

"Didn't realize. The night I saw her at church…"

"Glad we had this conversation, then."
He chuckles. "Plenty of other fish in the sea. The club seems

to attract a decent amount of nice chicks."

"You seen the new chef, Roxy?"

"Nah, man, but that new doctor in town is fuckin' hot. Frankie, right?"

I chuckle. "Oh, yeah, trouble with datin' a chick who works with pregnant women all day long is that they know more about how vaginas work than we ever will."

He laughs out loud, then covers his mouth with one arm. "You fuckin' kill me. They're probably always gonna know more, bein' they're the ones with the pussies, bro."

"Just sayin', she'll tell you where it's at, if you're not hittin' the mark and shit."

"Don't need to tell me. I hit the mark just fine," he says, rubbing his eyes. "Though, I'm okay with a chick takin' a little initiative, long as I get to ride it home in the end."

At least conversation is easy with him, that's a pleasant surprise, and he's opened up a little bit more. Lucy said he was always quiet growing up, as the pair of them didn't have the greatest of upbringings.

"Got that right."

Two hours go by, and nothing happens with anyone trying to break in.

It's three in the morning by the time we call it a night. Steel keeps Gears and Jax on the night shift in case anything happens in the wee hours. The junkyard is quiet, and so is Steel's neck of the woods. And while I'm glad they haven't struck the Stone Crow; it still leaves me uneasy.

The random attacks have gotten steadily worse over the last week. It's almost like whoever the fuck it is seems to be holdin' out. I fuckin' hope not. And the pigs have done nothing and found fuck all.

I don't dislike Jenkins, but seriously, the PD around here leaves a lot to be desired.

Thinking about Kennedy's office makes my blood boil. Her office got cleaned up and the glaziers replaced all the glass, but I know she's shaken. So much so, I told her to stay at mine tonight. I need her in my bed. I need her so fuckin' close. I don't care what differences we have. For now, we can put those aside, as long as she's safe.

When I get home, I rip my shirt off, then my jeans, and wander into my bedroom.

A mass of long, red hair splays out over my pillow, and I take a moment to admire her beauty in the dark light. She's fuckin' stunning at every which turn.

There is no greater feeling than seeing her in my bed, waiting for me, even though she's fast asleep. The fact that she came and stayed, that means everything to me.

I take a quick shower. Fuck knows I'm not heading into bed with my girl, stinking of dirt, grease, and oil. When I step out, dropping my towel on the floor, she stirs as I approach the bed.

"Bones?" she whispers.

Who else would it be in my house?

"Yeah, baby."

She pats the mattress next to her as I lift the duvet and climb under. I wrap my arms around her as we spoon. Her warm body feels like Heaven, with her ass pressing into me as I take in her scent. It's like some kind of flower, soft and delicate.

What this woman does to me so easily...

I'd love nothing more than to roll her over and devour her beautiful, naked body, but I'm not as selfish as some people might like to believe. I know she's tired, and it's been a long, stressful day.

I nuzzle my nose into her hair. "I don't want you to ever fuckin' ghost me again," I whisper in her ear. "Never."

She wiggles her ass against me as she murmurs something incoherent. That does nothing at all for the hard on I'm already sporting. I want to devour her so fuckin' much, but lying here like this is just as good as the sex.

She ignores me and murmurs. "How did it go tonight?"

"No go." I kiss her head.

"Bones?"

"Yeah, babe."

"We need to talk, about the fight we had."

"Know it, been on my mind all fuckin' weeklong, don't like not bein' able to see you." The words hang in the air and I know she's thinking about it.

"Does what we fought about have anything to do with that tattoo across your heart?" She asks, her voice barely a whisper.

I swallow hard.

"Perceptive," I mutter.

I have Abbey's name tattooed across my chest, and clearly, she's noticed. She probably thinks it's an ex-girlfriend.

"You don't have to talk about it, if you don't want to," she adds. "I know some things are hard to speak about."

I kiss her again. "Abbey was my sister," I say, the words feel lodged in my throat. "She…she died when she was ten." *Fuck.* Since talking to Nitro about it, it's brought it all to the surface. But I need to get it off my chest.

"Bones, I'm so sorry." She turns in my arms to face me, her hands reaching out for me.

"She had a rare form of leukemia. She fought hard, she was so strong for so long, but in the end, she was too weak to take any more chemo. It took her, after a long, horrible battle in and out of the hospital, it turned my dad gray overnight, it recked all of us for a long time. My other sister Caitlyn and I have been at odds ever since."

I swallow hard, my throat feels like it's thickening as I continue. "It's taken a long time to come to terms with it," I go on. "Wonderin' why her. Why not me? She was a little kid who never ever got to live her life, never got to grow up and be somethin', and those that loved her got to see her fade away. It's fucked."

She places her hand over my heart. "That must have been so awful for you, going through that, and your parents…"

"It was the worst time for everyone, I was a teenager when it happened. After she died, I became mixed up and confused, I went off the rails for a while. I couldn't deal with her bein' gone and seein' my parents so sad all the time, they were completely devastated and blamed themselves, it ate me up."

She stares at me, her eyes cloud over.

"And after a while of gettin' into trouble and causin' them more stress, I decided to turn my life around. I went into the military after graduation, the kind of discipline it offered seemed really good for me at the time. I needed it. I needed somethin' to focus my anger on and that helped, at least for a while."

"You must miss her," she whispers. "What was she like?"

"Every single fuckin' day." I stare at the ceiling. "She was smart and had a kick ass sense of humor. Sometimes I think I'm gonna forget her, you know? We only had ten years; it wasn't enough fuckin' time." Sometimes the gap in my heart doesn't seem to get any smaller. It's horse shit about time healing all wounds.

We're all broken, I've come to realize this, in some way, shape or form. We just have to live with brokenness and find the will to keep moving forward.

"Life's so fickle," she agrees. "Time should stop when

you go through grief, but it doesn't. Every day feels like a chore, like it may never actually end, and then you feel selfish because it didn't happen to you; it happened to someone you love and you couldn't stop it."

My eyes flick to hers as she snuggles into my shoulder.

"You're right. After the military I realized that I'd spent the last ten years or more takin' life too fuckin' seriously," I go on. "I didn't know how to have fun anymore. I was meticulous in everything I did, but I guess I just wanted to live like a normal person and not be tied down to a regime anymore. I was stuck in a box for a long time and wanted to break out of that whole mindset. I wasn't happy, so I changed it, and I left. It feels like every time I'm unhappy about somethin' stupid or inconsequential, I think about Abbey and what she'd give for another day, that's why I guess you could say I'm upbeat most of the time and kid around a lot. Life's too short to take it so seriously."

Her hand slowly rubs my bicep, her touch soft and soothing. "That definitely explains a lot, what you've accomplished so far Bones is incredible, which brings me to the question of why you always say that I'm slumming it by being with you."

I was hoping we'd never get to this question. I try to shrug it off. "I guess that's just how my mindset is. You're a hot-shot lawyer and I run a junkyard."

"Do you think that because I evaded you for so long and

didn't act on your advances, that it was because of what you do?" She sounds incredulous.

I turn to look down at her. "Isn't it?"

"No!" she cries, trying to lift off the bed as she cups my face. "I admit that I was concerned with you being in the Rebels, but that was before I knew what kind of club it was. It had nothing to do with you running a junkyard. I don't care about any of that. I don't care about what you do, it bothers me that you think that way."

I stare into her eyes and I know she's telling the truth. "You're a beautiful woman Kennedy, I see how other men look at you, I'm just sayin', they could give you a good life."

"And you couldn't?"

I stare at her, my heart thumping. "I know I could, but I've never had a girlfriend. What if I fuck up?"
She kisses me gently. "It's you I want, Bones. What if I fuck up? It works both ways."

I kiss her back as she lowers back down to the pillows. "It is kinda hot you're older than me."

"Older and wiser."

I smile then give her a chin lift. We're not done yet.

"Tell me about him."

A long silence ensues as she closes her eyes.

"I loved him," she says after a moment. "My husband. But I wasn't *in love* with him."

I feel her tense in my arms and I know this is a lot for

her to admit.

"And it feels wrong, to use him dying as a way to excuse all of my mistakes, but that's what haunts me the most. I tell myself we'd grown apart, that we were more like roommates then lovers. We were going in different directions and I planned to leave him. Then he got diagnosed and everything changed. In the end none of it was enough."

"And you blame yourself?"

"Of course, and it's not a pity party, but I feel guilt, so much fucking guilt, Bones. And I have to keep it bottled up inside because it wasn't *me* it happened to. He's the one who got taken, he's the one who wasted away and there was nothing anyone could do to stop it."

"You don't have to keep it bottled up, babe, not with me."

She's silent for a while. I feel her pain, it's a friend I know well.

"It feels so wrong, Bones," she whispers. "It's why I kept pushing you away and refused to let myself move on, I exiled myself to this torment that I created, to punish myself."

"Why can't you move on?" I tighten my grip around her. "It's safe Kennedy, I'll never judge you for anythin', you know that."

She takes a long time to answer. "There are things that I still need to come to terms with and I will in my own time, but I never want to dull his memory. He's gone and I'm here, it doesn't seem fair, Bones. It just isn't fair!"

I kiss her hair again as she holds me closer. I feel her shoulders shake quietly and I know how deep this hurt must run. I feel it too. Time waits for no one; the world should end but it doesn't. It just keeps fuckin' goin' like nothin' happened. That's what gets me the most.

She turns around in my arms and presses her body against me as I hold her.

"So, you're never ghostin' me again, like I said earlier," I whisper. "The one thing we can always do is talk. I don't want any secrets between us."

A few moments go by before I add, "I take it from your ass pressin' into my cock that you got me?"
She yawns, and I see her head nodding. "I got you, baby."

Her words spear me in the heart. She never calls me any kind of cute nickname.

I smirk into her hair. She astonishes me at every single turn. One minute, I think she's a spitfire who won't give me the time of day, the next we're rolling around in bed together, or we're fighting like an old married couple.

I obviously don't like the latter very much, but that's part of how relationships go, I guess. As I say, I've got a lot to learn in that department, but I know that I only wanna be with her.

At least she's made up her mind to be here; that's a start in the right direction. It's better than just beating around the bush, especially when I know I want her in my bed every night and no one else's. *She's here. She's mine.* That's all that matters.

I know she has demons, heck, don't we all? But there's nothing we can't work through, there's nothing she can say to me that will change the way I feel about her.

A few moments later, I hear her soft lull as she falls back asleep. Even when she's unconscious, she's a damn angel.

I marvel at her strength, at what she's had to go through, at how hard the road must have been, and while the details are sketchy, I get the idea.

Lying here in the dark for a long time, I hold her, keeping this feeling of contentment for as long as I can. I've had so little peace in my life, but with her, it comes to me easily.

I sleep better. I feel better. I *am* better. And I owe her for that. I'll give her the world, if only she'll let me.

I fall asleep feeling more at ease than I have in years.

All because of her.

I stir as I feel my dick twitch.

Lick.

I squeeze my eyes.

Lick. Lick.

I yawn.

Suck. Lick.

What the fuck is that?

I take a moment before opening my eyes, then I see red hair splayed out over my stomach and Kennedy under the sheet, giving me head. *Oh, fuck yeah.* What a way to be woken up.

"Babe?" I whisper, my voice hoarse.

She continues to swirl my tip with her tongue, cupping my balls as I groan and lay an arm over my eyes. *I could wake up to this more often.*

She takes more of me into her mouth as I try not to move my hips, because if I do, I know I'll ramrod her down her throat.

"Jesus," I grunt when she sucks me further into her mouth and bobs her head up and down on my dick over and over, setting the pace. I lift the covers and stare down at her.

Her eyes meet mine, and she gives me a big grin while my cock's still in her mouth.

She pulls out for a second and says, "Morning, sleepyhead." Then goes back to sucking, hollowing out her cheeks as I watch her take me.

I'll give her a good fuckin' mornin'...

"You do that so well, sweet cheeks," I mumble, closing my eyes again. If I keep watching her, I'll blow in seconds. Instead, I reach one hand into her hair, and she groans when I tug it.

"You miss me?" she asks sweetly, gripping my cock.

"What do you think?"

She grins again, her eyes shining with delight.

The truth is, I have fuckin' missed her, more than she'll ever know. This week has felt like a goddamn eternity.

"Keep teasin' me like that, and I'm gonna blow in your mouth," I add.

"Maybe I want you to."

I grin. "Careful what you wish for, babe."

That's all the encouragement I need. I pump my hips, gripping the other hand into her hair as she rides my mouth, her tongue swirling and licking as her head bobs up and down on me. When I hit the back of her throat, she gags. The sight is so fuckin' perfect, as are her moans of pleasure. I blow in seconds. My load shoots down her throat as she swallows and then I watch her clean me up. Every last drop. *Fuckin' perfect, infuriating woman...*

"That was so hot," I say, but before she can answer, I grab her under her arms and haul her up my body, then I flip her over. She gasps as I grab her by the thighs and lift her legs over my shoulders. "But it is only fair that I repay the favor, you have, after all, excelled in the art of oral skills, and I can't let this go unmatched."

"I didn't know we were grading," she groans when I part her with one hand and lick through her wet folds. I insert a finger and groan at how slick she is. So damn wet.

My balls ache to be inside her.

"So wet for me, babe. Suckin' me off turn you on?"

"Yes," she whispers. "I got lonely without you."

Her words hit me in the chest like a freight train.

"You just sayin' that because I'm eatin' your pussy?" I look up at her as she stills. "I might be a good attorney, Ryan, but one thing I don't do is lie."

"Good," I reply. "So be a good girl and shut that smart mouth of yours, *Ms. Hart*, and let me taste you."

She jumps when I thumb her clit, curling my fingers deep inside her at the same time.

"Oh… *oh…*"

There's nothing I like more than seeing her come apart and lose control. It's so satisfying.

I don't know what I ever did before this, but waking up with her in my arms is the damned nearest thing to perfection a man can get.

BRACKEN RIDGE
REBELS
ARIZONA
M · C

CHAPTER 24

KENNEDY

I can't even let the break-in yesterday dull my mood.

I know we've got shit to work on, and it's not perfect, but waking up like that with Bones after being cocooned around him all night felt so right. His hard body pressed against mine as we snuggled. I feel safe in his arms, like nothing in the world can ever touch me, and it's hard not to be drawn into that.

After we talked, it felt like a weight had been lifted and now I understand him so much more.

The truth is, I did miss him. He lights me up inside for the first time in a very long time, and maybe it's selfish of me because he makes me feel good, but I do have a sneaking suspicion that I make him feel good too. And I want to explore it. I need to work on my self-esteem, and I need to try harder to let go of the past. I loved Dean, and he died knowing as much.

My love for him is so very different to the love I have for… *wait…what?*

I stop what I'm doing and pinch the bridge of my nose. *I love Bones?* It isn't the first time I've thought about him and 'love' in the same sentence.

My heart kicks up a notch just thinking the words. Even when my brain is slow to catch up, my body never falters. It reminds me of what I need to do… and that's to *tell him.*

I need to let him know that I want to try. Try being in a relationship with him, not that I know what kind of a girlfriend I'd make. He's already told me he hasn't had a girlfriend since high school. This just went way past complicated.

Amelia pops her head in my doorway. "I'm off, if that's all right?"

We usually don't work Saturdays, but I had so much to catch up on after the break-in that we did a half day. I'll feel better for it come Monday morning, even if I don't right now.

"Of course, sweetie. I'm actually right behind you. Thanks for coming in." I stand and pick up my empty coffee cup.

"Anytime, happy to help."

I smile. "I feel better about things, knowing that we have security and bulletproof glass makes me feel a little more reassured."

Amelia squeezes me on the arm and asks, "Is it really bulletproof?"

I shake my head. "I don't think so, but it's double-glazed. The way Bones was carrying on, though, makes me believe it won't be shattering any time soon."

Colt spent all of last night installing a state-of-the-art security system, courtesy of Bones. I drew the line at bars on the windows, though I did agree to an alarm on those too.

The insurance will take care of the broken furniture and our computers. I'm lucky no confidential files were taken. It seems all these thugs really wanted was to cause a mess. All we've done today is tidy up and replace furniture, but at least it resembles an office now. And I'm grateful the prospects did all the heavy-lifting and cleaned up the glass.

"Well, have a nice rest of the weekend. I'll see you Monday."

"You too. Thanks, Amelia."

She leaves, and I wash up my coffee mug in the staff room. I switch my phone to message and pick up my purse. Just as I'm leaving the office, I hear a noise behind me, and when I turn, a young woman is coming up the path toward me.

"Sorry, we're closed," I say as she stops and then turns to point to her car.

"I'm really sorry. I just freaking broke down in the parking lot. I don't suppose you could give me a ride to town. I'd walk, but…" She glances up at the sky, and it looks like it is about to throw it down. The sky is an angry dark gray.

I wouldn't usually give a stranger a lift anywhere, but she seems harmless enough. Young. Blonde, unkempt hair. Pretty skin.

"Sure thing. I'm going to the Stone Crow. I can drop you there, if you like?"

"Perfect, thanks."

We make short work of getting to my car since it's right out in front of the lot.

"Wow, nice ride," she says, giving a low whistle as we climb in.

"Thanks."

"It must have cost a packet."

I laugh as I start the engine. "Something like that."

"How fast does it go?"

I pull out into the street. "Uh, fast enough. I'm a little bit of a law-abiding citizen, though. It kinda comes with the territory of the job."

She laughs too. "Yeah, kinda figured that."

"So, are you from around here?"

She taps her hand on the side of the door. "Born and raised."

My eyebrows pique in surprise. I am fairly new to town and don't get out much, so that could be the reason I don't recall seeing her before. She's probably around Stevie's age, maybe twenty-five.

"Oh, sorry, I'm new in town, not that that's any excuse but I don't know everyone yet."

She waves a hand at me. "It's fine. I don't get out much myself."

"Oh? What do you do."

"I actually just got laid off."

"I'm sorry to hear that. What did you do?"

"Office administration mainly." She gazes out the window, and like clockwork, the rain begins to pour.

"I think your car breaking down timed it about right," I muse, the wipers immediately coming on.

"Speaking of which, would it be a huge hassle to drop me at Steel's Garage? That way, I can see if he's still open, and if not, then I'll get a tow truck."

"Sure," I say. It's on the way anyway. "But I don't like your chances on a Saturday afternoon."

We ride in companionable silence until I pull into the lot at Steel's. I notice a closed sign on Rubble's front door, and then Sienna is sliding one of the barn doors closed as she looks up at us. Seeing my car, she waves through the blurry windscreen as I come to a stop. I wave back.

I know I'll get saturated if I head outside, but it seems impolite to not help this chick out, and sitting in the car while they work out the details is just plain rude.

"Looks like we may need to make a run for it," I note.

"Hey, thanks so much for the ride. I appreciate it."

I nod. "No trouble."

I make for the door, but something sharp stings me in the neck. I gasp and turn around; the chick is holding a syringe… and she just jabbed me with it… right into my neck.

"What did you –"

"Sorry, Kennedy, but this is the only way."

"The only way to wh–"

I don't even get to reach for the door handle when everything goes black.

"I told you, I had no choice… well, that isn't my issue. Get over here now... the warehouse, idiots. I'm lucky Steel wasn't there, or we'd be fucked."

I groan as I rub my neck. My mouth feels like I swallowed sandpaper.

I've no idea where I am or who is talking on the phone, but what I do know is it's dark out and it smells weird in here.

"I don't know, like I said, Kennedy and Sienna… no, I drugged her and tied the other one up… Steel's the one we wanted, remember? I had to improvise since my car broke down before I could get to the garage. My safest bet was to bring this bitch with me. She might be worth something too… whatever, just get over here. I think one of them just woke up."

I quickly snap my eyes closed and hear footsteps come closer to me. A few moments later, she shoves me with her boot.

"Motherfuckers," she says to herself, seemingly

satisfied I'm still out cold. "I do all the leg work and they can't even get their shit together and do one simple thing, like show up."

Who the fuck is this chick?

I didn't even get her name. I try to think, but I know that I don't know her from anywhere. More to the point, what the hell does she want?

She steps away, and I hear a door open and close, then silence. I quickly open my eyes. They dart around in the dark, looking for anything familiar. It's then I realize my hands and feet are tied.

The fucking bitch not only drugged me, but she tied me up? Oh, this piece of work is gonna pay when I get my hands free.

As my eyes begin to focus, and I blink the darkness away, I thank God I'm not gagged.

"Sienna!" I whisper-shout.

The woman did just say she nabbed Sienna and tied her up… surely she's here too then… *I need to get to her.*

I sit up, and in the dull light, I see we're in some kind of old warehouse, and it's completely full of old furniture and junk. I've no idea where the hell we are, but my head spins so bad it could fly off at any minute.

"Jesus, fuck," I whisper, rubbing my temples. I feel groggy like I can't move my arms or legs even if I wanted to.

Then I hear a noise. Looking to my right, I see her…

Sienna. She's tied to a chair, her arms and legs bound, and her mouth taped. She's trying to free herself.

"Holy fuck!" I whisper-shout again. "Sienna!"

I can't see her face because it's so dark, but she makes a strangled noise.

I have to get over to her. I try to shuffle along to get closer. It's a slow process because my body doesn't want to co-operate one iota, and my heads woozy and feels like it might roll. I manage to get to her, and her eyes go wide when I sit beneath her feet, and we stare at one another.

"Where the hell are we?" I whisper, realizing that's a fruitless question. It's not like she can answer me anytime soon, nor can I just reach up and rip the tape off her mouth.

"Do you know who this crazy bitch is?"

Sienna nods.

"Is it something to do with Jack?"

She nods again.

Shit.

The boys said that the family was bad news, but this is next level.

"Fucking bitch stuck a needle in my neck. She obviously jumped you in the shop?"

Sienna nods, her eyes darting frantically around, and I realize I need to try and get us out of this mess. She's tied to a chair and not moving. At least I can access the floor by shuffling. That's better than being tied *to* something.

I take in more of our surroundings and it's clear we're locked in pretty tight. There doesn't appear to be any windows that I can see. It's probably where Jack keeps all his shit. I turn back to Sienna.

"How long have we been here? An hour?"

She shakes her head.

"Two?"

Another shake.

"Three?"

She nods.

Tonight is Axton's homecoming party. I was meant to go and meet up with everyone. Surely someone will know we're in dire straits. Then I have a horrible thought… *What if nobody is coming?*

Bones will be missing me by now. I was meant to meet him at the clubhouse after work. Steel will be missing Sienna. They'll know… *won't they?*

I mean, he'd come looking for me and see I'm not at work or at home, and Amelia would tell him that I was right behind her, right? Panic washes through me and nausea sets in. Even so; *they don't know where we are.*

The only thing that gives me hope is that the cameras outside of Steel's would have caught everything that happened. That's if they realize we were kidnapped.

I glance around again, shaking, trying to locate something, *anything*, to use as a weapon or to get me untied.

But I don't get time to think, because a few moments later, I hear noise at the far end of the warehouse.

Shit!

I scuffle back as quick as I can to where I think I was dumped and lay down on the floor. I do not need them to know I'm awake… and I still can't feel my fucking fingers…

"I thought we were gonna stick to the plan," says a male voice.

"I took matters into my own hands," the girl replies. "Someone had to. You two weren't getting anywhere."

So there're at least three of them.

"Speak for yourself. You had one job to do and that was a complete balls up. I left Curly at the house. He's waiting for directions."

"You're forgetting they have their businesses locked up like Fort Knox. It's not like we got anything from the raids, nothing except seeing the satisfaction of them cleaning up, that's not nearly as satisfying as it should be."

"So why'd you drug that lawyer bitch?"

Their voices get closer.

"I had to get rid of her, didn't I? I couldn't have her poking around. It's not my fault that piece of shit car decided to die on me. Besides, I've got a new convertible now."

"Don't be fucking stupid. That's the first thing they'll look for."

"Not if I strip it down, change the plates, and repaint it. I'll leave this town in the dust anyway, so why not do it in style?"

The man grunts a laugh. "You're ambitious, I'll give you that."

"You're forgetting, I'm my father's daughter after all. He taught me every trick in the book."

"Pity that didn't extend to your brother. Could've done with his help tonight."

"Ugh, I could never count on that loser for anything," the girl says. "Pull the tape off her mouth. I need to ask her a few questions."

I hear movement, then a rip, and then Sienna panting as she gasps.

"Now," Psycho woman goes on, "we can make this really simple, or really hard, Sienna. The choice is yours in which way you want this to play out."

She nods to the large man standing next to her. He turns and looks at me. I squeeze my eyes closed.

"Why are you doing this, Stacey?" Sienna gasps. "You know what the club will do to you when they find out." She snorts a laugh. "Ah, the club. That took all of fifteen seconds. And what makes you think they'll find out? I covered my tracks. They expected another break-in, but this time, the stakes have changed."

I feel a sharp kick to my shins as I flinch, trying to keep pretending I'm still out cold. Then there's a kick to my ribs. I cry out this time, trying to curl up to protect myself.

"Knew the bitch was awake. She moved," the man grunts, pulling me up by the elbow as I struggle against him.

"What do you want?" I splutter out, my ribs feeling like they're on fire.

"You know that old saying?" Stacey prompts in a sing-song voice. "Revenge is a dish best served cold? That's a load of crap."

"Just tell us what you want, if it's money…"

"We'll get to that. First, though, we're going to play a little game."

I don't like the sounds of this at all.

"*Please,*" Sienna gasps, "we'll give you what you want."

Stacey snorts. "I seriously doubt that, unless you can erase the last twenty-something years of my life with my dead-beat dad who's in so much in debt that the sale of the business won't even cover closing costs. He's a gambler, always was a selfish son-of-a-bitch, and now that my mom has taken off, it's just us. And I'm not putting up with his shit for one second longer."

"If your beef is with your dad," I interject, "then why are we here?"

"Ah," she says, holding up a finger. Her wild blonde hair and what I once thought were pretty features, now just seem menacing. "Well, I need cash. And my two friends here are shit outta luck after being laid off, all thanks to the Bracken Ridge Rebels. That's where you come in."

"So you're the ones who smashed up all our businesses and offices?" I shake my head.

"Bingo. That was just for fun. It was a hoot watching y'all run around cleaning up, not knowing who was gonna be targeted next. But alas, those games can only go on so long. Now I need cash and to get the hell out of here."

"You don't actually think you'll get away with this, do you?" Sienna chokes out. I glance at her and become all the more frustrated that we can't move or defend ourselves.

"The club will kill you."

Stacey walks over to Sienna and slaps her hard across the face. The noise rings off the walls and makes me cringe. Tears rise in Sienna's eyes.

"Not if I kill you first."

"What do you want?" I repeat, trying to take the heat away from Sienna. "If it's money, we can get that for you, but you have to stop with the –" I get another kick to the side of my hip and curl into a ball to protect myself from the onslaught. He only boots me once this time, but it hurts like a motherfucker.

"Stop it!" Sienna yells. "Stop!"

"Shut the fuck up!" Stacey screams. This chick is clearly out of her mind. "Like I said, we're going to play a little game. Every time you give me a wrong answer or try to bullshit me, she'll get kicked and punched…" She points to me as my eyes go wide.

"We'll tell you anything you need to know," Sienna cries, "just stop hurting her."

"Aww! Isn't that sweet?" she fake gushes. "Loyalty, that's what you get with this club, David. Not that we would know what that's like, after Steel broke all my dad's fingers, shit got rough at home. My mom left. My brother is a lost cause. I thought he had potential, but he wouldn't join us. Would he, David?"

The big man cracks his knuckles and shakes his head. "His loss, our gain. Always was an asswipe anyway."

She smiles defiantly. "So, we'll start this again before I get to any of my demands. I need to know some things. Where does the club keep all their cash?"

Sienna shakes her head. "The club doesn't take any cash. They're not one percenters; everything that goes through the books is electronic…"

Crack. I get a swift kick to the shins again.

"If you expect me to believe that…"

"It's true," I blurt out. "I'm the club's attorney. All of the businesses, they have credit card machines…" I need to think fast, the club… *we need to get to the club.* "If there was any cash, it'd likely be kept with Hutch, the club Prez at church. Right, Sienna?"

I at least avoid another kick to my body.

Her breath is ragged as she says, "Yeah, I mean, we wouldn't have the combination to a safe or anything, but

Steel mentioned there is a place out behind the clubhouse bunker where they bury cash in a crate."

"They do?" I play along.

Sienna shrugs. "Anything to escape the IRS." Stacey is crazy enough to fall for it. "Perfect! The problem being that we can't exactly sneak into the clubhouse unnoticed."

"We can," I go on. "There's a huge party tonight. One of the boys just got out of the joint. One of us can slip in unnoticed."

"This sounds fishy," David says. "Too many bikers around at a party."

"And they'll all be drunk and partying," Stacey goes on like she's cracked it. "They won't be expecting anyone to sneak in and steal from right under their noses."

"Shouldn't be too hard," Sienna goes on. "Nobody goes out there at night. I'd know where to find it, I'm sure."

"Now we're getting somewhere." She claps her hands together, then turns to me. "In the meantime, you're going to wire me money from the club's bank account, just in case the cash buried in a crate is a myth. I think an even five hundred grand should cover things."

My eyes go wide. "Wait, I don't have access to the club's funds!" I splutter.

"Yes, but your boyfriend does. I'm sure with a little coaxing, we can get him to come around. After all, he does seem to be very protective of you. It would be a pity to fuck up that pretty little face of yours."

"What about her?" David points to Sienna. "Steel's gonna be fucking pissed. You know what he's like. If we get caught…"

"We'll be long gone by then," Stacey says. "And if we don't get what we want"—she points at me again—"this bitch can come with us as security until you can hack into the bank. If they put a hold on any funds, she's dead."

Oh shit.

"You won't get away with it," I repeat. "The club is going to find you, and when they do…"

A blow hits me in the side of the head as I slump back and begin to see stars. I hear Sienna scream. I never saw it coming.

"Oh, and don't worry, ladies." I hear Stacy laugh. "I already sent Steel a message telling him you and Kennedy are running a little late, so by the time they realize anything's up, we'll be long gone."

Then there's nothing except blackness.

Bones

BRACKEN RIDGE
REBELS
ARIZONA
M · C

CHAPTER 25
BONES

I look at my phone for the hundredth time. I've tried to call Kennedy, but she's not picking up. It's almost midnight, and as far as I was concerned, we were good. Yet, she's not here.

I stare across at Axton, who's getting a lap dance from one of the sweet butts, as he downs another beer and says something to her in her ear. Yeah, I'll bet he's packing tonight. It's been ten years since he's had any pussy.

He's a big dude. Like Brock. Blonde, short and spiked hair, and he's covered in tattoos. The chicks don't seem to rightly care that he just got out of the joint, and though he looks a little worse for wear due to the booze being shoved at him, he seems to be enjoying the attention.

"Been a long time comin'," Brock says, sidling up beside me.

"Yeah, good to have him here, brother."

"Can say that again. Big fuckin' day." He swipes a hand down his face. He looks like shit.

"How's Angel and the kids?"

"Good, bro. I'm gonna head off in a few. Think I got zero chance of Ax comin' home with me tonight."

We both glance over as he and the sweet butt suck each other's faces off, with Axon's hands grabbing her ass. I chuckle. "Did anyone tell him there's no sex on the couch?"

"Jesus, I mean, I know it's been a while, but there're plenty of rooms upstairs."

"Feel like he's still your little brother, huh?"

He turns to me and gives me a chin lift. "That'll never change. So many things I gotta fix. Startin' with our dad."

"That'll come in time," I remind him. "Rome wasn't built in a day. Small steps. Did Ax wanna see your parents?"

"Said he did. Mom wanted to be there, but I told her no. We'll visit sometime soon, when shit's settled down."

I glance over at Amelia, who's, yet again, chatting to Jax. I narrow my eyes.

"That guy got a cola-flavored dick or somethin'?"

"What'dya mean?" Then Brock glances over and straightens.

"First Kelsey, now Amelia."

"Fuck that, he shouldn't be talkin' to her."

"Damn straight."

Brock's about to march over there when Amelia sees us staring and quickly heads over to us instead. She seems in a hurry all of a sudden, which is smart. She knows how it works and Jax is still a prospect, he's got no business talking to her.

"What the fuck you doin' hangin' around a prospect?" Brock barks as she gives me a smile and a wave.

"Just talking. Don't get your knickers in knot."

I bark out a laugh as Brock gives me a side-eye. "Cut from the same cloth," I mutter.

"Don't be talkin' to him." Brock turns back to where Jax was, and magically, he's taken off, which is good. Don't wanna ruin Axton's night by starting a brawl. "Don't be lookin' at him, don't even think about him. Got me? He's a shitkicker, and if I see him around you again, I'll permanently rearrange his face."

"What's up your ass?" she sasses.

"You at the moment."

"You kicked Gunner's ass when you caught him with Lily and look how they turned out."

He glowers down at her. Ever the hothead. "Don't be givin' me any lip about that. He was a prospect then, like Jax, and Lil's a club sister, like you. I beat the shit outta Gunner, and trust me when I say I'll do the same to that little weasel."

"That won't be necessary," she says. "We were just talking. And you're overreacting."

I divert the conversation. "Hey, have you seen Kennedy? Apparently, she's with Sienna, but neither of them has shown up yet."

"No, not since we locked up," she says. "She was leaving right behind me. I think she may have got a client walk-in last minute, though. As I pulled out, a car was pulling in."

Something in my gut tells me that something's up, but I've spent too many years flying by the seat of my pants and looking over my shoulder. It's a perk of the job of being in an M.C. and being ex-military too. Some things you just can't shake.

"Seems weird," I say, scratching my head. "I think I'm gonna go take a drive over to her place."

"Shit, man, maybe take a prospect with you," Brock says just as I spot Steel over by the bar, looking down at his phone with a frown. Everyone's on hot bricks at the moment with the break-ins.

"I'll go see if he's heard from Sienna." I leave Amelia and Brock to walk over to Steel and give him a chin lift.

"You seen Kennedy or Sienna?" I ask as he turns to glance at me.

"Nah, man. Got a message hours ago. She said they were gettin' ready together. Just got Gash to go on over to my place to see if she's around."

A moment later, Steel's phone rings.

"Yeah." I listen as his face contorts. "So, it's locked up and her car's gone?" I wait as Steel frowns some more.

"What about a Mercedes convertible, was that in the drive? *Fuck!* This don't sound right to me. Where the fuck did the two of them go?"

"I'm gonna go by Kennedy's," I say.

Steel stops me. "What's her address?" he barks at me. I reel it off. "You get that? Nah, I'll meet you back at mine in five." Steel hangs up.

"Don't say we've got a problem."

"Gash found a phone on the side of the road, just outside the garage. Gonna head over there now. I don't like the sound of any of this."

"I'll come too. Maybe we should bring Gears along, just in case, he looks the most sober."

"I'll grab Brock. You should stay here in case they come back."

I shake my head. "I'm good."

"I insist," he says, giving me a hard look. "Everyone else is drunk out of their minds. Shit goes down, or they come here, then I need someone here who knows what's happenin'."

I don't like the sound of that. "Gotta find Colt, see if he can get a lead on the security cameras outside Kennedy's and your joint."

"He's over by the jukebox. I'll give him the heads up, and then I'll phone Hutch. He left not long ago."

I nod. I'm not happy, but I'm not gonna argue with

Steel, and while I want to know for myself, I figure that Kennedy will just walk through the door any minute… Thinking about what happened with me and Lucy though sends a cold shiver right through me. I don't trust anyone anymore, especially not with my girl.

I don't like this uneasy feeling. Not one bit.

"Call me the minute Gash lets you know if her cars in the lot."

"Got it." He stalks off toward Colt while I go for a walk around the front to see if either of the girls has arrived. There's a driveway at the side of the clubhouse that leads around to the back, so I take the long way around. Seeing neither Kennedy nor Sienna's ride parked there, I walk back down the gravel. Just as I'm rounding the corner, a dude runs right into me.

"Shit. Sorry, man," he says, trying to get away as fast as possible.

"Hey, watch it –" I squint. "Don't I know you from somewhere?"

He shakes his head. "I don't think so. I was looking for Steel." He puts his head down and his hands in his pockets.

"Well, you're not gonna find him out here in the bushes."

I frown. If he's a hang-around with the club, why does it seem like he's kinda holed up in the shadows, watching us?

I give him a chin lift as I move closer to him. "What do you want with Steel?"

He swallows hard as I wait, then it hits me… "You're fuckin' Jack's kid, right?"

My heart rate catches up with my brain a few seconds later, even though I've no fuckin' clue what he's doing here.

"Listen, I don't want any trouble…" He starts.

"Does this have to do with Sienna?"

"Is what to do with Sienna?"

"Oh, shit." His eyes go wide as I turn and see Steel heading my way. I motion him over as I grab the kid's shirt again so he can't slip away.

"Nathan?" Steel barks as he gets closer, then he looks at me. "What's he doin' here?"

"Just caught him prowling around, somethin' weird goin' on. I'm tryin' to get him to spit it out," I bark, my heart hammering even faster in my chest.

"So." Steel pokes him in the chest. "Start talkin', fuckface."

He runs a hand through his messy hair. "I… I should've come sooner, but I didn't think it'd go this far."
Steel and I exchange glances.

"It started off vandalizing the shops and causing a mess, then it went further, breaking in and trying to get cash. I thought they would stop…"

"Who's they?" Steel demands. "And where do we find them?"

Nathan blinks rapidly a couple of times. "That's just

it, I don't know where. Stacey didn't come home this last week…"

"Stacey?" I splutter.

He nods. "Yeah, my sister, she's gone completely crazy ever since my mom left and dad's now skipped town, then she got Curly and David on board."

The two hired idiot brothers that used to work for Jack. I run a hand over my face as Steel takes over from my grasp and literally yanks him to within a half inch of his face.

"Where the fuck are Sienna and Kennedy?"

"I don't know, I swear!" he yelps. "I came here to tell you. That's why I'm here… She's hellbent on paying you back after dad went down the tubes."

"He went down the tubes a long time ago. You sure you didn't come here to prowl around and watch our movements?" Steel continues. "Seems pretty convenient."

"I'm not suicidal!"

"Hey, what's he doin' here?" Colt asks, sidling up behind us.

"Fucker's involved with Kennedy and Sienna goin' missin'," Steel reports over his shoulder. "And he's about to tell us where they are, if he wants to keep his balls attached to his dick."

Nathan's eyes go wide. I think the fucker might even start crying.

"What the fuck?" Colt looks at each of us, then to Steel

he says. "Downloading the footage from your place first. Takes a few minutes on my phone, then we can head over to my office…"

"There's no time for that," Steel spits.

Steel's phone rings again, and he holds onto Nathan with one hand as he reaches into his cut to grab it with the other.

"Talk," he barks.

Gash is on speaker. "No car at Kennedy's either. I checked both lots, front and back, and neither of them are there or at Kennedy's office."

"The phone you found," I say, into Steel's phone. "Is it a silver blackberry?"

"Yeah, it's fucked, though. They smashed it."

I give Steel a chin lift. "How fast can Linc trace?"

"If they smashed Kennedy's phone, they sure as shit did the same to Sienna's."

"Kennedy has an I-watch," I say. "They may not have noticed. Could get a bead off that; has the same number."

"Stay put," Steel barks back into the phone. "I'll call you back." He hangs up, then dials again. "Linc, I need a location on…" I reel off the number for him. "Sorry to fuck your plans tonight, bro, but I got shit goin' down." He waits for a second. "I owe you one, Linc. Come to the club sometime. I'll hook you up."

"Good you got Linc at your beck and call," Colt says

once Steel hangs up. "He comes in handy."

A few moments later, Brock and Axton arrive behind us. "Fuck's goin' on?" Brock gives Steel a chin lift. "What the fuck's he doin' here?"

"Long story," I say. "Stacey's the one who's been terrorizing the businesses with the two goons Jack used to have workin' for him. He apparently came to warn us, though he claims he doesn't know where Kennedy and Sienna are located."

"Sounds like a big fuckin' lie if I ever heard one," Brock snorts, not looking one bit happy.

"Do we need to smash some skulls?" Axton asks, punching one fist into his palm.

"No. We don't," Steel retorts. "I've got Linc tracin' Kennedy's I-watch. Once we get a location, we go in."

"How many are there?" I ask Nathan. "Just the three of them?"

"Yes. David and Curly, along with Stacey."

"Fuck's sake," Steel whispers. "They've been gone for hours. Just thought they were gettin' their faces ready or whatever chicks do that takes so long."

Brock squeezes Steel on the shoulder. "We'll find them."

"Startin' with where Stacey lives, hangs out, that kinda thing," I go on. "If both the cars are missin', surely one of them is parked up somewhere."

"Not if they got dumped," Axton puts in. "Probably did

that the first chance they got."

"Kennedy's car is worth a bomb," I say. "Hundred grand easy. Smart thing to do would have been to keep it hidden somewhere until you can get it stripped and repainted."

Brock turns to Nathan. "Your dad still got the old warehouse out on Rockery?"

Nathan shakes his head. "He got rid of all the stuff in there before the sale went through," he replies. "It was either that or lose the gear. He was behind on the payments."

I rub my chin. "They've gotta be somewhere. They're gonna want a ransom, but fuck sittin' around here, waitin' for a call. We gotta move and look everywhere we can in the meantime until Linc gets back to us."

I don't need to look at Steel to see the worry etched on his face. Sienna was already involved in a kidnapping with her cousin, Cassidy, and while Sienna wasn't the one who was tied up at gunpoint, I know this will bring back all those unwanted memories of that night.

I grab Nathan by the scruff of the neck. "You're gonna show us all the places you think they might be. We need the addresses of where David and Curly live and where they've hung out, any relatives close by, and their plate numbers." *I only hope that it isn't too late.*

He nods, like we're giving him a choice.

One thing's for sure, it's a big ass desert out there; all the better to hide some dead bodies in, which is exactly what'll be happening like it did Tex. When I get my hands on them, I'm not gonna hold back. I don't care if it's a woman, if she hurt Kennedy or Sienna, that shit's not gonna stick with me.

"One chance," Steel grunts, shoving Nathan ahead of us. "If you fuck it up, you're gonna end up with my knife in your throat. You got me?"

He literally shakes in his boots. "I got you. We can start with their houses. I know where they live."

I let him go and shove him ahead of us.

It's gonna be a long night.

We kicked down the doors at David and Curly's house and found nothing there but a big fuckin' mess. The place was rundown and literally needs a match thrown on it.

Axton stayed behind with Jax and Gears and then we got hold of Gunner. Everyone is now on high alert, including Hutch who's waiting for the call about the trace on Kennedy's watch. Knuckles is with Dalton from Steel's shop, and Patch is keeping watch of anyone lurking around the grounds.

At least with some of the boys staying there, if anyone shows up back at the club, they'll be waiting.

Gotta hand it to Nathan, it took some guts to come here

to the clubhouse, knowing that he would be risking his life. The thing that pisses me off is he knew they were doing this from day one, and if he'd have told us then, none of this would have happened.

I try not to flip my lid thinking about what could be going on or how either of them are being treated. I sure as shit never would have picked Stacey as being the one to orchestrate this whole thing. It blows my mind.

"She hates the club," Nathan tells us as we drive to the next location. Steel, Brock, and me are sharing a ride as Colt and Rubble pick up Gears from downtown and go to check out the old warehouse.

A call comes through to Brock as we drive through town and by the house where Stacey's ex-boyfriend lives.

"Yeah?" he answers, then, "Sienna?"

"What the fuck?" Steel bellows as Brock turns his phone onto speaker.

"Ax said Sienna just showed up," he says, then lets Axton go on.

"Patch saw them pullin' up with some dude. We let them get toward the back of the club before I jumped him and knocked him out cold."

"Fuck," Steel yells. "What'd you do that for? We need the fucker conscious!"

"Sorry, dude, he's a big guy, but he fell harder than I thought…"

"Put Sienna on. Now!" Steel orders as he grips the steering wheel hard.

A few moments later, Sienna comes on the line.

"Babe?" she says, her voice shaky.

"Sienna. Fuck, I'm comin' back to get you."

"You have to get Kennedy first," she says. "They had us in some kind of warehouse. I don't know where; they kept me blindfolded when we came out. I don't know where we were."

"Describe it."

"It had some old furniture and cars covered over, but smelled weird, like oaky."

"Could be the old sawmill shed," Brock whispers. "That was where Jack used to store shit long before he got the yard, probably still has a key."

"So it's just Stacey and the other guy?" Steel goes on.

"Yes. She's on something, though. She's crazy. David is the one still there, and Curly is the guy that escorted me here. We lied and told her we had cash at the club because she needs it to get out of town. Kennedy made it up so one of us could get back here and try to signal the alarm. They're all stupid enough to believe they could get away with it."

"Desperate people," Brock mutters. "This ain't good, Steel. If the bitch is that crazy…"

I swallow hard, grabbing a fistful of my hair as I groan out loud in frustration.

"Then she wanted Kennedy to hack into the club's account and send her five hundred grand. They said if I don't go back with the money by the time she's cracked the code, she'll kill her."

"They won't be doin' anything of the sort." Steel tries to sound calm, but I know him.

I stare into space, not hearing any of it.

"I need to go back, pretend to make the drop," she cries. "This bitch isn't kidding around, Steel. She's already…"

"She's already what?" I choke out as silence stills the car.

"Sienna, did they hurt you?" Steel continues when I can't go on.

"Me, not so much," she cries openly now. "But David kept kicking her, then… then he punched her so hard, she blacked out… I'm sorry… I was tied up… I couldn't do anything…"

"I'm gonna kill him," I say without any doubt in my mind. "I'm goin' to fuckin' tie that bastard up and bleed him out slowly, and then I'm gonna gut him like a fish." My stomach wrenches. Kennedy has nothing to do with any of this. And trying to make her to get into the club's bank accounts? The chick is clearly off her rocker.

Steel's phone starts ringing.

"Got Linc," he says, then to Sienna, "Call you back, babe. Stay with Ax at the club. Do not go anywhere until I call back."

"Okay. I love you, please be careful."

"I will. Love you too," he mutters as he hangs up, running a hand through his hair. "This is so fucked up."

"Some fuckin' bastard has his hands on my woman?" I say through gritted teeth. "This is all because of me. If I hadn't have roped her into comin' around to the club and havin' her in my bed..."

"You couldn't have known this was gonna go down," Brock says, not that it helps any.

I know I've let her down. Even though we're not a one percent club with any other club beefs, shit still happens. Bad shit. Exhibit A.

Nathan stays quiet, anguish paling his features. At least he's got some redeeming qualities, though it's any wonder who he got it from.

"Fuckin' crazy bitch is gonna have a bullet in her head," I mutter.

Steel and Brock share a look.

I turn to Nathan. "Did your dad have any shit out at the old mill?"

He shrugs. "Not that I'm aware of, but I don't know... he kinda had stuff everywhere."

Steel's phone rings again. He puts it on speaker.

"Shoot," he says to Linc.

"Got a trace off a tower out on Woodlands industrial area."

"Gotta be the mill," I say. "That's out that way."

"We're on our way," Steel replies. "Owe you, brother."

"Sending the coordinates now."

He hands me his phone as a text comes through.

"How we gonna play this?" Brock asks, leaning over toward the front.

"I've got an idea," Steel says, nodding to Nathan. "And it involves him."

We all turn to look at the kid in the back seat.

He might just be our saving grace.

BRACKEN RIDGE
REBELS
ARIZONA
M · C

CHAPTER 26

KENNEDY

When I wake, my head hurts and my ears ring. I can feel one side of my face burning, most likely swollen from the blow I took when that bastard punched me. I feel my face hot and sticky, probably with blood marring my skin.

They've also gagged me.

Everything feels like it's so far away. It could have been hours since I was out cold, or minutes, I've no idea. When I can finally focus my eyes, I realize Sienna is gone from the chair, her restraints dropped on the floor. *Where did she go?*

Jesus, everything hurts. I try to open my jaw, but I'm met with more shooting pain, and I'm still tied up. This time, they've secured me to a pole farther in the back of the room.

It appears that I'm alone, so I look around the darkened space for something to help me get loose. Of course, it isn't like they left a knife or a pair of scissors hanging around.

Bones.

Will this morning's memory of us in bed together be the last memory I have of him? If it is, then what a way to go out. We're so perfect together. I don't know why I fought him for so long.

Maybe I always knew I'd fall for him. He always made me nervous when he chased me and made rude and crude remarks, even when I went home and fantasized about him doing those very things to me.

Now I may never get to tell him what he really means to me. That I… that I love him.

Despite the fact I'm in this mess because of the club and the situation with Jack, I still don't feel it inside me to be mad at any one of them. I should feel enraged. Sick to my stomach. Never wanting anything to do with them again. But a sense of peace falls over me because they have only ever welcomed me, like one of their own.

I close my eyes. So many missed opportunities. I let my pride get in the way. My career, wanting to have it all but not willing to put the time in and smell the roses when they were right under my nose. I *can* have it all, but that also includes him.

Family is everything, and that's what the Bracken Ridge Rebels are. A family. One I'd be happy to be a part of. Here I was, happy to take Kirsty's money to represent her business, yet still looked down my nose at the biker club because of my preconceived notions.

The thing that bothers me is when this shit happens, it seems to happen a lot with this club. Trouble does seem to follow them.

Everyone has the right to feel skeptical, especially someone like me who has seen and heard it all, and I let my judgment get in the way. For that, I feel a little ashamed. The shambles that I am aside, I had every right to proceed with caution, but not to judge Bones when I really didn't know him.

I only hope I get to tell him how much he means to me.

I hear the doors open again.

"Where the fuck is he?" I hear Stacey cry out, clearly agitated.

"Calm down. Curly said they got the cash. They're not far away. I'll check she's come around, then if she really is lying about not having access, I can try and hack into the system. It's gonna be okay."
Their voices echo all around the vast space.

They got the cash? I only hope that's code for someone is coming to rescue me…

"Well, we need that money, David. Sienna said there's only about fifty grand in cash. That's not gonna go far."

"So we'll take her with us."

I hear movement, then kissing. *So, she's taken up with fucking David? Talk about scraping the barrel.*

It hurts to move, and I think the bastard actually cracked

a rib. I feel so sore that my body has gone numb.

"What if we can't get the money?" She really is hellbent on getting the cash. I bet she's the type of woman that will dump him the minute he's not useful anymore.

"We will. Like I said, we'll take her if we have to."

"If we take her, we're more of a liability," Stacey goes on. "It's hard enough being on the run."

"She'll be our ransom. At least for now we'll have enough cash to start somewhere new and hide out until our demands are met. There's nothing they can do once we're outta this town. They're a fuckin' bunch of pussies. They'll pay to get her back."

"You're so sexy when you're dirty, David. I knew you'd come through in the end."

More kissing. "Fuck, you make me so hot, Stace. Wanna fuck you right now."

Please do not have sex in front of me…

"Not here," she says, in between kisses. "She's probably awake and listening."

"Who cares? Let her."

Stacey giggles. Actually fucking giggles, and I hear more movement as he groans.

Please no.

"What was that?" Stacey says a few moments later as they both stop their ministrations.

"I didn't hear anything."

I listen intently, though I'm too far away to make anything out.

"Babe, I heard something," she says again.

Then a mobile rings. Stacey answers it.

"Nathan? What the fuck? What? Why? Ugh." She curses, then says, "Did anyone see you? This isn't what we discussed… I don't understand why you'd do that? Fine… give me a second… are you sure nobody saw you? Okay, keep your hair on."

"What's going on?" David asks when she hangs up.

"That was Nathan. He thinks something went down at the club."

"Why's he helping all of a sudden?"

"I don't know, he sounded remorseful. He said he doesn't want me to get into trouble," she says. "And he's here, apparently."

"He's here, *here?*"

"Yeah, outside. He wanted to warn us, probably knows we've got cash and wants in now. Stupid fuck."

"Babe, I don't know…"

"I've got a better plan. We'll let him in, and you can knock him out. We'll leave him here tied up. He doesn't get to just come back after everything and pretend like he's sorry when he's done nothing to help us."

While they deliberate, I see movement at the top window, the only fucking window in here, and it's up high.

I'm sure I see a light… a shadow… in my mind Bones is up there, watching, waiting, trying to get to me…

Stacey goes to open the door. "Holy shit!" she says, trying to slam the door closed again.

"Don't fuckin' move, or I'll blow your brains out," I hear Steel, and my heart rate kicks up about seven hundred notches. I've never been so happy to hear his voice. I almost cry with sheer delight.

I can barely see what's going on, but it looks like Steel is holding a gun to Nathan's head and I spot Brock pointing another gun at David. They're both caught off guard, though I can see that David has a gun tucked in the back of his jeans. His hand hovers over the butt as Brock tells him to show his hands.

Where is Bones?

"Fucking Nathan!" Stacey yells. "What's going on?"

"Move inside," Brock orders, nodding behind the pair as they backtrack into the warehouse and he kicks the door shut.

"This can be real easy, Stacey, or it can get really fuckin' ugly," Steel goes on. "So let's make a switch. Your dear old brother for Kennedy. Bring her to me now, and he won't get harmed. We already have Curly. So, if David wants his brother back in one piece rather than several pieces, I suggest you don't take too long to think about it." *Oh my fucking God.*

"You think I care about this piece of shit?" Stacey

sneers. "Go ahead, shoot him."

It just goes to show you how far gone this lunatic is. She doesn't even care about her own brother being shot, or David's.

"What about Curly?" David asks, turning to look down at her. Clearly, he's a little more alarmed than she is. "We can't just –"

"Shut up, David!" she yells back at him.

"Stacey! These guys aren't kidding," Nathan goes on. "Think we're playin' around?" Steel barks, his tone harsh enough to cut glass. "I'll make what happened to your father look like a day at the beach."

I don't know how Stacey and her dickface boyfriend aren't shitting their pants right now.

"Just remember, we have Kennedy," David goes on. "And we won't be giving up her location unless you back off."

I squirm around, but nobody can hear me.

"Looks like we're the ones with the guns around here," Brock interjects. "I don't think you're in any position to be makin' any threats. Oh, and just so we're clear. You've got a mark on the back of your heads. You see, Kennedy's ol' man is ex-military, never misses his target. Don't worry, he'll feed you to the coyotes. They get real hungry this time of year."

My eyes go wide as I see a red dot hover between the back of Stacey's and David's heads.

Bones?

I turn my head to the window, but I only see shadows. *Bones is up there!*

"Kill us and you don't get her location, and let's just say, it's a pretty big ass desert out there," David fires back. "One call, and she's dead."

"You're lyin'," Brock counters. "There's only three of you, and we have Curly. Now, where the fuck is she?"

"You got some pretty big balls," Steel mutters. "Or you're really fuckin' stupid."

If I could slap my forehead, I would. They are clearly outmatched, and the frustrating thing is the boys have no idea I'm right back here.

"Stacey!" Nathan yells. "He's not kidding around. Do you really want my brains splattered all around? Do you really hate me that much?"

She laughs coldly. "I hate everyone in this family; for how we grew up, for the way we were treated, and the fact I was stuck here and couldn't get out. We used to be close, Nath, but you stopped being useful to me a while back."

I feel bad for Nathan. His own sister doesn't even care that he's got a gun to his head. And I thought I had family issues.

"I did everything I could, and you know it. Just because I wouldn't help you destroy other people's property and act like a crazy person, doesn't mean you get to just throw me away like I mean nothing."

"Like you drove away Mom?"

"That was our father, Stacey, not me. He's the one who was a drunk and couldn't hold his temper. He's the one you hate, not me."

A whipping sound shoots through the room and it takes a second for me to realize what just happened.

Then David cries out. "Holy fucking shit!" He reaches around to his shoulder and his fingers soak in blood. "He fucking shot me!"

"Looks like Bones doesn't have the same patience we have," Steel says, and a second later, Stacey darts to her right and ducks behind a box. Another shot rings out and ricochets off the used car she just hid behind.

Steel lets go of Nathan and follows after her. David drops to his knees, crying like a little girl when Brock kicks him down so he's laying sideways. "Don't fuckin' move, or the next shot will be to your head."

"Stacey, this won't end well for you," Steel calls behind her. "There's nowhere else for you to run."

I feel so useless sitting here, unable to do anything. I try to scream but just make garbled noises. Still, I wriggle against my restraints, knowing that I'm drawing blood and making the skin break, but I don't care... I want out of here.

She's trying to get to me. The bitch might just shoot me, knowing she's cornered... *shit!*

"You've nothing to gain from running, aside from a bullet." I hear Steel getting closer.

A few moments later, I jump. I realize that someone is next to me. "I'm Nathan," he whispers as he starts to untie the rope behind my head as he says, "I'm not gonna hurt you."

He must have crawled through the other side of the junk to get to me. I cry with relief.

It's then I hear the sirens.

"See, there's nowhere left to run," Steel calls out again. "The cops are on their way. You can't get out of this, Stacey. Your boyfriend's gonna die for nothing."

"Fuck you!" she yells out.

I struggle, trying to help Nathan but also needing to have my hands free.

"I've got her!" Nathan calls out, untying the rope around my hands as I gasp for air.

"Oh my God!" I cry out once I'm free. "My feet, please, my feet too…"

"You always were the little bitch of the family," Stacey says as both of us jump. She emerges from the shadows.

"Never understood how we're even related!"

She's grabbed a hammer from somewhere and lunges toward us, swinging it wildly, and it narrowly misses Nathan's head, but she manages to still sock him with it on the back swing as he falls sideways. Then Steel grabs her arms, holding her back as the hammer falls to the ground.

Then, I hear Bones call my name.

"She's over here!" Steel calls out as Bones flies through

the door and rushes to my side.

Stacey is wriggling around, trying to get away from Steel.

"You all right?" Bones calls to Nathan as he picks himself up off the floor, still bleeding, and starts to unravel the rest of my rope along with Bones.

He nods. "I'm good."

"Babe," Bones whispers frantically, cutting the rope away from my ankles with a large knife he pulls out of his jacket. *"Fuck..."*

Steel moves Stacey away, telling her if she doesn't stop struggling, he'll get her brother to sock her back with the hammer.

"Bones," I cry out. "Oh God…"

He touches my face and caresses me with a knuckle, but his expression darkens as he assesses my face. "Did that fuckface do this to you?"

I nod.

"I'm gonna slice his throat."

"No, Bones, please, don't do that. I can't get you off murder charges."

"Nobody touches my woman. Nobody."

"I love you," I whisper, barely, my head feeling light as my ropes are released. I can't seem to keep my eyes open, and I can't wait another second until he knows how I feel.

"Babe," he whispers back. "Stay with me."

"She's probably got a concussion," Nathan says, as I

feel the rope slip away.

"Careful," Bones warns. "We're gonna need a medic."

"Fuck." I hear Brock, I think.

"Where's that motherfucker?" Bones shouts, holding me with both hands.

"I knocked him out," Brock replies.

"Cops gonna be here soon. Steel shouldn't have called them," Bones mutters.

"He didn't. I did."

I feel Bones move. "What the fuck for?"

"Trust me," says Brock. "I didn't want to. We didn't have a bead on Kennedy at the time, and we needed all resources available."

"Well, he's not gonna be breathin' long."

"I know she's been beaten, brother, but –"

"Look at her!" Bones yells. "If you think I'm gonna let him get away with this, then you don't know me as well as I thought you did."

"I wanted to do the same when Angel's ex tried to kill her, remember? Look at what I'd have missed out on if I'd done it. Thirty years to life for murder. I'd never get to see my kids grow up, there would have been no Ethan Wolf."

"That's different."

"How?"

"It just is."

"You want a life with her?"

"You know I do."

I stare up at Bones, tears forming in my eyes.

"Then don't fuckin' do it. You've got time to beat the shit out of him, but keep him breathin'. We'll find a way to get to him in prison." Brock reaches out and clutches his shoulder in support.

Bones lifts me as I try to keep from going to sleep, and he starts to carry me out toward the entrance.

"Ambulance is enroute," I hear Steel say. "Five minutes, tops."

"Where's that crazy bitch?"

"Took her over to Colt. She's tied up and gagged. Fuckin' bitch is just like her old man."

"Take her," Bones says, and I feel a different set of arms around me.

"Bones…" I call.

"Remember what Brock said," I hear Steel mutter.

"Not fuckin' stupid," is Bones' reply.

I feel Steel grunt as we begin to move. The cold air hits me in the face as we step outside.

"Am I dying?" I ask him a few moments later.

He chuckles. "No, sweetheart, you're gonna be fine."

"I want Bones…"

"First time a woman's ever admitted that out loud. Should record you sayin' it. Clearly, you've hit your head hard."

"Very funny," I mutter.

Steel's boots crunch on the pea gravel.

"Fuck, is she okay?" I hear another voice. It could be Colt, I'm not sure.

"Yeah, Bones is havin' a chat with the perp."

"Great. He hasn't got long. Can see the cop lights."

"Yeah, Jenkins is gonna have a field day with this."

"She's cold. Grab the blanket out of my ride, and we'll stash her in the back till they arrive."
Something warm wraps around me as I struggle.

"Try and keep her lucid," Colt says.

"Tryin'," Steel mutters, then, "Babe, you gotta stay awake for me, yeah?"

"Bones," I whisper. "Tell him…"

"He knows, babe."

"But I didn't get to…"

"He knows."

That's all I remember as the blackness once again swallows me whole.

BRACKEN RIDGE
REBELS
ARIZONA
M · C

CHAPTER 27

KENNEDY

TEN DAYS LATER

Bones bundles me into his truck, and I wince as he lifts me onto the seat.

"Shit, babe, you okay?" His face is etched with concern as he takes me in.

"I'm fine, just a little sore." I force a smile as he frowns some more.

"Maybe they're lettin' you out too soon?"

"It's been ten days, Bones. I need to go home."

"You know you can't climb stairs."

"I have an elevator."

"You gonna argue with me about everything?" He tilts his head, amusement on his lips.

The man is infuriating. He will barely touch me, afraid he's going to hurt me, yet I know he wants to.

"Bones."

"Yeah, babe?"

"You can kiss me, you know."

He stares at me intently. "You know what the doc said about healin'…"

"Yes, but it's a kiss. I didn't mean throw me over the back seat and ravage me."

He doesn't seem to find me amusing. "That won't be happening for…"—he pretends to check his watch and counts on his other hand—"four weeks, three days, twelve hours, fifteen minutes, and twenty-seven seconds."

I snort out a laugh, then wince again. I keep forgetting that any kind of movement, even laughing, can cause me pain. My ribs are broken. The rest of my body is battered and bruised, but I'm physically fine aside from the broken bones. Mentally, I'm still shaken up. I have questioned things over and over in my mind, and I keep coming back full circle.

"Babe, you need to stop findin' me so funny."

"Tell me about it."

He closes the door once he straps me in and then dashes around to the driver's seat, then takes his cut off – true Sons of Anarchy style – and turns it around the other way, laying it down on the back seat. It's a bad omen, apparently, to wear your motorcycle jacket inside a car.

"I'm serious," he continues as he climbs in. "I feel bad enough as it is…"

"Bones, we talked about this. It's not your fault."

"It *is* my fault when I involved you with the club." He starts the engine, and we slowly take off from the lot. "If I hadn't chased you and basically stalked you, you wouldn't be in this mess right now. You'd be wining and dining with a man that's a little more up your alley. One who doesn't put you in harm's way."

"What's that supposed to mean?"

"Don't go all lawyer chick on me, but there's plenty of rich guys in suits who could woo you far better than I could."

I roll my eyes. "I don't need to be wooed. And I don't like rich guys in suits. They tend to be assholes."

He glances toward me, not convinced. "I work in a junkyard, babe. And I'm part of the Rebels and always will be. After what happened to you…"

My heart plummets. We're back to this again. "I don't care about that, Bones. We discussed this. And I like you in overalls covered in dirt, it's kinda sexy."

He turns back to the road, his lips twitching. "Cut me up about what happened."

He's taken it really hard, but the last thing I want is him blaming himself.

"You shot someone; I think we're good. Thank God you missed, though."

"You think I missed?" He snorts, unfazed.

I look over to him. "You clearly know what you're

doing with a rifle, if that's the case."

"Damn straight. If Brock hadn't called the cops already, it'd be a different story."

"When you say things like that, it scares me, Bones. It makes me think you really mean it, that you'd go to jail for murder."

"For you, I would. Look at what that prick did to you. Do you know how hard it was not lowering my rifle those last few centimeters?"

I shake my head. "Please don't tell me things like that."

"Why not? It's true, and I always wanna be honest with you, even if it's not what you wanna hear."

I look down at my hands. "There are things that I wasn't sure I'd ever get to say when I was tied up, things that I wanted you to know."

"Even though I dragged you into all of this?"

My eyes find his again as he turns back to the road the minute our eyes meet. "You didn't drag me anywhere. I'm a grown adult. I knew the risks getting involved with a motorcycle club. I knew all of that. I'm a big girl, and I took the risk."

"The point is, there's always gonna be some crazy bitch or disgruntled M.C. out for some kinda revenge. We attract attention because we're bikers," he goes on, his hands clenching the wheel. "Drawing you into this mess…"

"If you want me to be mad at you for this, then save

your energy. I was scared, sure. I admit as much. But I'd never blame you for someone else's crazy shit. Nobody could predict Jack's daughter was going to go AWOL and would freaking kidnap people."

He gives me a side-eye. "Why are you takin' this so well?"

"Do you want me to flip out instead?"

"No," he says, concern in his eyes. "But I never want you to feel like you need to paint a pretty picture."

"I wouldn't do that."

After a few moments silence, he says, "I wanted to kill that motherfucker. It took a lot of convincin' from Steel and Brock to not charge in there and blow his brains out."

"I know that's got to be tough, but I can't exactly date you through prison cell bars now, can I?"

"I'd have done it," he goes on, running a hand through his already disheveled hair. "I'd still do it to keep you safe."

"Bones," I say, laying a hand on his. "I know that you would, but I don't need you to think that I need wrapping in cotton wool. I've lived my life this far without having to look over my shoulder or live in fear. I think I'm gonna be fine."

"Exactly my point. Until you met me."

"That isn't what I meant," I sigh. "What I mean is, I'd do it all again, because the way I feel when I'm with you is worth any risk that comes along."

He turns to me again, the look in his dark eyes stunning me. There's heartbreaking sorrow there, and it breaks me.

"You can't just say shit like that unless you mean it." His voice is low as he turns back to the road. "Because I knew the first time I laid eyes on you that I wanted you to be mine."

"Bones…"

"That day, when I saw you with Angel, I knew. And because I didn't know how to talk to you properly, I made some stupid joke or remark. Figured if I made you laugh, you might overlook the fact you're a lawyer and I'm a biker."

"Stop it!" I snap. "I'm so tired of hearing you say things like that. I admit, knowing you were a biker didn't help put my nerves at ease the first time I met you, but I swear to God, I never judged you because of the fact you run a junkyard or are in an M.C. I don't want a fucking guy in a suit who drives a Bentley. You seem to think I want that, but I don't, and if I did, I'd be out there finding myself that kind of man. It seems you've put me on this pedestal with a stick up my ass that I never really asked for or wanted."

His lips twitch as he rubs his jaw with one hand. "I know what I'll stick up your ass once you're better."

I shake my head. "I'm serious, Bones, if we're to get to the next level of wherever it is we're going, you've got to stop thinking that you're less than me and I'm better than you. It's just simply not true."

He brushes my fingers with his and then brings my hand up to his mouth and kisses my knuckles.

"I just never wanna disappoint you or let you down."

"Well, if we're honest with each other, good or bad, we'll never have that problem."

He holds my hand close to his body, pressing it against his chest so I can feel his heartbeat. He's so warm. He's always warm, like a big teddy bear. "I just hate seein' you like this, all banged up."

The bruises on my face have turned an unsightly purplish green, but they are healing. I definitely look like I've been through the ringer and back. My body is worse, but I can cover that up.

At least they're locked up, awaiting trial. I don't know how, but the rifle Bones used to shoot David was one of Jack's. I assume Nathan got it for them.

Steel and Brock made it look like David shot at one of them, and one of the stray bullets ricocheted and hit him in the shoulder. Bones wasn't even on sight when the cops got there. If he was, he'd be back in jail for sure.

"I'm going to be fine. Thanks to you, we got out of it alive. And it got me to thinking."

"Oh no," he jokes. "Not sure I like the sound of this."

He squeezes my hand, settling it down between us as we interlink our fingers.

"I'm glad that we've been open an honest with each other, and though it was hard to talk about Dean and I've got a long way to go in terms of healing, I want to try

Bones. I want to be with you."

He turns to look at me briefly, his eyebrows lift and it's as if he fights a smile.

"The truth is, you're not the only one that feels unworthy or not good enough," I whisper.

"For real?"

I nod. "Dean wanted to keep at it, give it another go, and we'd discussed having a break. I was even looking at rental properties. Then he got diagnosed and you know the rest. He was a good man, Bones. I never want to tarnish what we had, but a big part of why I feel guilty is because the relationship I have with you was nothing like that, there was never any passion. I didn't know what it even was until I met you."

"You've nothing to feel guilty about," he tells me. "You hear me?"

"I know, but we're only human. And it may take some time until I don't feel so broken, no pun intended."
His face darkens as he pulls to the side of the road and puts the truck into park.

"Don't make jokes about broken bones or I may just go break into county and murder Stacey and fuckface David."

I wipe a stray tear from my eye as he cups my face.

"Babe, don't cry." He holds me to him, and I nod, holding back tears.

"I really loved him, Bones, despite everything."

"I know, babe."

"This is why it's taken me so long to get back in the saddle. I've punished myself for not being a good person…"

"But you are a good person. You stuck by him, took care of him, nursed him until he died. You never put yourself first, babe. That's the most unselfish thing I've ever heard."

I snivel as he pulls me back to face him. "I'm a mess."

"You're the furthest thing from a mess, babe. Trust me."

"How do I make this better?" I whisper.

He brushes my hair back off my face, then wipes my tears with his thumbs. "I think you need to make peace with it. I don't think you can move on until you do."

"But that's just it," I whisper. "I'm in love with you, Bones."

He stares at me, his brow still creased, as if he's waiting for the punchline.

"Don't say that unless you mean it, babe." His voice is barely audible. "Because if that's really true, I ain't ever gonna let you go."

I run a hand up his chest and feel his pec muscles. "It's true, all of it."

His eyes are intense as he says, "I've been in love with you since the first time I saw you and that curvy, sexy body I love so much."

My heart warms as he smiles.

Our lips touch and his kisses are feather light. He

immediately pulls back.

"Bones…"

"I don't want to hurt you."

"Kissing doesn't hurt!" I yell back as he grins at my annoyance.

"Defiant little thing, aren't you?" He brushes his lips back over mine as I scrunch his tunic in my hand, wanting so much more.

"I want you, Bones."

He chuckles against my lips. "Not here, and sorry to burst your bubble, but your ribs are broken. Need I remind you again of the timeline I'm workin' with. Gonna have to watch me jerk my cock every night."

I sigh in frustration, then my frown turns into a grin.

"Every night?"

"Every night, babe."

"Does that mean you want sex every night when I'm better?"

"Fuckin' oath."

I laugh as I shake my head, then turn serious. "I think you're right, about making peace. I think I need to finally let it go. Forgive myself, I can't attempt to make a life with you until I do."

"I'll wait as long as it takes."

I close my eyes and laugh without humor. "How did I ever get to deserve a man like you?"

He puts a finger to my lips. "There you go again. We both have to promise we're not gonna talk like that. If I can't, then you can't either. You're kind, beautiful, sexy, smart, have a whiplash tongue, and a body made for sin, but most of all, you're a good woman, Kennedy Hart, and I'm gonna do everything I can to make you see that."

I bite my lip, trying to stop it from trembling. "Even if I need to get my ducks in a row?"

He smiles kindly. "Yup, even then."

"What if—"

"Will you just shut the fuck up and let a man kiss his woman?"

My eyes go wide as he gently tilts my head and we kiss slowly, softly, our tongues meeting as his hand touches my knee. The touch of his fingers feels like fire on my flesh.

I need him so damn much.

When we pull back, he has a lustful look in his eyes as I clutch on to him.

"I love you, Ryan Romero," I whisper. "I'll never be sorry you pursued me, even when I made your life hard."

He grins into my neck.

"What's so funny?" I demand.

He kisses my pulse point carefully, biting my flesh gently. It hits me right between the legs as I let out a small moan. "I like how you said that to me while you're not concussed."

I look at him sharply. "What do you mean?"

He brings his face back to mine. "You told me you loved me at the warehouse, I thought you were just sayin' it cause you thought you were gonna die."

"I don't remember…"

"Exactly my point." He kisses me again. "So, I like how you said again, while not under the influence of a concussion or heavy mediation. And for the record, I love you too, so fuckin' much."

He caresses me so gently; I've never seen this soft side to him but I like it a lot.

"I liked what you said, about us always being honest and talking things through, I need that Bones."

He nods. "I know, babe. I just don't need you talking shit though, with my brothers."

I frown again. "What do you mean?"

"You told Steel he was a good man."

I chuckle. "Well, what's wrong with that? He is."

"Then you said he had pretty eyes."

My eyes go wide. "I did?"

He smirks. "Don't worry, he'll get over it."

"Wait, when did that happen?"

"When he carried you out to the van with Colt, it was while I kicked the shit out of David."

I close my eyes. "I don't remember any of that."

"Clearly." He rubs his nose with mine. "You're mine, sweet cheeks, and I'm yours. Got me?"

I smile as I stare into his eyes that look back at me full of that exact promise. "Got you."

You and only you, Mr. Romero.

BRACKEN RIDGE
REBELS
ARIZONA
M · C

EPILOGUE

BONES
FOUR AND HALF WEEKS LATER

I walk into the house and immediately smell something delicious in the oven.

Ever since Kennedy took up residence in my house, she's also taken the keys to the banquet hall. Not that I was fighting her or anything, since we can't exactly live on grilled cheese and tinned spaghetti for the rest of our lives.

"Somethin' smells good, babe," I call out, pulling my boots off and kicking them out of the doorway.

I've had a long day at the office. Ever since the club bought out Jack and the sale went through; we've had a shit ton of stuff to sort out. Mainly all the crap Jack liked to hoard.

"Where are you?" I shout when I get no response.

"In here!" she calls back as I make my way down the hall and into the bedroom.

She's fresh out of the shower, wearing sweats and

zipping up a hoodie as I come toward her and kiss her. I pull back as she stares up at me, her eyes dancing, and I know what that means…

"What did the doc say?" I prompt.

"He said…"

"He?"

She rolls her eyes. "My doctor is a man, yes."

"Does he like… look at your pussy and shit?"

She bursts out laughing. "Umm… no, babe. I have a *female* gynecologist who looks at my lady bits when the time calls for it, and he's old anyway, so eww."

"Just 'cause he's old don't mean shit."

She sighs, shaking her head as I unzip her hoodie. "Any other questions before I can get to the point?"

I reach a hand inside and find she has no bra or top on, so I unzip it all the way as her large, beautiful tits pop out. I tweak both nipples as I stare at them, my cock grows hard.

She groans, and I'm tempted to bend down and play with them with my tongue, then I remember myself and look back up at her for confirmation…

"He said my ribs are still cracked."

I stop. "What?"

"I know. There's like a small hairline fracture or something, and just to be on the safe side, we shouldn't probably do anything too strenuous for at least three more weeks."

I stare at her. "Three. More. Weeks?" I spell the words out slowly. "Does the man have a death wish or somethin'?" She shrugs. "I don't know, but I guess you can never be too careful with these things."

I blink a few times. I mean, it's been fun, I've jerked off a lot, and she's helped of course, but it's not the same thing. She's tried to convince me to give it a try and go slow, but I didn't want to put her at risk.

It's a testament to my sanity that I've been able to sleep with her naked every night and be able to hold back. I wasn't kidding when I said I'd wait for her, but it's so damn hard when she's like a fallen angel, one that's been sent down from Heaven just to torture me.

"Uh, babe." I palm the back of my neck. "We probably shouldn't… uh… continue."

She reaches down and rubs her palm over the bulge at the front of my jeans, and I groan.

"We can do other stuff, though."

I put my hand over hers and rub it up and down my hardened cock. "It's not quite the same." I reach into her hair and peck her on the lips. "Though I could eat that sweet pussy, long as you keep really, really still." Her eyes go wide as I grin.

"Could we, I mean, *should* we?" she splutters, her eyes blazing.

Her sweet lips are like fuckin' torture, but this isn't

about me and my needs. It's about hers.

"You know how rough I get," I whisper in her ear, my hands cupping her breasts again gently. "And as frustrating as this is, I guess I'll have to improvise where possible. I *am* pretty good with my tongue after all, as you well know."

She sighs and then starts to giggle. I pull back to look at her.

"Why you laughin'?"

"You're such a good man, Ryan Romero."

"Save those compliments for when you can ride my face again like a rodeo."

She laughs out loud, pulling me closer, her hand gripping my cock harder. "And I was kidding."

"Kiddin' about me eatin' you out? That's happenin', babe, just gotta take a quick shower…"

She rolls her eyes, slamming her body into mine. "No, dummy, about the doctor. There is no fracture."

I stare back at her as she laughs at me. "You cooked this up?"

She nods, not afraid of me, she never has been. In fact, she loves nothing more than winding me up.

"You realize three more weeks without bein' able to be inside you would be as bad as trappin' my dick in a vice." I walk her back to the dresser, pressing into her so she can feel what she's done to me. I waste no time in hitching her onto the top of the flat surface, planting her ass so I can rip her bottoms off.

"Bones!" she gasps when I spread her legs and move between them. I cup her tits and squeeze them together, tweaking her nipples as I take her mouth at the same time.

"You think you're funny, huh?" She wraps her arms around my neck and nods, still chuckling. "The look on your face was priceless, but it was kinda sweet."

"Nothin' sweet about what I'm gonna do to you," I grunt, moving my mouth to one nipple as I suck it into my mouth, then lick it back and forth. I do the same to the other. "Gonna shoot my load all over these babies."

"I need you, Bones. I need you so bad," she groans, pulling my hair with her fingers as I continue my slow, sweet torture. I snake one hand down her body, still tentative across her ribs, and cup her pussy.

"Fuck," I mutter as I slip two fingers though her slickness. "So wet for me, babe."

"Bones, I need it. Hurry, put it in me."

I chuckle as I meet her eyes. "Who's impatient now, *Ms. Hart*? Wanna spank an orgasm out of you first."

"No time for that," she groans, moving her hand to my wrist in an attempt to speed things up. "I'm almost there, yeah, just there… oh, babe…" She rubs her pussy in time with our hands, and I look down at the sight and almost blow.

I keep up her demands and insert two fingers as she

gasps, then I place my thumb on her clit, and she detonates. Shaking, she impales my fingers as I move them in and out of her while sucking on her nipple.

"Like that, babe?" I muse, dipping down her body as I grasp her throat with one hand, and she rests back against the wall. I lick through her folds as she squirms, and I taste her on my tongue. *Fuck, this feels like home.*

"Ryan… oh, babe, oh God…" she cries out when I suck her clit into my mouth and finger her pussy while she digs her feet into my shoulders, all the while I squeeze her throat. She comes hard as I revel in her sweet, soft curses. I lift her off the dresser and she wraps herself around me, our kisses heated, fumbled and all over the place.

"Get my dick out," I grunt.

She brushes my cock with her fingers in her haste to unbutton me. I help her, shoving my jeans down when I sit on the edge of the bed, and she straddles me. She fists my cock, pulling it, jerking me off slowly as our tongues collide and precum leaks out of my tip. I want her to suck me so bad, but I know I'll blow too soon. Instead, I break the kiss and whisper in her ear.

"Across my knee. You've got punishment I need to inflict."

She rubs against me, her soft, sweet pussy dripping for me as I try to contain my urge to push into her and fuck her stupid.

"I need you inside me," she groans, her tits rubbing against my chest as I grin.

"You sure we're good to go?" I say, just checking that I'm not gonna do any damage. It's been a long, slow healing process, and I don't wanna be super rough with her until she's ready.

"I'm sure. Green light. So go."

I push her hair back off her face. "Over my knee," I repeat.

She pouts but does as she's told.

Her bare ass laying across me makes me groan out loud. I love her curves, always have, always will.

"Gonna take this ass," I tell her as she wiggles it over my cock, sticking it up in the air.

I smooth a hand over her plush cheeks, then I spank one as she yelps on contact. I rub it gently, then smack the other side, loving how turned on she gets when I do this.

"*Ryan...*" she calls out.

"Shhh," I tell her, and spank her again, then the other side. I rub both cheeks again, loving how pink they turn. I spread her legs and smack her pussy gently.

"I'm gonna come," she cries.

"No, not till I say." I stare down at her ass and pussy, and I want in so bad. I slide two fingers into her, lovin' how she takes me as I thumb over her back entrance, rubbing her slickness there as she moans. "Just relax."

She does as she's told, squirming against me, trying to rub herself as I move my fingers in and out faster. Thumbing her ass, I slip the tip inside, then a little more, reveling in her soft moans.

"How does that feel?"

"So good," she replies, her voice muffled into the duvet.

The sight alone is gonna make me come if I keep at it.

"Imagine my cock inside you there," I say as my cock jerks in response. *Fuck yeah.*

"I want that, babe… I want all of you…"

I replace my thumb with my middle finger, slowly letting her take more of me in and out until she lets me insert another. She's so slippery and wet as she comes again, her orgasm spiraling so hard she cries out over and over. I spank her ass with my other hand as she climaxes.

I lean down and bite her ass cheek gently, then flip her over, climbing up her body as she scampers back on the bed.

"I love you so fuckin' much," I tell her, stroking my cock.

"Right back at you, big boy." She smiles. "Come here."

"So, you'll forgive me if this is really fast the first time?"

"Stop talking and put your fat cock inside me."

I grin and place my hands on either side of her head as she wraps her legs around me.

Placing my cock at her entrance, I shove inside her full tilt, and she cries out as I still, then I slowly move out of her, doing it again and again.

"Oh… Oh… *Ryan*… you feel so good…"

I throw my head back as I move faster, her hot little pussy choking my dick as I ride her.

"Your pussy's made for me," I tell her. "I've missed this so fuckin' much. You're callin' in sick tomorrow."

She slaps my ass as I move my hands to the headboard and grip onto it, moving my hips even faster. I'll never grow tired of seeing her splayed out on her back, taking me.

"And the rest of the week if this is what you have planned," she replies as she drops her head back into the pillows.

The way our bodies move, her soft, sweet skin taunting me, making me fuck her harder. It feels like a lifetime since we were this physically close, but I admit, getting to know her and just being near to her has made us that much closer.

"I'm at your service, sweet cheeks."

She grips my ass as the bed rocks and she says, "I'm gonna come, oh, oh, *Ryan!*"

I come too, fucking her harder as I grip her hips, stilling as I empty my load and call out her name.

Collapsing on top of her, we both lie there, breathless.

"So worth the wait," I say, lifting up to kiss her sweaty forehead. "Four weeks of torture."

I roll off her and we lay for a while, catching our breath. She cuddles into my side and traces across the tattoo that reads: *Abbey.*

I stare into her eyes, and I know that there is no other place I'd rather be than right here, right now.

"Say you'll be my ol' lady," I whisper.

She snuggles closer to me. "Does that mean you think you get to own me?"

I snort. "Trust you to ruin a moment."

She chuckles into my shoulder, kissing my chest as her hand reaches down to my cock.

"If it means I get to own this."

"You already do, babe," I say, as I roll her on top of me. "You had me at hello."

I pull her to me, and we kiss with a fiery passion that I hope never goes out.

She's my forever. And I'll make sure to tell her every single day what she means to me, if it's the last thing I do.

HENNEDY
SIX MONTHS LATER

I grin as I look at the text message Bones just sent me. He's always sending me dirty messages but this takes the cake.

It's his birthday and I told him to swing by my office since I had to work late. I know he's always had this fantasy about doing me in my office, and tonight I'm going to make that happen. I had to omit the clients out in the waiting room, while it was a thrilling thought, I'd rather not have an audience.

It's dark, all the lights are out and I've locked the office,

Bones has a key to get in.

I reply back telling him to come to the office, and that I've got a problem with the alarm not setting. I know that'll get him over here in no time.

The last six months have been great. We've done a lot. I've been on club runs around Arizona and I've been at church a lot, getting to know everyone and helping Stevie settle into her new role at the Stone Crow. Life's been great.

Bones and I have gone from strength to strength.

I still have the occasional days where I have to check in on myself whenever I feel doubt creeping in, that old connotation of not being allowed to feel joy has long gone. Bones makes me happy, and he's made such a difference in my life, we've helped each other heal.

While the memory of being drugged and tied up haunts me from time to time, I've realized that I am one tough cookie. It's gonna take a lot for someone to knock me off my perch. Rather than be scared of what happened, I've learned to embrace it. I lived. I got through it, and I have the club and Bones to thank that I'm still here to tell the tale.

My phone pings and the message says he's on his way. A few moments later, I hear the roar of his motorcycle.

I sit behind my desk in my chair and drop my silk robe. I brought it this morning in my purse, as well as the tie I'm now wearing and the heels Bones loves, and nothing else.

I cross my legs and fold one arm over my breasts and

wait. My heart thumps in my chest, not because I'm naked, but because of what this means. I want Bones to be mine and not just his ol' lady. I want to ask him a very important question over dinner…

His motorcycle roars into the lot and then he cuts the engine, a few moments later, I hear the keys in the door. Then he calls out, "Kennedy?"

"In here!" I call back.

He fumbles around for a few minutes then I see the hallway light go on under the door.

Then the doorhandle to my office turns.

He stands in the doorway. My beautiful, cheeky, bad ass biker.

He's cut his hair again, shaved at the sides. He's kept the slightly longer beard I like and he's oh, so sexy. I will never tire of looking at this gorgeous man.

"Good evening, *Mr. Romero,*" I drawl, flicking the tie over one shoulder as he stares at me. "Glad you could make it."

"Holy fuck," he mutters.

We often have this roleplay game to turn the heat up where I'm his naughty attorney and he's my client who can't keep his hands to himself…a lot like real life.

"Happy Birthday," I add.

He rubs his chin, his eyes flicking down my body as I move my arm so my breasts are visible. "*Ms. Hart.* Do you do this for all your clients or am I the exception?"

He falls into the role so easily.

"The minute I represented you, *Mr. Romero,* I knew I had to have you, in fact, I wanted you to drag me back here and pound me across my desk."

His eyes are wild as he steps closer to me, adjusting his dick. "Fuck, you're a sight for sore eyes."

I uncross my legs as his eyes shift down and he groans. "And I've been a very bad girl."

"What did you do?" His voice is thick.

"I played with myself, imagining it was you…while I had clients out in the waiting room."

He always gets off on hearing about me pleasing myself when he's not around.

He grunts, unbuttoning his jeans and lowers his zipper. "You know how I feel about you pleasing yourself without my say-so."

I lick my lips. "Are you going to punish me?" I move a hand between my legs and start playing with myself as he watches.

He stares at my hand and drops his jeans, his huge cock springing free as he reaches down pulls his boots off and then his jeans. He rounds my desk and pushes my chair back, as it's on wheels I scoot back but he catches it with his hands. He leans down and kisses me, his tongue forcing his way into my mouth.

"Been thinkin' about you all day, Ms. Hart, and how I'm

gonna punish you."

"Is that right?"

"Yep. And I've come up with all sorts of dirty things."

"Before we get into it. I've got a present for you," I whisper as he drops to his knees, shrugging his cut off and then his shirt. He stares up at me.

"Aside from you?"

I nod. "Yes."

He grins. "What is it?"

He starts to rub a thumb through my folds as I try to keep my voice coherent.

"I want you, Bones."

"You have me, all of me."

"What if I asked you to be more?" I know I can't wait a moment longer. Screw dinner.

He looks up at me. "What do you mean?"

We've discussed having a family, someday, though my biological clock is ticking I'm not ready for a baby yet. But, I know that I believe in the sanctity of marriage and maybe one day, children may come. I've never thought about kids until Bones, he'd make such a great father. He's so good with little Avery and with Ethan and Rawlings.

"I know it's not traditional, but…"

He grins. I know that he's up for anything, even this.

"But what?"

"Marry me," I say. "Be my husband."

His eyebrows shoot up, he leans up, pulling me to the edge of the seat. "Aren't I supposed to be the one asking you to be my wife?"

"You know I'm not one for tradition, Ryan."

"Did you ask me this while you're naked to ensure victory?"

I swat him with my hand. "I was planning on asking you over dinner, actually."

"Right, but the sight of my cock hard for you, had you jumping the gun."

"You're ruining the moment."

He leans up and kisses me hard. "I'll marry you tonight, tomorrow, any day of the week if it means I get to have you and only you for the rest of my life."

I cup his face in my hands. "I didn't just get naked to do this," I whisper. "But I love you so damn much, and I always want you to know it, every second."

"Not as much as I love you."

"So that's a yes, then?"

He grins. "Wait, aren't I supposed to seal the deal with a diamond?"

"We can get to that."

He kisses me again. "As long as I get to be with you Kennedy Hart, you can lead me any which way you want."

"Forever," I say.

"Forever," he agrees.

"Come here." I pull him closer.

"I'm already here babe, and I always will be. Like I said, you had my heart a long time ago."

"I'm sorry it took me a while to realize it," I say. "I'll never be so glad you persisted."

He shushes me with one finger to my lips. "Do you always have to have the last word?"

"At least you know what you're marrying into." I shrug.

My gift to him is giving him my heart. He already had my soul a long time ago.

He chuckles. "Touché, sweet cheeks."

"Can't wait to call you hubbie," I whisper as our lips meet.

"Does that mean I get to call you wifey?"

"It's *Ms. Hart* to you, Mr. Romero."

He grins. "Kennedy Romero, I like the sound of that."

"I was thinking I'd hyphenate my name."

He rolls his eyes. "Of course you did."

"Kennedy Hart-Romero. It has a ring to it."

"Speaking of rings, yours is about to get pounded."

I shake my head. "You always ruin the moment."

"You've got a lifetime to try and smack it out of me. Sound fair?"

I laugh as he looks up at me with eyes I'll forever be lost in. "Sounds like a deal."

My heart pounds with what it means, but I know I want this and I'm so glad he does too.

"Should we shake on it?"

"How about I impale you instead?" I chuckle as he adds, "Or are you gonna have the last word on, that too?"

I raise a finger and I yelp as he lifts me suddenly and throws me over his shoulder.

"Bones!"

He sets me on my feet, then turns and bends me over my desk as I sweep the papers and files on the floor with dramatic flair, I've always wanted to do that.

"You want it," he growls in my ear, his hand stoking my skin. "Admit it."

"I'll always want it with you."

"Me too, babe." He smooths his hands down my body, kissing me on the shoulder. "Me too."

THE END

ACKNOWLEDGMENTS

It's been a journey this release! I'm forever grateful to my P.A. duo powerhouse Savannah and Brianna. I couldn't do this without your help, thank you so much.

Thank you to my sister D for being my proofreader and always being in my corner. I promise I will not stress out on the next release *I say this with tongue in cheek*

Thank you to Michelle, Kerri, Tianna, Brenda and Gemma my Beta team once again for taking the time to read, leave me notes and correct all my horrendous mistakes.

Thank you to my ARC readers and I hope you enjoy Bones as much as I enjoyed writing him.

A big shout out to my blogger friends for sharing my posts, graphics and your positive and lovely messages. I feel so lucky to have you in my corner.

Love and hugs to my fellow indies, some of which I've grown close to over the last year and half. Please know I am championing in your corner always x

Special thanks to my awesome editor Mackenzie @ nicegirlnaughtyedits for everything you do and your notes and comments which I appreciate, it helps me so much!

Thanks LJ from Mayhem Cover Creations for another

awesome cover.

And as always, thank you to you guys, the readers. You took a chance on a little indie author from Australia and I'm so thrilled that you want to read my books. I feel so lucky to be able to bring my characters alive and that you want more. I literally pinch myself every day that I get to be an author. Without you, I couldn't do this. Much love x

If you can spare the time to leave a review on GR and/or Amazon if you loved Bones or any of my books that would be greatly appreciated and helps me so much as an indie author. Links are on the following pages.

I can't wait to bring you all many more books this year and I have so much fun stuff planned.

Be sure to check out my private facebook group (links below) as I update regularly in there before anything gets released on other social media channels.

Love from Australia, MF xx

FIND ME AT

Facebook: https://www.facebook.com/mackenzy.foxauthor.5

Instagram: https://www.instagram.com/mackenzyfoxbooks/

Tiktok: https://www.tiktok.com/@mackenzyfoxauthor

Linktree: https://linktr.ee/mackenzyfox

Goodreads: https://bit.ly/2TKp7ck

https://books2read.com/Steel-BRR

Website: https://mackenzyfox.com

Join my private Facebook group for all the juicy gossip, giveaways and spicy reveals first at The Den - A Mackenzy Fox Reader Group - https://bit.ly/3dgQfKk

ABOUT THE AUTHOR

Mackenzy Fox is an author of contemporary, romantic and erotic themed romance novels. When she's not writing she loves vegan cooking, walking her beloved pooch's, reading books and is an expert on online shopping.

She's slightly obsessed with drinking tea, testing bubbly Moscato, watching home decorating shows and has a black belt in origami. She strives to live a quiet and introverted life in Western Australia's North West with her hubby, twin sister and her dogs.

ALSO BY MACKENZY FOX

Bracken Ridge Rebels MC:
Steel
Gunner
Brock
Colt
Rubble
Bones
Axton
Nitro
Gears
Knox

Medici Mafia:
Fortress of the King
Fortress of the Queen
Fortress of the Heart
Fortress of the Soul
Fortress of the Damned
Fortress of the Brave

Bad Boys of New York:
Jaxon

Standalone:
Broken Wings

www.ingramcontent.com/pod-product-compliance
Lightning Source LLC
Chambersburg PA
CBHW030837190726

48285CB00004B/1252